From the library of:

THE
LYLE
OFFICIAL
ANTIQUES
REVIEW 1989

THE LYLE

OFFICIAL

ANTIQUES
REVIEW 1989

A PERIGEE BOOK

Perigee Books
are published by
The Putnam Publishing Group
200 Madison Avenue
New York, NY 10016

Published simultaneously in Canada

Library of Congress Catalog Card Number 74-640592

ISBN 0-399-51484-8

Printed in the United States of America
1 2 3 4 5 6 7 8 9 10

The publishers wish to express their sincere thanks to the following for their
involvement and assistance in the production of this volume:

KAREN DOUGLASS (Art Editor)
JANICE MONCRIEFF (Assistant Editor)
ANNETTE CURTIS
SALLY DALGLIESH
TANYA FAIRBAIRN
FRANK BURRELL
ROBERT NISBET
LOUISE SIMPSON
JONN DUNLOP
EILEEN BURRELL
SARAH RITCHIE
MACDONALD GREEN
LISA JONES
ALAN KIDD

INTRODUCTION

This year over 100,000 Antique Dealers and Collectors will make full and profitable use of their Lyle Official Antiques Review. They know that only in this one volume will they find the widest possible variety of goods — illustrated, described and given a current market value to assist them to BUY RIGHT AND SELL RIGHT throughout the year of issue.

They know, too, that by building a collection of these immensely valuable volumes year by year, they will equip themselves with an unparalleled reference library of facts, figures and illustrations which, properly used, cannot fail to help them keep one step ahead of the market.

In its nineteen years of publication, Lyle has gone from strength to strength and has become without doubt the pre-eminent book of reference for the antique trade throughout the world. Each of its fact filled pages are packed with precisely the kind of profitable information the professional Dealer needs — including descriptions, illustrations and values of thousands and thousands of individual items carefully selected to give a representative picture of the current market in antiques and collectibles — and remember all values are prices actually paid, based on accurate sales records in the twelve months prior to publication from the best established and most highly respected auction houses and retail outlets in Europe and America.

This is THE book for the Professional Antiques Dealer. 'The Lyle Book' — we've even heard it called 'The Dealer's Bible'.

Compiled and published afresh each year, the Lyle Official Antiques Review is the most comprehensive up-to-date antiques price guide available. THIS COULD BE YOUR WISEST INVESTMENT OF THE YEAR!

ANTHONY CURTIS

CONTENTS

Acknowledgements

Abridge Auction Rooms, Market Place, Abridge, Essex RM4 1UA
Anderson & Garland, Anderson House, Market Street, Newcastle-upon-Tyne NE1 6XA
Bagshaws, 17 High Street, Uttoxeter
Ball & Percival, 132 Lord Street, Southport, Merseyside PR9 0AE
Banks & Silvers, Fine Art Dept, 66 Foregate Street, Worcester
Barbers Fine Art Auctioneers, Smarts Heath Road, Mayford, Woking, Surrey
Bearnes , Rainbow, Avenue Road, Torquay TQ2 5TG, Devon
Bermondsey Antique Market, Tower Bridge Road, London
Biddle and Webb, Ladywood Middleway, Birmingham, West Midlands B16 0PP
Blackhorse Agencies, Ambrose, 149 High Road, Loughton, Essex IG10 4LZ
Bloomsbury Book Auctions, 3 & 4 Hardwick Street, London EC1R HRY
Boardman — Fine Art Auctioneers, Station Road Corner, Haverhill, Suffolk CB9 0EY
Bonhams, Montpelier Galleries, Montpelier Street, Knightsbridge, London SW7 1HH
Bracketts, 27-29 High Street, Tunbridge Wells TN1 1UU, Kent
British Antique Exporters, 206 London Road, Burgess Hill, West Sussex RH15 9RX
Broader & Spencer, 18 Quay Road, Bridlington, East Yorkshire YO15 2AP
Brown & Merry, 41 High Street, Tring, Herts HP23 5AB
Wm. H. Brown, Westgate Hall, Grantham, Lincs NG31 6LT
Lawrence Butler & Co., Butler House, 86 High Street, Hythe, Kent CT21 5AJ
Capes Dunn and Co., The Auction Galleries, 38 Charles Street, Manchester, Lancashire M1 7DB
Chancellors Hollingsworth, 31 High Street, Ascot, Berkshire SL5 7HG
Christie's, Cornelis Schuystraat 57, 1071 JG, Amsterdam
Christie's (International) S.A., 8 Place De La Talonwerie, 1204 Geneva
Christie's (Hong Kong) Ltd., 3607 Edinburgh Tower, 15 Queens Road, Hong Kong
Christie's, 8 King Street, St James's, London SW1Y 6QT
Christie's (Monaco) S.A.M., Park Palace, 98000 Monte Carlo
Christie's, 502 Park Avenue, New York, NY 10022
Christie's, 219 East 67th Street, New York, NY 10021
Christie's Scotland, 164-166 Bath Street, Glasgow, Scotland G2 4TG
Christie's South Kensington Ltd., 85 Old Brompton Road, London SW7 3LD
Chrystals Auctions, Unit 32, Spring Valley Industrial Estate, Braddan, Isle of Man
Coles, Knapp & Kennedy, Georgian Rooms, Ross-on-Wye, Herefordshire HR9 5HL
Bruce D. Collins, Fine Arts Gallery, Box 113, Denmark, Maine
Cooper Hirst, Goldlay House, Parkway, Chelmsford, Essex CM2 7PR
County Group, 102 High Street, Tenterden TN30 6AU, Kent
Dacre, Son and Hartley, 1-5 The Grove, Ilkley, West Yorkshire LS29 8HS
Dee & Atkinson, The Exchange Saleroom, Driffield YO25 7LJ, North Humberside
Dickinson, Davy & Markham, New Saleroom, Elwes Street, Brigg, DN20 8JH, North Humberside
Dreweatt Neate, Donnington Priory, Donnington, Newbury, Berkshire RG13 2JE
Du Mouchelles Art Galleries Co., 409 E. Jefferson Avenue, Detroit, Michigan 48226
Hy Duke & Son, Fine Art Salerooms, Weymouth Avenue, Dorchester DT1 1DG
Peter Eley, Western House, 98-100 High Street, Sidmouth, Devon EX10 8EF
Elliott & Green, Emsworth Road, Lymington, Hampshire SO41 9BL
R. H. Ellis and Sons, 44/46 High Street, Worthing, West Sussex BN11 1LL
Fellows and Sons, Bedford House, 88 Hagley Road, Edgbaston, Birmingham, West Midlands
John D. Fleming & Co., 8 Fore Street, Dulverton, Somerset TA22 9EX
John Francis, S.O.F.A.A., Chartered Surveyors, Curiosity Sale Rooms, King Street, Carmarthen
Geering & Colyer, 22/26 High Street, Tunbridge Wells, Kent TN1 1XA
Glendining's, Blenstock House, 7 Blenheim Street, New Bond Street, London W1Y 9LD
Goss & Crested China Co., 62 Murray Road, Horndean, Hants PO8 9JL
Andrew Grant, St Mark's House, St Mark's Close, Cherry Orchard, Worcester WR5 3DJ
Graves, Son & Pilcher, 71 Church Road, Hove, East Sussex BN3 2GL
W. R. J. Greenslade & Co., 13 Hammet Street, Taunton, Somerset TA1 1RN
Hamptons Fine Art, 93 High Street, Godalming, Surrey
Giles Haywood, The Auction House, St John's Road, Stourbridge DY8 1EW, West Midlands
Harvey's Auctions Ltd., 14-18 Neal Street, London WC2H 9LZ
Hetheringtons Nationwide, The Amersham Auction Rooms, 125 Station Road, Amersham, Bucks
Andrew Hilditch and Son Ltd., 19 The Square, Sandbach, Cheshire CW11 0AT
Hobbs & Chambers, 'At the Sign of the Bell', Market Place, Cirencester, Gloucestershire
Hobbs Parker, Romney House, Ashford Market, Ashford, Kent TN23 1PG
Holloways, 49 Parsons Street, Banbury, Oxfordshire OX16 8PF

Edgar Horn, Auction Galleries, 46/50 South Street, Eastbourne, BN21 4XB
Jacobs & Hunt, Lavant Street, Petersfield, Hampshire GU32 3EF
Kent Sales, Giffords, Holmesdale Road, Dartford, Kent
G. A. Key, Aylsham Salerooms, Palmers Lane, Aylsham, Norfolk NR11 6EH
King & Chasemore, West Street, Midhurst, West Sussex GU29 9NG
Lacy Scott (Fine Art Dept.), 10 Risbygate Street, Bury St Edmunds, Suffolk IP33 3AA
Lalonde Fine Art, 71 Oakfield Road, Clifton, Bristol, Avon BS8 2BE
Lambert & Foster, The Auction Sale Rooms, 102 High Street, Tenterden, Kent
W. H. Lane & Son, Fine Art Auctioneer & Valuers, 64 Morrab Road, Penzance Cornwall
Langlois Ltd., Westaway Rooms, Don Street, St Helier, Jersey, Channel Islands
Lawrence Fine Art, South Street, Crewkerne TA18 8AB, Somerset
Lawrence's, Fine Art Auctioneers, Norfolk House, 80 High Street, Bletchingley, Surrey
David Lay, The Penzance Auction House, Alverton, Penzance, Cornwall TR18 4RE
Lewes Auction Rooms, 56 High Street, Lewes
Locke & England, Walton House, 11 The Parade, Leamington Spa
Lots Road Chelsea Auction Galleries, 71 Lots Road, Chelsea, London SW10 0RN
R. K. Lucas & Son, 9 Victoria Place, Haverfordwest, SA61 2JX
Lyon & Turnbull, 51 George Street, Edinburgh, Midlothian, Scotland
Mallams, Fine Art Auctioneers, 24 St Michaels Street, Oxford, Oxfordshire
Michael G. Matthews, The Devon Fine Art Auction House, Dowel Street, Honiton, Devon
McKenna's Auctioneers & Valuers, Bank Salerooms, Harris Court, Clitheroe, Lancashire
Miller & Company, Lemon Quay Auction Rooms, Truro, Cornwall TR1 2LW
Moore, Allen & Innocent, 33 Castle Street, Cirencester, Gloucestershire GL7 1QD
Morphets, 4-6 Albert Street, Harrogate, North Yorkshire HG1 1JL
Neales of Nottingham, 192 Mansfield Road, Nottingham, Nottinghamshire NG1 3HX
D. M. Nesbit & Co., 7 Clarendon Road, Southsea, Hampshire PO5 2ED
James Norwich Auctions Ltd., Head Office, 33 Timberhill, Norwich, Norfolk NR1 3LA
Olivers, 23/24 Market Hill, Sudbury, CO10 6EN
Onslow's Auctioneers, 14-16 Carroun Road, London SW8 1JT
Osmond, Tricks, Regent Street, Auction Rooms, Clifton, Bristol, Avon BS8 4HG
Outhwaite & Litherland, "Kingsway Galleries", Fontenoy Street, Liverpool, Merseyside L3 2BE
J. R. Parkinson Son & Hamer Auctions, The Auction Room, Rochdale Road, Bury, Lancashire
Parsons, Welch & Cowell, The Argyle Salerooms, Argyle Road, Sevenoaks, Kent
Phillips, 65 George Street, Edinburgh EH2 2JL
Phillips, 207 Bath Street, Glasgow G2 4DH
Phillips, Blenstock House, 7 Blenheim Street, New Bond Street, London W1Y 0AS
Phillips New York, 406 East 79th Street, New York, NY 10021
Phillips, The Old House, Station Road, Knowle, Solihull, West Midlands B93 0HT
Prudential Fine Art Auctioneers, 5 Woodcote Close, Kingston Upon Thames, Surrey KT2 5LZ
Prudential Fine Art Auctioneers, Trinity House, 114 Northenden Road, Sale, Manchester
Reeds Rains Prudential, Trinity House, 114 Northenden Road, Manchester M33 3HD
Rendells, Stone Park, Ashburton, Devon TQ13 7RH
Ernest R. De Rome, 12 New John Street, Westgate, Bradford BD1 2QY
Russell, Baldwin & Bright, The Fine Art Saleroom, Ryelands Road, Leominster HR6 8JG
Sandoe Luce Panes, Wotton Auction Rooms, Wotton-Under-Edge, Gloucestershire GL12 7EB
Sentry Box Military Antiques, 2 Market Street, Brighton, Sussex
Robt. W. Skinner Inc., Bolton Gallery, Route 117, Bolton, Massachusetts
Southgate Antique Auction Rooms, Rear of Town Hall, Green Lanes, Palmers Green, London N13
Henry Spencer & Sons, 20 The Square, Retford, Notts. DN22 6DJ
St John Vaughan with John Hogbin, 8 Queen Street, Deal, Kent CT14 6ET
David Stanley Auctions, Stordan Grange, Osgathorpe, Leicestershire LE12 9SR
G. E. Sworder & Sons, Northgate End Salerooms, 15 Northgate End, Bishops Stortford, Herts
Louis Taylor & Sons, Percy Street, Hanley, Stoke-on-Trent, Staffordshire ST1 1NF
Tiffen King Nicholson, 12 Lowther Street, Carlisle, Cumbria CA3 8DA
Duncan Vincent, Fine Art & Chattel Auctioneers, 105 London Street, Reading RG1 4LF
Wallis and Wallis, West Street Auction Galleries, West Street, Lewes, East Sussex BN7 2NJ
Warners, Wm. H. Brown, The Warner Auction Rooms, 16/18 Halford Street, Leicester LE1 1JB
Warren & Wignall Ltd., The Mill, Earnshaw Bridge, Leyland Lane, Leyland PR5 3PH
J. M. Welch & Son, Old Town Hall, Great Dunmow, Essex CM6 1AU
Wellington Salerooms, Mantle Street, Wellington, Somerset TA21 8AR
Peter Wilson Fine Art Auctioneers, Victoria Gallery, Market Street, Nantwich, Cheshire
Woolley and Wallis, The Castle Auction Mart, Salisbury, Wiltshire SP1 3SU
H. C. Wolton & Son, 6 Whiting Street, Bury St Edmunds, Suffolk IP33 1PB
Worsfolds Auction Galleries, 40 Station Road West, Canterbury, Kent
Wright-Manley, Beeston Sales Centre, Beeston Castle Smithfield, Tarporley, Cheshire

ANTIQUES
REVIEW 1989

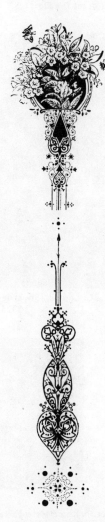

THE Lyle Official Antiques Review is compiled and published with completely fresh information annually, enabling you to begin each new year with an up-to-date knowledge of the current trends, together with the verified values of antiques of all descriptions.

We have endeavoured to obtain a balance between the more expensive collector's items and those which, although not in their true sense antiques, are handled daily by the antiques trade.

The illustrations and prices in the following sections have been arranged to make it easy for the reader to assess the period and value of all items with speed.

You will find illustrations for almost every category of antique and curio, together with a corresponding price collated during the last twelve months, from the auction rooms and retail outlets of the major trading countries.

When dealing with the more popular trade pieces, in some instances, a calculation of an average price has been estimated from the varying accounts researched.

As regards prices, when 'one of a pair' is given in the description the price quoted is for a pair and so that we can make maximum use of the available space it is generally considered that one illustration is sufficient.

It will be noted that in some descriptions taken directly from sales catalogues originating from many different countries, terms such as bureau, secretary and davenport are used in a broader sense than is customary, but in all cases the term used is self explanatory.

Tizer 'The Appetizer'. (Street Jewellery) $75

Milkmaid Brand Milk. (Street Jewellery) $370

Monsters. (Street Jewellery) $230

Rowntree's Pastilles. (Street Jewellery) $100

'Black Cat' Virginia Cigarettes. (Street Jewellery) $325

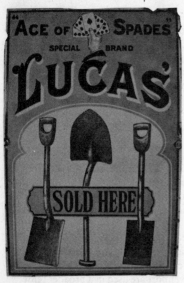

Lucas 'Ace of Spades'. (Street Jewellery) $275

Duckham's Oils. (Street Jewellery) $140

Komo Metal Paste. (Street Jewellery) $275

Hall's Distemper. (Street Jewellery) $220

Martini. (Street Jewellery)
$160

Singer Sewing Machines.
(Street Jewellery)
$175

Nestle's Milk. (Street Jewellery)
$140

'Matchless' metal polish. (Street
Jewellery) $465

Belga Vander Elst. (Street
Jewellery) $120

Player's 'Drumhead' cigarettes.
(Street Jewellery) $185

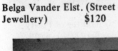

Shell. (Street Jewellery) $75

Anti-Laria Sparkling Wine. (Street
Jewellery) $140

'Ovum' Thorley's Poultry Spice. (Street Jewellery) $140

'Redgate' Table Waters. (Street Jewellery) $110

Van Houtens Cocoa. (Street Jewellery) $160

Phipp's 'Diamond Ale'. (Street Jewellery) $200

Fry's Pure Breakfast Cocoa. (Street Jewellery) $160

Taylor's Depository. (Street Jewellery) $370

Drink Coca Cola. (Street Jewellery) $140

Mazawattee Tea. (Street Jewellery) $220

Nectar Tea. (Street Jewellery) $130

Veno's 'Cough Cure'. (Street Jewellery) $140

Sunlight 'Guarantee of Purity. (Street Jewellery) $700

Ogden's 'Coolie Cut Plug'. (Street Jewellery) $140

Colman's Starch. (Street Jewellery) $85

18

A Navajo silver and turquoise Concho belt, hand-hammered silver, comprised of seven oval conchos and six butterflies. (Robt. W. Skinner Inc.) $1,600

Plains beaded and fringed hide pipebag, Sioux/Arapaho, 1880's, 23½in. long. (Robt. W. Skinner Inc.) $1,400

California coiled basketry bowl, Pomo gift basket, oval, 10½in. long, 4in. high. (Robt. W. Skinner Inc.) $1,200

A North American Plains Indian leather drawstring purse with blue and white bead decoration. (Phillips) $151

A Navajo silver Concho belt, comprised of nine open-center conchos and a repoussed buckle. (Robt. W. Skinner Inc.) $750

A Navajo silver Concho belt, comprised of seven oval conchos, six butterflies and open center buckle. (Robt. W. Skinner Inc.) $1,600

Two Cascades/Plateau imbricated coiled baskets, Klikitat, 19th century, 10¼in. and 7¼in. high. (Robt. W. Skinner Inc.) $1,300

Plains beaded hide cradle cover, Sioux, 1880's, 19in. long. (Robt. W. Skinner Inc.) $1,500

Northwest Coast polychrome wood totemic carving, 19th century, cedar, 29½in. high. (Robt. W. Skinner Inc.) $2,300

Northwest Coast polychrome wood rattle, cedar, carved in two sections and joined with square metal nails, 11¼in. long. (Robt. W. Skinner Inc.) $350

Plains polychrome and fringed hide doll, Northern, 1880's, 18½in. high. (Robt. W. Skinner Inc.) $1,800

California coiled basketry bowl, Pomo, diam. 12in., 5¾in. high. (Robt. W. Skinner Inc.) $500

Nez Perce twined cornhusk bag, 13½ x 18in. (Robt. W. Skinner Inc.) $475

Southwestern polychrome pottery jar, San Ildefonso, black on red, Powhoge Period, 12½in. diam. (Robt. W. Skinner Inc.) $1,100

Hopi polychrome wood Kachina doll, early 20th century, 'Topsy', 7¾in. high. (Robt. W. Skinner Inc.) $425

Tlingit twined spruce root rattle top basket, 5¼in. diam. (Robt. W. Skinner Inc.) $500

Hopi polychrome wood Kachina doll, 'Ang-ak-China', early 20th century, 9in. high. (Robt. W. Skinner Inc.) $425

Tonita Pena, (Quah Ah), (San Ildefonso), Winter Dancers, tempera on white paper, signed, 5¾ x 6¾in. (Robt. W. Skinner Inc.) $550

Hopi polychrome wood Kachina doll, 'Bule Mana', early 20th century, 13in. high. (Robt. W. Skinner Inc.) $1,000

Tonita Pena, (Quah Ah), (San Ildefonso), Ceremonial Dancers, tempera on white paper, signed, 5½ x 7in. (Robt. W. Skinner Inc.) $325

Hopi polychrome wood Kachina doll, possibly the clown figure, 'Piptuka', early 20th century, 8½in. high. (Robt. W. Skinner Inc.) $900

Richard Martinez, (Opa Mu Nu), (San Ildefonso), Bonnet Dancer, tempera on white paper, signed, 10½ x 12¾in. (Robt. W. Skinner Inc.) $650

Nez Perce twined cornhusk bag, false embroidered in homespun wool and natural grass, 19 x 24in. (Robt. W. Skinner Inc.) $400

Southwestern polychrome pottery jar, Zia, 14in. diam. (Robt. W. Skinner Inc.) $2,100

Nez Perce twined cornhusk bag, false embroidered in natural dyed cornhusk and grass, 19½ x 26in. (Robt. W. Skinner Inc.) $475

Plains beaded and fringed hide doll, Northern, 1880's, 13½in. high. (Robt. W. Skinner Inc.) $1,600

Jimmy Toddy (Beatien Yazz), (Little No Shirt), (Navajo), Running Antelope, circa 1940, tempera on white paper, signed, 14 x 15½in. (Robt. W. Skinner Inc.) $375

Great Lakes beaded cloth bandolier bag, early 20th century, 42in. long. (Robt. W. Skinner Inc.) $600

Southwestern coiled basketry bowl, Pima, 16in. diam. (Robt. W. Skinner Inc.) $850

An Indian-style covered woven basket, 1916, 8¼in. high, 10½in. diam. (Robt. W. Skinner Inc.) $450

California coiled basketry tray, Pomo gift basket, with cotton twine and shell disk handle. (Robt. W. Skinner Inc.) $1,200

Southern Ojibwa engraved birchbark instruction scroll, Mide Ghost Lodge Menominee, 67in. long. (Robt. W. Skinner Inc.) $1,300

Late 19th century Hopi polychrome wood Kachina doll, possibly 'Qoia', a Navajo singer, 16½in. high. (Robt. W. Skinner Inc.) $4,000

Navajo fringed Germantown rug, woven on a bright red ground in navy-blue, dark red, pink, white and green, 76 x 83in. (Robt. W. Skinner Inc.) $7,750

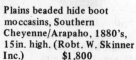

Plains beaded and fringed hide cradleboard, Ute Reservation Period, 39in. high. (Robt. W. Skinner Inc.) $650

A four-color Chocktaw Indian plaited basket, 4½in. high, and a handled three- color Cherokee basket, 11½in. high. (Robt. W. Skinner Inc.) $275

Plains beaded hide boot moccasins, Southern Cheyenne/Arapaho, 1880's, 15in. high. (Robt. W. Skinner Inc.) $1,800

Southwestern pre-historic pottery bowl, late 13th/early 14th century, 16½in. diam. (Robt. W. Skinner Inc.) $3,300

Plains beaded and quilled hide 'Possible' bag, Sioux, late 19th century, 20¾in. long. (Robt. W. Skinner Inc.) $1,500

Late 19th century Plains carved red Catlinite pipehead, in the form of an eagle's claw clutching an ovoid-shaped bowl. (Robt. W. Skinner Inc.) $275

Plains pony beaded and fringed hide dress, 19th century, formed of two skins, 51in. long. (Robt. W. Skinner Inc.) $7,200

American Indian wood Kachina doll, Hopi of flattened form, probably 'Shalako Mana', 11in. high. (Robt. W. Skinner Inc.) $2,800

Navajo pictorial weaving, woven on a burgundy ground in white, green, brown, black and pink, 43 x 57in. (Robt. W. Skinner Inc.) $900

Eskimo/Northwest Coast polychrome wood mask, 19th century, cedar, 8½in. long. (Robt. W. Skinner Inc.) $2,200

Southern Ojibwa engraved birchbark document scroll, Mide-Wiwim Society, 61in. long. (Robt. W. Skinner Inc.) $1,700

Great Lakes loom beaded cloth bandolier bag, late 19th century, 36in. long. (Robt. W. Skinner Inc.) $850 £477

An officer's single epaulette of the 1st or the Royal Regt., gilt lace ornamental embroidered scarlet strap, 2½in., GC for age (gilt lace tarnished). (Wallis & Wallis) $650

A Chinese horse armor with hemp backing, the body comprising two crupper and peytral panels of overlapping fish-scale plates. (Christie's) $401

A composite Cuirassiers three-quarter armor, circa 1600, fingers lacking from gauntlets, pitted and cleaned overall. (Phillips) $4,536

A Grenadier Guards Drummer's richly laced full dress tunic, a buff leather belt, full dress trousers, and a Guardsman's bearskin. (Christie's) $545

A composite Continental armor mainly in early 17th century style, mounted on a fabric-covered wooden dummy, with realistically-carved, painted and bearded head set with glass eyes. (Christie's) $6,674

ARMS & ARMOR

Grenadier Guards: Drum Major's sash extremely richly embroidered with a magnificent trophy of arms, thirty-four battle honours ending with France and Flanders 1914-18. (Christie's) $1,278

A left hand gauntlet circa 1580, deep roped knucklepiece, four lames, and cuff. (Wallis & Wallis) $270

A composite Continental armor in mid 16th century style, with roped borders and etched decoration, on a wooden stand. (Christie's) $3,560

A fine Black Watch broadsword by Wilkinson Sword Co. Ltd, London with 32½in. blade, an officer's Black Watch full dress doublet, a kilt and Black Watch sporran by Wm. Anderson & Sons Ltd. (Christie's) $1,550

A decorative composite armor mainly in 16th century style, on a wooden display-stand with square base. (Christie's) $1,602

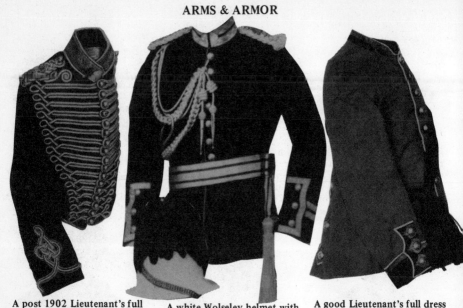

A post 1902 Lieutenant's full dress blue jacket of The Royal Horse Artillery, with scarlet collar, gilt cord and lace trim including 17 loops to chest. (Wallis & Wallis) $475

A white Wolseley helmet with gilt chin-chain, a dark blue tunic with black velvet facings and with General's buttons, white leather gloves. (Christie's) $637

A good Lieutenant's full dress scarlet tunic circa 1865 of the 18th (Royal Irish) Regt., with its crimson silk shoulder sash. (Wallis & Wallis) $455

Pre-1914 Major's blue tunic of The Royal Regt. of Artillery. (James Norwich Auctions) $40

A composite armor comprising: lacquered iron four-plate momonari kabuto with four lame shikiro and modern kuwagata, all contained in a wood box, some restoration. (Phillips) $2,464

A yellow Skinner's kurta with plain shoulder chains, a fine pouchbelt and its Skinner's Horse title scroll. (Christie's) $4,500

A good post 1902 Lt. Colonel's full dress scarlet doublet of The Gordon Highlanders, and a pair of tartan trews. (Wallis & Wallis) $365

A pre-1914 officer's scarlet tunic of The Prince of Wales Leinster Regt. (James Norwich Auctions) $48

A Prussian Rittmeister's dress tunic of the 14th Uhlan Regt., dark blue with maroon piping and cuffs. (Wallis & Wallis) $300

An Edward VII blue mess jacket and waistcoat of The King's Own Norfolk Yeomanry, worn by Regt. Sgt. Major Hudgell. (James Norwich Auctions) $120

A 19th century sugake-laced okegawa-do, unsigned, lacking armor-box. (Christie's) $4,928

A fine Colonel's full dress scarlet tunic of The Royal Warwickshire Regt., with a crimson silk waistsash and tassels. (Wallis & Wallis) $400

DAGGERS

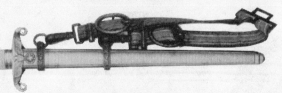

A Nazi Army officer's dagger, by Kolping, plated mounts, white grip, in its plated sheath with hanging straps and belt lug. (Wallis & Wallis) $192

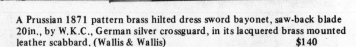

A Prussian 1871 pattern brass hilted dress sword bayonet, saw-back blade 20in., by W.K.C., German silver crossguard, in its lacquered brass mounted leather scabbard. (Wallis & Wallis) $140

A Nazi Red Cross Man's dagger, blade retaining all original polish, plated mounts, diced black grips, in its black painted steel sheath. (Wallis & Wallis) $239

An Imperial German Naval officer's dirk, blade with WKC, Knight's head trade mark, gilt mounts, crown pommel, real ivory grip, original dress bullion knot, in its lacquered brass sheath. (Wallis & Wallis) $576

A Nazi model 1936 S.S. officer's dagger, by Boker, German silver mounts, in its metal sheath with plated mounts and hanging chains and belt clip. (Wallis & Wallis) $1,200

A Nazi Naval officer's dirk, by W.K.C., blade retaining virtually all original polish, wire bound white celluloid grip, in its gilt brass sheath. (Wallis & Wallis) $239

An Imperial German Naval Applicanten Naval dirk, blade 12½in., steel hilt with double small folding shell guards, in its leather sheath. (Wallis & Wallis) $416

DAGGERS

A Nazi Naval officer's dirk, plain blade by Eickhorn, gilt mounts, wire bound white celluloid grip, in its gilt sheath with original bullion dress knot. (Wallis & Wallis) $184

A Nazi Hitler Youth bayonet, blade 8in., steel mounts, stylized eagle's head pommel, diced black grips, in its black painted metal scabbard. (Wallis & Wallis) $128

A Nazi Wehrmacht dress bayonet, plated blade 9¾in., by Everitz, plated mounts, stylized eagle's head pommel, real staghorn grips, in its black painted steel scabbard with leather frog. (Wallis & Wallis) $112

A Nazi Naval officer's dirk, by Eickhorn, plain double fullered blade, gilt mounts, white grip, in its gilt sheath with bullion dress knot. (Wallis & Wallis) $240

A 3rd Reich Naval officer's dirk, by Eickhorn, blade retaining all original polish, gilt mounts, wire bound white celluloid grip, bullion dress knot tied naval style, in its gilt sheath. (Wallis & Wallis) $429

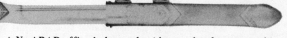

A Nazi RAD officer's dagger, by Alcoso, plated mounts, white celluloid grip, in its plated sheath. (Wallis & Wallis) $455

A South African Air Force officer's dress dagger, plain, plated blade 9in., gilt brass crosspiece in form of eagle with wings spread, round fish-skin covered grip, gilt band mounts, in its leather covered sheath. (Wallis & Wallis) $160

29

DAGGERS

A Georgian Naval Officer's dirk circa 1790, straight double edged blade 15in., with single fullers, etched with crowned G. R., trophies of arms and other trophies. (Wallis & Wallis) $140

An unusual all steel Indian katar, 15in., blade 9½in. with swollen armor piercing tip and raised ribs, hilt with broad flared sides deeply chiselled overall with flowers and foliage in relief. (Wallis & Wallis) $105

A scarce 1907 Presentation bayonet, blade 17in., by Wilkinson, ordnance stamp at forte, etched: Presented to J. Clayton by The Wilkinson Sword Co. Ltd. on the completion of 2,000,000 Bayonets, 1915-1918' (Wallis & Wallis) $140

A rare 1st Pattern Field service fighting knife, tapering double edged blade 7in., by Wilkinson Sword, also etched at forte 'The Field Service Fighting Knife'. (Wallis & Wallis) $455

A large late 19th century Ottoman enamelled jambiya, 22in., broad curved tapered double edged blade 11in. with twin narrow fullers. (Wallis & Wallis) $440

A large late 19th century Ottoman enamelled jambiya, 22in., broad curved tapered double edged blade 11in. with twin narrow fullers.

An unusual 19th century all steel Tibetan dagger, broad single edged blade 11in. with narrow fuller, steel hilt and large sheath mounts nicely chiselled overall with scrolling foliage. (Wallis & Wallis) $78

An Australian M.1944 Machete Paratroopers bayonet Bolo blade 11in., steel mounts, wood grip. (Wallis & Wallis) $130

DAGGERS

An unusual 19th century Burmese/Thai dagger, straight single edged blade 11½in., stamped 'Manipurhaih', downturned brass crosspiece with chiselled lion's head terminals in full relief. (Wallis & Wallis)$300

A scarce U.S.M.C. Stiletto fighting knife, double edged blade 6¾in., checkered solid alloy hilt with integral crosspiece, in a brown leather M6 sheath. (Wallis & Wallis) $315

A large Wahabite dagger jambiya, 27¼in. overall, curved tapered double edged blade 14½in., silver colored metal hilt and sheath embossed with foliage. (Wallis & Wallis) $500

An attractive 19th century Indian bowie knife, blade 7in. with false edge, polished ivory grip, silver colored metal mounts, recurved crosspiece chiselled with foliage. (Wallis & Wallis) $210

A good quality Victorian Scottish dirk of The 78th (Ross-shire Buffs) Regt., straight single edged bifullered blade 12in. etched with crowned 'VR' cypher, '78 Highland' beneath elephant. (Wallis & Wallis)
$1,650

A good Spanish Ripol type knife, 17½in., broad tapered single edged blade 11½in. chiselled brass sheath and hilt mounts. (Wallis & Wallis)
$140

An unusual 19th century Turkish H.M. silver mounted trousse, 15½in., the three knives with curved fullered single edged blades 6¼in. to 4½in., hilts made from jade. (Wallis & Wallis) $630

FLASKS

A good embossed copper powder flask (R. 355) 8in., graduated nozzle stamped G. & J. W. Hawksley. (Wallis & Wallis) $90

A powder horn circa 1800, brass circular base plate engraved with the device of the Percy Tenantry, 13½in. long. (Wallis & Wallis) $135

An embossed copper powder flask (R.535), 8in. embossed with panel of geometric and foliate ornament, patent brass top stamped James Dixon & Sons. (Wallis & Wallis) $87

An 18th century Persian all steel powder flask, of swollen boat or swan form. (Wallis & Wallis) $107

A good scarce Japanese cow horn powder flask, 5½in. very well made and polished, turned ivory spout and collar emanate from fluted horn tehenkanemono. (Wallis & Wallis) $160

An engraved rifle horn with carved horntip powder measure, Midwest, dated 1843, in cartouche, 4½in. long. (Robt. W. Skinner Inc.) $1,200

A good 18th/19th century Transylvanian stag horn powder flask, 6in. decorated overall with geometric devices. (Wallis & Wallis) $175

A brass mounted Continental lanthorn powder flask, fixed baluster turned nozzle swivels on knuckle joint for cut off. (Wallis & Wallis) $150

A 17th/18th century Persian Circassian walnut powder flask, 6in., sprung steel lever charger with shaped top. (Wallis & Wallis) $400

An unusually large and scarce American embossed copper gun flask 'Indian Hunting Buffalo', 9½in. overall, (Wallis & Wallis) $175

A scarce 18th century Persian silver mounted brass powder flask of swollen form, 5½in., engraved overall with flowers and foliage. (Wallis & Wallis) $265

A good small copper pistol sized powder flask, 4¾in., common brass charger. (Wallis & Wallis) $87

FUCHI-KASHIRA

An 18th century shakudo nanakoji fuchi-kashira decorated with serpents in takabori, gilt detail. (Christie's) $1,267

A shibuichi migakiji fuchi-kashira, signed Hidekatsu, early 19th century. (Christie's) $880

A 19th century shakudo nanakoji fuchi-kashira, inscribed Ishiguro Masayoshi. (Christie's) $968

A 19th century fuchi-kashira, silver takazogan, inscribed Omori Eishu. (Christie's) $2,195

A shakudo nanakoji fuchi-kashira, signed Kondo Mitsuyasu, circa 1800. (Christie's) $1,091

An 18th century shakudo nanakoji gilt rimmed in fuchi-kashira, Soten style. (Christie's) $704

A shibuichi fuchi-kashira, decorated with carp among gilt water-weeds, signed Tomohisa, Mito School, circa 1800. (Christie's) $844

Early 19th century copper fuchi-kashira depicting Raiden among clouds on the kashira, unsigned. (Christie's) $440

A shakudo nanakoji fuchi-kashira, iroe takazogan, reed warblers on branches of blossoming plum, signed Ganshoshi Nagatsune and kao. (Christie's) $739

A 19th century shakudo migakiji fuchi-kashira decorated with Gentoku, signed Yasumasa. (Christie's) $563

A shakudo migakiji fuchi-kashira decorated in takazogan with ants and their eggs, 19th century. (Christie's) $563

A 19th century shakudo nanakoji fuchi-kashira, unsigned. depicting a cuckoo in flight. (Christie's) $563

HELMETS

An officer's 1855 pattern shako bearing gilt plate of the 82nd Regiment with VR cypher on the gilt ball, upper lining missing. (Christie's) $728

An interesting WW1 steel helmet in the form of a tropical helmet, khaki painted overall. (Wallis & Wallis) $100

A good other ranks helmet of the 1st Dragoon Guards, brass skull and fittings, brass and white metal helmet plate, red horse hair plume. (Phillips) $810

A Prussian M.1915 Ersatz (Pressed Felt) O.R's Pickelhaube of a Pioneer Battalion. (Wallis & Wallis) $245

A good Spanish Officers shako, fawn cloth, leather peak and headband, simulated leather top. (Wallis & Wallis) $380

A Hesse M.1915 Infantryman's Pickelhaube, gray painted helmet plate and mounts leather lining and chinstrap. (Wallis & Wallis) $260

Queen's Own Cameron Highlanders: officer's feather bonnet by W. Cater, Pall Mall. (Christie's) $584

A well made modern copy of an English close helmet from a Greenwich armor, of good form and weight. (Wallis & Wallis) $500

A Cabasset circa 1600, formed in one piece with 'pear stalk' finial, plain narrow brim. (Wallis & Wallis) $230

34

HELMETS

A large round black hat with pale drab cotton cover bearing a large elaborate badge in wire embroidery of the Bersaglieri. (Christie's) $127

An English civil war period pikeman's 'pot', made in two pieces with sunken edges and steel rivetted borders. (Wallis & Wallis) $800

An Italian black velvet fez by Unione Militare, Roma with an embroidered badge surmounted by Fasces. (Christie's) $218

An officer's bearskin cap of the Royal Welsh Fusiliers with fine white metal mounted gilt grenade. (Christie's) $475

A Bavarian M.1915 Uhlan ORs Tschapska, gray painted helmet plate and mounts. (Wallis & Wallis) $315

5th (Northumberland Fusiliers): officer's bearskin cap with regimental gilt grenade, inside is marked H.W. Archer, Esq., 5th Fusiliers. (Christie's) $639

A very rare helmet of an experimental pattern for French Dragoon regiments circa 1900, bearing manufacturer's stamp: B. Franck et ses fils, Aubervilliers. (Christie's) $728

An interesting composite close helmet made up for the Pisan Bridge Festival, the skull from a very rare Milanese armet circa 1440-1450. (Wallis & Wallis) $2,750

A Rifles officer's Astrakhan busby, a tunic with scarlet facings and a composite pouch-belt with a whistle, chin-boss and badge. (Christie's) $435

HELMETS

A Prussian Artillery officer's pickelhaube of The 10th Field Artillery Regt. (Wallis & Wallis) $496

A scarce American Civil War Officers Dark Blue Kepi, black lace edge trim and side welts. (Wallis & Wallis) $475

A Prussian Cuirassier trooper's helmet with gray metal helmet plate and spike. (Wallis & Wallis) $576

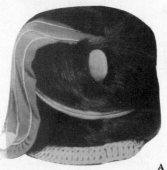

A Prussian Cuirassier officer's helmet with brown leather and silk inner lining. (Wallis & Wallis) $1,089

An officer's fur busby of The 20th Hussars. (Wallis & Wallis) $544

A Prussian Cuirassier officer's helmet, green leather lining to lobster tail and stepped peak. (Wallis & Wallis) $1,122

A Victorian officer's blue cloth spiked helmet of The Royal Scots. (Wallis & Wallis) $478

A closed cuirassier's Savoyard type burgonet with raised comb and pointed peak. (Christie's) $1,909

A tall Cabasset circa 1600, formed in one piece with smooth finish and vestigial 'pear stalk' finial. (Wallis & Wallis) $350

HELMETS

A Prussian Jager Zu Pferd trooper's helmet with gray metal finish to spike and mounts. (Wallis & Wallis) $600

A Prussian Infantryman's ersatz (pressed felt) pickelhaube of The 87th Infantry Regt. (Wallis & Wallis) $432

A distinctive beige/gray helmet of the Harrow Rifles with matching leather binding, label inside marked Chamberlayne. (Christie's) $690

An Other Rank's brass 1871 pattern helmet of The 1st King's Dragoon Guards. (James Norwich Auctions) $520

A Prussian NCO's lance cap of The 1st Guard Uhlan Regt. (Wallis & Wallis) $1,040

Officer's helmet of The King's Own Norfolk Imperial Yeomanry, circa 1915. (James Norwich Auctions) $1,240

Trooper's helmet of The King's Own Norfolk Imperial Yeomanry, circa 1910. (James Norwich Auctions) $577

An early 17th century pikeman's pot helmet, formed in two pieces with engraved line decoration and brass rivets. (Wallis & Wallis) $455

A French 1858 pattern Dragoon officer's helmet. (Wallis & Wallis) $2,145

HELMETS

Early 19th century kabuto with a russet-iron sixty-two plate hoshi-bachi, rear plate signed Nagamichi. (Christie's) $2,816

A post-1902 R.N. Flag officer's dark blue peaked cap. (Wallis & Wallis) $352

A Nazi Naval officer's cocked hat with silk lining. (Wallis & Wallis) $192

An officer's blue cloth peaked forage cap of The Somersetshire Light Infantry. (Wallis & Wallis) $304

A Victorian officer's blue cloth spiked helmet of The Royal Engineers. (Wallis & Wallis) $400

A Prussian other rank's lance cap as worn by The 1st and 2nd Uhlan Regt. (Wallis & Wallis) $800

A Victorian officer's blue cloth spiked helmet of The Royal Scots. (Wallis & Wallis) $800

A post-1902 officer's shako of The Highland Light Infantry. (Wallis & Wallis) $336

A post-1902 officer's blue cloth spiked helmet of The Dorsetshire Regt. (Wallis & Wallis) $400

HELMETS

An Imperial German Hussar officer's busby of The 2nd Leib Hussar Regt. (Queen Victoria of Prussia). (Wallis & Wallis) $2,887

A 17th century kabuto with russet-iron hoshi-bachi, unsigned. (Christie's) $2,816

A post-1902 officer's blue cloth ball-topped helmet of The Royal Army Medical Corps. (Wallis & Wallis) $315

A Volunteer Artillery Officer's blue cloth ball topped helmet, silver plated mounts. (Wallis & Wallis) $265

A Victorian officer's peaked forage cap of The Derbyshire Regt. (Wallis & Wallis) $304

An Imperial Austrian Dragoon officer's helmet with silk and leather lining. (Wallis & Wallis) $1,732

Helmet from the uniform of Col. Pilkington, 4th Vol. Bn. The King's Regt. (Wallis & Wallis) $1,320

An officer's fur busby of The Royal Corps. of Signals, with leather lining. (Wallis & Wallis) $152

An officer's blue cloth spiked helmet of The Royal Warwickshire Regt. (Wallis & Wallis) $496

A steel barrelled flintlock blunderbuss pistol circa 1820, 12in. overall, swamped barrel 7in. with B'ham proofs and stamped 'London' at breech, trade quality flat lock with swan neck cock and unbridled frizzen. (Wallis & Wallis) $820

A 40-bore all-metal Scottish percussion dress belt pistol, circa 1850, 9½in., 3 stage barrel, 6in., silvered metal stock, ram's horn butt, button trigger, pricker to butt, steel ramrod, sprung steel belt hook and stock profusely engraved overall. (Wallis & Wallis) $1,980

A 22-bore Prussian model 1850 percussion Cavalry trooper's pistol, 15in., barrel 8¾in., halfstocked, regulation brass mounts, steel lanyard ring, side-plate and backstrap. (Wallis & Wallis) $660

A 16-bore New Land pattern flintlock holster pistol, 15in., browned barrel 9in., Tower proved, fullstocked, stepped lockplate, regulation brass mounts, swivel ram-rod and stock struck with inspector's marks. (Wallis & Wallis) $792

A flintlock boxlock pocket pistol, by W. Bond, circa 1820, 5¼in. overall, turn-off barrel 1½in. with fern-tip engraved muzzle, Birmingham proved. (Wallis & Wallis) $363

A 14-bore miquelet flintlock Spanish belt pistol, by Torento, circa 1800, 10in., half octagonal barrel 5½in., fullstocked, brass furniture with applied silver foil bosses to buttcap, trigger guard bow and escutcheon. (Wallis & Wallis) $726

PISTOLS

A 14-bore French model 1777 brass framed Cavalry trooper's flintlock belt pistol, 13in., barrel 7½in. with arsenal stamp and 83 at breech. (Wallis & Wallis) $858

A 16-bore E.I.G. percussion holster pistol, 13½in., blued barrel 8in., Tower proved, fullstocked, regulation brass furniture, swivel ramrod and steel lanyard ring. (Wallis & Wallis) $495

A 48-bore flintlock sidelock travelling pistol, by Tatham, circa 1815, 8in. overall, browned octagonal twist barrel 3½in. with gold line at breech engraved 'Tatham, London', walnut fullstock and scroll-engraved lion trigger guard with pineapple finial. (Wallis & Wallis) $1,320

A 5-shot 54-bore Kerr's patent back action single action percussion revolver, No. 11282, 11in., octagonal blued barrel 5½in., London proved, underlever rammer, steel lanyard ring to buttcap and onepiece chequered walnut grip. (Wallis & Wallis) $660

A .577in. 1856 pattern rifled percussion Yeomanry Cavalry pistol, 16in., blued barrel 10in., Tower proved, hinged leaf sights stamped 2 and 3, fullstocked, regulation brass mounts, swivel ramrod and steel lanyard ing. (Wallis & Wallis) $1,039

Late 18th century 64-bore Italian miquelet flintlock holster pistol, 17½in., stepped barrel 12in., fullstocked, stepped Roman style lock, brass furniture, longspur buttcap engraved with trophies and brass tipped wooden ramrod. (Wallis & Wallis) $907

A 7.63mm. Mauser model 96 cone hammer semi-auto pistol No. 6622 (matching), 11½in., barrel 5½in., ramp rearsight to 300 metres, two-piece ribbed walnut grips with steel lanyard ring, in its wooden holster acting as detachable stock. (Wallis & Wallis)   **$3,300**

A pair of slender mid 18th century English 22-bore flintlock holster pistols of provincial quality, 17in. overall, round barrels 10in., with tapered panel and acanthus engraving at breeches, London proofs, plain fullstocks with carved apron round barrel-tang and brass mounts including long-spurred butt caps. (Wallis & Wallis)   **$1,650**

An 1856 pattern .577in. Yeomanry Cavalry trooper's rifled percussion holster pistol with detachable shoulder stock, 26¼in. overall, pistol 16in., barrel 10in., Tower proved. (Wallis & Wallis) **$1,485**

A pair of 36-bore percussion duelling pistols, by Henry Tatham, Jnr., circa 1840, 15½in. overall, rifled octagonal twist barrels 10in., platinum vents and lines at breeches, figured walnut halfstocks with rounded checkered butts and oval horn buttcaps. (Wallis & Wallis)
        $2,392

A pair of early 19th century horse pistols with walnut stocks, Turkish stamp. (Woolley & Wallis)   **$340**

PISTOLS

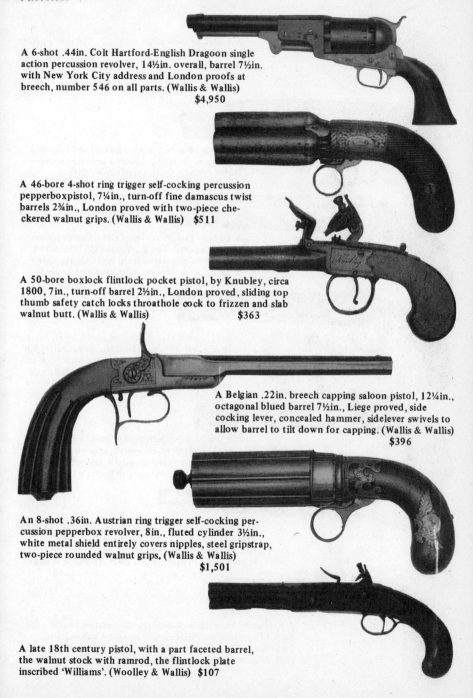

A 6-shot .44in. Colt Hartford-English Dragoon single
action percussion revolver, 14½in. overall, barrel 7½in.
with New York City address and London proofs at
breech, number 546 on all parts. (Wallis & Wallis)
$4,950

A 46-bore 4-shot ring trigger self-cocking percussion
pepperboxpistol, 7¼in., turn-off fine damascus twist
barrels 2¾in., London proved with two-piece checkered walnut grips. (Wallis & Wallis) $511

A 50-bore boxlock flintlock pocket pistol, by Knubley, circa
1800, 7in., turn-off barrel 2½in., London proved, sliding top
thumb safety catch locks throathole cock to frizzen and slab
walnut butt. (Wallis & Wallis) $363

A Belgian .22in. breech capping saloon pistol, 12¼in.,
octagonal blued barrel 7½in., Liege proved, side
cocking lever, concealed hammer, sidelever swivels to
allow barrel to tilt down for capping. (Wallis & Wallis)
$396

An 8-shot .36in. Austrian ring trigger self-cocking percussion pepperbox revolver, 8in., fluted cylinder 3½in.,
white metal shield entirely covers nipples, steel gripstrap,
two-piece rounded walnut grips. (Wallis & Wallis)
$1,501

A late 18th century pistol, with a part faceted barrel,
the walnut stock with ramrod, the flintlock plate
inscribed 'Williams'. (Woolley & Wallis) $107

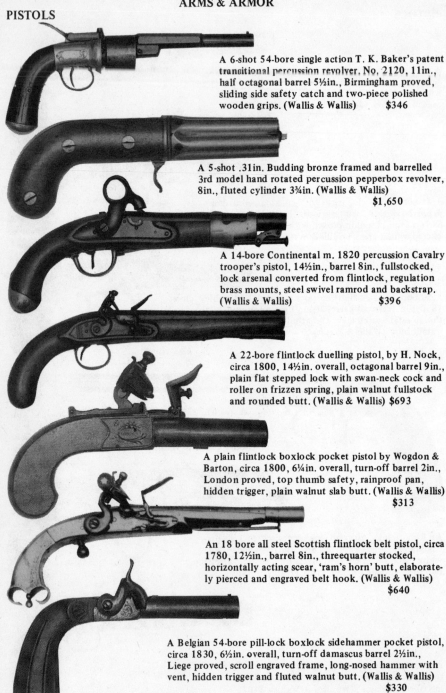

A 6-shot 54-bore single action T. K. Baker's patent transitional percussion revolver, No. 2120, 11in., half octagonal barrel 5½in., Birmingham proved, sliding side safety catch and two-piece polished wooden grips. (Wallis & Wallis) $346

A 5-shot .31in. Budding bronze framed and barrelled 3rd model hand rotated percussion pepperbox revolver, 8in., fluted cylinder 3¾in. (Wallis & Wallis)
$1,650

A 14-bore Continental m. 1820 percussion Cavalry trooper's pistol, 14½in., barrel 8in., fullstocked, lock arsenal converted from flintlock, regulation brass mounts, steel swivel ramrod and backstrap. (Wallis & Wallis) $396

A 22-bore flintlock duelling pistol, by H. Nock, circa 1800, 14½in. overall, octagonal barrel 9in., plain flat stepped lock with swan-neck cock and roller on frizzen spring, plain walnut fullstock and rounded butt. (Wallis & Wallis) $693

A plain flintlock boxlock pocket pistol by Wogdon & Barton, circa 1800, 6¼in. overall, turn-off barrel 2in., London proved, top thumb safety, rainproof pan, hidden trigger, plain walnut slab butt. (Wallis & Wallis)
$313

An 18 bore all steel Scottish flintlock belt pistol, circa 1780, 12½in., barrel 8in., threequarter stocked, horizontally acting scear, 'ram's horn' butt, elaborately pierced and engraved belt hook. (Wallis & Wallis)
$640

A Belgian 54-bore pill-lock boxlock sidehammer pocket pistol, circa 1830, 6½in. overall, turn-off damascus barrel 2½in., Liege proved, scroll engraved frame, long-nosed hammer with vent, hidden trigger and fluted walnut butt. (Wallis & Wallis)
$330

PISTOLS

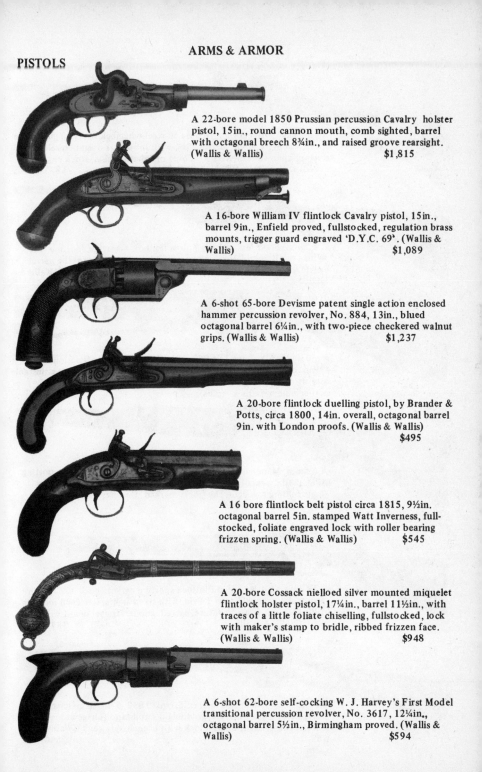

A 22-bore model 1850 Prussian percussion Cavalry holster pistol, 15in., round cannon mouth, comb sighted, barrel with octagonal breech 8¾in., and raised groove rearsight. (Wallis & Wallis) $1,815

A 16-bore William IV flintlock Cavalry pistol, 15in., barrel 9in., Enfield proved, fullstocked, regulation brass mounts, trigger guard engraved 'D.Y.C. 69'. (Wallis & Wallis) $1,089

A 6-shot 65-bore Devisme patent single action enclosed hammer percussion revolver, No. 884, 13in., blued octagonal barrel 6¼in., with two-piece checkered walnut grips. (Wallis & Wallis) $1,237

A 20-bore flintlock duelling pistol, by Brander & Potts, circa 1800, 14in. overall, octagonal barrel 9in. with London proofs. (Wallis & Wallis) $495

A 16 bore flintlock belt pistol circa 1815, 9½in. octagonal barrel 5in. stamped Watt Inverness, fullstocked, foliate engraved lock with roller bearing frizzen spring. (Wallis & Wallis) $545

A 20-bore Cossack nielloed silver mounted miquelet flintlock holster pistol, 17¼in., barrel 11½in., with traces of a little foliate chiselling, fullstocked, lock with maker's stamp to bridle, ribbed frizzen face. (Wallis & Wallis) $948

A 6-shot 62-bore self-cocking W. J. Harvey's First Model transitional percussion revolver, No. 3617, 12¼in., octagonal barrel 5½in., Birmingham proved. (Wallis & Wallis) $594

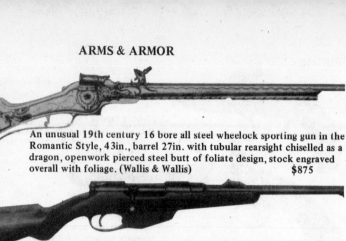

An unusual 19th century 16 bore all steel wheelock sporting gun in the Romantic Style, 43in., barrel 27in. with tubular rearsight chiselled as a dragon, openwork pierced steel butt of foliate design, stock engraved overall with foliage. (Wallis & Wallis) $875

A 6.5mm. Steyr Model 1899 bolt-actionbox magazine sporting rifle, 47in. overall, barrel 26in., number 8493 on trigger guard, the barrel engraved 'Charles Lancaster, 151 New Bond St. London, W.' (Wallis & Wallis) $115

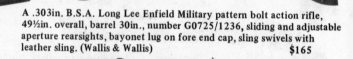

A .303in. B.S.A. Long Lee Enfield Military pattern bolt action rifle, 49½in. overall, barrel 30in., number G0725/1236, sliding and adjustable aperture rearsights, bayonet lug on fore end cap, sling swivels with leather sling. (Wallis & Wallis) $165

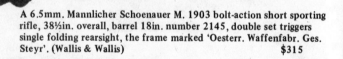

A 6.5mm. Mannlicher Schoenauer M. 1903 bolt-action short sporting rifle, 38½in. overall, barrel 18in. number 2145, double set triggers single folding rearsight, the frame marked 'Oesterr. Waffenfabr. Ges. Steyr'. (Wallis & Wallis) $315

A 24 bore Austrian rifled flintlock sporting carbine circa 1770, 34in., swamped octagonal barrel 19½in. with fixed sights, flattened lock, un-bridled frizzen, brass furniture, carved wooden trigger guard with brass inlay. (Wallis & Wallis) $875

An attractive Indian flintlock rifle, circa 1830, 57in. damascus twist barrel with swollen muzzle, gold inlaid scrolls and foliage at breech and muzzle, fullstocked, English lock with Frenchstyle cock. (Wallis & Wallis) $840

A matchlock gun with oak butt and stock, brass match-holder, spring, lock-plate, trigger and guard, the octagonal iron barrel signed Goshu Hino Yoshihisa saku, barrel length 77.8cm. (Christie's) $792

An interesting Irish military style flintlock blunderbuss by Pattison of Dublin circa 1800, 34in., flared steel barrel 18in. stamped on octagonal breech 'Pattison Dublin', fullstocked, military style lock with throat-hole cock. (Wallis & Wallis) $700

A 16-bore Austrian military flintlock carbine, 30in., barrel 14½in., two-third length stock, regulation steel mounts, finger scrolls to trigger guard, carved cheekpiece, steel ramrod and lanyard rings to extended side-plate. (Wallis & Wallis) $495

A good .22in. LR Remington semi-auto take-down Model 24 rifle No. 101927, 45½in. overall including blued 7in. Parker Hale sound moderation, blued barrel 21in. with Remington address and Browning patent 1916, blued telescopic sight stamped with Winchester address. (Wallis & Wallis) $315

A U.S. .30in. M1-A1 semi-automatic carbine with folding skeleton stock for airborne troops, 36in. overall, barrel 18in., number 370180, the action stamped 'InlandDiv', with sling swivels and webbing sling. (Wallis & Wallis) $455

A French 11mm. Gras Model 1874 bolt action single shot military rifle 46¼in. overall, barrel 28in., number 18015, the frame stamped 'Manu-facture d'Armes St.Etienne Mle 1874'. (Wallis & Wallis) $160

A Greene's patent 28-bore breech loading Maynard's tape primed percussion carbine, No. 503, 35in., blued barrel 18in. released by front trigger, turns and swings out for loading, ladder rearsight to 600 yards. (Wallis & Wallis)
$1,815

A .450in. Westley Richards 'monkey-tail' breech loading percussion sporting rifle, No. 5550.C, 42½in., octagonal barrel 25in., Birmingham proved, five-leaf rearsights to 500 yards, ladder rearsight to 1000 yards. (Wallis & Wallis)
$792

A 40-bore Austrian percussion sporting rifle, by W. Leithner of Ischl, circa 1850, 38½in., octagonal barrel 23½in., fullstocked, swivel safety catch and foliate engraved steel furniture, carved cheekpiece, staghorn ramrod pipe, and brass tipped mahogany ramrod. (Wallis & Wallis) $1,773

A 9-shot 36-bore P. W. Porter's patent vertically revolving turret percussion rifle, No. 630, 45in., octagonal barrel 26in., lever at side of frame allows action to hinge away for removing cylinder, underlever cocking lever cocks hammer and revolves cylinder. (Wallis & Wallis) $2,640

A 30-bore Hall's patent American breech loading military flintlock Harper's Ferry rifled, dated 1837, 53in., barrel 32¾in., regulation steel mounts, 3 barrel bands, finger scroll to trigger guard, steel sling swivels and cleaning rod. (Wallis & Wallis) $1,980

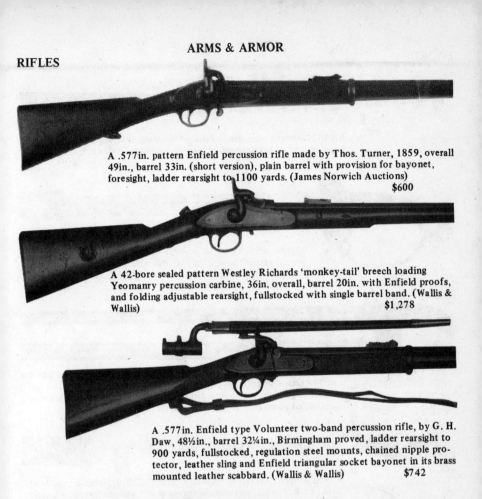

A .577in. pattern Enfield percussion rifle made by Thos. Turner, 1859, overall 49in., barrel 33in. (short version), plain barrel with provision for bayonet, foresight, ladder rearsight to 1100 yards. (James Norwich Auctions)
$600

A 42-bore sealed pattern Westley Richards 'monkey-tail' breech loading Yeomanry percussion carbine, 36in. overall, barrel 20in. with Enfield proofs, and folding adjustable rearsight, fullstocked with single barrel band. (Wallis & Wallis)
$1,278

A .577in. Enfield type Volunteer two-band percussion rifle, by G. H. Daw, 48½in., barrel 32¼in., Birmingham proved, ladder rearsight to 900 yards, fullstocked, regulation steel mounts, chained nipple protector, leather sling and Enfield triangular socket bayonet in its brass mounted leather scabbard. (Wallis & Wallis)
$742

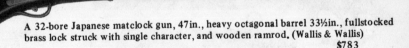

A 32-bore Japanese matclock gun, 47in., heavy octagonal barrel 33½in., fullstocked brass lock struck with single character, and wooden ramrod. (Wallis & Wallis)
$783

A .44-40in. Winchester model 1873 underlever repeating carbine No. 51949, 39in., barrel 20in., London proofs with flip-up rearsight to 500 yards, tube magazine under barrel, brass receiver, steel lanyard ring to side of frame, steel furniture and barrel band. (Wallis & Wallis)
$1,815

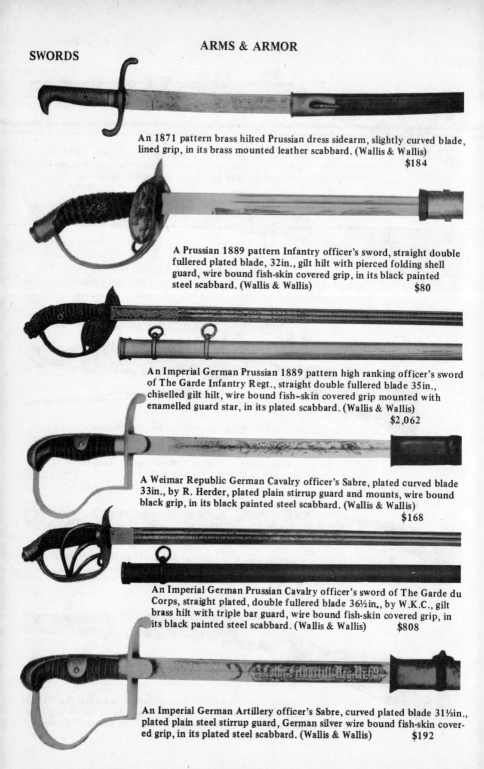

An 1871 pattern brass hilted Prussian dress sidearm, slightly curved blade, lined grip, in its brass mounted leather scabbard. (Wallis & Wallis) $184

A Prussian 1889 pattern Infantry officer's sword, straight double fullered plated blade, 32in., gilt hilt with pierced folding shell guard, wire bound fish-skin covered grip, in its black painted steel scabbard. (Wallis & Wallis) $80

An Imperial German Prussian 1889 pattern high ranking officer's sword of The Garde Infantry Regt., straight double fullered blade 35in., chiselled gilt hilt, wire bound fish-skin covered grip mounted with enamelled guard star, in its plated scabbard. (Wallis & Wallis) $2,062

A Weimar Republic German Cavalry officer's Sabre, plated curved blade 33in., by R. Herder, plated plain stirrup guard and mounts, wire bound black grip, in its black painted steel scabbard. (Wallis & Wallis) $168

An Imperial German Prussian Cavalry officer's sword of The Garde du Corps, straight plated, double fullered blade 36½in., by W.K.C., gilt brass hilt with triple bar guard, wire bound fish-skin covered grip, in its black painted steel scabbard. (Wallis & Wallis) $808

An Imperial German Artillery officer's Sabre, curved plated blade 31½in., plated plain steel stirrup guard, German silver wire bound fish-skin covered grip, in its plated steel scabbard. (Wallis & Wallis) $192

SWORDS

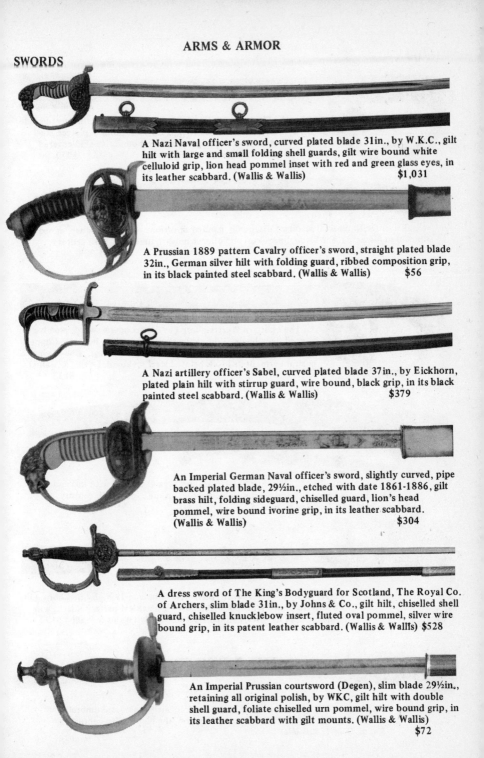

A Nazi Naval officer's sword, curved plated blade 31in., by W.K.C., gilt hilt with large and small folding shell guards, gilt wire bound white celluloid grip, lion head pommel inset with red and green glass eyes, in its leather scabbard. (Wallis & Wallis) $1,031

A Prussian 1889 pattern Cavalry officer's sword, straight plated blade 32in., German silver hilt with folding guard, ribbed composition grip, in its black painted steel scabbard. (Wallis & Wallis) $56

A Nazi artillery officer's Sabel, curved plated blade 37in., by Eickhorn, plated plain hilt with stirrup guard, wire bound, black grip, in its black painted steel scabbard. (Wallis & Wallis) $379

An Imperial German Naval officer's sword, slightly curved, pipe backed plated blade, 29½in., etched with date 1861-1886, gilt brass hilt, folding sideguard, chiselled guard, lion's head pommel, wire bound ivorine grip, in its leather scabbard. (Wallis & Wallis) $304

A dress sword of The King's Bodyguard for Scotland, The Royal Co. of Archers, slim blade 31in., by Johns & Co., gilt hilt, chiselled shell guard, chiselled knucklebow insert, fluted oval pommel, silver wire bound grip, in its patent leather scabbard. (Wallis & Wallis) $528

An Imperial Prussian courtsword (Degen), slim blade 29½in., retaining all original polish, by WKC, gilt hilt with double shell guard, foliate chiselled urn pommel, wire bound grip, in its leather scabbard with gilt mounts. (Wallis & Wallis) $72

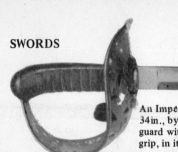

An Imperial Wurttemberg Cavalry trooper's sword, plain curved blade 34in., by Lunceschloss, issue stamps for 1915, foliate pierced steel guard with state arms, steel mounts, wire bound fish-skin covered grip, in its steel scabbard. (Wallis & Wallis) $272

A wakizashi with unusual scabbard diagonally banded in various styles of lacquer, signed Choshu ju Masasada, the blade, hirazukuri and almost musori, unsigned, 19th century, 36.5cm. long. (Christie's) $1,309

An 1889 pattern Wurttemberg Cavalry trooper's sword, pipe back, clipped back blade, 32in., issue stamps for 1891, by Alex. Coppel, steel guard with marking of the 25th Dragoon Regt., ribbed composition grip, in its black painted steel scabbard. (Wallis & Wallis) $123

A finely mounted aikuchi tanto, the kuroronuri saya decorated with kiri and kikumon in hiramakie and a gilt saya-kanamono en suite, mid 19th century, the blade 27.2cm. long, circa 1573. (Christie's) $6,688

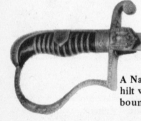
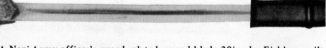

A Nazi Army officer's sword, plated curved blade 29in., by Eickhorn, gilt hilt with flattened stirrup knucklebow with oakleaf pattern, black, wire bound grip, in its black painted steel scabbard. (Wallis & Wallis) $192

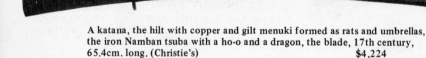

A katana, the hilt with copper and gilt menuki formed as rats and umbrellas, the iron Namban tsuba with a ho-o and a dragon, the blade, 17th century, 65.4cm. long. (Christie's) $4,224

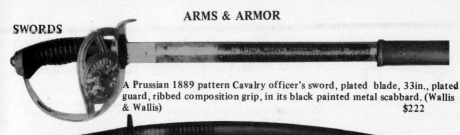

A Prussian 1889 pattern Cavalry officer's sword, plated blade, 33in., plated guard, ribbed composition grip, in its black painted metal scabbard. (Wallis & Wallis) $222

A wakizashi with natural wood scabbard, iron kojiri and fuchi-kashira, the cast iron tsuba depicting a woodcutter and a packhorse, the blade, signed Masatomi, 17th century, 39.1cm. long. (Christie's) $1,309

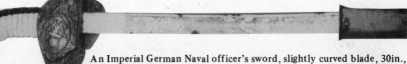

An Imperial German Naval officer's sword, slightly curved blade, 30in., brass hilt, chiselled large and small folding shell guards, lion's head pommel, ribbed white grip, in its brass mounted leather scabbard. (Wallis & Wallis) $363

An aikuchi tanto with fittings by Goto Ichijo, the blade signed Shinsoku, probably mid 15th century, 29.5cm. long. (Christie's) $7,744

A Prussian 1889 pattern Cavalry officer's sword, plated blade 31in., German silver hilt with folding sideguards, ribbed composition grips, in its black painted steel scabbard. (Wallis & Wallis) $144

A tanto blade signed Tairyusai Sokan horu dosaku, and dated Bunkyu ninen nigatsu no hi (February 1862), in brown leather covered scabbard with copper kojiri and fuchi-kashira depicting the Chinese heroes Kan U, Chohi and Gentoku, 33cm. long. (Christie's)
$3,366

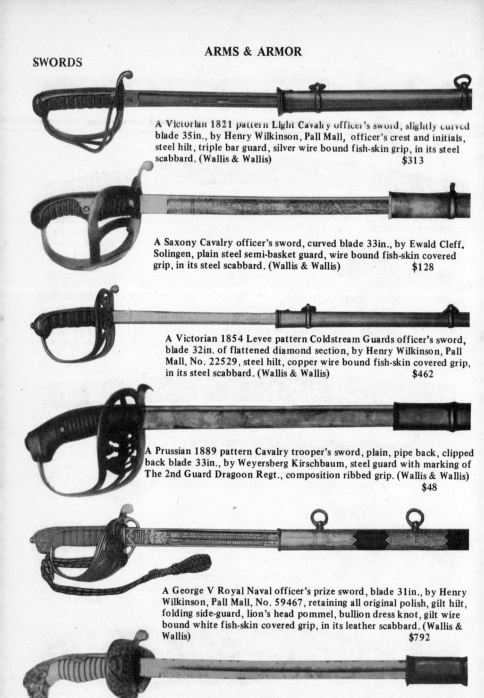

A Victorian 1821 pattern Light Cavalry officer's sword, slightly curved blade 35in., by Henry Wilkinson, Pall Mall, officer's crest and initials, steel hilt, triple bar guard, silver wire bound fish-skin grip, in its steel scabbard. (Wallis & Wallis) $313

A Saxony Cavalry officer's sword, curved blade 33in., by Ewald Cleff. Solingen, plain steel semi-basket guard, wire bound fish-skin covered grip, in its steel scabbard. (Wallis & Wallis) $128

A Victorian 1854 Levee pattern Coldstream Guards officer's sword, blade 32in. of flattened diamond section, by Henry Wilkinson, Pall Mall, No. 22529, steel hilt, copper wire bound fish-skin covered grip, in its steel scabbard. (Wallis & Wallis) $462

A Prussian 1889 pattern Cavalry trooper's sword, plain, pipe back, clipped back blade 33in., by Weyersberg Kirschbaum, steel guard with marking of The 2nd Guard Dragoon Regt., composition ribbed grip. (Wallis & Wallis) $48

A George V Royal Naval officer's prize sword, blade 31in., by Henry Wilkinson, Pall Mall, No. 59467, retaining all original polish, gilt hilt, folding side-guard, lion's head pommel, bullion dress knot, gilt wire bound white fish-skin covered grip, in its leather scabbard. (Wallis & Wallis) $792

An Imperial German Naval officer's sword, curved blade, 32in., gilt chiselled hilt, large and small folding sideguards, lion's head pommel, wire bound ivorine grip, in its leather scabbard with three gilt mounts. (Wallis & Wallis) $320

SWORDS

A scarce 1887 pattern 19th Hussar officer's sword by Wilkinson, No. 42910 (made 1911), slightly curved fullered single edged blade, 35in., wire bound checkered patent solid grip, in its steel scabbard. (Wallis & Wallis) $313 .

A late 19th century pattern Saxony Cavalry trooper's sword, pipe back, clipped back blade 30in., by Gebr. Weyersberg, steel guard with pierced state device, with issue marks of The 19th Hussar Regt., ribbed composition grip. (Wallis & Wallis) $96

An Imperial German Naval officer's sword, curved blade 29½in., steel chiselled hilt, large and small folding sideguards, lion's head pommel, wire bound bone grip, in its leather scabbard. (Wallis & Wallis) $173

A Prussian 1889 pattern Infantry officer's sword, straight double fullered blade, 32in., by Alex. Coppell, brass guard, wire bound leather covered grip, in its black painted steel scabbard. (Wallis & Wallis) $128

A George V officer's sword of The Royal Horse Guards, blade 35in., retaining all original polish, original wash leather liner and bullion dress knot, silver wire bound fish-skin covered grip, in its plated scabbard. (Wallis & Wallis) $924

An Imperial Bavarian Infantry officer's Sabre, plated curved blade 32in., gilt hilt with stirrup knucklebow, ribbed fish-skin covered grip, in its steel scabbard. (Wallis & Wallis) $112

TSUBAS

A 19th century sentoku tsuba formed as a serpent in marubori, signed Nagatsugu, 8.4cm. (Christie's) $3,344

A 19th century iron tsuba with a crayfish in marubori, with gilt hirazogan seal of Munenori, 6.9cm. diam. (Christie's) $860

Late 19th century otafuku-mokko sentoku hari-ishimeji tsuba decorated with two carp, signed Nagamasa. (Christie's) $8,800

A shallow mokkogata tsuba decorated with Susano-o no Mikoto attacking the monster Yamata no orochi, Meiji period, 8.9cm. (Christie's) $1,672

An iron higo tsuba formed as a blossoming plum tree, circa 1725, 7.8cm. diam. (Christie's) $561

Mid 19th century hakkaku copper tsuba carved as a tree-trunk with an eagle, signed Ryuo (Ittosai). (Christie's) $7,040

A large mokkogata iron tsuba, branches of bamboo in takabori, Kyo-shoami school, circa 1800, 8.7cm. (Christie's) $486

Late 18th century iron tsuba, signed Bushu ju Masakata, 7.7cm. diam., and another, early Echizen school, 7cm. diam. (Christie's) $561

Late 19th century hari-ishimeji tsuba decorated with Emma-O and a demonic attendant, inscribed Hamano Noriyuki, 9.6cm. (Christie's) $4,928

TSUBAS

A hexagonal copper ishimeji tsuba decorated with a swallow-tail butterfly, signed Mitsumasa, Meiji period, 9.6cm. (Christie's) $2,464

Late 18th century ju-mokko-gata migakiji iron tsuba, Awa Shoami style. (Christie's) $748

A 19th century sentoku and copper tsuba formed as the eight-headed snake, signed Katsuchika, 8.8cm. (Christie's) $4,576

An 18th century gilt rimmed shakudo mokkogata tsuba, unsigned, 7.6cm. (Christie's) $1,122

An iron tsuba with maple leaves and pine needles in ikizukashi, signed Suruga Takayoshi saku, circa 1850, 7.8cm. diam. (Christie's) $935

An 18th century mokkogata shakudo-nanakoji tsuba, Mino-Goto style, 7.1cm. (Christie's) $860

An aorigata copper ishimeji tsuba decorated with Emma-o the King of Hell holding a shaku, 9.1cm. (Christie's) $4,400

A 19th century mokkogata iron tsuba, Edo Bushu school, 7.4cm. (Christie's) $448

A sentoku tsuba with canted corners decorated with a carp in copper takazogan, signed Tenkodo Hidekuni, 1825-91, 9.6cm. (Christie's) $6,160

TSUBAS

An 18th century oval iron tsuchimeji tsuba, Nara school, 7.7cm. (Christie's) $374

Late 19th century copper migakiji tsuba with wavy rim, signed Sadakatsu, 9.2cm. (Christie's) $2,992

Late 18th/early 19th century oval shakudo migakiji tsuba, Shoki in shishiaibori with gilt and silver detail, 7cm. (Christie's) $1,672

An iron tsuba, sections of a saddle frame in yosukashi, signed Choshu Hagi ju Tomotsune saku, circa 1775, 7.5cm. diam. (Christie's) $561

Late 16th century Momo-yama period tsuba decorated with two men towing a boat, 8.6cm. (Christie's) $1,144

A 19th century iron migakiji tsuba decorated in takabori and iroe takazogan with Chinnan and Gama sennin, 7.6cm. diam. (Christie's) $1,271

A 17th/18th century circular iron tsuba decorated with the takaramono in cloisonne enamels, unsigned, 8.5cm. diam. (Christie's) $1,936

A mokko-shaped Shakudo tsuba chiselled with grass-hoppers amidst numerous flowers, gilt detail, 7.7cm. (Phillips) $264

An 18th century iron tsuba, signed Choshu Hagi ju Kawaji, 7.4cm. diam. (Christie's) $374

TSUBAS

An iron migakiji tsuba, signed
Kageaki, with kao, and dated
Bunsei junen (1827), 7.9cm.
diam. (Christie's) $1,028

Late 18th century oval iron
tsuba, signed Chosu ju Masa-
asada, 7.5cm. (Christie's)
$561

An oval iron migakiji tsuba
decorated with branches of
bamboo in kosukashi, circa
1875, 8.5cm. (Christie's)
$2,057

An 18th century iron soten
tsuba depicting Kyoyu and
Sofu in hikone-bori, 8.3cm.
diam. (Christie's) $860

An oval shakudo-nanakoji
tsuba decorated in gilt, silver
and copper takazogan with
seven horses, 7.3cm.
(Christie's) $1,320

Mid 18th century circular
iron tsuba formed as the
madogiri or paulownia and
window design in yosukashi
and kebori, 8.5cm. (Christie's)
$1,760

A rounded-square shinchu
and sahari tsuba decorated
with Taira no Kiyomori
seated on an engawa, signed
Masanaga, Meiji period,
8.8cm. (Christie's)
$1,936

An oval shakudo-nanakoji
tsuba decorated in silver and
gilt takazogan with three
rats and branches of mochi-
bana, circa 1800, 6.6cm.
(Christie's) $1,215

A mokko-shaped Shakudo
Nanako Tsuba decorated with
flowers in gilt, the rim with
gilt kiri-mon, 7.6cm. (Phillips)
$563

AUTOGRAPH LETTERS & DOCUMENTS

Sir Winston Churchill, LS 1 page 4to, Home Office, Whitehall, 28th June 1911, to King George V. (Onslow's) $581

Benito Mussolini, document 1 page folio, Rome 15th Feb. 1940, promotion for an Air Force General, counter signed by King Victor Emmanuel. (Onslow's) $199

Edith Cavell, ALS on postcard to her mother in Mundesley, Norfolk, 24th January 1913. (Onslow's) $249

Edith Cavell (1865-1915), a worn German identity document, said to have been forged by Edith Cavell in order to assist a soldiers escape. (Onslow's) $166

Anatoli V. Lunacharski (1875-1933), Lunacharski was a Bolshevist and served as Commissar for Education 1917-1929, signed, 6 x 4in. (Onslow's) $132

Richard Strauss (1864-1949), Composer, portrait photograph, inscribed and signed Vienna, 5th February 1931, 10 x 8in., together with another of Strauss in 1917. (Onslow's) $166

Rudolf Hess, Hitler's Deputy, TLS on NSDAP letterheading 1 page 4to, Munich 8th May 1937, to A. Rosenberg. (Onslow's) $199

Winston Churchill and Franklin D. Roosevelt, 'Short Snorter', an English £1 note, signed by Winston Churchill, F. D. Roosevelt and Stanley Matthews. (Onslow's) $830

Heinrich Himmler (1900-1945), TLS 1 page 8vo, Berlin, 30th March 1938, to Nazi Politician Alfred Rosenberg. (Onslow's) $282

King George V and Queen Mary, studio portrait photo, 14 x 18in., signed by both on mount, dated 1911. (Onslow's) $166

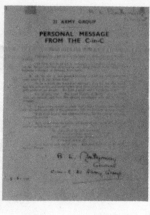

Archduke Franz Ferdinand (1863-1914), ALS 1 page 8vo with integral leaf, Cannes 23rd March 1896 to his accountant, Velicogna, in pencil. (Onslow's) $249

D-Day, 6th June 1941, a printed Personal Message from the C-in-C of 21st Army Group General Sir Bernard L. Montgomery to be read out to all troops', 1 page 4to, dated 5th June 1941. (Onslow's) $166

Samuel Pepys (1633-1703), manuscript letter, signed, 1 page legal folio, Navy Office 17th April 1671, also signed by two other officials. (Onslow's) $697

Lawrence of Arabia (1888-1935), signature as T. E. Shaw, 12/2/29, together with an ALS of Lawrence's mother, 1 page 8vo. (Onslow's) $332

The Beatles, signatures of all four on album sheet, 5½ x 4in., an unsigned photo, greetings card signed by Brian Epstein and a signed pcm. on verso of Maharishi Yogi. (Onslow's)$315

King Charles II, document signed as King, 1 page folio, 22nd June 1665, Whitehall, counter signed by Sir Wm. Morice, Secretary of State. (Onslow's) $348

A clockwork fur covered rabbit automaton, emerging from a green cotton covered cabbage, 7½in. high, French, circa 1900. (Christie's) $544

A varicolored gold musical fob seal with commemorative portraits of Napoleon I and Josephine and an erotic automaton, Swiss, early 19th century, 42mm. high. (Christie's) $17,600

Mid 19th century Swiss musical automaton of singing birds, 38in. high. (Christie's) $935

A Leopold Lambert musical automaton doll, 'The Flower Seller', the Jumeau bisque head impressed 4, 19½in. high. (Lawrence Fine Art) $6,265

A French musical clock diorama, signed Hy Marc, 37¾ x 26¾in. (Lawrence Fine Art) $2,774

Mid 19th century automaton of a singing bird in a cage, the movement signed Bontems, Paris, 21½in. high. (Christie's) $1,760

Mid 19th century Swiss gilt metal automaton with three singing birds, 21in. high. (Christie's) $3,300

Early 20th century mother rocking baby automaton, German, the oak base contains the mechanism. (Robt. W. Skinner Inc.) $700

A French automaton dancing couple by Theroude, on velvet lined circular base, 12in. high. (Lawrence Fine Art) $1,700

An oak stick barometer, signed A. Ortelli, Birmingham, 38in. high. (Christie's) $814

An unusually small mahogany wheel barometer, signed Spelzini, London, 35in. high. (Christie's) $1,548

An early 19th century mahogany stick barometer, the plate signed J. Minolla, London, 38in. high. (Christie's) $631

A large Victorian oak wheel barometer, inscribed Fletcher and Sons, London, 46½in. high. (Christie's) $569

An early 19th century mahogany Sheraton shell wheel barometer, signed J. & P. Noseda, Walsall, 96cm. high. (Phillips) $470

A stained oak stick barometer, inscribed Troughton and Simms, London, 39in. high. (Christie's) $1,003

A 19th century rosewood wheel barometer, signed F. Amadio & Son, London, 100cm. high, circa 1840. (Phillips) $2,534

A mahogany stick barometer, signed Josh. Croce, London, 39in. high. (Christie's) $1,645

BAROMETERS

A George III maho-
gany barometer, the
dial signed Malacrida,
London, 37½in. high.
(Christie's)
$3,052

A mahogany wheel
barometer, inscribed
Dring and Fage,
London, 38½in. high.
(Christie's) $447

George II mahogany
stick barometer with
silvered face, signed
F. Watkins, London,
40½in. high: $39,204
(Christie's)

A late 19th century
mahogany wheel baro-
meter, dial signed
Leoni Taroni & Co.,
London, 36¼in. high.
(Christie's) $865

An oak wheel baro-
meter, inscribed
Gulliford, Dunster,
42in. high. (Christie's)
$407

A good Georgian
mahogany bow-front
mercury barometer, in-
scribed J. Pastorelli,
Liverpool, 37½in. high.
(Christie's)
$3,750

A Victorian mahogany
wheel barometer with
architectural pediment,
inscribed A. Corti, Fecit,
38in. high. (Christie's)
$794

A late 18th century
mahogany stick baro-
meter, signed Cary,
London, 96cm. high.
(Phillips) $1,086

BAROMETERS

A mahogany wheel baro-
meter with boxwood
and ebony inlay, inscrib-
ed Rowe, Cambridge,
42in. high. (Christie's)
$877

A good mahogany bow-
front mercury baro-
meter, signed J. Blatt,
Brighton. (Christie's)
$610

A George III satin-
wood barometer, the
pewter dial signed C.
Gaina, 43¼in. high.
(Christie's)
$1,972

An early 19th century
mahogany stick baro-
meter, dial signed
Manticha Fecit, 37in.
high. (Christie's)
$685

An early 19th century
mahogany stick baro-
meter, signed Joseph
Somalvico & Co.,
London, 98cm. high.
(Phillips) $995

A mahogany stick baro-
meter with crested pedi-
ment, signed J.J. Wilson,
38in. (Christie's)
$1,258

A mahogany stick baro-
meter, signed W. Field,
Aylesbury, 39in. long.
(Christie's)
$1,548

A mahogany wheel baro-
meter, signed Vittory
and Dannelli, Man-
chester. (Christie's)
$1,452

A 19th century mahogany ship's barometer, stamped J. Blair, Bristol, 36¼in. high. (Christie's) $2,164

Early 19th century mahogany stick barometer, signed Rizzi Fecit, 37in. long overall. (Prudential Fine Art) $660

A large 19th century rosewood wheel clock barometer, signed J. Amadio, 128cm. high, circa 1835. (Phillips) $3,620

An 18th century George Adams Jnr. mahogany stick barometer, the scale signed G. Adams, London, 99cm. high. (Phillips) $1,810

A 19th century mahogany ballooning barometer signed on the thermometer scale G & C Dixey, London, 36½in. high. (Christie's) $1,353

A good walnut Admiral Fitzroy's barometer (some damage), 48½in. high. (Christie's) $813

A mid-19th century rosewood stick barometer, signed J. Somalvico & Co., 97cm. high. (Phillips) $579

A very rare portable mercury barometer in ebonized carrying case, length of case 37in. (Christie's) $1,149

BOOKS

Book of Devotions, 146 leaves printed in Latin on vellum, 18 full-page wood engravings, engraved pictorial borders. (Phillips)
$1,814

Agricola (G.): Vom Bergwerck XII Bucher, First German Edition. (Phillips)
$4,202

Dickens (C.): Dombey and Son, 20 orig. parts bound in 1 vol., 40 engr. plates, by G. Bellew of Dublin, 1848. (Phillips) $687

Surtees (R.S.): Jorrocks's Jaunts and Jollities, second edition, hand-col. front. title and 13 plates by Henry Alken. (Phillips) $1,050

Rosel von Rosenhof (A.): Der Monatlich-Herausgegeben Insecten-Belustigung, 4 vol.s, port. by J. M. Windler. (Phillips) $3,960

Combe (William): The English Dance of Death, 2 vol.s, hand-col. front. and vig. title, 72 hand-col. plates by Rowlandson, 1 cover detached. (Phillips) $1,337

Dixon (W.S.): Loose Rein, 11 orig. parts, col. plates, 1887. (Phillips) $787

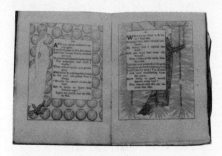

' The Last Ride', by Robert Browning,
printed by Roycrofters , East Aurora, N.Y.,
1900, copy no. 359. (Robt. W. Skinner Inc.)
$450

'Fringilla or Tales in Verse', by Richard D.
Blackmore, published by Burrows & Co.,
Cleveland, 1895, illustrated by Will A.
Bradley, no. 490 of 600 copies. (Robt. W.
Skinner Inc.) $800

Walton (I.) and Cotton (C.): The Complete
Angler, ed Sir H. Nicolas, extended to 4 vol.s
with specially printed titles. (Phillips)
$3,490

Combe (W.): The Tour(s) of Doctor Syntax.
(Phillips) $930

Dickens (C.): The Mystery of Edwin Drood,
6 orig. parts, engr. port., title and 12 plates.
(Phillips) $537

Moliere (J. B. P.): Oeuvres, 6 vol.s, Nouvelle
Edition, port., 33 plates by F. Boucher.
(Phillips) $1,650

A leather bound visitors book, 1909-1922, Used at Windsor Castle and St. James' Palace. (Prudential Fine Art) $478

'Magic Lanterns: how made and how used with practical hints to unpractised lecturers', re-bound, London, E. G. Wood, 74 Cheapside, 1875. (Christie's) $110

'Catalogue of Optical Lantern Slides', rebound in original wrappers, Bradford, Riley Brothers Ltd., n.d. ca 1911. (Christie's) $157

George R. Sims — 'Ballads and poems' the complete works of Sims, with a portrait of the author, London, T. Vernon & Co. Ltd., n.d. (Christie's) $36

A collection of ephemera relating to the cruise of Cunard's R.M.S. Lancastria from Liverpool to Gibraltar, North Africa and the Atlantic Isles, a quantity of menu cards and other literature. (Christie's) $83

A Catalogue of Parts for Rolls-Royce, August 1914. (Onslow's) $305

'The Story of a Passion", by Irving Bacheller, published by Roycrofters, 1901, hand-illuminated by Abby Blackmar, suede cover. (Robt. W. Skinner Inc.) $150

Eleven lantern readings including 'Daisy's Influence', 'Labour and Victory' and 'A Famous Orator, An Evening with J. B. Gough' and others. (Christie's) $36

Bassett-Lowke, New Illustrated Catalogue of Model Flying Machines, Aeroplanes, Balloons, Motor Fittings and Materials, May 1910. (Onslow's) $112

A pair of Louis XVI ormolu mounted marble vases with fruiting finials and circular covers, 9in. high. (Christie's) $1,653

A pair of French figural bronze candelabra in the rococo style, 35cm. high. (Phillips) $1,394

A pair of Regency ormolu candlesticks, the bases with gardeners, the girl with a rake and the boy with a spade, 13in. high. (Christie's) $1,623

Pair of Regency ormolu candlesticks of George II style, fitted for electricity, 9½in. high. (Christie's) $631

A set of early 19th century bronze statuettes of the Four Seasons, with rectangular marble bases, 23cm. high. (Christie's) $1,194

Late 19th century bronze vase, signed Seiya zo, 32cm. high. (Christie's) $654

A Viennese cold painted bronze of a lion attacking an Arab mounted on a camel, incised beneath with the Bergman seal, 22cm. high. (Phillips) $1,467

Pair of bronze oviform vases, signed Saito, Meiji period, 31.5cm. high. (Christie's) $3,872

A 19th century bronze of Actaeon kneeling on a wounded stag, incised Holme. Cardwell Fect. Roma 1857, 83cm. high. (Christie's) $14,520

An early 20th century Swiss bronze statuette of a nude man hurling a rock entitled 'Der Steinstosser', cast from a model by Hugo Siegwart, 37cm. high. (Christie's) $2,904

'Penthesilia, Queen of the Amazons', a bronze figure cast from a model by A. Bouraine, 48.2cm. long. (Christie's) $1,443

A 19th century French bronze statuette of Fanny Elssler, signed A. Barre fct. 1837, 43cm. high. (Christie's) $5,511

A 19th century French bronze group of Hercules slaying the Cretan bull, after a model from the school of Giambologna, 56 x 61cm. (Christie's) $3,674

Bronze bust of 'Dalila', by E. Villanis, circa 1890, seal of Societe des Bronzes de Paris. (Worsfolds) $1,440

A 19th century French gilt bronze equestrian statuette of King Francois I, 42 x 41cm. (Christie's) $826

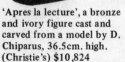

'Apres la lecture', a bronze and ivory figure cast and carved from a model by D. Chiparus, 36.5cm. high. (Christie's) $10,824

Three bronze groups, camel and rider, Arab horse and rider and mounted Indian, circa 1930, each 9in. high. (Prudential Fine Art) $2,268

A 20th century French bronze group of a Scottish huntsman holding up a dead fox with a hound below, after P. J. Mene, 52cm. high. (Christie's) $1,102

A late 19th/early 20th century Japanese bronze group of Death and a Maiden, with foundry stamp Dai Nippon Genryusai Seiya Zo. (Christie's) $1,837

A 19th century French bronze group of the Voyage of the Nations, cast from a model by Edouard Drouot, 49cm. high. (Christie's) $2,722

A late 19th century French 'Chryselephantine' bronze and ivory figure of 'La Liseuse', base signed A. Carrier-Belleuse, 62cm. high. (Christie's) $2,939

A 19th century French bronze group of a putto riding a lion, 39.5cm. high. (Christie's) $1,102

A bronze bust of a woman cast from a model by Dora Gordine, Paris, 1925, 36.8cm. high. (Christie's) $1,533

A 19th century English bronze figure of a groom and a rearing horse, cast from a model by Joseph E. Boehm, 59cm. high. (Christie's) $7,260

A 19th century French bronze statuette of the 'Tribunal', cast from a model by Paul Dubois, 50.5cm. high. (Christie's) $2,722

A late 19th century French bronze model of a pointer called Aro, cast from a model by Alfred Barye, 18.5 x 25.5cm. (Christie's) $1,996

A 19th century French gilt bronze statuette of Joan of Arc kneeling in prayer, signed Fremiet, 49cm. high. (Christie's) $2,939

'Torch Dancer', a bronze and ivory figure cast and carved from a model by F. Preiss, 41.5cm. high. (Christie's) $6,314

A late 19th/early 20th century bronze memorial relief, attributed to Sir Alfred Gilbert, 25cm. high. (Christie's) $551

Bronze figure of Sagittarius, by E. M. Geyger, H. Gladenbeck u. Sohn, Berlin, 13in. high. (Worsfolds) $159

A 19th century French bronze group of an Arab falconer, signed on the base P. J. Mene, 78 x 76cm. (Christie's) $14,520

An early 20th century French patinated bronze bust of Omphale, cast from a model by E. Villanis, 53cm. high. (Christie's) $2,178

A 19th century gilt bronze group of an 18th century scientist with pen and manuscript, seated beside a plate electrical machine, 13in. wide. (Christie's) $902

A fine bronze cast from a model by Le Faguays, of a female archer, 46cm. high. (Christie's) $1,353

A 19th century English bronze of the Prince Consort, base incised Elkington on an ebonized wood stand, 54cm. high. (Christie's) $2,722

'Russian Dancer', a bronze and ivory figure cast and carved after a model by F. Preiss, 32.4cm. high. (Christie's) $5,051

Bronze figure of a woman,
signed Oscar Glandebeck,
circa 1900, 12in. high.
(Lots Road Chelsea Auction
Galleries) $304

An Art Deco bronze and ivory
figurine of a young bather
reclining on a large rock.
(Biddle & Webb)
        $7,498

A bronze figure, 'Egyptian
Priestess', 80cm. high.
(Christie's) $1,443

A 19th century French
bronze statue of Cupid, after
Denis-Antoine Chaudet,
60cm. high. (Christie's)
        $3,122

An early 20th century
Italian bronze bust of a
maiden in folk costume,
cast from a model by E.
Rubino, 44cm. high.
(Christie's) $762

A 19th century French
bronze figure of a nude
woman, cast from a model
by Aime Jules Dalou, 33cm.
high. (Christie's)
        $10,890

A bronze figure, cast from a
model by H. Molins, as a
female dancer, 58.5cm. high.
(Christie's) $1,443

A 19th century French bronze
model of a stag, signed on the
base Isidore Bonheur, 80 x
56cm. (Christie's)
        $11,022

One of a pair of Charles X
ormolu vases with pierced
scrolling foliate handles,
14¼in. high. (Christie's)
$2,755

A 19th century French
bronze group of Theseus
combating the Minotaur,
signed Barye, 44.5cm. high.
(Christie's) $20,207

A French bronze group of a
mare and foal, base inscribed
P. J. Mene and dated 1868,
46cm. high. (Christie's)
$11,940

An early 20th century
Austrian bronze bust of
Edward VII, cast from a
model by J. Muhr, dated
1908, 40cm. high.
(Christie's) $1,377

A pair of mid 19th century
gilt metal, bronze and white
marble six-light candelabra,
26in. high. (Christie's)
$3,630

An early 19th century
French bronze statuette of
a Greek warrior on a giallo
antico marble pedestal,
57.5cm. high. (Christie's)
$2,087

Pair of 19th century bronze
figures of Mercury and Hebe,
2ft.9in. and 2ft.6in. high.
(Lots Road Chelsea Auction
Galleries) $800

One of a pair of ormolu
and white marble five-branch
candelabra, 35in. high.
(Christie's) $2,939

A set of three French 19th century
bronze and steel fire-irons, 33in.
long, and smaller. (Christie's)
$1,102

'Girl with a riding crop', a
bronze figure cast from a
model by Bruno Zack, Made
in Austria, 46cm. high.
(Christie's) $3,968

A bronze head of a negro
girl, signed indistinctly A.
Memiller(?), 43cm. high.
(Christie's)
$3,674

A late 19th century French
bronze model of a grazing
sheep, signed Rosa Bonheur,
14 x 21.5cm. (Christie's)
$1,194

A 19th century French
bronze head of a child, 'Bebe
Endormi', cast from a model
by Aime-Jules Dalou, 19cm.
high. (Christie's)
$3,993

A pair of Charles X ormolu
and bronze three-light
candelabra, 21in. high.
(Christie's) $3,306

'Con Brio', a bronze and
ivory figure cast and carved
from a model by F. Preiss,
29cm. high. (Christie's)
$9,020

Pair of ormolu and bronze
candlesticks formed as
winged putti, 10¾in. high.
(Christie's) $1,653

One of a pair of Empire bronze
and ormolu four-light candelabra, 30¼in. high.(Christie's)
$6,429

A pair of ormolu and porcelain
twin-branch wall-lights of
Louis XV style, fitted for
electricity, 14½in. high.
(Christie's) $3,306

One of a pair of late 19th
century bronze vases formed
in two sections, 68cm. high.
(Christie's) $3,520

An Oriental bronze architectural decoration with onion-shaped finial for a post top, 31in. high, 13in. diam. (Robt. W. Skinner Inc.) $700

A mid 19th century French bronze group 'L'Accolade', base inscribed P. J. Mene, 34cm. high. (Christie's) $12,491

A 19th century bronze group of Louis XIV on horseback, after a model by Girardon, 38cm. high, on ebonized and bronze mounted plinth. (Phillips) $20,375

A 19th century English bronze figure of the young Prince of Wales standing on a bronze plinth inscribed T. Fowke Sc., London, 1864, 84cm. high. (Christie's) $15,427

A 19th century French bronze group of a python attacking an Arab horseman, cast from a model by Antoine Louis Barye, circa 1835-40, 22 x 29cm. (Christie's) $23,595

A 19th century bronze bust of a young boy, stamped Dalou, Cire Perdue A. A. Hebrard, 31cm. high. (Phillips) $2,934

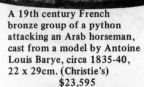

A 19th century bronze bust of a bearded 16th century scholar, his cloak cast with allegorical figures, 28cm. high. (Phillips) $1,304

A 16th century gilt bronze plaque of the dead Christ supported by the Virgin and St. John, after Moderno, 7.5 x 5cm. (Phillips) $1,385

One of a pair of Empire ormolu vases with overhanging lips, 6½in. high. (Christie's) $2,571

A 19th century French bronze group of St. George and The Dragon, by E. Fremiet, 50cm. high. (Christie's) $4,719

Late 19th century bronze models of elephants rearing in pain, signed Seiya and Saku, 29cm. and 22cm. long. (Christie's) $2,112

A bronze figure cast from a model by Rudolf Kuchler, modelled as a male fencer, 37cm. high. (Phillips) $448

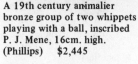

A late 19th century French bronze group of a Scottish huntsman restraining two wolfhounds, cast from a model by P. J. Mene, 51cm. high. (Christie's) $3,674

A 19th century animalier bronze group of two whippets playing with a ball, inscribed P. J. Mene, 16cm. high. (Phillips) $2,445

'Au But', a bronze group of three male athletes, the base inscribed A. Boucher and foundry mark Siot Decauville, 28cm. high. (Phillips) $1,630

An ancient Egyptian bronze mirror, 600 B.C., 8in. wide. (Robt. W. Skinner Inc.) $850

A pair of late Louis XVI ormolu and white marble three-light candelabra, 18¼in. high. (Christie's) $2,939

A 19th century French bronze group of Hebe and the Eagle of Jupiter, inspired by Rude, the base inscribed E. Drouot, 78cm. high. (Phillips) $4,564

One of a pair of bronze statues of Abyssinian cats, 32in. tall. (Chancellors Hollingsworths) $972

An early 20th century German or French bronze group of Saint George on horseback, 55.5 x 36cm. (Christie's) $918

An early 20th century bronze model of a seated blood-hound bitch, base signed Paolo Troubetskoy, 22.5cm. high. (Christie's) $1,542

A 19th century bronze group of a whippet carrying a dead hare in its mouth, inscribed P. J. Mene, 7in. wide. (Woolley & Wallis) $1,166

Art Deco bronze and ivory figurine of a young woman on a jetty holding a canoe paddle. (Biddle & Webb) $3,586

One of a pair of ormolu and bronze chenets of Louis XVI style, 8¼in. high. (Christie's) $642

One of a pair of ormolu mounted pink granite urns, 17½in. high. (Christie's) $7,715

'Bat Dancer', a bronze and ivory figure cast and carved from a model by F. Preiss, 23.5cm. high. (Christie's) $5,412

A George III ormolu mounted blue-john pot-pourri vase, by Matthew Boulton, 11in. high. (Christie's) $2,851

One of a pair of French 19th century bronze figures in Egyptian taste, on siena marble bases, 37cm. high. (Christie's) $907

An early 20th century German bronze group of Europa and the Bull, cast from a model by A. Grath, 60 x 51cm. (Christie's) $3,306

A 19th century bronze group of The Danseuses, after a model by Jean Baptiste Carpeaux, 53cm. high. (Christie's) $1,815

A 19th century French bronze model of a lion crushing a serpent, after Barye, 40cm. high. (Christie's) $4,776

A bronze and ivory figure cast and carved from a model by Kovats, 39cm. high. (Christie's) $12,628

A 19th century bronze group of a retriever with a dead goose in its mouth, inscribed P. J. Mene, 7½in. wide. (Woolley & Wallis) $1,555

A pair of Charles X bronze tazze with foliate rims and ribbed bases and handles, 10¼in. high. (Christie's) $2,939

A mid 19th century French bronze figure of the 'Cheval Turc', signed Barye, 38.5 x 29.5cm. (Christie's) $82,665

One of a pair of ormolu mounted crackle-glazed baluster vases, now converted to lamps, 13½in. high. (Christie's) $2,020

A bronze mounted coconut shell in the form of a caricature of Louis Philippe, 18cm. high. (Phillips) $521

One of a pair of George III ormolu cassolettes, 7¼in. high. (Christie's) $1,782

A Viennese cold painted bronze of a seated Indian brave, bearing the inscription C. Kauba and stamped Geschutzt 5806, 17cm. high. (Phillips) $1,271

An early 20th century English bronze statuette of Peter Pan, after Sir George Frampton, 47.5cm. high. (Christie's) $4,900

A pair of French 19th century bronze busts of a Nubian man and woman, also known as 'Venus Africaine', both signed Cordier, 83cm.and 79cm. high. (Christie's) $166,980

An Art Deco bronze figure cast from a model by Lorenzl, modelled as a dancing girl, 43.9cm. high. (Phillips) $1,040

'Valkyrie Rider', a parcel gilt bronze and ivory equestrian figure statue, signed L. Chalon, 54.5cm. high. (Christie's) $8,118

An Australian 'New Sculpture' bronze figure of Diana, by Sir Bertram Mackennal, 1905, 37cm. high. (Christie's) $21,780

A 19th century animalier bronze of a cock pheasant perched on a stump with weasel hiding beneath, the base inscribed J. Moigniez. (Phillips) $1,304

A 19th century French bronze figure of La Baigneuse, cast from a model by Aime Jules Dalou, 41cm. high. (Christie's) $6,352

A bronze figure of Herakles, Etruscan, 11.3cm. high. (Phillips) $852

A 19th century bronze group of a mounted African Hunter, incised P. J. Mene, 46cm. high. (Phillips) $3,423

A bronze and ivory figure cast and carved from a model by Marquetz and modelled as a girl with a long robe tied at the waist, 28.5cm. high. (Phillips) $608

Pair of 19th century French bronze, copper and silver plated busts of 'La Juive d'Alger' and the 'Cheik Arabe de Caire', by Charles-Henri-Joseph Cordier, 86cm. high. (Christie's) $161,656

A Roman bronze figure of Venus mounted on a wood base, 8.5cm. high, 1st-2nd century A.D. (Phillips) $902

Mid 19th century bronze and ormolu inkwell, with shaped fitted top and pierced Gothic arcaded frieze, 6in. wide. (Christie's) $635

A French bronze figure of a Neapolitan mandolin player, bearing the inscription Duret, 55cm. high. (Phillips) $1,222

One of a pair of ormolu and tole peinte jardinieres of Louis XVI style with white porcelain flowerheads, 15½in. high. (Christie's) $10,103

A Roman bronze bust of
Athena, 8.5cm. high, 2nd
century A.D. (Phillips)
$309

A pair of Roman bronze model
feet, socketed, both 8cm. long,
circa 2nd century A.D. (Phillips)
$254

Ming type miniature bronze
horse. (G. A. Key) $97

An Art Deco 'erotic' cold
painted bronze figure case
from a model by Nan Greb,
10¾in. high. (Christie's)
$1,247

Pair of Oriental bronze lions
standing, approx. 18in. long.
(G. A. Key) $708

Bronze, 'Young Girl Looking
Down at Frog', circa 1900, 18in.
high. (J. M. Welch & Son)
$688

An 18th century bronze bell
shaped mortar and pestle,
5in. high. (Christie's)
$123

A cold painted bronze figure
of Cleopatra cast from a
model by Nan Greb, 10in.
across. (Christie's)
$1,247

A 19th century bronze two-
handled koro with pierced
lid and lion finial, 12½in. tall.
(J. M. Welch & Son)
$336

BRONZE

A Roman bronze figure of the child, Harpokrates, 4.7cm. long, circa 2nd century A.D. (Phillips) $145

A large bronze figure of a mountain lion. (Lawrences) $2,002

A Romano British bronze fibula with linear decoration and onion-shaped terminals, 6.5cm. long, 3rd-4th century A.D. (Phillips) $58

'Sword Dancer', a large cold painted bronze figure cast from a model by Nan Greb, 21¼in. high. (Christie's) $2,138

A group of painted bronze miniature figures of animals, mainly characters from Beatrix Potter's books. (Christie's) $907

An Egyptian bronze figure of Osiris, Late Dynastic Period, 15cm. high. (Phillips) $400

Pair of bronze floriform candlesticks, attributed to Jarvie, Chicago, circa 1902, 14in. high. (Robt. W. Skinner Inc.) $3,100

A bronze gun muzzle plate in the form of a King George V sovereign, 17.2cm. diam. (Christie's) $258

Late 19th century bronze equestrian group of Louis XIV on horseback, the figure and saddle-cloth of gilt bronze, 10in. high. (Lalonde Fine Art) $280

A George III brass bound mahogany peat bucket, 16in. diam. (Christie's) $2,904

A George III brass bound mahogany peat bucket with later detachable tin liner, 15in. diam. (Christie's) $902

A George III brass bound mahogany bucket of navette shape with brass liner, 13½in. wide. (Christie's) $631

A George III brass bound mahogany peat bucket with carrying handles, 16in. diam. (Christie's) $2,706

A pair of painted leather fire buckets, Newport, Rhode Island, 1843, 12¼in. high. (Christie's) $1,210

A Regency brass bound mahogany plate bucket with carrying handle, 16½in. high. (Christie's) $1,434

A George III mahogany brass bound plate pail with brass carrying handles. (Phillips) $1,804

A Regency brass bound mahogany bucket with tin liner, 12in. wide. (Christie's) $1,434

A Georgian mahogany caned plate bucket with brass liner and loop handle, 14in. (Worsfolds) $3,520

A leather fire bucket, red painted rim, body painted black, legend reads 'No. 11 Daniel Waldo, 1756', Mass., 11in. high. (Robt. W. Skinner Inc.) $650

A Georgian brass bound mahogany plate bucket with swing handle. (Geering & Colyer) $1,424

A painted leather fire bucket, America, 1822, 12½in. high. (Robt. W. Skinner Inc.) $8,500

A 19th century pair of painted and decorated leather fire buckets, New England, 12.3/8in. high. (Robt. W. Skinner Inc.) $1,600

1st World War water carrier of kidney section, painted red and bearing crest, rope carrying handles, 21in. high. (Peter Wilson) $70

Pair of 19th century painted leather fire buckets, New England, 13½in. high. (Robt. W. Skinner Inc.) $950

A painted leather fire bucket, America, 11¾in. high. (Robt. W. Skinner Inc.) $850

A George III brass bound mahogany bucket with lead lined body and foliate ring carrying handles, 8in. diam. (Christie's) $3,256

A George III brass bound mahogany peat bucket with ribbed slatted sides and later tin liner, 14¾in. diam. (Christie's) $1,936

A 17th century oak box, the molded edge lid with iron hinges, 20.5in. long. (Woolley & Wallis) $198

A French straw-work workbox worked in a three-colored diapered pattern, pink, gold and green, 7½ x 5½ x 4in., circa 1750. (Christie's) $1,443

An early 19th century veneered Anglo-Indian Colonial rectangular sarcophagus shape workbox, 14in. wide. (Woolley & Wallis) $2,970

A 19th century mahogany domestic medicine chest by Fischer & Toller, 9½in. wide. (Christie's) $1,232

A travelling dressing set with silver mounts, dated 1901, Birmingham, in an alligator skin case. (Lots Road Chelsea Auction Galleries) $680

An Anglo-French silver and silver mounted dressing table set contained in a brass inlaid rosewood case, by C. Rawlings, 1821, and P. Blazuiere, Paris, 1819-38. (Christie's) $25,740

Mid 19th century Victorian rosewood and mother-of-pearl inlaid sewing box with fitted interior. (G. A. Key) $462

A George III mahogany cutlery urn with fitted interior, 25½in. high. (Christie's) $1,255

A William and Mary trinket cabinet with star inlaid panels, fitted with ten drawers and enclosed by single door, 9½in. wide. (Prudential Fine Art) $1,444

A rectangular box, containing two fitted boxes, the interiors nashiji, Meiji period, 8.7cm. long. (Christie's) $2,618

A 19th century miniature stencilled sewing box, American, 10in. high, 14in. wide. (Christie's) $286

An Indian fruitwood, ivory and micro-mosaic workbox with mirror-backed interior, 18in. wide. (Christie's) $1,996

Regency mahogany tea caddy of sarcophagus form with brass lion ring handles. (G. A. Key) $264

A mid 19th century wall salt box, inlaid with different woods, back inlaid with a sailing ship. (Woolley & Wallis) $429

Early 19th century painted tin tea caddy, America, 5¼in. wide, 5in. high. (Robt. W. Skinner Inc.) $500

A George IV mahogany veneered sarcophagus shape decanter box, the divided interior with two sets of six original hobnail cut glass decanters, 18.5in. wide. (Woolley & Wallis) $1,815

An 18th century suzuribako, the inside with suzuri and gourd-shaped shinchu tsuiteki, 21.3 x 18cm. (Christie's) $13,090

Victorian bird's-eye walnut and rosewood crossbanded cigar casket with lift-up folding top, 11½in. wide. (Hobbs & Chambers) $445

An oblong chased silver gilt singing bird box, circa 1900, 4½in. long. (Christie's) $1,540

An oblong enamelled gilt singing bird box, circa 1900, 4in. long. (Christie's) $2,200

A 19th century leather covered document box, the dome top with brass bail handle, 11½in. wide. (Christie's) $242

A Spanish 17th century rosewood and ivory inlaid table cabinet, 40cm. wide. (Phillips) $2,624

A mahogany rotunda, the hinged fitted spherical box with three pairs of drawers with spreading pillars, 16in. wide. (Christie's) $3,048

Late 16th century Momoyama period rectangular box with cover decorated in hiramakie, 19 x 12 x 11cm. (Christie's) $14,960

Early 19th century tortoiseshell veneered tea chest with pagoda-shaped lid, 8in. wide. (Woolley & Wallis) $864

An oak cigar box carved in the form of a kennel with a boxer, 10½in. wide. (Christie's) $871

A George III burr-yew veneered tea chest, the interior with two lidded compartments, 7½in. wide. (Woolley & Wallis) $368

Early Victorian Macassar ebony veneered sarcophagus-shaped workbox inlaid with mother-of-pearl, 12in. wide. (Woolley & Wallis) $486

A 19th century box of double clam shell shape, the interior nashiji, 13.4cm. long. (Christie's)
$2,805

A William & Mary oyster walnut veneered lacemaker's box with brass escutcheon, 21in. long. (Woolley & Wallis) $1,360

A 19th century cylindrical cosmetic box with an inner tray and three small containers, 9.3cm. diam., 8.8cm. high. (Christie's)
$15,895

A 19th century rounded rectangular suzuribako, 23 x 19.8cm. (Christie's)
$3,366

A Georgian fruitwood tea caddy in the form of an apple, 11cm. high. (Phillips) $820

A Momoyama church-style chest with drop front, the interior with various-sized drawers, 89 x 65 x 52cm. (Christie's) $24,310

Late 18th century document box (bunko), decorated in gold and silver hiramakie, takamakie and hirame on a nashiji ground, 40 x 30 x 15cm. (Christie's)
$9,350

A George III fiddle-back mahogany veneered tea chest with ivory escutcheon, 9¼in. wide. (Woolley & Wallis)
$384

Mid 18th century Batavian silver mounted burr-walnut casket, 13in. high. (Christie's) $1,194

A grain-painted document box, probably New Hampshire, circa 1831, 24½in. wide. (Christie's) $440

Late 16th century Momoyama period small domed travelling casket, 21 x 12 x 10.5cm. (Christie's) $748

Late 16th/early 17th century gourd-shaped roironuri suzuribako, 25.5cm. long. (Christie's) $11,220

Mid 19th century gilt metal mounted tulipwood and kingwood coffre a bijoux in the style of B.V.R.B., 40in. high. (Christie's) $4,408

Late 19th century mahogany slide cabinet of twenty-one drawers, containing slides by various makers, 12in. high. (Christie's) $1,172

An Italian parcel gilt and painted casket on claw feet, 18in. wide. (Christie's) $1,745

Late 16th century Momoyama period Christian host box or pyx, 9cm. diam. (Christie's) $38,720

A 19th century document box, the exterior covered with cherry-tree bark, 41.3 x 30.8 x 12.2cm. (Christie's) $14,080

CADDIES & BOXES

A 19th century silver rimmed suzuribako shaped as a koto, the interior fitted with a suzuri and an oval kikugata tsuiteki, 22.5cm. long. (Christie's) $11,220

Victorian mother-of-pearl inlaid and painted papier mache two-division tea caddy, 7½in. wide. (Hobbs & Chambers) $136

Early 19th century Indian ivory and micro-mosaic work-box with fitted interior. (Christie's) $1,270

A grain-painted document box, 19th century, 11½in. wide, and another possibly Amish, 7¾in. wide. (Christie's) $770

Eastern silver colored metal Scribes box engraved with stylized script and geometric patterns. (Prudential Fine Art) $2,025

A Victorian two bottle tantalus with silver plated mounts, 13¼in. long overall.   (Christie's) $495

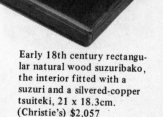

A 19th century leather covered document box, with brass bail handle and brass stud trim, 5¾in. high, 14in. wide. (Christie's) $275

One of a pair of Chippendale mahogany urns, 24½in. high. (Woolley & Wallis) $8,000

Early 18th century rectangular natural wood suzuribako, the interior fitted with a suzuri and a silvered-copper tsuiteki, 21 x 18.3cm. (Christie's) $2,057

A painted and decorated 'Tree of Life' domed top box, American, circa 1840, 33in. long. (Robt. W. Skinner Inc.) $1,900

A William and Mary walnut crossbanded marquetry lace box with hinged top, 50cm. wide. (Phillips) $1,755

An Italian olivewood box with Tunbridgeware style crossbanding, approx. 9 x 6in. (G. A. Key) $67

An early 19th century blond tortoiseshell tea chest, the hinged lid reveals two lidded compartments with silver plated knobs, 7in. long. (Woolley & Wallis) $429

A Georgian Stilton box. (Hobbs Parker) $3,192

A George III satinwood travelling necessaire box, the hinged lid enclosing a well-fitted interior, with leather label inscribed 'Manufactured by Bayley & Blew, 5 Cockspur Street, London', 15½in. wide. (Christie's) $2,645

Mid 18th century George III inlaid mahogany tea caddy, English or American, 6½in. high, 9in. wide. (Christie's) $462

Mid 19th century chip carved high domed painted poplar box, 13¾in. long. (Robt. W. Skinner Inc.) $325

Victorian burr-walnut stationery box in the form of a miniature piano, 9¾in. wide. (Hobbs & Chambers) $332

A William IV mahogany and rosewood writing slope, inlaid with cut brass, 44.5cm. long. (Osmond Tricks) $215

A 19th century oval putty grained Shaker box, America, 5.7/8in. long. (Robt. W. Skinner Inc.) $3,300

Bird's-eye maple Academy painted polychrome box, circa 1820, 12¼in. long. (Robt. W. Skinner Inc.) $3,600

Mid 19th century coromandel veneered writing box inlaid with brass stringing, 16in. wide. (Peter Wilson) $334

Mahogany collector's box decorated with brass stringing and vacant name plate, circa 1850, 7½in. wide. (Peter Wilson) $228

A 19th century brass inlaid coromandel writing box, the interior with blue velvet lining, 14in. wide. (Hobbs & Chambers) $525

A French tortoiseshell and enamel singing bird box, circa 1900, 4in. long. (Christie's) $2,200

Late Georgian mahogany decanter box, oblong with lift-up top and compartmented interior, 1ft.9½in. wide. (Hobbs & Chambers) $1,602

A painted box by Rufus Cole, N.Y., circa 1830, 13½in. long. (Robt. W. Skinner Inc.) $7,500

Early 19th century inlaid sailor's art writing box, 20½in. long. (Robt. W. Skinner Inc.) $1,800

A painted and decorated Bentwood box, Germany, circa 1780, oval form with fitted lid, 18¾in. long. (Robt. W. Skinner Inc.) $1,750

A walnut writing box inlaid with broad Greek Key pattern borders, enclosing a blue leather-lined writing slope, 12in. wide. (Lalonde Fine Art) $198

A Regency tortoiseshell tea caddy. (Hetheringtons Nationwide) $704

A painted maple lap desk, New York State, circa 1840, 19in. wide. (Christie's) $2,200

An early 19th century French satinwood workbox, 12 x 35.5 x 26cm. (Phillips) $2,492

One of a pair of ivory and gilt decorated three-tier Oriental boxes, 4in. square. (J. M. Welch & Son) $142

A William and Mary oyster walnut veneered lace maker's box, the divided interior with pink satin padding and a frame, 23in. long. (Woolley & Wallis) $1,122

An Italian green stone inkstand, the cover set with seven lava cameos, 11.5cm. diam. (Lawrence Fine Art) $699

A two-compartment Tunbridge-ware tea caddy. (David Lay) $250

A smoke grained dome-top box, American, circa 1830, 18¼in. long. (Robt. W. Skinner Inc.) $1,200

A miniature putty grained blanket box, American, circa 1825, 14in. long. (Robt. W. Skinner Inc.) $1,800

A Victorian Baccarat liqueur set, in an amboyna and marquetry case, signed, 13in. wide. (Hy. Duke & Son) $1,044

A French gilt metal mounted velvet and leather small cartonnier with six drawers, the bases stamped L. Dromard F. cant Paris, 18, Rue St. Lazare, Ft. de Sieges, 12in. wide. (Christie's) $881

A Regency tea caddy. (Hobbs Parker) $504

A rosewood portable writing desk with countersunk brass handles, late Regency period, 14in. wide. (Lalonde Fine Art) $462

A miniature Tunbridgeware cabinet with domed top and hinged door, 18cm. wide. 15cm. high. (David Lay) $360

A George III laburnum tea caddy with a divided interior, on bracket feet, 10in. wide. (Christie's) $1,180

A chrome Leica III camera No. 330547 with body cap, back plate engraved 'Leitz-Eigentum'. (Christie's) $865

A Leica IIIa camera No. 252835 with 'R.P.' engraving on top plate. (Christie's) $99

A gray Luftwaffen Leica IIIc camera No. 388254 engraved 'FI No. 38079' on top plate. (Christie's) $1,804

A chrome Leica IIIc No. 379660 engraved 'Heer' on top plate. (Christie's) $2,525

A Leica IIIc camera No. 476488 with a Leitz Summarit 5cm. f 1.5 No. 1500400 in Leitz box. (Christie's) $757

A Leica IIIc camera No. 482153 with 'shark skin' vulcanite covering and a Leitz Summitar 5cm. f 2 No. 705438. (Christie's) $500

A Leica I camera No. 176 with a Leitz Anastigmat f 3.5 50mm. and cap, a Leitz black enamelled rangefinder and double Leica film cassette holder. (Christie's) $17,138

A replica UR-Leica camera top plate engraved and picked out in white 'Nachbildung der Ur-Leica'. (Christie's) $2,345

A Leica I camera No. 8011 with a Leitz Elmar f 3.5 50mm. (Christie's) $902

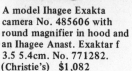

A black Leica MP camera No. 72 with the Leicavit MP rapid winder. (Christie's) $9,922

A model Ihagee Exakta camera No. 485606 with round magnifier in hood and an Ihagee Anast. Exaktar f 3.5 5.4cm. No. 771282. (Christie's) $1,082

A Leica IIIa camera No. 197512 with a Leitz Summar 5cm. f 2 No. 409322 and a Leica-Motor No. 2388. (Christie's) $992

A chrome Leica IIIb camera No. 351154 with a Leitz Elmar 5cm. f 3.5 No. 175134, camera baseplate engraved 'Robt. Ballantine, Glasgow'. (Christie's) $1,082

A Leica I camera No. 17917 with a Leitz Elmar f 3.5 50mm. (Christie's) $1,082

A gray Leica IIIc camera No. 372091 engraved on back plate 'Luftwaffen-Eigentum' with a Leitz Elmar 5cm. f 3.5 No. 547997. (Christie's) $2,525

A Leica MDa camera No. 1379203 stamped on the top plate 'Y' (indicates Bundeswehr (German army) use). (Christie's) $1,443

A Leica IIIc camera No. 364893 with a Leitz Summar 5cm. f 2 No. 218400. (Christie's) $577

A Leica IIIb camera No. 280422 with body cap. (Christie's) $234

A black dial Leica If camera No. 563478 back stamped in red 'A.P. 8886', with special mounting attachment on back. (Christie's) $1,353

An E. Leitz Leica M2 camera No. 982920 with a Leitz Elmar 5cm. f 2.8 lens No. 1602272 in maker's leather e.r.c. and original box plus other accessories. (Christie's) $591

A Leica I camera No. 740 with a Leitz Elmax f 3.5 50mm and cap, a Leitz black enamelled rangefinder and double Leica film cassette. (Christie's) $4,510

A Leica 24 x 36mm. Post camera No. 987591 engraved 'DPB' on top plate and with a Leitz Summaron f 2.8 35mm. No. 1931466 and cap. (Christie's) $2,164

A black Leica M2 camera No. 956651 with push button rewind control. (Christie's) $1,172

A Leica I camera No. 6460 with a Leitz Elmar f 3.5 50mm. (Christie's) $1,082

A postcard Newman and Guardia Sibyl camera model No. 10 No. PC136 with a Zeiss Tessar f 4.5 15cm. No. 176722. (Christie's) $324

An E. Leitz Leicaflex camera No. 1119417 with a Leitz Summicron-R f.2 50mm. lens, plus another two, in plastic case in maker's box. (Christie's) $1,016

A Musashino Koki 6 x 9cm. Rittreck IIa s.l.r. camera No. 2747 with two Luminant lenses, one f3.5 10.5cm. and another f4.5 21cm. lens. (Christie's) $369

A falling plate Svenska Express camera No. 2067 in black leather stamped in gilt on reverse 'Hasselblad Svenska Express'. (Christie's) $739

An E. B. Koopman 28 x 28mm. 'The Presto' camera with four glass plates in situ and instruction book 'Presto Pocket Camera Primer'. (Christie's) $739

An Eastman Kodak Co. 7 x 5in. No. 5 Folding Kodak camera (early satchel type) with lens set into an early sector shutter and an E.K. Co. roll film pack. (Christie's) $443

An Ernemann-Werke 6½ x 9cm. Ermanox camera No. 1168134 with an Ernemann Ernostar f 1.8 12.5cm. No. 165405, film pack adapter and cloth dark slides. (Christie's) $1,443

A 35mm. Globuscope 360° Panoramic camera No. 1094 with a Globuscope 25mm. f 3.5 - 22 lens with pouch case, film case and film resin all in maker's box. (Christie's) $1,623

A 6 x 4½cm. Dallmeyer Speed camera No. D639 with a Dallmeyer Pentac f 2.9 3in. lens, film pack adapter and three d.d.s., all engraved and in maker's leather case. (Christie's) $240

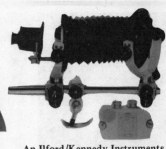

A Houghtons Ltd. 5 x 4in. tropical Sanderson camera, struts numbered '22425' with a Zeiss Tessar f 4.5 15cm. No. 600133 in a dial set Compur shutter. (Christie's) $757

A Franke & Heidecke 4 x 4cm. grey Baby Rolleiflex camera with a Schneider Xenar f3.5 60mm. lens, in case. (Christie's) $203

An Ilford/Kennedy Instruments 35mm. K.I. Monobrar camera in polished and cream enamelled metal with removable bellows, 35mm. film magazine and a Leica-fit lens panel. (Christie's) $811

A black Leica M4-M camera No. 1206841 with an E. Leitz New York remote control winder No. 02787 and 'AA' battery pack. (Christie's) $6,133

A Franke & Heidecke Rolleiflex Wide Angle camera No. W 2492220 with a Zeiss Distagon f.4 55mm. taking lens and a Heidosmat f.4 55mm. viewing lens. (Christie's) $1,663

A half-plate brass and mahogany camera with a brass bound lens and focussing cloth, all in canvas bag. (Christie's) $277

A C. P. Stirn No. 1 Concealed Vest camera No. 8364 with glass plate inside camera and two other circular glass plates. (Christie's) $887

A Zeiss Ikon twin lens Contaflex camera No. Y84783 with a Zeiss Sonnar f 2 5cm. No. 1538892, and a rare Zeiss Sonnar f 2 8.5cm. No. 1799751. (Christie's) $1,804

'The Rover Patent' detective camera by J. Lancaster & Son with a Lancaster Patent see saw shutter and internal brass plate holders. (Christie's) $406

One of a pair of gilt metal
and cut glass twelve-light
chandeliers, fitted for
electricity, 41in. high,
38in. diam. (Christie's)
$5,511

An Empire gilt metal twelve-
branch hanging light, fitted
for electricity, 18in. high,
excluding chain suspension.
(Christie's) $1,174

An early Victorian brass
eighteen-light chandelier
in the Gothic style, 56in.
high. (Christie's)
$8,167

A Regency bronze and ormolu
colza oil chandelier, 38in. high,
including chain suspension.
(Christie's) $12,798

Early 20th century hammered
copper and bronze chandelier
with seven Steuben shades,
20in. diam. (Robt. W. Skinner
Inc.) $3,000

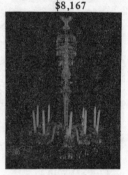

Mid 19th century cut glass
ten-light chandelier, fitted
for electricity, 65in. high.
(Christie's) $8,019

A George III cut glass six-
light chandelier with double
inverted dish corona hung
with pear shaped drops,
50in. high. (Christie's)
$9,451

An Art Deco glass and
chromium plated metal
chandelier of star form, circa
1930, 71cm. wide.
(Christie's) $9,922

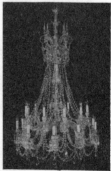

A large cut glass twenty-light
chandelier with scalloped
corona issuing eight scrolls
with arrow-head finials, 72in.
high, 44in. diam. (Christie's)
$47,256

One of a set of four George III style five-light crystal wall lights, fitted for electricity, 23in. high, 21in. wide. (Christie's) $1,650

A glass chandelier, the six branches complete with drops and glass chains. (G. A. Key) $743

A Lalique plafonnier, hemispherical clear and opalescent glass, 31.5cm. diam. (Christie's) $1,804

A George III style eight-light crystal chandelier, approx. 41in. high, 34in. diam. (Christie's) $962

An 18th century Dutch brass six-light chandelier, fitted for electricity, 32in. high. (Christie's) $3,309

A 19th century Swedish brass and cut glass twelve-light chandelier, 37in. high, 27in. diam. (Christie's) $7,348

A Regency bronze and ormolu eight-branch chandelier, each leaf cast double scroll arm supporting twin sconces, 100cm. diam., 123cm. drop. (Phillips) $12,250

A Regency gilt bronze colza oil ceiling light, the foliate corona, with beaded and faceted drops hung with a cut glass dish, 99cm. drop, 59cm. diam. (Phillips) $14,000

A 19th century French gilt bronze twelve-light chandelier, the extensively decorated baluster stem cast with triple cherub heads, circa 1880, 115cm. drop. (Phillips) $4,200

A 19th century creamware covered pitcher, entire surface in checkerboard pattern, brown glaze cut to cream, 6¼in. high. (Robt. W. Skinner Inc.) $125

A pearlware plate, bowl and ladle with American Eagle decoration, early 19th century, plate 7¾in. diam., bowl 13½in. diam. and the ladle 2¾in. diam. (Christie's) $770

Early 20th century Dedham pottery crackleware vase, decorated with blue iris, 7in. high. (Robt. W. Skinner Inc.) $550

One of a pair of pearlware plates and a creamware plate, one 9¾in. diam., 1810-30. (Christie's) $286

A Fulper pottery centerpiece on pedestal base, hammered olive-green on paler green glaze, circa 1915, 10½in. high. (Robt. W. Skinner Inc.) $1,600

A Clifton Art pottery 'Indian Ware' vase, circa 1910, 10½in. high, 12in. diam. (Robt. W. Skinner Inc.) $300

A two-color Grueby pottery vase, Boston, Mass., circa 1905, 8¼in. high. (Robt. W. Skinner Inc.) $2,400

One of two 19th century slip-decorated Redware dishes, American, 9¼in. and 11¾in. diam. (Christie's) $385

Late 19th/early 20th century creamware mug, 4¾in. high, together with a jar and a castor. (Christie's) $528

Late 19th century Chelsea Keramic Art Works pottery 'oxblood' vase, 8in. high. (Robt. W. Skinner Inc.) $2,000

A five-piece Picard China Co. porcecelain breakfast set, decorated with the 'Aura Argenta Linear' design, artist signed by Adolph Richter, circa 1910-30. (Robt. W. Skinner Inc.) $550

A Teco pottery molded lotus flower vase, Chicago, circa 1905, designed by F. Moreau, 11½in. high. (Robt. W. Skinner Inc.) $3,000

A mid 19th century Moravian slip-decorated Redware bowl, probably Salem, N. Carolina Jacob Christ type, 13½in. diam. (Christie's) $264

A Weller Sicard twisted pottery vase, iridescent purples and greens with snails in the design, circa 1907, unsigned, 7½in. high. (Robt. W. Skinner Inc.) $600

A 19th century slip-decorated Redware dish, American, 10½in. diam., and a bowl 7½in. diam. (Christie's) $352

A glazed ceramic grotesque face jug, by H. B. Craig, N. Carolina, ovoid with two applied strap handles, 16½in. high. (Christie's) $330

A pair of late 19th century painted chalkware doves, American, 11½in. high. (Christie's) $528

A manganese decorated Redware jar, by John W. Bell, 1880-95, 12½in. high. (Christie's) $528

AMERICAN

Late 19th century painted chalkware horse, 10in. high. (Christie's) $286

Saturday Evening Girls decorated planter, Boston, Mass., 1918, 9½in. long. (Robt. W. Skinner Inc.) $650

A two-color Grueby pottery vase, artist's initials A.L. for Annie Lingley, circa 1905, 8¼in. diam. (Robt. W. Skinner Inc.) $3,300

A Grueby pottery vase, Boston, Mass., circa 1905, 13½in. high. (Robt. W. Skinner Inc.) $3,900

A Zuni pottery jar, decorated in brown and red on a white ground, 27cm. high. (Phillips) $2,184

A Rookwood pottery standard glaze portrait vase, decorated with portrait of a black African with a cap, 1897, 12in. high. (Robt. W. Skinner Inc.) $2,500

A large Redware bowl or pot, probably Penn., 1870, 12in. diam. (Robt. W. Skinner Inc.) $1,100

A 19th century painted chalkware cat, America, 10¾in. high. (Robt. W. Skinner Inc.) $850

A Rookwood pottery jewelled porcelain vase, signed by Kataro Shirayamadani, Ohio, 1924, 7in. high. (Robt. W. Skinner Inc.) $1,400

AMERICAN

A Clifton Art pottery 'Indian Ware' vase, circa 1910, 8in. high, 10in. diam. (Robt. W. Skinner Inc.) $325

Saturday Evening Girls pottery decorated bowl, Mass., circa 1915, 11½in. diam. (Robt. W. Skinner Inc.) $600

Grueby pottery butterscotch glazed vase, artist's initials W.P. for Wilamina Post, dated 3/12/06, 9in. diam. (Robt. W. Skinner Inc.) $6,500

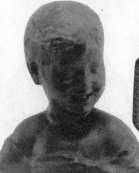

One of a pair of octagonal creamware plates and a similar soup plate, 1810-30, 8¾in. diam. (Christie's) $220

Late 19th century Grueby Faience Co. bust of 'Laughing Boy', based on a statue by Donatello, 11in. high. (Robt. W. Skinner Inc.) $1,800

One of a pair of pearlware plates, each octagonal painted with swags of lemons with brown leaves, 1810-20, 7¾in. diam. (Christie's) $198

Early 20th century Dedham pottery crackleware vase, decorated with white iris on blue ground, signed, 7½in. diam. (Robt. W. Skinner Inc.) $2,200

One of two 19th century slip-decorated Redware plates, American, 11¼in. and 12in. diam. (Christie's) $385

A Newcomb pottery floral vase, New Orleans, circa 1928, initialled by Henrietta Bailey, 5¼in. high. (Robt. W. Skinner Inc.) $900

A Shawsheen pottery vase, probably Billerica, circa 1906, 6in. high. (Robt. W. Skinner Inc.) $200

A Teco pottery double-handled vase, Illinois, circa 1910, 7in. high. (Robt. W. Skinner Inc.) $350

One of two 20th century Van Briggle pottery vases, Colorado, one 2¾in. high, the other 5½in. high. (Robt. W. Skinner Inc.) $360

A 19th century glaze and slip decorated redware platter, New England, 13½in. long. (Robt. W. Skinner Inc.) $2,600

A Grueby pottery two-color vase, elongated bottle neck on spherical cabbage form, circa 1905, 9¼in. high. (Robt. W. Skinner Inc.) $4,500

A Teco Art pottery fluted vase, Illinois, circa 1905, 10½in. high. (Robt. W. Skinner Inc.) $1,200

Saturday Evening Girls decorated pitcher, Mass., 1911, 9¾in. high. (Robt. W. Skinner Inc.) $950

Early 20th century Grueby pottery vase, Mass., 4¾in. high. (Robt. W. Skinner Inc.) $450

A Teco pottery four-handled vase, circa 1910, 7¼in. high. (Robt. W. Skinner Inc.) $650

AMERICAN

Louwelsa Weller pottery
Indian portrait vase, Ohio,
circa 1915, 10¾in. high.
(Robt. W. Skinner Inc.)
$475

Early 20th century Fulper
pottery candle lantern,
10½in. high. (Robt. W.
Skinner Inc.) $600

A Grueby pottery vase,
signed with logo, circa 1905,
11.7/8in. high. (Robt. W.
Skinner Inc.) $2,600

Late 19th century Chelsea
Keramic Art Works covered
jar, Mass., impressed CKAW,
5½in. high. (Robt. W. Skinner
Inc.) $150

A Merrimac pottery decorated
vase, Mass., circa 1893, 4in.
diam. (Robt. W. Skinner Inc.)
$400

Early 20th century pottery
pitcher, New Hampshire,
8¼in. high. (Robt. W.
Skinner Inc.) $150

A Jervis Art pottery motto
mug, 1906, 5¾in. high, 4in.
diam. (Robt. W. Skinner Inc.)
$200

Early 20th century Dedham
pottery decorated crackleware vase, 7½in. high. (Robt.
W. Skinner Inc.)
$2,000

Early 20th century Grueby
pottery two- color vase,
Mass., 10¼in. high. (Robt. W.
Skinner Inc.) $3,000

ARITA

One of a pair of early 18t!
century Arita blue and
white lobed dishes, Ming
six-character marks, 15.5cm.
wide. (Christie's)
$7,854

One of two Arita oviform
bottle vases decorated in
kakiemon style, circa
1675, approx. 30cm. high.
(Christie's) $12,320

One of a pair of 17th century
Arita standing puppies,
24cm. long. (Christie's)
$37,400

Late 17th/early 18th
century Arita blue and
white oviform jar, 27cm.
high. (Christie's)
$1,496

A fine pair of Arita blue
and white oviform jars and
covers, Genroku period,
88cm. high, wood stands.
(Christie's) $10,560

One of a pair of late 17th/
early 18th century Arita
Dutch decorated apothecary
bottles, 26.5cm. high.
(Christie's) $4,862

Late 17th century Arita blue
and white charger, 39cm.
diam. (Christie's)
$2,112

Late 17th century Arita blue
and white oviform ewer with
loop handle, 17cm. high.
(Christie's) $2,464

An 18th century Arita
armorial foliate-rimmed
shallow dish, 22cm. diam.
(Christie's) $9,680

ARITA

An 18th century Arita blue and white shallow dish decorated with the design of the 'Hall of One Hundred Boys', 20cm. diam. (Christie's) $3,179

Late 17th century large Arita blue and white baluster vase and cover, 47cm. high. (Christie's) $8,800

Early 18th century Arita foliate rim shallow dish, 20.5cm. diam. (Christie's) $1,776

One of two Arita oviform bottle vases decorated in Kakiemon style, circa 1680, approx. 30cm. high. (Christie's) $7,480

An Arita blue and white garniture comprising three oviform jars and covers and two trumpet-shaped beakers, Genroku period, jars and covers 37cm. high, the vases, 22.5cm. high. (Christie's) $9,350

Late 17th century Arita blue and white ewer with loop handle, 24cm. high. (Christie's) $880

Late 17th century Arita blue and white charger. (Christie's) $2,805

A 19th century Arita model of a tiger climbing on rocks among dwarf bamboo, 71cm. high. (Christie's) $5,610

An Arita shallow dish decorated with a scene entitled 'Entering the Enemy's Camp', Meiji period, 24.5cm. diam. (Christie's) $1,496

BERLIN

A KPM Berlin oval porcelain plaque painted with two cherubs, by Zapf, signed,10½in. across, impressed KPM. (Christie's) $1,322

A Berlin Reliefzierrat rectangular indented tea caddy and cover, painted in colors with putti playing on clouds, circa 1700, 14.5cm. high. (Christie's) $4,114

A Berlin rectangular plaque, painted at the Lamm decorating establishment by G. Meisel, after Boucher, 26.5 x 32.5cm., impressed KPM. (Phillips) $3,465

A Berlin plaque painted after Murillo. with two peasant boys eating grapes and melon, circa 1875, 28 x 22.5cm. (Christie's) $3,085

A Berlin two-handled campana vase painted in the neo-classical taste, 1803-1810, 45cm. high. (Christie's) $13,365

A German porcelain rectangular plaque painted with a three-quarter length portrait of a young girl, 7½in. high. (Christie's) $855

An 18th century Berlin figure of the Farnese Hercules, blue scepter mark, 16cm. high. (Christie's) $78

A Berlin rectangular plaque painted after Rubens, impressed scepter, KPM and numeral marks, circa 1880, 33 x 20cm. (Christie's)
$5,878

A Berlin cylindrical coffee-cup and saucer with garlands of flowers between blue bands gilt with foliage, blue scepter mark and gilt dot circa 1795. (Christie's) $1,260

BERLIN

A KPM Berlin oval plaque painted by Zapf, signed, 10½in. across, impressed KPM and scepter mark. (Christie's) $3,866

A Berlin Celadon ground Tasse D'Amitie the saucer inscribed Le tems s'envole; votre amour est bien plus constant, circa 1805. (Christie's)$2,468

A Berlin ecuelle and cover with Ozier molded borders, blue scepter mark, circa 1780, 19cm. wide. (Christie's) $1,682

A Berlin plaque painted after Peter Paul Rubens, 39 x 31cm., KPM and scepter mark. (Phillips) $8,684

A pair of Berlin blue and white octagonal vases and covers, painted in the Oriental style with chinoiserie figures in landscapes (repairs to one neck), circa 1725, 44cm. high. (Christie's) $5,740

A Berlin plaque painted after Raphael with a detail of the 'Madonna di San Sisto', late 19th century, 25.5 x 19cm. (Christie's) $1,542

A Berlin oval plaque painted after A. Kauffmann with a Vestal Virgin, impressed KPM, scepter, F and 5 marks, late 19th century, 27cm. high. (Christie's) $2,541

A Berlin two-handled campana vase, on spreading foot and square base, circa 1825, 31cm. high. (Christie's) $10,760

A K.P.M. oval portrait plaque of the young Christ, impressed marks, the plaque 10 x 8in. (Christie's) $393

A Bow leaf molded pickle-dish of ovate form, circa 1760, 11.5cm. wide. (Christie's) $1,828

A Bow figure of a shepherd playing the bagpipes, circa 1757, 26.5cm. high. (Christie's) $1,732

A Bow blue and white oval sauceboat, 1747-50, 22cm. wide. (Christie's) $1,089

A pair of Bow figures of Eastern dancers, the lady wearing a purple coat over puce-fringed yellow skirt and flowered underskirt, the man with fur-lined yellow cloak, 24cm. (Phillips) $1,567

A Bow figure candlestick, formed of a cupid kneeling on a rococo base (slight damage), anchor in red circa 1765. (Phillips) $1,076

A pair of Bow candlestick figures of a stag and doe with mottled brown coats, circa 1765, 23.5cm. high. (Christie's) $4,356

A Bow candlestick group of musicians, after Meissen models by Kaendler, circa 1760-65, 8¾in. high. (Christie's) $1,300

A rare early Bow 'Muses' figure of Hope, the lady rest-ing one arm on a puce column, her other on an anchor, 21.5cm. high. (Phillips) $1,472

A Bow circular plate painted in famille rose with a Chinese lady, probably Lan Ts'ai Ho, 22.5cm. diam. (Phillips) $1,586

BOW

A Bow leaf molded sauce-boat, circa 1765, 16cm. long. (Christie's) $621

A Bow porcelain figure of a nurse. (Hobbs Parker) $1,152

A Bow leaf molded sauce-boat with green stalk handle, circa 1765, 16cm. long. (Christie's) $3,272

A pair of Bow candlestick figures of the New Dancers, circa 1765, 29cm. high. (Christie's) $1,996

A rare Bow 'Muses' figure of Justice, the lady standing and wearing a black helmet and flowered white robe, 21cm. high. (Phillips) $1,067

Two Bow figures symbolizing the Elements, water depicted as Neptune, air as a nymph, 28.5cm. (Phillips) $1,656

A Bow spirally molded cane handle of tapering form, circa 1750, 5.5cm. high. (Christie's) $1,942

A Bow flared pierced circular basket, painted in the Kakiemon palette with The Quail Pattern, circa 1756, 16.5cm. diam. (Christie's) $3,167

A rare early Bow figure of Harlequin modelled in white, standing on a square base leaning against a tree trunk, 13.5cm. high. (Phillips) $1,656

A pearlware Toby jug
painted in Pratt colors,
perhaps Yorkshire, circa
1800, 23.5cm. high.
(Christie's) $907

An English porcelain group of
a recumbent cat with kittens,
4½in. wide, perhaps Derby,
circa 1825. (Christie's)
$887

A pearlware figure of
Napoleon as an Artillery
Officer, circa 1840, 29cm.
high. (Christie's)
$1,089

One of a pair of Yorkshire
models of cows, one with a
gardener, the other with a
woman, 14.5cm. long.
(Phillips) $4,676

Early 20th century Arts &
Crafts ceramic umbrella stand,
stamped with logo, 'The Foley
"Intarsio" England', 27½in.
high. (Robt. W. Skinner Inc.)
$700

A Portobello cow creamer,
with milkmaid on a stool,
16cm. wide. (Phillips)
$734

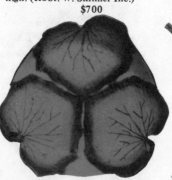

An H. & R. Daniel deep cream-
ground vase, pattern no. 196,
197, circa 1830, and another
similar. (Christie's)
$235

A Longton Hall triangular
dish molded with three
cucumber leaves, circa
1755, 15cm. wide.
(Christie's) $1,089

A pearlware pipe modelled
as a man seated astride a
green barrel, perhaps Yorkshire, circa 1800, 15.5cm.
high. (Christie's)
$1,542

116

BRITISH

A flask of Prince Albert, standing beside a pillar on which rests a crown, 28cm. high. (Phillips) $250

A rectangular plaque, painted with Highland cattle and sheep, signed E. Townsend, 23.5 x 36cm. (Phillips) $1,753

A creamware pipe modelled as a lady seated on a green barrel, perhaps Yorkshire, circa 1800, 17cm. high. (Christie's) $1,542

A George Jones 'majolica' circular cheese dish and cover, circa 1880, 28cm. diam. (Christie's) $577

A candle extinguisher in the form of a young lady's head, by James Hadley, 9cm. high, date code for 1892. (Phillips) $668

A Holdcroft majolica jardiniere, square with canted corners, 21.1cm. high. (Christie's) $551

A pearlware pipe modelled as a man, impressed with the name 'Jolly Pickman', circa 1800, 14.5cm. high. (Christie's) $1,542

One of a pair of Caughley plates from the Donegal Service, painted at Chamberlain's factory, circa 1793, 21cm. diam. (Christie's) $1,724

A pearlware puzzle jug, the serpent handle with three spouts, circa 1820, 29cm. high. (Christie's) $689

A Longton Hall cabbage-leaf molded teapot and cover, circa 1755, 11cm. high. (Christie's) $19,965

A large English delft bowl, painted in light blue with panels of parrots alternating with flower sprays, 34.5cm. diam. (Phillips) $1,528

One of a pair of Caughley quatrefoil two-handled sauce tureens and covers, circa 1785, 15cm. wide. (Christie's) $2,178

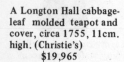

A creamware tall cylindrical mug, circa 1785, 12.5cm. high. (Christie's) $726

An H. & R. Daniel blue-ground part tea service, comprising an 'Etruscan' shape teapot, cover and stand, a two-handled sugar bowl and cover, a milk jug, a slop-basin, eight teacups and saucers, pattern no. 3859, circa 1825. (Christie's) $726

An 18th century blue and white pottery jug with loop handle, 7.75in. high. (Prudential Fine Art) $214

A Barr, Flight & Barr plate, decorated probably in London and in the manner of the Baxter workshop, 23.5cm. diam. (Phillips) $501

Hadley's porcelain vase and lid with cone finial, 4in. high. (G. A. Key) $280

A London delft 'bleu persan' plate painted in white enamel with a seated Chinese figure, in Nevers style, 21.5cm. diam. (Phillips) $5,730

BRITISH

A late Wemyss small model of a pig, 15.5cm. high, painted mark Wemyss, printed mark Made in England. (Phillips) $1,337

Late 18th century creamware circular dish with petal-shaped rim, painted in Pratt-type colors, 14in. diam. (Lalonde Fine Art) $627

A Foley 'Intarsio' 'Kruger' teapot and cover, designed by Frederick Rhead, modelled as the South African Statesman, 12.7cm. high. (Phillips) $563

Carlton Ware lustre jug with gilt loop handle, the body painted and gilded with stylized floral and fan decoration, 5in. high. (Prudential Fine Art) $189

A Ralph Wood figure of a harvester, circa 1775, 20cm. high. (Christie's) $3,085

A Maw & Co. circular pottery charger painted in a ruby red lustre with winged mythical beast, 13½in. diam. (Christie's) $382

A Maw & Co. pottery vase, the body painted in a ruby red lustre with large flowers and foliage all on a yellow ground, 13in. high. (Christie's) $644

A Portobello cow creamer and cover, 13cm. wide. (Phillips) $601

A Carlton Ware ginger jar and cover, the oviform body painted with clusters of stylized flowerheads, 10¾in. high. (Christie's) $801

A Cistercian ware tyg, the conical cup with three loop handles, the black glaze stopping just above the foot, 6.8cm. high. (Phillips) $382

A pair of pearlware figures of Mansion House dwarfs, their costumes in shades of yellow, brick-red, lime-green and brown, 16cm. and 16.5cm. high. (Phillips) $1,375

A Longton Hall leaf dish, painted in the manner of the Trembley Rose painter, circa 1755, 22.5cm. wide. (Christie's) $653

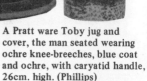

Belleek cream-ground shaped handled jug, black factory mark 'Robinson & Cleaver, Belfast', circa 1935. (Giles Haywood) $295

Two George Jones majolica cheese dishes and covers, 25cm. and 24cm. high respectively, circa 1885. (Christie's) $1,815

A Pratt ware Toby jug and cover, the man seated wearing ochre knee-breeches, blue coat and ochre, with caryatid handle, 26cm. high. (Phillips) $1,107

A Leeds creamware tea canister of octagonal shape, 12.5cm. high, incised no. 25. (Phillips) $2,087

A Swansea porcelain crested shaped rectangular dish with gilt twig handles, from the service made for T. Lloyd of Bronwydd, in 1819, 11in. long. (Dacre, Son & Hartley) $1,732

A Sampson Hancock, Derby, group of Dr. Syntax chased up a tree by a bull, 17.5cm. high, red painted mark. (Phillips) $573

BRITISH

A Pratt ware cow creamer, the animal with ochre sponging on a white body, the milkmaid wearing a blue bodice and spotted yellow skirt, 22cm. long. (Phillips) $802

A Plymouth group of two putti emblematic of Spring, 14.5cm. high, impressed letters S & D (flower festoon R). (Phillips) $687

A Victorian china two-handled footbath with 'bird' decoration. (J. M. Welch & Son) $623

A Ralph Wood Vicar and Moses group, circa 1780, 24.5cm. high. (Christie's) $866

Art Deco 'Shelley' teaset of five cups, six saucers, six side plates, cake plate and bowl, numbered R11792E. (J. M. Welch & Son) $134

A 19th century pearlware transfer-printed coffee pot and cover, 10in. high. (Christie's) $528

A Bretby pottery jardiniere, formed as a lion's head with glass eyes, 31cm. (Osmond Tricks) $710

A 'scratch blue' saltglaze puzzle jug, the rim with three pinecone molded spouts (two missing), 21.5cm. high. (Phillips) $5,348

Early 19th century porcelain commemorative pottery jug with motto 'Success to Queen Caroline', 5.25in. high. (Prudential Fine Art) $247

A late Wemyss model of a pig of small size, the body painted in green with scattered shamrock, 16cm. high. (Phillips) $1,566

A pearlware cylindrical teapot and cover, applied with figures of Lord Rodney and Plenty, circa 1785, 13cm. high. (Christie's) $653

A Longton Hall leaf dish, painted in the manner of the Trembley Rose painter, circa 1755, 27.5cm. wide. (Christie's) $1,452

A Pilkington Lancastrian pottery vase by Richard Joyce, impressed Bee mark and date code for 1909, 11¾in. high. (Christie's) $1,006

A pair of shell sweetmeat dishes, attributed to James Hadley, 22cm. wide, impressed and printed marks for 1882. (Phillips) $1,002

'Guardian Vessel', a porcelain form by Ruth Barrett-Danes, 22.2cm. high. (Christie's) $1,262

A Longton Hall strawberry leaf molded plate, circa 1755, 23cm. diam. (Christie's) $3,448

A Longton Hall white figure of a turkey of so-called 'Snowman' type, circa 1750, 18.5cm. high. (Christie's) $2,904

An English slipware circular baking dish, 20.3cm. diam. (Phillips) $1,050

A West Pans blue and white leaf molded sauceboat with stalk handle, circa 1766, 20.5cm. wide. (Christie's) $508

A pair of 19th century ironstone crescent-shaped serving dishes, 16in. long. (Prudential Fine Art) $218

Shelley rectangular shaped cheese dish.with matching handled cover 'Cloisello ware', 8in. long. (Giles Haywood) $106

A creamware swelling jug painted in iron-red and black, circa 1770, 20.5cm. high. (Christie's) $1,270

Pair of 'majolica' squirrel vases with branch handles, circa 1885, 31.5cm. high. (Christie's) $770

A Caughley pounce pot, printed in underglaze blue with fruit and flower sprigs and insects, 8.5cm. high. (Phillips) $1,336

An 18th century decorated baluster two-handled 'leech' jar with cover, approx. 14in. tall. (J. M. Welch & Son) $2,584

A majolica glazed Stilton cheese dish and cover, probably by George Jones & Sons, late 19th century. (G. A. Key) $140

'Bestiary Form', a porcelain jug form by Ruth Barrett-Danes, 28.5cm. high. (Christie's) $1,262

CANTON

A Cantonese circular bowl richly painted with panels of male and female figures within gilt cartouches, 16in. diam. (Anderson & Garland) $1,274

A 19th century oval covered Canton vegetable dish, China, 11in. long. (Robt. W. Skinner Inc.) $225

Canton salad bowl, 19th century, shaped rim with notched corners, usual Canton scene. (Robt. W. Skinner Inc.) $650

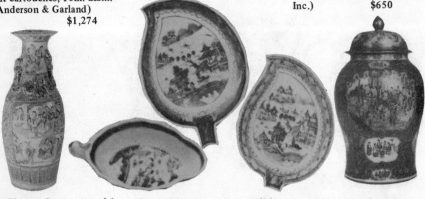

A Chinese Canton porcelain vase decorated in famille rose colors with panels of geishas on a floral ground, 2ft.½in. high. (Hobbs & Chambers) $313

Three 19th century Canton dishes, two leaf-shaped relish dishes and an oval shallow sauceboat, 6¾in., 8in. and 7in. long. (Robt. W. Skinner Inc.) $325

A 19th century Cantonese vase and cover decorated with Chinese household scenes. (Osmond Tricks) $3,217

Canton cider jug, mid 19th century, the domed cover with foo dog finial, height 8½in. (Robt. W. Skinner Inc.) $800

Canton spittoon, 19th century, deep wide rim with Rain Cloud border, height 6¾in., rim diam. 7¾in. (Robt. W. Skinner Inc.) $600

Shaped Canton shrimp dish, 19th century, typical Canton scene, diam. 10¼in. (Robt. W. Skinner Inc.) $275

CARDEW

A stoneware casserole and cover by Michael Cardew, Wenford Bridge seals, circa 1970, 32cm. diam. (Christie's) $704

An earthenware coffee pot and cover by Michael Cardew, impressed MC and Winchcombe Pottery seals, circa 1933, 17cm. high. (Christie's) $457

A large stoneware teapot by Michael Cardew with strap handle and grip, Wenford Bridge seals, circa 1970, 23.4cm. high. (Christie's) $1,020

An earthenware inscribed platter by Michael Cardew, decorated by Henry Bergen, Winchcombe Pottery seals, 42.7cm. diam. (Christie's) $1,760

An unglazed stoneware teapot and cover by Michael Cardew, with bound cane handle, circa 1950, 17.8cm. high. (Christie's) $844

A stoneware plate by Seth Cardew, impressed SC and Wenford Bridge seals, 35.6cm. diam. (Christie's) $228

An earthenware cider flagon by Michael Cardew, circa 1970, 41cm. high. (Christie's) $704

An Abuja large deep bowl on shallow foot, 34cm. wide. (Christie's) $246

A large stoneware jar by Seth Cardew, the cylindrical body with four strap handles to the shoulder, 61.8cm. high. (Christie's) $492

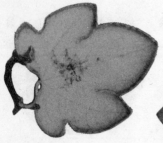

A Chelsea leaf dish with green vine-stock handle, red anchor mark, circa 1755, 21cm. wide. (Christie's) $3,850

A Chelsea knife handle of facted octagonal shape, 11.5cm. long, red anchor period. (Phillips) $668

An 18th century Chelsea 'Red Anchor' decorated bird of Paradise on a tree stump, 9in. high. (J. M. Welch & Son) $688

A Chelsea cauliflower tureen and cover, red anchor mark to inside of base, circa 1755, 12cm. long. (Christie's) $4,235

One of a pair of Chelsea-Derby groups of Renaldo, Armida, Cephalus and Procris, 20cm. high, incised numbers 75 and 76 with the initials J. W. (Phillips) $1,840

A Chelsea-Derby Jardiniere of 'U' shape, Chelsea style with fabulous birds on rockwork and in the branches of leafy trees, 17cm. high. (Phillips) $1,485

A Chelsea group of two children, naked except for a pink drapery, with large fish, 24cm. high. (Lawrence Fine Art) $1,458

A Chelsea octagonal dish, painted in the Kakiemon palette with pheasants, circa 1750, 20.5cm. wide. (Christie's) $1,925

A Chelsea white top of a Bonbon Nierre, modelled as Cupid and another, 5.5cm. high. (Lawrence Fine Art) $486

CHELSEA

A red anchor Chelsea butter tub and cover, of circular straight sided shape, with two upright rectangular handles, set on three curved scroll feet, 13.5cm. diam., (one handle restored) circa 1752-6. (Phillips) $1,246

A rare Chelsea model of a crouching leveret, 9cm. high. (Phillips) $9,936

An 18th century Chelsea 'Red Anchor' half-circular flower holder, 12in. wide, 6½in. high. (J. M. Welch & Son) $885

A Chelsea candlestick group, with leaf molded candle nozzle and drip guard, 16.8cm. high, red anchor mark. (Phillips) $955

A Chelsea group of two children, naked except for a white and gold drapery, seated on a rocky mound, 17.5cm. high. (Lawrence Fine Art) $1,539

A Chelsea blue-ground square tapering vase, gold anchor mark, circa 1765, 32cm. high. (Christie's) $1,925

A Chelsea-Derby figure of Diana, standing on a rocky, flower encrusted base, a stag at her feet (slight damage), circa 1770-5. (Phillips) $1,068

A Chelsea cinquefoil scolopendrium dish, circa 1755, 20.5cm. diam. (Christie's) $3,850

A rare Chelsea 'toy' figure of a gardener, pushing a roller over a grassy base strewn with applied flowers, 6.3cm. high. (Phillips) $1,196

A Chinese famille verte armorial teapot, Yongzheng, circa 1724, (spout restored). (Woolley & Wallis) $928

One of a pair of water-buffalo-head rhytons, 4½in. long. (Christie's) $3,262

A fine blue and white bowl, painted in bright violet tones with a stylized lotus spray at the centre, 19.5cm. diam., fitted box. (Christie's) $3,495

A large famille verte fish bowl with interior decoration, 45cm. high. (Dee & Atkinson) $480

A blue and white pear-shaped vase, Yuhuchunping, painted with two mandarin ducks (minor rim chip), 26cm. high. (Christie's)$42,725

A Chinese famille verte plate, Kangxi, circa 1725, 9¼in. diam. (Woolley & Wallis) $672

Large mid 19th century Chinese Nanking ashet, 16½in. wide. (Peter Wilson) $721

A rare Robin's egg blue Yixing wine ewer and cover, 18th century, 7¾in. high. (Christie's) $6,991

A rare Chinese teapot and cover, decorated in London, the reverse inscribed '57 Miles to London', a milestone inscribed 'XIV Miles from London', 16cm., 1750-1760. (Phillips) $759

CLARICE CLIFF

A Clarice Cliff Bizarre bowl, painted with crocus, 22.4cm. diam. (Osmond Tricks) $196

A Clarice Cliff wall pocket in the form of a pair of budgerigars, 23cm. high. (Osmond Tricks) $93

A Clarice Cliff Bizarre 'Fantasque' octagonal bowl, painted with foxgloves and canterbury bells, 20.6cm. diam. (Osmond Tricks) $93

A Clarice Cliff Bizarre Latona vase of lotus shape with single handle, 30cm. high. (Osmond Tricks) $1,140

A Clarice Cliff Bizarre biscuit barrel with wicker handle, 16cm. (Osmond Tricks) $252

A Clarice Cliff 'Delicia' patterned jug. (Hobbs Parker) $574

A large Clarice Cliff 'Fantasque' circular wall plate, 45.50cm. diam., printed marks and facsimile signature. (Phillips) $1,568

A large Clarice Cliff 'Churchill' Toby Jug, inscribed on base 'Going into Action, May God Defend the Right', 30.5cm. high, signed 'Clarice Cliff' No. 292'. (Phillips) $1,365

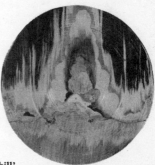

.A Wilkinson Bizarre pottery circular charger, by Clarice Cliff, 18¼in. diam. (Dacre, Son & Hartley) $2,310

COALPORT

One of two Coalport two-handled ecuelles and covers, painted in black with silhouette portraits of Queen Charlotte and George III, circa 1810, 16.5cm. wide. (Christie's) $4,356

Part of a Coalport dessert service, the center panels painted with floral bouquets on fawn ground, the compote 12¾in. wide, circa 1840. (Anderson & Garland) $1,699

One of a pair of Coalport porcelain lozenge-shaped dessert dishes, painted in the manner of Thos. Baxter, circa 1810, 10¾in. by 8in. (Dacre, Son & Hartley) $1,732

A late Coalport 'ramshead' vase and cover of shield shape, 18cm. high. (Phillips) $601

A Coalport rectangular plaque with Cupid holding a dove, signed J. Rouse, 1856, 36.5 x 30.5cm. (Christie's) $1,996

One of a pair of late Coalport vases with views of 'Dryburgh Abbey' and 'Hawthorndean', 29.5cm., green printed marks. (Phillips) $1,320

A Coalport porcelain dessert plate from the service presented by Queen Victoria to the Emperor of Russia in 1845, 10in. wide. (Dacre, Son & Hartley) $2,557

A Coalport vase of shield shape with scroll handles and square base, painted in the Baxter workshop, 32cm. (Phillips) $625

A Coalport cabinet plate, signed by F.H. Chivers, with ripened fruit on an earthy ground, 10½in. across. (Christie's) $529

COALPORT

A 19th century Coalport porcelain peacock in gold and white on a rococo base, 6in. high. (G. A. Key) $222

A pair of rare Coalport mantelpiece vases in neo-Classical style, painted almost certainly by Thomas Baxter, 29cm. high. (Phillips) $1,288

A Coalport Bough pot decorated in the Baxter workshop, 28.5cm. wide. (Phillips) $956

Large Coalport vase of baluster form, heavily applied with floral leaf decoration and griffin type handles, approx. 24in. high. (G. A. Key) $660

A garniture of three early Coalport vases attributed to Charles Muss, 22cm. and 32cm. high, all signed underneath in gold CM. (Phillips) $1,072

A Coalport vase of campana shape, with double scroll handles and leaf scroll molded stem, on square base, 44cm. high. (Phillips) $3,056

COPELAND

A Copeland 'orchid' vase, painted by T. Sadler, signed and dated 1904, 62.5cm. high. (Phillips) $1,910

A Copeland part dessert service, the centers painted with named views, comprising twenty-four pieces, printed marks (some damage). (Christie's) $1,628

A Copeland & Garrett rectangular shaped ceramic panel in oak frame, circa 1840, 32 x 8in. (Giles Haywood) $343

COPER, HANS

A stoneware 'spade-form' vase by Hans Coper, circa 1970, 19.8cm. high. (Christie's) $10,912

An early small stoneware bowl by Hans Coper, with undulating rim, circa 1955, 14cm. diam. (Christie's) $7,920

A stoneware 'poppy head' shaped vase by Hans Coper, circa 1958, 13.8cm. high. (Christie's) $5,632

A tall bulbous stoneware vase by Hans Coper, with narrow neck and flared rim, circa 1958, 33.4cm. high. (Christie's) $7,920

A bottle vase by Hans Coper, oviform body with short cylindrical neck, circa 1958, impressed HC seal, 65.2cm. high, (Christie's) $23,760

A stoneware 'spade-form' vase by Hans Coper, circa 1972, 23.4cm. high. (Christie's) $16,720

A tall 'hour-glass' vase by Hans Coper, impressed HC seal, 45.5cm. high. (Christie's) $29,920

A stoneware 'spade-form' vase by Hans Coper, 17.8cm. high. (Christie's) $6,688

A waisted cylindrical stoneware vase by Hans Coper, impressed HC seal, circa 1957, 18.6cm. high. (Christie's) $2,112

DELFT

An English delft polychrome posset pot, either London or Bristol, circa 1695, 24.5cm. wide. (Christie's) $2,359

One of two Bristol delft blue and white small rectangular flower-bricks painted with huts, circa 1760, 11.5cm. wide. (Christie's) $808

A Bristol delft blue and white footed bowl, circa 1730, 26.5cm. diam. (Christie's) $2,178

A London delft blue and white Royalist portrait plate, circa 1690, 22cm. diam. (Christie's) $2,541

A Delft mantel garniture, comprising two covered jars and a vase, vase 13in. high. (Christie's) $770

A Lambeth delft blue and white octagonal pill slab, circa 1780, 26cm. high. (Christie's) $3,085

A Bristol delft plate painted in a bright palette with a peacock, circa 1740, 21cm. diam. (Christie's) $1,540

A London delft vase painted in blue 24cm. high. (Phillips) $835

A late 17th century Lambeth blue and white delftware dish, 14in. wide. (Dacre, Son & Hartley) $656

DERBY

A Derby Crown porcelain small lobed jardiniere, 19cm. wide, black printed mark. (Phillips) $768

A pair of Derby figures of a sailor and his lass, Wm. Duesbury & Co., circa 1765, approx. 24cm. high. (Christie's) $1,996

Bloor Derby porcelain sauce tureen and cover, Japan polychrome pattern with gilt work, circa 1820. (G. A. Key) $300

A Derby figure of Justice represented by a blind lady in richly decorated Classical robes, 32cm. (Phillips) $1,104

A Derby (Sampson Hancock) documentary rectangular plaque, signed and dated on the reverse Sampson Hancock May 31, 1865, 21.5 x 15.5cm. (Christie's) $726

A Derby figure of a gallant seated on a tree stump, Wm. Duesbury & Co., circa 1760, 13cm. high. (Christie's) $1,179

A Derby baluster jug, painted by Richard Dodson, 17cm. high, crown, crossed batons and D mark in red. (Phillips) $2,865

Two Derby figures of John Wilkes and General Conway, Wm. Duesbury & Co., circa 1765. (Christie's) $2,178

An attractive early Derby bell-shaped mug, painted with a bouquet of colored flowers and scattered sprigs, the rim edged in brown, 11cm. (Phillips) $1,564

DERBY

Derby handled cup and
saucer, white ground with
floral and gilded decoration,
red mark to base, circa 1815.
(Giles Haywood) $68

A fine set of three 18th
century Derby flower vases
with named views.
(Worsfolds) $4,704

A Derby porcelain wine taster,
circular with scalloped rim,
leaf-shaped handle, circa 1770,
3.1/8in. long. (Christie's)
$717

A Derby figure of a flautist,
Wm. Duesbury & Co., circa
1758, 15.5cm. high.
(Christie's) $2,178

A Derby set of the 'Four Quarters
of the Globe', circa 1770, 22.5cm.
high. (Phillips) $6,346

An early Derby figure of a
flautist, on a circular base with
molded puce scrolls, 14cm.
(Phillips) $1,140

An attractive small Derby
model of a Pug, modelled
and colored with a gold
studded collar around its
neck, 6cm. high. (Phillips)
$699

A pair of Derby groups, both
of a cow with calf in front
of a flowering bocage back-
ground, 16cm. high. (Phillips)
$840

One of a pair of Derby plates,
the centers painted with roses,
thistles, bluebells, ferns and
other flowers, 22.5cm. diam.
(Phillips) $1,050

DOULTON

'Smuts', Royal Doulton character jug, large, no number, designed by H. Fenton, introduced 1946, withdrawn circa 1948. (Louis Taylor) $676

'The Wandering Minstrel' HN1224, designed by L. Harradine, introduced 1927, withdrawn 1938, 7in. high. (Louis Taylor) $1,402

''Ard of 'Earing', large, D6588, designed by D. Biggs, introduced 1964, withdrawn 1967. (Louis Taylor) $792

Royal Doulton stoneware pottery jug, black leather ware, circa 1903, 8in. high. (G. A. Key) $108

'North American Indian', a Royal Doulton character jug, 7in. high. (Anderson & Garland) $60

'Coquette', no number, designed by Wm. White, introduced 1913, withdrawn 1938, 9.25in. high. (Louis Taylor) $1,567

'Jarge', a Royal Doulton character jug, 6¾in. high. (Anderson & Garland) $177

A large Doulton Lambeth stoneware vase by Hannah Barlow and Frank Butler, 21in. high. (Christie's) $1,425

'The Mikado', a Royal Doulton character jug, small, D6507, designed by M. Henk, introduced 1959, withdrawn 1969. (Louis Taylor) $123

DOULTON

'Brown-Haired Clown', a Royal Doulton character jug, large, D5610, designed by H. Fenton, introduced 1937, withdrawn 1942. (Louis Taylor) $1,730

Royal Doulton china model of a Siamese cat, 5½in. high, HN1655. (Prudential Fine Art) $33

'Granny', Royal Doulton character jug, large, no number, designed by H. Fenton and M. Henk, introduced 1935. (Louis Taylor) $346

Royal Doulton character jug, 'Old King Cole', with yellow crown and grey/white hair, 6in. high. (Prudential Fine Art) $5,445

A Doulton Lambeth stoneware vase by Francis C. Pope, 16½in. high, impressed and incised artist monogram. (Christie's) $644

'Jockey', a Royal Doulton character jug, large, D6625, designed by D. Biggs, introduced 1971, withdrawn 1975. (Louis Taylor) $255

Doulton Lambeth stoneware jug decorated with bacchanalian figures and verse, circa 1895, 7in. high. (G. A. Key) $183

'Boy with Turban', HN1210, designed by L. Harradine, introduced 1926, withdrawn 1938, 3.75in. high. (Louis Taylor) $495

'Drake' (hatless), a Royal Doulton character jug, large, D6115, designed by H. Fenton, introduced 1940, withdrawn 1941. (Louis Taylor) $2,970

DOULTON

A Lambeth stoneware figure, 'The Toiler', bearing initials LH, (Leslie Harradine), circa 1912, 9.25 in. high. (Louis Taylor) $445

Royal Doulton Dickens' ware part-toilet set, special back-stamp, 19th century. (Peter Wilson) $615

A Sung flambe figure 'Boy on a Seahorse', signed Frederick Moore, 8.5 in. high, probably a pilot. (Louis Taylor) $907

A Royal Doulton flask, modelled by Leslie Harradine as Asquith, 18cm. high. (Phillips) $133

Two Doulton Lambeth brown saltglazed stoneware figures, by George Tinworth, one playing a pipe, the other a tambourine, the tallest 4¾in. high. (Christie's) $1,181

Royal Doulton figure, 'Harlequinade', HN585. (Warren & Wignall Ltd.) $640

'Kathleen', HN1252, a Royal Doulton figure designed by L. Harradine, 7¾in. high. (Christie's) $433

'Monty', D6202, a Royal Doulton character jug, 6in. high. (Anderson & Garland) $46

'The Coming of Spring', HN1723, designed by L. Harradine, introduced 1935, withdrawn 1949, 12.5 in. high. (Abridge Auctions) $875

DOULTON

'One of the Forty', no number first version design, undecorated, hair crack in base, date 1924, 9.5in. high. (Louis Taylor) $330

A flambe figure of a Seated Rabbit, 5.75in. high. (Louis Taylor) $132

'Lady of the Georgian Period', HN41, designed by E. W. Light, introduced 1914, withdrawn 1938, 10.25in. high. (Louis Taylor) $1,072

'Dog Begging with Lump of Sugar on nose', produced 1929, probably a prototype, 8in. high. (Louis Taylor) $759

A pair of Royal Doulton stoneware vases by Hannah B. Barlow and Florrie Jones, 5½in. high. (Christie's) $354

'Midinette', HN2090, a Royal Doulton figure designed by L. Harradine, 7¼in. high. (Christie's) $255

'One of the Forty', no number, treacle glaze decoration, 6.5in. high. (Louis Taylor) $198

Pair of Doulton Faience vases, dated 1885, 9½in. high. (Geering & Colyer) $356

'Young Miss Nightingale', HN2010, a Royal Doulton figure designed by M. Davies, 9½in. high. (Christie's) $590

DOULTON

'Gladys', HN1740, designed
by L. Harradine, introduced
1935, withdrawn 1949, 5in.
high. (Louis Taylor)
$528

'The Lady Jester', style two,
HN1284, designed by L.
Harradine, introduced 1928,
withdrawn 1938, 4.25in. high.
(Louis Taylor) $1,089

'Sweet and Twenty', HN1360,
a Royal Doulton figure designed
by L. Harradine, 5¾in. high.
(Christie's) $315

A Doulton, Burslem, ovoid
vase, the panel painted by
Fred Sutton, 17cm. high.
(Phillips) $668

A Royal Doulton group, 'The
Flower Seller's Children',
HN1342, 20cm. high. (Dee &
Atkinson) $152

A Royal Doulton Chang
vase, 9in. high. (G. A. Key)
$513

'White Haired Clown' Royal
Doulton character jug, D6322
designed by H. Fenton,
introduced 1951, withdrawn
1955. (Abridge Auctions)
$840

A Royal Doulton Limited
Edition Tower of London
jug. (Hobbs Parker)
$785

'Dick Whittington', a Royal
Doulton character jug, large,
D6375, designed by G.
Blower, introduced 1953,
withdrawn 1960. (Louis
Taylor) $239

DOULTON

'Delight', HN1772, a Royal Doulton figure designed by L. Harradine, 7½in. high. (Christie's) $130

Seated Bulldog with Union Jack, hat and cigar, 7.5in. high. (Louis Taylor) $858

A Royal Doulton figure, 'Rebecca', HN2805, 19cm. high. (Dee & Atkinson) $136

'Jarge', large, no number, designed by H. Fenton, introduced 1950, withdrawn 1960. (Louis Taylor) $189

'The Farmer's Boy', HN2520G, 9.25in. high. (Louis Taylor) $759

'Samuel Johnson', a Royal Doulton character jug, large no number, designed by H. Fenton, introduced 1950, withdrawn 1960. (Louis Taylor) $247

A Doulton Lambeth style stoneware conservatory planter in the form of a weathered tree trunk. (Locke & England) $978

'Old King Cole', a Royal Doulton character jug, 5¼in. high. (Anderson & Garland) $150

A Doulton Lambeth stoneware jug, impressed factory mark and incised monograms for Florence Barlow and Mary Aitken, 8in. high. (Peter Wilson) $486

CHINA

An earthenware two-handled motto tankard by Michael Cardew, impressed MC and Winchcombe Pottery seals (circa 1930), 10.1cm. high. (Christie's) $356

'Vertical Vessel', an earthenware vase by Gordon Baldwin, dated '83, 50.7cm. high. (Christie's) $528

A small oval earthenware slip-decorated dish by Charles Tustin, impressed CT and Winchcombe Pottery seals (circa 1935), 20.4cm. diam. (Christie's) $108

A Poole pottery earthenware oviform vase, painted by Anne Hatchard, 28cm. high. (Christie's) $425

An earthenware cider flagon, by Michael Cardew, Wenford Bridge seals, circa 1970, 39cm. high. (Christie's) $1,450

A black earthenware hand-built coiled amphora by Fiona Salazar, 24.6cm. high. (Christie's) $457

A large earthenware jug by Sidney Tustin, with strap handle, impressed ST and Winchcombe Pottery seals (circa 1935), 16.5cm. high. (Christie's) $99

An earthenware charger by Ljerka Njers, inscribed on the reverse L. Njers 1983, 39.4cm. wide. (Christie's) $554

An early St. Ives slip deco-rated earthenware jug with elaborate strap handle, 22.5cm. high. (Christie's) $70

EARTHENWARE

'Painting in the form of a bowl', an earthenware bowl by Gordon Baldwin, circa 1980, 38.4cm. diam. (Christie's) $563

'Painting in the form of a bowl', an earthenware bowl by Gordon Baldwin, dated '82, 45.5cm. diam. (Christie's) $739

A grey earthenware bowl by Birch, with shaped double flanged rim, 26.5cm. wide. (Christie's) $158

An early St. Ives small earthenware jug with strap handle incised St. Ives 1927, 6.5cm. high. (Christie's) $1,056

A 16th century mediaeval jug in buff colored earthenware, probably Surrey, 18.5cm. high. (Phillips) $764

A Linthorpe earthenware vase molded on each side with grotesque fish faces, 17.9cm. high. (Christie's) $589

A large earthenware dish by Michael Cardew, impressed MC and Winchcombe Pottery seals (circa 1930), 36.6cm. wide. (Christie's) $950

A small earthenware jug by Michael Cardew, impressed MC and Winchcombe Pottery seals, 12.4cm. high. (Christie's) $167

'Vessel in the form of a Gray Voice', an earthenware sculpture in two parts by Gordon Baldwin, dated '84, base 38cm. square. (Christie's) $633

Early 20th century Gouda pottery covered urn, Holland, 16½in. high. (Robt. W. Skinner Inc.) $400

Pair of 19th century Continental glazed and decorated stoneware figures, 'Policeman' and 'Woman', 12in. and 11in. tall. (J. M. Welch & Son) $151

A mid 19th century Russian Toby jug from the Korniloff factory, 21.5cm. high. (Phillips) $1,085

A model of a roistering Dutchman astride a Dutch gin cask, 37.5cm. high. (Christie's) $52,360

A set of four Continental ceramic plaques, square, each depicting industrial and artisan subjects in the purist style, 10½in. sq., printed marks, each painted with Cocrah. (Christie's) $1,167

Early 17th century Netherlands majolica syrup jar, painted in blue with scrolling foliage and plant pods, 23.5cm. high. (Phillips) $955

A Russian Imperial porcelain dinner plate, 23.5cm. diam., cypher mark of Nicholas I in blue. (Phillips) $668

A Zurich figure of a shepherd, modelled by J. J. Meyer, 20cm. high, incised mark N I. (Phillips) $8,404

A Cheese dish in the form of a bull's head. (Worsfolds) $184

FAMILLE ROSE

A Chinese famille rose sauce-boat, Qianlong, circa 1760, 8¼in. across handle. (Woolley & Wallis) $640

A pair of famille rose 18th century octagonal plates with the 'pseudo' 'tobacco pattern', 22in. diam. (Phillips) $356

One of a pair of famille rose octagonal jardinieres, 10½in. wide. (Reeds Rains) $4,258

An ormolu mounted famille rose baluster jar and cover with fruiting finial, the porcelain circa 1800, 21¾in. high. (Christie's) $2,388

An 18th century Chinese famille rose plate, 43cm. diam. (David Lay) $450

A famille rose Oviform vase with a scene of the eight Daoist Immortals below pine trees, 28cm. high. (Christie's) $10,098

One of a pair of famille rose bowls, Yung Cheng marks and of the period, 7in. diam. (Phillips) $13,104

A rare famille rose marbled-ground oviform vase, 15.5cm. high. (Christie's) $13,206

A famille rose punch bowl, enamelled with panels of courtiers within key and floral pattern borders, 15½in. diam. (Greenslade & Co.) $1,780

A 19th century Samson porcelain figure of Minerva, approx. 15in. high. (G. A. Key) $371

Pair of French sweetmeat dishes formed as seated figures of a Girl and Boy, 5in. high. (G. A. Key) $495

An 18th century French biscuit group modelled as a bearded god attended by two cupids, 40cm. high. (Christie's) $1,069

One of a pair of Luneville shaped circular dishes painted in polychrome with chinoiserie figures with umbrellas, circa 1770, 33cm. diam. (Christie's) $5,667

A pair of early 19th century Jacob Petit baluster vases on square bases with gilt mask handles, 71cm. high. (Wellington Salerooms) $6,720

One of a pair of mid 18th century Strasbourg hexafoil plates, 24cm. diam. (Christie's) $796

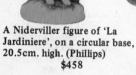

A Niderviller figure of 'La Jardiniere', on a circular base, 20.5cm. high. (Phillips) $458

Pair of Samson porcelain figure ornaments, 'Presentation of Ribbons' and 'The Hairdresser', 7in. high. (G. A. Key) $672

A 'Henri Deux style' candlestick, by Charles Toft, 34cm. high. (Phillips) $1,336

FRENCH

Late 18th/early 19th century French biscuit group emblematic of America, 29cm. high. (Christie's) $801

A Rouen shaped circular plate painted in a famille verte palette, circa 1740, 25cm. diam. (Christie's)
$1,948

An 18th century French biscuit figure emblematic of Africa, 31.5cm. high. (Christie's) $1,158

Late 19th century Lachenal Art pottery pitcher, French, 15¾in. high. (Robt. W. Skinner Inc.) $400

A Limoges teaset for six, the whole covered in a mauve glaze, comprising teapot, hot water jug, sugar bowl and cover, milk jug, six cups and saucers, teapot 9¼in. high. (Christie's) $483

A Primavera pottery figure depicting a female in broadly flared pantaloons, 29cm. high, stamped 'Primavera, France', signed Levy. (Phillips)
$228

One of a pair of Marseilles (Veuve Perrin) shaped circular plates painted en camaieu vert with bouquets of flowers, circa 1765, 25cm. diam. (Christie's) $743

An 18th century French biscuit group emblematic of Plenty, 34cm. high. (Christie's) $801

One of a pair of Moustiers (Ferrat) shaped circular plates painted with pairs of parrots, circa 1770, 25cm. diam. (Christie's)
$619

GERMAN

A Frankenthal figure of Pantolone from the Commedia dell'Arte, blue lion and monogram of Joseph Adam Hannong to base, circa 1760, 11.5cm. high. (Christie's) $6,058

A Furstenberg globular teapot and cover, blue script F and figure 3 to base, circa 1765, 19cm. wide. (Christie's) $3,029

A Brunswick Faience figure of a standing bagpiper, circa 1730, 18cm. high. (Christie's) $8,553

Early 18th century Westerwald oviform tankard (Birnkrug) painted in blue and manganese on the gray body, 24cm. high. (Christie's) $534

A Florsheim Faience inkstand, modelled as a chest of three serpentine-fronted drawers, 15cm. high. (Phillips) $2,254

A German Faience tankard with pewter footrim mount, and cover with ball thumbpiece and engraved 'H. J. 1751', 25cm. high overall, the tankard circa 1730. (Christie's) $1,416

A German plaque by Louis Renders, after David Neal, with Mary Queen of Scots' first encounter with Rizzio, signed, circa 1887, 29 x 21.5cm. (Christie's) $1,089

Pair of Sitzendorf figurines, depicting flower girl and gardener boy, impress marks to base 'S' 'DEP' '15024', circa 1880. (Giles Haywood) $229

A Hochst figure of harlequin wearing a multi-colored suit and a conical hat, circa 1755, 16cm. high. (Christie's) $5,667

GERMAN

An early Frankenthal figure of Pulchinella, impressed PH3 (for Paul Hannong) on base, circa 1755, 12cm. high. (Christie's) $8,910

A Frankfurt Faience teapot and cover, painted in a bright blue with Chinese style figures, 13.5cm. high. (Phillips) $1,670

A German Faience tankard painted in colors by a Nuremberg Hausmaler, with hinged pewter cover, the Faience 1740, 25.5cm. high. (Christie's) $16,929

A Bottger gold Chinese milk jug and later domed cover gilt in the Seuter workshop, the porcelain circa 1725, 18cm. high. (Christie's) $1,211

A Dresden Wolfsohn late 19th century china lobed dish, cover and stand. (Graves Son & Pilcher) $572

A German Faience tankard (Walzenkrug), circa 1740, probably Erfurt, 24cm. high. (Christie's) $1,692

Part of a Nymphenburg tea and coffee service painted in green and black with sprays of flowers and with iron-red borders, circa 1765. (Christie's) $2,302

A Frankenthal group of four children, 23cm. wide, Carl Theodor mark in underglaze blue and dated 1783. (Phillips) $7,348

A Dorotheenthal polychrome tankard, blue 'D' mark to base, circa 1735, with later cover, 25.5cm. high overall. (Christie's) $1,416

GERMAN

Early 18th century German white Faience figure of a Callot dwarf modelled as a smoker, 46cm. high. (Christie's) $6,198

Late 17th century Habaner Ware inscribed and dated beer jug, 30cm. high. (Christie's) $6,237

A Hochst figure of a dancing girl modelled by Johann P. Melchior, blue crowned wheel mark, circa 1775, 13.5cm. high. (Christie's) $796

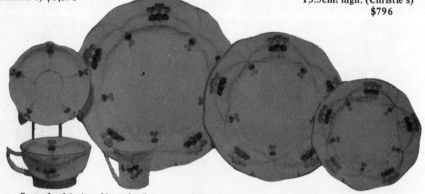

Part of a 36-piece Nymphenburg porcelain dinner service painted in purple, green and yellow enamels with stylized scrolling, flower-heads and stems. (Christie's) $992

A Hochst group of Wandering Musicians, modelled by J. P. Melchior, underglaze blue wheel mark to base, circa 1770, 23cm. high. (Christie's) $7,128

A German porcelain oval plaque painted with a portrait of a young girl, 14cm. high. (Christie's) $881

A Frankenthal group of card players modelled by J. F. Luck, crowned CT mark and letter B for Adam Bergdoll to base, circa 1765, 17cm. high. (Christie's) $8,910

A Hochst figure of a lady modelled by Johann P. Melchior as a sultan, circa 1770, 18cm. high. (Christie's) $1,239

A pair of Nymphenburg plates , one of the five 'engravings' pinned to it with red and gilt nails, signed G. Sator inv. et Fecit, 24cm. diam. (Christie's) $2,851

A Ludwigsburg figure of a lady with a muff modelled by Pierre F. Lejeune, circa 1760, 12.5cm. high. (Christie's) $1,328

A pair of Hochst figures of musicians, blue wheel marks to bases, circa 1765, 16.5cm. high. (Christie's) $5,313

A pair of Furstenberg white portrait busts modelled by J. C. Rombrich, probably of Schrader von Schiestedt and his wife, circa 1758/9, 15cm. high. (Christie's) $9,740

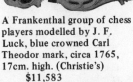

A Frankenthal group of chess players modelled by J. F. Luck, blue crowned Carl Theodor mark, circa 1765, 17cm. high. (Christie's) $11,583

A Bottger rectangular teapot and cover painted in Schwarzlot enriched in gilding by I. Preissler, circa 1720, 15cm. high. (Christie's) $60,214

A Ludwigsburg group of dancers modelled by Franz Anton Pustelli, blue crowned crossed-C mark and incised UM 3 to base, circa 1760, 16cm. high. (Christie's) $19,602

CHINA

GERMAN

A German bisque porcelain figure group on oval base, 15in. high. (G. A. Key) $75

Pair of Dresden Wolfsohn late 19th century china vases and covers, 12in. high. (Graves Son & Pilcher) $751

A Sitzendorf porcelain classical figure group with polychrome decoration, 10in. high. (G. A. Key) $477

Pair of German porcelain figures, decorated in blue and white, 13in. high. (G. A. Key) $379

Late 19th century German porcelain table centerpiece, underglazed blue 'R' mark, 11½in. high. (Peter Wilson) $704

Late 19th century pair of German porcelain figures, a dandy fruit gatherer with his female companion, 12in. tall. (G. A. Key) $354

GOLDSCHEIDER

A Goldscheider ceramic wall plaque molded as the head, neck and hand of a young woman, 7½in. high, printed marks. (Christie's) $194

A Goldscheider alabaster figure carved by Dakon, of a clown, 30cm. high. (Christie's) $631

A Goldscheider tin-glazed earthenware wall mask, Wien, Made in Austria, inscribed 8874, 36cm. high. (Christie's) $811

GOSS

Parian bust of Southey. (Goss & Crested China Ltd.) $260

Glazed Florence Goss wall vase, with radiating hair and feathers, 120mm. high. (Goss & Crested China Ltd) $435

Rye Cannon Ball without plinth. (Goss & Crested China Ltd.) $54

Kirk Braddon Cross in brown washed parian. $140 £82 Unusually, the white parian example is more valuable. (Goss & Crested China Ltd) $325

Parian bust of Lord Palmerston on socle base and fluted column, 335mm. high. (Goss & Crested China Ltd.) $270

Shakespeare's House, half size. (Goss & Crested China Ltd.) $144

The Trusty Servant of Winchester. (Goss & Crested China Ltd.) $2,430

Large Carnarvon Ewer with Welsh Antiquities design of mistletoe and sickle, crossed daggers. (Goss & Crested China Ltd.) $72

Colored Parian bust of The Beautiful Duchess, who was Georgiana, Duchess of Devonshire. (Goss & Crested China Ltd.) $2,250

IMARI

An Imari tall oviform jar decorated in colored enamels and gilt on underglaze blue, Genroku period. (Christie's) $3,344

An Imari charger decorated in iron-red enamel and gilt on underglaze blue, Genroku period, 55cm. diam. (Christie's) $2,057

One of a pair of Imari double-gourd bottle vases, Genroku period, 33.5cm, high. (Christie's) $12,320

One of a pair of pierced Imari plates, 8in. diam.. (R. K. Lucas & Son) $159

An Imari model of a bijin decorated in iron-red, green, aubergine and black enamels and gilt, Genroku period, 37cm. high. (Christie's) $2,431

A mid 19th century Japanese Imari goldfish bowl. (Miller & Co.) $787

An Imari molded kendi of typical form decorated in iron-red on underglaze blue, Genroku period, 27cm. high. (Christie's) $1,584

An Imari jar decorated with a ho-o bird and a cockerel, Genroku period, wood cover, 39.5cm. high. (Christie's) $2,805

An octagonal faceted Shoki-Imari bottle vase, circa 1660, 29cm. high. (Christie's) $4,288

IMARI

An Imari globular bottle vase with tall neck decorated in colored enamels and gilt with two cranes, circa 1700, 24.5cm. high. (Christie's) $523

An Imari bowl, Ming four-character mark, Genroku period, 25cm. diam. (Christie's) $2,244

An Imari jar and cover decorated in iron-red and black enamels and gilt on underglaze blue, Genroku period, 63cm. high. (Christie's) $2,992

An Imari barber's bowl, Genroku period, 28cm. diam. (Christie's) $704

An Imari model of an actor decorated in iron-red, green, aubergine and black enamels and gilt on underglaze blue, Genroku period, 39cm. high. (Christie's) $3,553

An Imari plate painted in underglaze blue, iron-red, colored enamels and gilt with 'La Dame au Parasol', circa 1740, 22.5cm. diam. (Christie's) $2,992

One of a pair of 19th century Chinese Imari style lidded vases of high shouldered ovoid form. (Peter Wilson) $915

Late 17th century Ko-Imari jar decorated in iron-red, black, green and yellow enamels, 34cm. high.(Christie's) $96,800

One of a pair of late 19th century Imari molded rectangular sake bottles, 27.5cm. high. (Christie's) $1,122

IMARI

Late 17th/early 18th century
Imari molded condiment
ewer, 9cm. high.
(Christie's) $633

Pair of Imari ewers decorated in iron-red, green
enamels and gold on underglaze blue, Genroku period,
16.5cm. high. (Christie's)
$3,168

An Imari model of a leaping
carp on rockwork, Genroku
period, 32cm. high.
(Christie's) $2,992

Late 17th century Ko-Imari
shaped square shallow dish,
14cm. square. (Christie's)
$3,168

Late 17th century Ko-Imari
model of a seated karashishi,
48.5cm. high. (Christie's)
$56,100

A large Imari fish bowl,
40cm. high. (Dee &
Atkinson) $496

An Imari charger decorated
in iron-red and black enamels
and gilt on underglaze blue,
Genroku period, 54cm. diam.
(Christie's) $11,220

An Imari octagonal jar,
Genroku period, 46cm.
high. (Christie's)
$12,320

An Imari charger, the roundel
containing a vase of cascading
chrysanthemum and peony
sprays on a veranda, Genroku
period, 55cm. diam.
(Christie's) $3,179

IMARI

An Imari circular tureen and cover with applied loop finial, Genroku period, 23cm. diam. (Christie's) $2,992

An Imari model of a bijin decorated in iron-red, green, black enamels and gilt on underglaze blue, 36cm. high. (Christie's) $3,553

An Imari condiment set, ewer and cover decorated in iron-red and black enamels and gilt on underglaze blue, Genroku period, 9cm. high. (Christie's) $316

Early 18th century Imari armorial dish decorated in iron-red and gilt on underglaze blue. (Christie's) $4,675

A large Imari jar and a cover decorated in iron-red enamel and gilt on underglaze blue, Genroku period, the vase 61cm. high. (Christie's) $9,350

An Imari charger decorated in iron-red and black enamels on underglaze blue, Genroku period, 60cm. diam. (Christie's) $2,244

An Imari charger decorated in iron-red and gilt on underglaze blue, Genroku period, 53cm. diam. (Christie's) $6,545

A pair of late 19th century Imari bijin, 48cm. high. (Christie's) $2,431

An Imari shallow dish decorated in iron-red and gilt on underglaze blue, Genroku period, 25.5cm. diam. (Christie's) $841

A Deruta blue and gold lustre
charger, early 16th century,
41.5cm. diam. (Phillips)
$7,258

One of a pair of mid 16th
century Venetian vasi a
palli, 33cm. high. (Christie's)
$21,252

A Castelli armorial plate from
the Grue workshop, 25cm.
diam. (Phillips)
$9,168

A Faenza or Tuscan vase,
circa 1500-20, 32.5cm.
high. (Phillips) $1,753

A Castelli rectangular plaque
painted by Saverio Grue with
Joseph sold by his brothers to
the Midianites, circa 1770,
32.5 x 23.5cm. (Christie's)
$10,626

Early 17th century Central
Italian circular plaque with
a raised rim dated 1606,
probably Deruta, 27cm.
diam. (Christie's)
$891

Mid 16th century Castel
Durante plate, 22cm. diam.
(Phillips) $2,292

An Urbino small albarello,
workshop of Orazio Fontana,
circa 1665-70, 15cm. high.
(Phillips) $4,966

A Venice vaso a palla with
the portrait heads of two
saints in cartouches, circa
1550, 28cm. high.
(Christie's) $8,855

ITALIAN

Early 16th century siena maiolica dish center, probably from a tondino, the shield with the arms of the Penalva family of Portugal, 9.5cm. diam. (Phillips) $993

A small pair of 19th century Italian albarello pots, the bases signed R.B., 4½in. high. (Christie's) $316

An 18th century Savona polychrome tazza, painted in yellow, blue and green, mark in ochre, 35cm. high. (Phillips) $835

A Deruta gold lustre circular dish with the arms of Colonna in the central raised well, circa 1520, 29cm. diam. (Christie's) $7,128

A pair of siena maiolica vases by Bartholomeo Terchi, one vase signed Bar: Terc(h)i: Romano: 1726, 56cm. high overall. (Phillips) $4,008

Mid 17th century Montelupo circular dish painted with oak leaves, 32cm. diam. (Christie's) $566

A Castelli small plate, painted with a putto in flight holding a book, 17cm. diam. (Phillips) $802

An Urbino maiolica wet drug or syrup jar, workshop of Orazio Fontana, 1565-70, 34cm. high. (Phillips) $22,920

Late 17th century Castelli plate painted in colors with a mounted hunting party, 23cm. diam. (Christie's) $4,633

ITALIAN

A Naples creamware white group of the Madonna with the Infant Christ and St. John, inscribed Laudato Fecit 1794, 35cm. high. (Christie's) $7,128

A 17th century Italian square tray, probably Deruta. (Christie's) $1,514

One of a pair of 17th century Sicilian wet-drug jars with scroll handles, 25cm. high. (Christie's) $2,302

An Urbino dish painted in the Patanazzi workshop with Abraham sacrificing Isaac, circa 1580, 35cm. diam. (Christie's) $8,910

A Sicilian oviform vase painted with a portrait of a helmeted soldier, dated 1662, 37cm. high. (Christie's) $974

A Castelli armorial circular dish, the center painted with equestrian figures hawking, circa 1720, 40.5cm. diam. (Christie's) $8,500

One of three 17th century Sicilian waisted albarelli, approx. 24cm. high. (Christie's) $891

Two siena polychrome plates with scenes of the deer hunt and wolf hunt, circa 1740, 23.5cm. diam. (Christie's) $1,416

A Sicilian waisted albarello painted with the head of a man in quatrefoil cartouche, 30cm. high, also another albarello and a wet-drug jar, all 18th/19th century. (Christie's) $2,125

ITALIAN

A Deruta bottle for A. Graminis painted with the figure of Santa Barbara, circa 1530, 40cm. high. (Christie's) $8,910

A Castelli rectangular plaque painted in the Grue workshop with the Flight into Egypt, circa 1720, 20 x 25.5cm. (Christie's) $2,479

An 18th/19th century South Italian maiolica plaque painted with Christ, 38cm. high. (Christie's) $743

A Deruta tondino painted in a palette of green, yellow, blue and orange, circa 1550, 21cm. diam. (Christie's) $1,960

A 17th century baluster vase painted with yellow and green stylized flowers and foliage on a blue ground, 25cm. high. (Christie's) $1,069

An Italian istoriato plate with the Judgement of Paris painted in colors, 1544, 27cm. diam. (Christie's) $17,820

A Naples two-handled ecuelle, cover and stand painted with vignettes of five dated nocturnal eruptions of Vesuvius, circa 1794, stand 23.5cm. diam. (Christie's) $21,384

A Pesaro istoriato tazza painted in colors by Sforza di Marcantonio with Anchises and Aeneas arriving at Pallanteum, circa 1550, 27cm. diam. (Christie's) $4,989

A Castelli oval plaque painted by Saverio Grue with St. Francis, circa 1730, 38cm. high. (Christie's) $6,198

ITALIAN

A 19th century Italian alabaster bust of an allegory of Sculpture, inscribed on the reverse Vichi Firenze, 67cm. high. (Christie's) $1,745

An Urbino maiolica shallow dish painted with Cain slaying Abel, circa 1540, 25cm. diam. (Christie's) $4,276

Late 17th century S. Italian Holy Water stoup, 33cm. high. (Christie's) $1,514

A Castelli circular tondo painted with the Dispute in the Temple, circa 1725, 43cm. diam. (Christie's) $1,062

An Italian maiolica waisted albarello painted with a saint, circa 1600, 28cm. high. (Christie's) $1,593

An early 18th century siena circular dish painted with two women with children, 31.5cm. diam. (Christie's) $1,771

A South Italian waisted albarello painted with the goddess Victory in a landscape, circa 1550, 28cm. high. (Christie's) $1,328

A Castelli rectangular plaque painted with the Meeting between St. John and the Infant Christ, circa 1690, 30 x 40cm. (Christie's) $2,656

One of three 17th century Sicilian waisted albarelli painted in yellow, green and blue, approx. 23cm. high. (Christie's) $1,514

ITALIAN

Late 17th century S. Italian maiolica Holy Water stoup painted in colors , 31cm. high. (Christie's) $801

An Urbino istoriato tazza painted in colors in the circle of Francesco Xanto Avelli with Marcus Curtius on horseback, circa 1545, 26.5cm. diam. (Christie's) $16,038

A Savona blue and white fountain with loop-over handle, circa 1700, 59cm. high. (Christie's) $6,729

An Urbino istoriato plate painted with the Temptation of Adam, circa 1560, 23cm. diam. (Christie's) $5,702

A 17th century South Italian armorial waisted albarello, probably Sciacca, 29.5cm. high. (Christie's)$1,505

An Urbino istoriato dish painted with the Death of Achilles, by Nicola Pellipario, circa 1535, 25.5cm. diam. (Christie's) $14,256

One of two 17th century Sicilian drug jars with narrow necks, 23cm. high. (Christie's) $1,336

Two Urbino armorial circular dishes, the centers with classical figure panels, circa 1580, 27.8cm. diam. (Christie's) $2,851

A Castelli campana vase, probably painted by Liborio Grue, circa 1740, 41.5cm. high. (Christie's) $2,302

JAPANESE

One of a pair of Kakiemon oviform jars and covers, circa 1680, 29.5cm. high. (Christie's) $24,640

Late 18th century foliate shaped Kakiemon bowl decorated in iron-red, blue, green, yellow and black enamels, 18cm. diam. (Christie's) $3,740

Late 19th century Kinkozan oviform vase and cover, impressed seal mark, signed Kinkozan zo, 15.5cm. high. (Christie's) $2,431

One of a pair of late 18th century Kakiemon style underglaze blue globular bottle vases, 23.5cm. high. (Christie's) $5,610

Late 17th century model of a Kakiemon seated tiger, 18.5cm. high. (Christie's) $35,530

A large octagonal oviform jar and domed cover with knop finial, Genroku period, 89cm. high. (Christie's) $14,025

A Kakiemon oviform vase and cover, circa 1660, the mounts 18th century, 19.5cm. high. (Christie's) $14,960

Late 18th century Kakiemon type underglaze blue koro and cover, 14.3cm. diam. (Christie's) $1,870

One of a pair of Kaga ware sake bottles (tokkuri), 21cm. high. (Christie's) $3,179

JAPANESE

Late 19th century Kinkozan baluster vase, signed Dai Nihon Teikoku Kinkozan zo Kyoto Awata-yaki Shozan hitsu, 31cm. high. (Christie's) $5,610

Late 17th/early 18th century Kakiemon type shallow dish, decorated in various colored enamels and underglaze blue, 24.5cm. diam. (Christie's) $4,114

Late 17th century Kakiemon underglaze blue oviform vase and cover, 36cm. high. (Christie's) $5,510

Late 19th century Kinkozan oviform vase decorated in various colored enamels and gilt on a dark green ground, 14cm. high. (Christie's) $2,244

Pair of Kakiemon cockerels standing on rockwork bases, circa 1680, 28cm. high. (Christie's) $35,200

A Kakiemon globular bottle vase, circa 1680, 28cm. high. (Christie's) $28,050

Late 19th century Kinkozan oviform bottle vase decorated in colored enamels and gilt, signed Kinkozan zo, 12.5cm. high. (Christie's) $2,805

Late 19th century Yabu Meizan koro and cover with knop finial, signed, 9cm. diam. (Christie's) $1,870

Late 19th century Kinkozan globular bottle vase, impressed seal mark, 26cm. high. (Christie's) $2,992

Late 17th century Kakiemon teabowl with later ormolu mounts, the bowl 6.75cm. diam., fitted box. (Christie's) $1,870

An ormolu mounted Kakiemon porcelain vase of bombe shape, the porcelain late 18th century, 5in. wide. (Christie's) $1,653

A decagonal Kakiemon foliate rim bowl, circa 1680, 18.5cm. wide. (Christie's) $4,114

A 19th century Japanese Satsuma pottery coffee service of fifteen pieces, all decorated with panels of geishas and other figures on a gilt brocade ground. (Hobbs & Chambers) $330

A Kakiemon shallow plate in iron-red, green, black, blue and yellow enamels on under-glaze blue lines, circa 1680, 22cm. diam. (Christie's) $3,179

A pair of late 19th century Japanese polychrome bottle vases, 25in. high. (Woolley & Wallis) $2,480

One of a pair of late 17th/ early 18th century foliate rim Kakiemon type under-glaze blue dishes, 20cm. diam. (Christie's) $528

KANGXI

A Kangxi 'egg and spinach' bowl, a finely mottled glaze of green, yellow and brown splashes, 17.5cm. diam. (Christie's) $2,019

A Kangxi Famille Verte deep bowl, painted in vivid enamels, 23cm. diam. (Christie's) $2,485

A Kangxi yellow-glazed bowl, sides flaring into an everted rim, all under a lustrous yellow glaze, 19cm. diam. (Christie's) $2,330

A Kangxi Famille Verte Foliate dish, painted in the Kakiemon style, 8¾in. diam. (Christie's) $1,398

A Kangxi blue and white Yanyan vase with baluster body and flaring neck, 46cm. high. (Christie's) $2,175

A Kangxi blue and white baluster jar, 10.8cm. high. (Christie's) $1,165

A Kangxi rare documentary dated white-glazed stem cup, 10cm. high. (Christie's) $10,098

An early Kangxi blue and white baluster vase, 20.5cm. high. (Christie's)$1,398

A Kangxi Langyao dish, 7¾in. diam.(Christie's) $201

A stoneware flask, by Bernard Leach, circa 1957, 33cm. high. (Christie's) $5,385

A stoneware bowl by Bernard Leach, covered in a speckled olive-green glaze, circa 1970, 19.2cm. diam. (Christie's) $475

A stoneware pear-shaped vase by Bernard Leach, covered in a blue-grey glaze over which brushed hakeme is incised with bell flowers, circa 1960, 26cm. high. (Christie's) $563

A stoneware rectangular slab bottle by Bernard Leach, covered in a tenmoku glaze with shiny black and rich russet areas, circa 1962, 19.4cm. high. (Christie's) $457

A stoneware oviform jar by John Leach, with everted rim decorated in wax-resist, 30.5cm. high. (Christie's) $352

A Yingqing porcelain globular vase by Bernard Leach, covered in a bluish white glaze with blue black rim, circa 1965, 15cm. high. (Christie's) $492

A Yingqing porcelain bowl by Bernard Leach, the exterior covered in a pale greenish white glaze, circa 1970, 17.5cm. diam. (Christie's) $704

A tapering stoneware cylindrical vase by Bernard Leach, covered in an olive-green and pale green ash glaze with areas of russet brown, circa 1965, 30.4cm. high. (Christie's) $1,408

A stoneware 'leaping deer' plate with everted rim decorated by Bernard Leach, circa 1965, 23.9cm. diam. (Christie's) $3,520

A porcelain bowl with compressed sides by Bernard Leach, circa 1960, 20.6cm. diam. (Christie's) $668

A large stonewar jar by Bernard Leach, with lobed sides, circa 1965, 19.3cm. high. (Christie's) $1,232

A stoneware bowl by Bernard Leach, on shallow foot, 25.2cm. diam. (Christie's) $880

A stoneware flattened rectangular slab bottle by Bernard Leach, covered in an olive-green tea-dust glaze, 18.6cm. high. (Christie's) $668

A large stoneware globular vase by Janet Leach, covered in a mottled olive-green ash glaze, circa 1980, 29.4cm. high. (Christie's) $281

A tall stoneware jug by Bernard Leach, with incised strap handle, circa 1970, 27cm. high. (Christie's) $880

A large stoneware 'fish' vase by Bernard Leach, circa 1970, 37.5cm. high. (Christie's) $9,680

A pair of early slip decorated earthenware dishes attributed to Bernard Leach, circa 1935, 19.5cm. diam. (Christie's) $1,056

A Yingqing porcelain slender oviform vase, by Bernard Leach, circa 1969, 36cm. high. (Christie's) $1,598

LIVERPOOL

A Liverpool tin-glazed stone-ware small cylindrical mug, circa 1760, 6.5cm. high. (Christie's) $3,267

A Liverpool blue and white molded oval sauceboat, attributed to Wm. Ball's factory, circa 1758, 14.5cm. wide. (Christie's) $3,993

A Liverpool Delft blue and white bottle painted with chrysanthemum and other flowers, 9¾in. high, circa 1750. (Christie's) $612

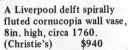

A Liverpool creamware jug, 21cm. high. (Phillips) $1,252

Two 19th century Liverpool transfer-printed pitchers, 10¾in. and 5½in. high respectively. (Christie's) $935

A Liverpool delft spirally fluted cornucopia wall vase, 8in. high, circa 1760. (Christie's) $940

A Liverpool creamware oviform jug, inscribed in black script W.B., 6¾in. high, circa 1800. (Christie's) $209

An English delft blue and white dish, perhaps Liverpool, circa 1740, 30.5cm. diam. (Christie's) $2,722

A 19th century Liverpool transfer-printed pitcher of baluster form with pulled spout and applied C-scroll handle. (Christie's) $1,100

LOWESTOFT

A Lowestoft bell-shaped mug, painted in colors, in the manner of the Tulip Painter, 14cm. high. (Phillips) $1,837

An 18th century Lowestoft porcelain miniature sparrow-beak jug, 3½in. high. (Hy Duke & Son) $106

A Lowestoft cylindrical mug, the scroll handle with thumb rest, 15cm. high. (Phillips) $3,173

LUSTRE

A large Pilkingtons Lancastrian pottery vase, designed by Gordon Forsyth, painted in a golden lustre of foliage, 17in. high, circa 1919. (Christie's) $880

Royal Lancastrian lustre pottery vase by W. S. Mycock, dated 1925, 9in. high. (Prudential Fine Art) $206

Pilkington's Royal Lancastrian lustre two-handled baluster vase decorated by William S. Mycock, 8.25in. high. (Prudential Fine Art) $156

MARTINWARE

A Martin Brothers stoneware vase, 23.5cm. high, signed 'Martin Bros. and dated '8-1903' and 'No. 6'. (Phillips) $296

A Martin Brothers stoneware 'Gourd' vase, 17.5cm. high, signed 'Martin Bros., London & Southall', dated '2-1910. (Phillips) $222

A Martin Bros. grotesque bird, covered in blue and olive-green glaze, 1915, 18.3cm. high. (Christie's) $2,692

MASON'S

A Miles Mason rectangular sugar bowl and cover, pattern no. 328 in gold, 17.5cm. wide, an oval teapot stand and a trio, circa 1815. (Christie's) $127

Mason's ironstone jug decorated with Imari pattern, 8in. high. (G. A. Key) $136

A Miles Mason sugar bowl and cover painted with 'The Dragon in Compartments' pattern, 16cm. wide, with two others, 15cm. and 19cm. wide, 1810-15. (Christie's) $707

A Mason's ironstone part dinner service each piece decorated in the Imari colors, meat dish 48cm., circular underdish, 33cm., two vegetable dishes, 35cm., twelve dinner plates, 26cm. diam., five soup plates, 26cm., two smaller dishes and two sauce tureen underdishes, 25 pieces. (Lacy Scott) $1,456

A Miles Mason pale apricot-ground D-shaped bough pot and pierced dome cover, circa 1805, 25cm. high. (Christie's) $2,359

A very rare garniture of Mason vases, 19.5cm and 17cm. high., two vases impressed M. Mason. (Phillips) $1,980

Mason's pottery jug painted and stamped mark, with lizard handle and Imari pattern, 8in. high. (G. A. Key) $192

MEISSEN

A Meissen snuff box with hinged silver gilt mount, 7.5cm., the interior with KPM and crossed swords in blue, circa 1725. (Phillips) $8,786

A Meissen shaped plate, blue crossed swords mark and Pressnummer 16, circa 1755, 24cm. diam. (Christie's) $13,370

A Meissen large mythological centerpiece in three sections, 63cm. overall length, crossed swords mark. (Phillips) $5,730

One of a pair of Meissen vases with flared necks, 20.5cm. high, crossed swords marks (SR). (Phillips) $4,775

An early Meissen teapot and cover, painted by J. G. Horoldt, 12.5cm. wide. (Phillips) $7,515

A Meissen yellow ground quatrefoil coffee-pot and domed cover, blue crossed swords mark, gilder's mark M. to both pieces, circa 1742, ·23cm. high. (Christie's) $11,313

A Meissen porcelain group of three Bacchantes, 8in. high. (Prudential Fine Art) $825

A Meissen tureen and cover, painted in the manner of C. F. Herold, 26cm. wide, crossed swords mark. (Phillips) $5,921

A 19th century Meissen porcelain group of the Reveller, 18th century style, 13½in. high. (Christie's) $935

MEISSEN

A Meissen figure of Dr. Boloardo modelled by J. J. Kandler, circa 1742, 18.5cm. high. (Christie's) $8,553

A Meissen KPM baluster teapot and domed cover, painted by P. E. Schindler, circa 1724, 15cm. wide. (Christie's) $12,474

A Meissen figure of a tailor from the series of craftsmen modelled by J. J. Kandler, circa 1753, 23.5cm. high. (Christie's) $2,656

A Meissen hunting group, blue crossed swords marks and incised X to base, circa 1755, 16cm. high. (Christie's) $1,603

A Meissen deckelpokal, blue crossed swords mark to the base, and gilder's mark c to both pieces, circa 1725, 18cm. high. (Christie's) $13,282

A Meissen group of a Mother and Children modelled by J. J. Kandler and P. Reinicke, circa 1740, 23.5cm. high. (Christie's) $2,673

A Meissen tea caddy with domed shoulder, circa 1755, 10.5cm. high. (Christie's) $623

A Meissen crinoline group of the gout sufferer modelled by J. J. Kandler, circa 1742, 19.5cm. wide. (Christie's) $9,740

A Meissen cylindrical pomade pot and domed cover, painted in the manner of Gottfried Klinger, circa 1745, 15cm. high. (Christie's) $2,851

MEISSEN

A Meissen figure of a Turkish woman playing the lute modelled by P. Reinicke, trace of blue crossed swords mark to base, circa 1755, 16.5cm. high. (Christie's) $980

A Meissen KPM inverted baluster teapot and domed cover, painted in colors perhaps by Mehlhorn, circa 1724, 16cm. wide. (Christie's) $7,128

A Meissen figure of a youth holding a rooster under his arm, circa 1755, 14.5cm. high. (Christie's) $531

A large Meissen group of Count Bruhl's tailor on a goat, blue crossed swords and incised numeral marks, circa 1880, 43cm. high. (Christie's) $4,041

A Meissen clock case and stand, blue crossed swords mark and Pressnummer 25 to the stand, circa 1745, the movement by LeRoy, 50cm. high overall. (Christie's) $7,969

A pair of Meissen figures of a shepherd and shepherdess, faint blue crossed swords marks on bases, circa 1755, 14.5cm. high. (Christie's) $2,316

A Meissen coffee pot and a cover, gilder's marks L. to cover and 65. , circa 1725, 19.5cm. high. (Christie's) $2,833

A Meissen quatrefoil tureen, cover and stand, painted in colors with Watteaumalerei vignettes of amorous couples, circa 1750, the stand 28.5cm. wide. (Christie's)$8,553

A Meissen kinderbuste, blue crossed swords and incised numeral marks, circa 1880, 25cm. high. (Christie's) $918

MEISSEN

A Meissen green-ground quatrefroil teacup and saucer with ombrierte gilt cartouches of figures in landscapes, circa 1740. (Christie's) $1,151

A Meissen two-handled quatrefoil tureen stand with shell and scroll handles, circa 1740, 41cm. wide. (Christie's) $5,346

A Meissen baluster cream jug (small chip to spout), blue crossed swords mark to base, circa 1740, 9cm. high. (Christie's) $213

A Meissen figure of a Turkish woman modelled by P. Reinicke, circa 1745, 17cm. high. (Christie's) $1,062

A Meissen garniture of five vases and three covers, blue crossed swords marks and Pressnummern 21 to bases, circa 1738, the largest vase 46.5cm. high. (Christie's) $85,536

A Meissen figure of Cupid as a soldier, blue crossed swords mark at back, circa 1755, 9.5cm. high. (Christie's) $354

A Meissen baluster coffee pot and a cover, blue crossed swords mark and Dreher's mark +, circa 1728, 16.5cm. high. (Christie's) $1,682

One of a pair of Meissen circular dishes, blue crossed swords marks, Pressnummern 20 and 21, circa 1745, 30.5cm. diam. (Christie's) $3,920

A Meissen figure of a Gallant Dressing A Mops, modelled by J. F. Eberlein, circa 1745, 12cm. high. (Christie's) $2,138

MEISSEN

A Meissen teacup and saucer, blue underglaze crossed swords marks and Pressnummern 64 and 66, circa 1750. (Christie's) $619

An early Meissen sugar box and cover, the cover with half-length figures of Chinese, by J. G. Horoldt, 11cm. wide. (Phillips) $1,670

A Meissen goldmalerei globular teapot and cover, 1725-30, 17cm. wide. (Christie's) $3,207

A Meissen chinoiserie silver mounted tankard painted by J. E. Stadler, circa 1728, the Augsburg silver cover and thumbpiece by Hans J. Wild II, 18cm. high. (Christie's) $26,730

An early Meissen beaker or chocolate cup with twisted stem handles. (Phillips) $1,002

A Meissen small cylindrical tankard by Johann G. Horoldt, circa 1728, 10.5cm. high. (Christie's) $28,336

A Meissen circular two-handled tureen and cover with Turk's head finial and Frauenkopf scroll handles, circa 1730, 32.5cm. high. (Christie's) $6,771

A Meissen model of an elephant modelled by Kandler, 15cm. long. (Phillips) $1,336

A Meissen figure of a musician in theatrical costume playing a lute, modelled by J. J. Kandler, circa 1745, 16.5cm. high. (Christie's) $8,910

MEISSEN

A Meissen figure of the Marquis from the Cris de Paris series, circa 1756, 13cm. high. (Christie's) $3,385

A Meissen shaped oval jagd tureen and cover with boar's head and shell finial, painted in the manner of C. F. Herold, circa 1740, 31.5cm. wide. (Christie's) $9,801

A Meissen figure of a seamstress modelled by J. J. Kandler, circa 1753, 22.5cm. high. (Christie's) $2,656

A Meissen two-handled ecuelle, cover and stand of round lobed form, circa 1745, the stand 18cm. diam. (Christie's) $2,656

A Meissen monkey band of eighteen figures, from 11cm. to 18cm. high; two German monkey band figures, about 12.5cm. high; a Continental monkey figure of a drummer, 13.5cm. high and a faience music stand, 10cm. high, all late 19th century. (Christie's) $4,592

AMeissen gold Chinese globular teapot and domed cover gilt at Augsburg by B. Seuter, circa 1725, 16.5cm. wide. (Christie's) $9,801

A Meissen figure of Pulchinella from the Commedia dell'Arte modelled by J. J. Kandler, circa 1740, 14cm. high. (Christie's) $3,010

A Meissen oviform rococo molded teapot and cover painted in the manner of C. J. Albert, circa 1755, 15.5cm. wide. (Christie's) $908

MEISSEN

A Meissen figure of the Courtesan from the Cries of London series, modelled by J. J. Kandler and P. J. Reinicke, circa 1754, 14cm. high. (Christie's) $2,851

A pair of Meissen dancing children on rococo scroll bases, impressed numerals 24 to base, 12cm. high. (Christie's) $2,673

A Meissen figure of harlequin with a jug modelled by J. J. Kandler, on an ormolu base in Louis XV style, circa 1737, 17.5cm. high. (Christie's) $3,896

A pair of Meissen condiment groups modelled as a man and a woman, blue crossed swords and incised numeral marks, circa 1880, 20cm. high. (Christie's) $1,010

Pair of Meissen Hausmalerei teacups and saucers painted by F. F. Meyer von Pressnitz, circa 1740. (Christie's) $4,958

A Meissen three-footed cream pot and cover painted in colors with Watteaumalerei scenes of figures from the Commedia dell'Arte in park landscapes, circa 1745, 11cm. high. (Christie's) $1,782

A Meissen figure of Cupid as a harlequin, circa 1765, 12cm. high. (Christie's) $1,416

A Meissen baluster teapot and domed cover, blue crossed swords mark, gilder's mark 42, circa 1730, 15cm. wide. (Christie's) $16,929

A Ming white-glazed Anhua-decorated bowl, 20.8cm. diam. (Christie's) $20,197

A Ming Imperial yellow saucer-dish, a glaze of rich, warm yellow tones, 22.1cm. diam. (Christie's) $3,107

A Ming blue and white stem bowl, painted in a vivid blue with two five-clawed dragons, 16.2cm. diam. (Christie's) $4,364

A Ming Wucai saucer-dish, with a youthful Shoulao on a deer's back, 19cm. diam. (Christie's) $3,884

A Ming blue and white vase, 4½in. high, wood stand. (Christie's) $7,379

One of a pair of Ming dishes, in iron-red with three fish swimming, 8½in. diam. (Christie's) $8,545

A Ming blue and white baluster jar, painted in violet-blue tones, 12.5cm. high. (Christie's) $4,364

A fine Ming blue and white saucer-dish, 14.5cm. diam. (Christie's) $4,661

An early 16th century large Ming blue and white baluster jar, Guan (minor restoration), 36.5cm. high. (Christie's) $7,768

MINTON

A Minton pink-ground cabinet cup and saucer, circa 1825. (Christie's) $272

A pair of Minton 'Dresden Scroll' vases and pierced covers in neo-rococo style, 29cm. high. (Phillips) $2,101

A Minton Pilgrim vase, painted probably by A. Boullemier after W. S. Coleman, 20cm. high, date code possibly 1873. (Phillips) $434

One of a pair of Minton porcelain dessert plates, one with swallow in flight, signed Leroy, the other with a bird perched on fuchsia branch, 9½in. diam. (Dacre, Son & Hartley) $2,062

A massive Minton 'majolica' peacock after the model by P. Comolera, circa 1875, 153cm. high. (Christie's) $30,800

A Minton porcelain dessert plate, the central pate-sur-pate panel signed L. Solon, circa 1880, 9¼in. wide. (Dacre, Son & Hartley) $495

A Minton white and celadon glazed centerpiece modelled as three putti holding a basket, circa 1868, 26cm. high. (Christie's) $731

A pair of Minton candlestick figures, both in richly decorated costumes and with flowered and striped designs, 22cm. high. (Phillips) $2,769

A Minton 'majolica' garden seat modelled as a crouching monkey, circa 1870, 47cm. high. (Christie's) $12,512

MINTON

A large Minton majolica umbrella stand modelled as a stork, impressed Minton 1916, 102cm. high. (Christie's) $4,592

A Minton majolica jardiniere, the handles formed as satyrs impressed Minton and with date code for 1871, 26.5cm. high. (Christie's) $642

A Minton majolica figure, 'Basket Carrier', with date code for 1868, 22.9cm. high. (Christie's) $514

A Minton majolica bowl, impressed marks, numerals and date code for 1874, 31.5cm. diam. (Christie's) $1,452

A Minton pale turquoise-ground 'Munster pot-pourri' vase and cover, circa 1830, 26cm. high. (Christie's) $544

A Minton oval sugar bowl and cover, 13.5cm. wide, together with a trio and a saucer dish, circa 1805. (Christie's) $580

A pair of Minton blue-ground 'Wellington' vases, the gilding perhaps by Thomas Till, circa 1830, 35cm. and 34.5cm. high. (Christie's) $3,630

A Minton dark brown-ground pate-sur-pate plate, date code for 1873, 23.5cm. diam., together with another two plates. (Christie's) $471

A Minton majolica barrel-shaped garden seat in the Oriental taste, date code for 1873, 50cm. high. (Christie's) $871

MINTON

A Minton blue-ground center-piece, circa 1835, 66cm. high. (Christie's) $5,445

A Minton majolica cheese dish and cover with reclining bull finial, 29cm. high. (Christie's) $1,285

A Minton majolica figure of a partially draped putto holding a lyre-shaped viol seated on a conch-shell, impressed Minton 1539 and with date code for 1870, 46.5cm. high. (Christie's) $3,674

A Minton globular jug with loop handle, pattern no. 248, circa 1805, 16.5cm. wide. (Christie's) $308

A Minton majolica vase, 'Monkey Match Pot', impressed Mintons 1692 and date code for 1873, 19cm. high. (Christie's) $551

A Minton shaped rectangular basket of 'Clarence' shape, blue crossed swords mark, circa 1835, 18.5cm. wide. (Christie's) $580

One of a pair of Minton yellow-ground cabinet plates, pattern no. G1276, 1874 and 1881, 24cm. diam. (Christie's) $726

One of a pair of Minton majolica vases, twelve-sided oviform shape, date code for 1859 on one vase, 29cm. high. (Christie's) $918

A pair of Minton majolica figures, 'Grape Gatherers', with date codes for 1866, 24.5cm. high. (Christie's) $734

A Minton majolica-ware teapot and cover in the form of a Chinese actor holding a mask, 14cm. high, impressed Mintons, model no. 1838, date code for 1874. (Phillips) $660

A Minton vase and cover by Louis Jahn, 50cm. high, impressed and printed marks. (Phillips) $1,670

A Minton majolica-ware teapot and cover in the form of a monkey, 15.5cm. high, impressed Mintons, model no. 1844, date code for 1876. (Phillips) $1,023

One of a pair of Minton majolica-ware figures of boys leaning on tall vine baskets, 23cm. high, model no. 421, date codes for 1868. (Phillips)   £561

A Minton aesthetic movement 'Cloisonne' vase, 18.5cm. high, impressed 'Minton'. (Phillips) $481

A Mintons Kensington Gore pottery moon flask, 34.2cm. high. (Phillips) $555

A Minton majolica-ware Neptune shell dish, 17cm. high, impressed Minton, shape no. 903 and date code for 1861. (Phillips) $462

A Minton pate-sur-pate vase and cover by Marc Louis Solon, 35cm. high, date code for 1903. (Phillips) $3,340

A fine Minton pate-sur-pate plate, signed Louis Solon, 24cm. high., printed Minton and A. B. Daniell & Sons retailer's mark. (Phillips) $1,380

MOORCROFT

A bellied vase with waisted neck and foot rim, by Wm. Moorcroft, 6in. high. (Hetheringtons Nationwide) $140

A twin-handled bowl, by Wm. Moorcroft, made for Liberty & Co., 23cm. wide. (David Lay) $306

A ginger jar and cover, by Walter Moorcroft, factory mark and potter to the Queen, circa 1945, 11in. high. (Peter Wilson) $528

PARIAN

Maisons bisque porcelain bust of Minerva, Charenton, France, late 19th century, marked base, 34½in. high. (Robt. W. Skinner Inc.) $2,500

A Parian figural group of sleeping children 'Le Nid', circa 1875, signed 'Croisy', 15in. high. (Robt. W. Skinner Inc.) $750

A Goss Parian bust of Queen Victoria, for Mortlock's of Oxford Street, 236mm. high. (Phillips) $400

A Goss Parian wall vase with head of Georgiana Jewitt, white unglazed, chipped and marked. (Phillips) $116

A large Parian group entitled 'Detected', signed R.J. Morris, 41cm. high. (Dee & Atkinson) $284

A Sam Alcock & Co Parian seated portrait figure of Wellington with joined hands and crossed legs, 28cm. high. (Phillips)$498

A Paris (Nast) green-ground cabinet cup and saucer, gilt marks, circa 1810. (Christie's) $220

A pair of Paris (Jacob Petit) pink-ground vases of inverted baluster form, circa 1840, 18cm. high. (Christie's) $1,089

A Paris veilleuse, the body painted with panels of buildings in extensive country landscapes, 9¾in. high. (Christie's) $437

A pair of Paris royal-blue-ground two-handled vases, the oviform bodies painted after Teniers, circa 1820, 37cm. high. (Christie's) $3,630

One of a pair of Paris (Jacob Petit) Mayblossom vases and covers, blue J.P. marks, circa 1830, 39.5cm. high. (Christie's) $1,653

A pair of Paris gold-ground two-handled vases on square richly gilt bases, circa 1825, 42.5cm. high. (Christie's) $10,890

A Paris (Schoelcher) royal-blue-ground cabinet cup and saucer, reserved and painted with a portrait of Helene, circa 1820. (Christie's) $404

A massive Paris blue-ground 'Medici' vase, painted with Cupid, circa 1820, 54.5cm. high. (Christie's) $2,904

A large Paris biscuit group entitled 'Le Nid' after the original sculpture by A. O. Croisy, circa 1880, 38.5cm. high. (Christie's) $2,388

A Paris (Jacob Petit) two-handled cup, cover and trembleuse-stand, blue JP marks, circa 1840, the stand 16.5cm. diam. (Christie's) $580

Pair of early 19th century Paris (Dart Freres) white china elliptical dessert dishes, covers and fixed stands, 13in. diam. (Graves Son & Pilcher) $1,467

A Paris (Jacob Petit) neo-renaissance oval two-handled pot-pourri vase and cover, circa 1840, 21.5cm. high. (Christie's) $235

A Paris (Restoration) purple-ground tea service, each piece painted with a different scene after the fables of La Fontaine in a gilt panel, circa 1820. (Christie's) $4,455

One of a pair of Paris ice-pails and covers with white and gilt caryatid handles, circa 1810, 39cm. high. (Christie's) $2,788

A pair of Paris (Jacob Petit) vases modelled as figures of a boy and a girl, circa 1850, about 22cm. high. (Christie's) $508

A Paris gilt bronze mounted vase, imitation incised interlaced L and blue marks, circa 1900, 44cm. high. (Christie's) $1,285

RIE, LUCIE

One of a pair of stoneware bowls by Lucie Rie and Hans Coper, on shallow feet with compressed sides, circa 1958. (Christie's) $1,760

A porcelain sgraffito bowl by Lucie Rie, circa 1958, 15.3cm. diam. (Christie's) $1,056

A small stoneware sgraffito bowl by Lucie Rie, covered in a translucent finely crackled mustard-yellow glaze, circa 1955, 6.1cm. high. (Christie's) $1,232

A tall stoneware bottle vase, by Lucie Rie, circa 1967, 38.7cm. high. (Christie's) $6,688

A sgraffito inlaid bowl and cover by Lucie Rie, the exterior with radiating inlaid purple lines, circa 1966, 18.2cm. diam. (Christie's) $3,872

A stoneware bottle vase by Lucie Rie, with flared waves rim, flattened cylindrical neck, circa 1975, 27.2cm. high. (Christie's) $2,112

A small porcelain sgraffito bottle vase by Lucie Rie, 16.5cm. high. (Christie's) $668

An early stoneware vase by Lucie Rie, covered in an olive-green glaze oxidizing in places to a lustrous black, 27.1cm. high. (Christie's) $1,320

A stoneware baluster vase by Lucie Rie, covered in a shiny deep-blue glaze with run matt-manganese rim, circa 1955, 31.7cm. high. (Christie's) $2,640

RIE, LUCIE

A small stoneware sgraffito bowl by Lucie Rie, circa 1960, 12.2cm. diam. (Christie's) $616

One of a pair of stoneware bowls by Lucie Rie and Hans Coper, each impressed with LR and HC seals, circa 1958, 8cm. high. (Christie's) $704

A small stoneware sgraffito bowl by Lucie Rie, covered in a translucent finely crackled mustard-yellow glaze, circa 1950, 6cm. high. (Christie's) $1,144

A porcelain bottle vase by Lucie Rie, with trumpet-shaped neck and rim, circa 1980, 26.7cm. high. (Christie's) $2,640

A small stoneware bowl by Lucie Rie, covered in a mirror-black manganese glaze with white rim, circa 1953, 10cm. diam. (Christie's) $739

A stoneware bottle vase by Lucie Rie, covered in a chalky-white glaze with puce and turquoise spiral, circa 1975, 24cm. high. (Christie's) $2,112

A large stoneware milk jug with pulled handle by Lucie Rie, 15.8cm. high. (Christie's) $299

A stoneware vase by Lucie Rie, covered in a pitted and mottled pale-pink, olive-green and brown glaze, circa 1966, 24cm. high. (Christie's) $5,280

A stoneware bottle vase by Lucie Rie, covered in a finely pitted shiny white glaze thinning in places, circa 1968, 27.4cm. high. (Christie's) $5,984

ROCKINGHAM

A Rockingham cottage pastille burner and stand, lavender color with gilt details, 13cm. high. (Lawrence Fine Art) $435

A Rockingham porcelain octagonal plate, decorated in famille verte enamels, 35cm. diam. (H. Spencer & Sons) $435

A Rockingham Cadogan teapot, of peach shape, 4½in. high, impressed Brameld. (Dreweatt Neate) $103

ROOKWOOD

Rookwood pottery Spanish water jug, Cincinnati, Ohio, 1882, cobalt blue glaze on strap handled, double spout round pitcher, 10in. high. (Robt. W. Skinner Inc.) $125

Rookwood Pottery Flower vase, Cincinnati, Ohio, 1886, spherical clay body, impressed 'RP/189/Y' and signed 'M.A.D.' by Matt Daly, 7½in. diam. (Robt. W. Skinner. Inc.) $200

Rookwood pottery scenic vellum vase, signed and artist initialled by Sallie E. Coyne, 1913, 9in. high. (Robt. W. Skinner Inc.) $900

Rookwood pottery silver overlay mug, Cincinnati, Ohio, 1891, marked 'Gorham Mfg. Co.' 6¼ in. high. (Robt. W. Skinner. Inc.) $1,200

A Rookwood pottery vase with sterling silver overlay, initialled C.C.L., for Clara C. Linderman, 1906, 7¼in. high. (Robt. W. Skinner Inc.) $1,600

Rookwood pottery flower pitcher, Cincinnati, Ohio, 1884, bulbous white clay body, signed 'AMB' by Anne Marie Bookprinter, 8¼in. high. (Robt. W. Skinner Inc.) $250

ROOKWOOD

A Rookwood pottery decorated pitcher, artist's initials MLN for Maria Longworth Nichols, 1882, 6in. high. (Robt. W. Skinner Inc.) $750

Rookwood pottery dish, Cincinnati, Ohio, 1882, ginger clay body, signed by Nathaniel J. Hirschfield, diam 6½in. (Robt. W. Skinner Inc.) $125

A Rookwood pottery decorated creamer, Ohio, 1893, artist's initials O.G.R. for Olga Geneva Reed, 4¼in. high. (Robt. W. Skinner Inc.) $175

A Rookwood pottery scenic vellum vase, Ohio, initialled by artist Harriet E. Wilcox, 1918, 8in. high. (Robt. W. Skinner Inc.) $850

A Rookwood pottery standard glaze pillow vase, 1889, artist's initials ARV for Albert R. Valentien, 14in. high. (Robt. W. Skinner Inc.) $1,000

A large Rookwood pottery standard glaze vase, Ohio, 1899, initialled AMV for Anna Marie Valentien, 19in. high. (Robt. W. Skinner Inc.) $1,300

A Rookwood pottery wax-resist floral vase, Ohio, 1929, artist initialled LNL for Elizabeth N. Lincoln, 17in. high. (Robt. W. Skinner Inc.) $950

A Rookwood pottery scenic vellum loving cup, initialled by Frederick Rothebusch, 1908, 7¼in. high. (Robt. W. Skinner Inc.) $1,000

A Rookwood pottery vase, decorated by K. Shirayama-dani, Roman II for 1902, 38cm. high. (Christie's) $2,345

ROYAL DUX

Royal Dux 'Austria' Art Nouveau vase having fold-over leaf top, 14in. high. (Giles Haywood) $124

Pair of Royal Dux figurines, flower girl carrying flower basket and boy with apron carrying basket, signed F. Otto, pink triangle to base. (Giles Haywood) $574

Czechoslovakian Royal Dux figure of an Indian Boy playing a flute with a half nude female dancer, 9in. high. (G. A. Key) $284

Royal Dux-style centerpiece designed as a young lady holding water lily, impress mark 8335, 12in. high. (Giles Haywood) $90

A Royal Dux pottery toilette mirror, depicting an Art Nouveau maiden. (Phillips) $1,091

A Royal Dux porcelain ornament formed as two Sirens near Conche Shell on a stemmed base, 18in. high. (G. A. Key) $447

A Royal Dux group of two figures in classical dress on oval base with red triangle mark no. 1980, 16½in. high. (Prudential Fine Art) $439

Pair of Royal Dux figurines, signed F. Otto, pink triangle to base, 17in. high. (Giles Haywood) $574

A Royal Dux figure of a peasant boy leaning on a wooden pitcher, 59cm. high.   (Abridge Auctions) $675

Late 19th century Kyo-
Satsuma oviform tea caddy,
signed Hakuzan, 12.5cm.
high. (Christie's)
$1,496

Late 19th century Satsuma
model of a caparisoned
elephant decorated in
colored enamels and gilt,
31cm. high. (Christie's)
$2,640

Late 19th century Kyo-
Satsuma shallow dish, signed
Dai Nippon Setsuzan, 31.5cm.
diam. (Christie's)
$3,168

A pair of Satsuma pottery
vases, decorated in a pink
and blue palette, 14in. high.
(G.A. Key) $264

Late 19th century Satsuma
model of a lantern decorated
in various colored enamels
and gilt, 50cm. high.
(Christie's) $3,344

Pair of late 19th century Kyo-
Satsuma oviform vases, signed
Mitsu, 25cm. high. (Christie's)
$1,848

A Satsuma oviform vase
decorated in various thickly
applied colored enamels and
gilt, 152cm. high. (Christie's)
$9,350

A 19th century Satsuma
pottery plaque decorated
with shaped panels of figures
dancing and feasting, 14in.
diam. (Hobbs & Chambers)
$1,248

Late 19th century Satsuma
molded oviform jar and
cover, depicting the story of
Bishamon and Kichigo-ten,
42cm. high. (Christie's)
$2,464

SEVRES

Late 19th century Sevres pattern gilt bronze mounted two-handled centerpiece, 27.5cm. wide. (Christie's) $998

A Sevres reeded cup and fluted saucer, date letter for 1768, and painter's mark of Thevenet Pere. (Christie's) $677

A Sevres seau a demi-bouteille from the Duchesse du Barry service, date letters for 1771, and decorator's mark LB for Le Bel junior, 13cm. high. (Christie's) $8,553

A Sevres plate, 23.5cm. diam., LL mark enclosing date letters EE for 1782, painter's marks for Capelle and probably Huny. (Phillips) $6,847

Late 19th century Sevres pattern green-ground Napoleonic tapering oviform vase and cover, decorated by Desprez, 138cm. high. (Christie's) $8,712

A Sevres plate, 24.3cm. diam., LL mark enclosing date letters EE for 1782, painter's mark probably for Huny. (Phillips) $3,674

One of a pair of ormolu mounted and bleu celest Sevres style three-branch candelabra, 19th century, 24½in. high. (Christie's) $2,939

A pair of late 19th century Sevres pattern blue-ground Napoleonic tapering oviform vases and covers, painted by J. Pascault, 152.5cm. high. (Christie's) $39,930

Late 19th century Sevres pattern turquoise-ground gilt bronze mounted two-handled vase, fitted for electric light, the vase 31.5cm. high. (Christie's) $698

SEVRES

A Sevres green-ground cup and saucer, interlaced L marks, date letters D for 1756 and R for 1770, decorators' marks L B and E. (Christie's) $891

A Sevres circular tazza for the Paris Exhibition of 1878, 36.5cm. high. (Christie's) $1,724

A Sevres green-ground large cup and deep saucer, interlaced L marks and date letter V for 1774 and painter's mark B.g. (Christie's) $392

One of a pair of late 19th century Sevres pattern turquoise-ground gilt bronze mounted jardinieres, 27cm. high overall. (Christie's) $2,204

One of a pair of late Sevres vases of 'Stephanus' shape, designed by Carrier-Belleuse in 1880, 55cm. high, mark and date code for 1894. (Phillips) $1,469

A Sevres two-handled ecuelle, cover and stand, blue interlaced L marks, date letter for 1775, and blue decorator's mark for Thevenet, 25.5cm. wide. (Christie's) $1,603

One of a pair of late 19th century Sevres pattern gilt bronze mounted ewers, 24.5cm. high. (Christie's) $762

A Sevres rose pompadour lobed quatrefoil dish, blue interlaced L marks enclosing the date letter for 1762, painter's mark of Micaud, 28cm. wide. (Christie's) $2,494

One of a pair of late 19th century Sevres pattern green-ground vases and covers, 42cm. high. (Christie's) $2,359

A Sevres blue-ground milk jug, incised os, interlaced L's enclosing the date letter for 1760, and the painter's mark of Aloncle, 10.5cm. high. (Christie's) $1,748

A Sevres yellow ground ecuelle, cover and oval lobed stand, interlaced L's enclosing the date letter kk for 1788, the painter's mark cm for Commelin, 20cm. wide. (Christie's) $5,759

A Sevres sucrier and cover interlaced L's enclosing date letter s for 1771 and mark possibly of Mereaud, 11.5cm. high. (Christie's) $2,262

A Sevres baluster hot milk jug and cover, interlaced L's enclosing date letter u for 1773 and the painter's mark for Xhrouet, 15cm. high. (Christie's) $2,674

A pair of Charles X Sevres plates, one painted with the Chateaux de Montargis, the other with the Grande Chartreuse a Grenoble, 22.3cm. diam., crowned entwined C's and dated 1824-25. (Phillips) $1,184

A Sevres bleu lapis ground hot milk jug and cover, interlaced L's enclosing the letter D for 1756, two dots, and the mark of the painter Evans, 11cm. high. (Christie's) $4,731

A Sevres blue-ground small cup and saucer with the date letter c for 1755. (Christie's) $2,057

A Sevres tripod cream jug, interlaced L's enclosing date letter s for 1771 and the painter's mark b for Boulanger, 12.5cm. high. (Christie's) $2,674

A Sevres bleu celeste ground cup and saucer, interlaced L's enclosing date letter M for 1765 and the painter's mark Cp for Chapuisaine. (Christie's) $1,748

A Spode miniature taperstick with pattern no. 1166, 7.5cm. high., marked in red. (Phillips) $1,237

Part of a Spodes new stone dinner service, impressed mark Spodes New Stone and pattern no. 3875 in red. (Lawrence Fine Art) $5,994

An attractive pair of Spode candle extinguishers on a small rectangular tray with loop handle, 12.5cm., impressed workman's mark. (Phillips) $883

A comprehensive Spode stone china dinner service, blue printed Spode stone china mark, and pattern no. in red. (Phillips) $2,392

A Spode porcelain 'Beaded New Shape' jar and cover with gilt ball finial and loop handles, pattern No. 1166, 10½in. high. (Dacre, Son & Hartley) $7,410

A pair of Spode porcelain cabinet cups, covers and stands marked in puce 'Spode 711' (circa 1805). (Dacre, Son & Hartley) $4,180

A Spode footed vase with flared rim, decorated with 'Japan' pattern, 15.5cm. high. (David Lay) $322

STAFFORDSHIRE

A Staffordshire pearlware sailor Toby jug, circa 1800, 29.5cm. high. (Christie's) $1,270

A Staffordshire pearlware figure of a cow, circa 1800, 32.5cm. wide. (Christie's) $1,089

A Staffordshire creamware Toby jug, circa 1800, 25.5cm. high. (Christie's) $635

A Staffordshire saltglaze bear jug and cover, circa 1740, 24cm. high. (Christie's) $9,982

A Staffordshire figure of a gentleman, circa 1810, 22.5cm. high. (Christie's) $544

A Staffordshire figure of a doe of Ralph Wood type, circa 1770, 15.5cm. wide. (Christie's) $1,179

A Staffordshire equestrian group of Obadiah Sherratt type, circa 1830, 22cm. high. (Christie's) $3,267

A Staffordshire pearlware figure of a recumbent stag, circa 1800, 20.5cm. high. (Christie's) $635

A Staffordshire creamware group of St. George and the Dragon of conventional Ralph Wood type, circa 1780, 28.5cm. high. (Christie's) $3,630

STAFFORDSHIRE

A Staffordshire Toby jug of conventional type, circa 1780, 26cm. high. (Christie's) $907

A Staffordshire creamware figure of a standing lion, circa 1810, 16cm. wide. (Christie's) $1,179

A Staffordshire creamware Toby jug of Ralph Wood type, circa 1780, 25cm. high. (Christie's) $1,179

A Staffordshire creamware spill-vase of Ralph Wood type, modelled as a gallant, circa 1780, 20cm. high. (Christie's) $635

A pair of Staffordshire figures of a gardener and companion of Ralph Wood type, circa 1780, 19.5cm. high. (Christie's) $4,356

A Staffordshire bust of Maria Foot of Obadiah Sherratt type, circa 1816, 29cm. high. (Christie's) $2,904

A Staffordshire porcelain pastille-burner modelled as a two-storeyed pavilion, circa 1845, 16.5cm. high. (Christie's) $762

A Staffordshire creamware recumbent stag, circa 1800, 15cm. wide. (Christie's) $762

A Staffordshire spill vase musician group, circa 1830, 22.5cm. high. (Christie's) $2,541

Large Staffordshire ornament of a recumbent lion, 12in. long. (G. A. Key) $85

Pair of 19th century Staffordshire lions decorated in brown and cream with glass eyes and painted mouths, 12in. long. (G. A. Key) $280

A Staffordshire saltglazed teapot and cover, modelled by Wm. Greatbatch for J. Wedgwood at Lane Delf, 11.5cm. high. (Phillips) $5,348

A pair of South Staffordshire opaque tea caddies for Bohea and Green, circa 1760, about 13.5cm. high. (Christie's) $7,088

One of a pair of Staffordshire pearlware dinner plates and two soup plates, early 19th century, one 10in. diam. (Christie's) $99

A Staffordshire figure of Maritta Alboni as Cinderella seated in a shell-shaped carriage, circa 1850, 8¾in. high. (Christie's) $924

A pair of Staffordshire models of the British lion, both holding beneath their paws the figure of Napoleon III, 24.2cm. high. (Phillips) $993

A Staffordshire tipstaff molded with Royal Garter, circa 1840, 11in. high. (Christie's) $332

Pair of Victorian Staffordshire pottery flat-back deer spill vases, 12in. high. (Hobbs & Chambers) $347

STAFFORDSHIRE

A Staffordshire model of a seated rabbit eating a lettuce leaf, 3½in. high, circa 1860. (Christie's) $314

Early Staffordshire Walton type pottery model of a seated deer and a similar model of a standing deer, both 5¾in. high. (Hobbs & Chambers) $391

Death of the Lion Queen, a Staffordshire pottery group of Ellen Bright, 36cm. high. (Phillips) $1,375

A Staffordshire figure of the actor Menier in the part of Thelsitor from the play, 'Porga, circa 1850, 10¼in. high. (Christie's) $646

Set of three early Staffordshire pottery figures on circular grassy mounds and square plinth bases, 6½in. high. (Hobbs & Chambers) $373

A Staffordshire Phrenology bust by L. N. Fowler, late 19th century, 30cm. high. (Christie's) $1,058

A Staffordshire Pratt type model of a deer, strongly colored in ochre, 13.5cm. high. (Phillips) $668

Pair of Staffordshire pottery spirit barrels with metal taps, 12in. high. (G. A. Key) $272

A 19th century Staffordshire spill vase, 'Milk Sold Here', 13½in. tall. (J. M. Welch & Son) $699

A Staffordshire glazed red-ware hexagonal teapot and cover, circa 1745, 14.5cm. high. (Christie's)
$816

A Staffordshire white porcelain triple pastille burner, modelled as three Gothic pavilions, circa 1848. (Christie's) $816

A Staffordshire saltglaze pecten-shell molded baluster teapot and a cover, circa 1755, 13cm. high. (Christie's)
$1,996

A Staffordshire erotic figure of a barmaid, circa 1820, 19cm. high. (Phillips)
$1,369

A pair of Staffordshire pearlware figures of Mansion House dwarfs, after the Derby porcelain originals, 15cm. and 17cm. high. (Phillips) $2,254

A Staffordshire saltglaze baluster milk jug and cover, circa 1755, 15.5cm. high. (Christie's) $3,630

A pearlware 'Birds in Branches' group, probably Staffordshire, circa 1790, 19.5cm. high. (Christie's) $1,089

An early creamware cow creamer and cover, 18cm. wide. (Phillips)
$2,254

A Staffordshire pearlware figure of a cockerel, circa 1820, 25cm. high. (Christie's) $1,179

STAFFORDSHIRE

A Staffordshire creamware oviform 'pebble-dash' teapot and cover of Whieldon type, circa 1760, 13cm. high. (Christie's) $18,150

A 19th century Staffordshire cow creamer with willow pattern decoration in blue, 5¼in. high. (Robt. W. Skinner Inc.) $350

A Staffordshire saltglaze globular teapot and cover, circa 1760, 6in. wide. (Christie's) $1,145

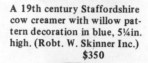

Early 19th century Staffordshire bust of John Wesley mounted on a marbleized pedestal base, 11½in. high. (Robt. W. Skinner Inc.) $175

A Staffordshire spill-vase modelled as a ram, circa 1845, 4½in. high. (Christie's) $147

A Staffordshire group of children, entitled 'Scuffle', 19cm. high. (Phillips) $412

A Staffordshire seated dog, circa 1790, 3½in. high. (Christie's) $240

A pair of early Staffordshire figures of Whieldon type, depicting a sailor and a soldier, 15cm. and 15.5cm. high. (Phillips) $7,682

A Staffordshire figure of James Blomfield Rush, circa 1850, 10in. high. (Christie's) $1,626

STONEWARE

A Westerwald stoneware inverted baluster kanne molded all over with relief rosettes on a blue-ground, 32cm. high. (Christie's) $566

A stoneware flask-shaped vase by Alan Wallwork, 32.1cm. high. (Christie's) $387

A Bottger brown stoneware cylindrical tankard and hinged cover, circa 1715, 21.5cm. high. (Christie's) $31,878

A stoneware cut-sided bottle vase by Shoji Hamada, with short neck and shallow foot, circa 1960, 29.1cm. high. (Christie's) $2,640

A stoneware saltglazed press-molded jar by Shoji Hamada, with paper label inscribed 56, 22cm. high. (Christie's) $2,816

A stoneware oviform vase by Thomas Samuel Haile, covered in a gray-white glaze with dark olive-green splashes, 20.4cm. high. (Christie's) $158

A tall St. Ives commemorative stoneware jug with strap handle, 29.1cm. high. (Christie's) $211

A stoneware dish by Kitaoji Rosanjin, partly covered in a pale olive-green glaze, 19.1cm. diam. (Christie's) $1,408

A stoneware teapot by Shoji Hamada, the cut-sided body with short spout and arched handle, 18.7cm. high. (Christie's) $1,496

STONEWARE

Late 17th century Westerwald stoneware square flask, 22.5cm. high. (Christie's) $708

A stoneware pinched and coiled bulbous vase by Betty Glandino, 28.4cm. high. (Christie's) $281

A Pierre Fondu stoneware amphora vase, covered in an olive-brown and blue crystalline glaze, 57.9cm. high. (Christie's) $1,082

A tall flattened stoneware cylindrical vase by Joanna Constantinidis, 33.2cm. high. (Christie's) $264

A stoneware dish by Ewen Henderson, with irregular rim, 35cm. wide. (Christie's) $528

A stoneware asymmetrical sack-shaped vase by Ewen Henderson, 56cm. high. (Christie's) $1,760

A St. Ives stoneware jug covered in a translucent inky-blue glaze, 19.2cm. high. (Christie's) $123

A stoneware platter by Raymond Finch, decorated by Henry Bergen, Winchcombe Pottery seals, 39cm. diam. (Christie's) $1,056

A stoneware jug by Janice Tchalenko, with pulled lip and strap handle, 24cm. high. (Christie's) $211

STONEWARE

A stoneware bowl by Kitaoji Rosanjin, covered in a finely crackled pale lavender translucent glaze with iron-brown rim, 25.2cm. diam. (Christie's) $5,984

An unmarked stoneware butter crock with cover, American, circa 1850, 8¼in. diam. (Robt. W. Skinner Inc.) $450

One of three early 18th century Westerwald salt-glazed stoneware rectangular inkwells, 14cm. wide. (Christie's) $566

A decorated stoneware vase, attributed to Russell G. Crook, 1906-12, 9½in. high. (Robt. W. Skinner Inc.) $750

A stoneware vase by John Ward, with oval undulating rim, 18.7cm. high. (Christie's) $158

A narrow waved stoneware vase by Joanna Constantinidis, with sagged rim, 1984, 46.3cm. high. (Christie's) $616

A large stoneware vase, by Seth Cardew, Wenford Bridge seals, circa 1984, 61cm. high. (Christie's) $302

A saltglazed stoneware two-gallon batter jug, by Cowden & Wilcox, Penn., 1870-90, 11in. high. (Christie's) $1,870

A stoneware elongated oviform vase by Shoji Hamada, 27.9cm. high. (Christie's) $1,760

STONEWARE

A stoneware saltglazed deep bowl with flared rim by Shoji Hamada, 28.2cm. diam. (Christie's)
$2,112

A three-gallon saltglaze stoneware crock, J. & E. Norton, Bennington, Vt., 10½in. high. (Robt. W. Skinner Inc.) $700

A stoneware globular vase by Ruth Duckworth, covered in streaked and run green, brown and copper-red glazes, 23.9cm. high. (Christie's)
$528

A stoneware vase, by John Ward, impressed JW seal, circa 1984, 22.4cm. high. (Christie's) $336

A brown stoneware torso by Roger Perkins, 74.2cm. high. (Christie's) $281

A stoneware oviform jar by Charles Vyse, 1928, 17cm. high. (Christie's) $252

Two gallon Bennington stoneware jar, circa 1855, 13¾in. high. (Robt. W. Skinner Inc.)
$1,500

'The Bull', a Poole pottery stoneware figure, designed by Harold and Phoebe Stabler, 33.5cm. high. (Christie's) $252

An English saltglazed brown stoneware tobacco jar, modelled as a bear, probably early 19th century, 21cm. high. (Phillips) $4,202

A saltglazed stoneware three-gallon jar, by Cowden & Wilcox, Penn., 1870-90, 12in. high. (Christie's) $418

A stoneware jug by Thomas Samuel Haile, with strap handle, 19.9cm. high. (Christie's) $528

'J. & E. Norton, Bennington, VT' two-gallon stoneware croek, 1850-59, 9¼in. high. (Robt. W. Skinner Inc.)
     $1,200

A cobalt blue decorated and incised stoneware jug, New York, circa 1822, 13¾in. high. (Robt. W. Skinner Inc.)
     $21,000

A stoneware bowl, by Eric James Mellon, dated 1982, 33.2cm. diam. (Christie's) $437

One of two 19th century saltglazed stoneware jugs, N. Carolina, 8½in. and 10½in. high. (Christie's) $770

A saltglazed stoneware two-gallon jar, by G. A. Satterlee and M. Morey, 1861-85, and a two-gallon crock by P. Riedinger and A. Caire, 1857-78, 11½in. and 9½in. high. (Christie's) $385

A large stoneware watercooler, double handled slightly ovoid form, America, 1866, 24¾in. high. (Robt. W. Skinner Inc.)
     $800

A three-gallon saltglazed stoneware crock, J. & E. Norton, Bennington, Vt., 1850-59, 13½in. high. (Robt. W. Skinner Inc.)
     $1,500

TERRACOTTA

A Cypriot terracotta chariot drawn by two horses, 7th-6th century B.C., 13cm. long. (Phillips) $656

A terracotta figure of Eros, 4th-3rd century B.C., Boetia, 7.5cm. high. (Phillips) $426

A Cypro-geometric bowl raised on three looped supports, circa 1700 B.C., 15cm. high. (Phillips) $1,230

A 19th century French group of Bacchus and a Bacchante, cast from a model by Clodion, 33cm. high. (Christie's) $734

A 19th century French terracotta bust of a little girl, attributed to Houdon, 39cm. high. (Christie's) $1,837

A Cypriot terracotta equestrian figure, slight traces of red and black pigment, 7th-6th century B.C., 11.5cm. high. (Phillips) $311

A Cypriot terracotta equestrian figure, 7th-6th century B.C., 15cm. high. (Phillips) $360

A pair of 19th century French terracotta busts of 'L'Espiegle' and 'Le Printemps', signed J.-Bte-Carpeaux, 48cm. and 55cm. high. (Christie's) $5,143

A terracotta figure of Eros, naked except for a drape across the shoulders, Boetia, 4th-3rd century B.C., 7cm. high. (Phillips) $328

A Vienna (Dupaquier) covered 'pastetentopf' with loop handle, circa 1735, 15.5cm. wide. (Christie's) $14,168

A Vienna (Dupaquier) rect-angular casket and liner, circa 1728, in a contemporary fitted leather box, 16.5 x 12cm. (Christie's) $35,420

A Vienna (Dupaquier) two-handled, double-lipped baroque molded sauceboat painted in the Imari style, circa 1740, 24.5cm. wide. (Christie's) $7,969

Late 19th century 'Vienna' rectangular porcelain plaque, painted with three vestal virgins, 32 x 26cm. (Christie's) $1,285

A Vienna (Dupaquier) cream-pot and cover painted by Johann P. Dannhoffer, circa 1725. (Christie's) $5,313

A 'Vienna' rectangular plaque painted by C. Meinelt after Murillo, signed and impressed blue enamelled beehive mark, circa 1880, 44 x 35cm. (Christie's) $16,533

A pair of large Vienna-style ewer vases with gilt scrolled handles and ovoid bodies, 60cm. high. (Phillips)　　$4,008

One of a set of six 'Vienna' porcelain plates, signed Wagner, 9½in. diam. (Capes Dunn)　　$3,043

A Vienna Commedia dell'Arte group of Scaramouche and Pulchinella, circa 1750, 14.5cm. high. (Christie's)　　$14,168

WEDGWOOD

A rare Wedgwood 'Willow' lustre bowl, 23.5cm., Portland Vase mark, pattern Z5407. (Phillips) $495

A Wedgwood majolica-ware three-piece strawberry set, 24.5cm., impressed Wedgwood, registration mark and GBX. (Phillips) $528

A Wedgwood large octagonal Fairyland lustre bowl, 27.8cm. diam., Portland Vase mark and Z5125. (Phillips) $1,567

An extensive Wedgwood creamware dinner service, impressed Wedgwood marks 116 pieces. (Phillips) $10,725

A Wedgwood majolica-ware 'Kate Greenaway' jardiniere, modelled as a lady's straw bonnet, 16.5cm., impressed Wedgwood and molded registration mark. (Phillips) $379

A rare and important Wedgwood Sydney Cove medallion, titled below Etruria 1789, the reverse impressed, 5.7cm. overall diam. (Phillips) $27,600

A Wedgwood Fairyland lustre 'Malfrey Pot' and cover, 18cm. high, 26cm. diam., Portland Vase mark, Z5257, incised shape number 2308. (Phillips) $907

WEDGWOOD

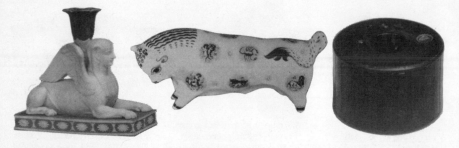

One of a pair of Wedgwood dipped blue and white jasper sphinx candlesticks, circa 1810, 16.5cm. wide. (Christie's) $4,235

A Wedgwood pottery figure of a bull designed by Arnold Machin, 15½in. long. (Christie's) $315

A Wedgwood & Bentley black basalt cylindrical ink-well, circa 1775, 7.5cm. diam. (Christie's) $500

A Wedgwood creamware oval sauce tureen, cover and pierced stand, painted in the manner of James Bakewell, circa 1770, the stand 26.5cm. wide. (Christie's) $3,630

A pair of mid 19th century Wedgwood black basalt triton candlesticks of conventional type, 28cm. high. (Christie's) $1,452

A Wedgwood white biscuit tripod vase and domed cover, circa 1810, 25cm. high. (Christie's) $1,925

A Wedgwood Masonic handled jug, white ground, cobalt-blue neck and gilded rim, circa 1935, 7in. high. (Giles Haywood) $65

A Wedgwood black basalt rectangular plaque molded with 'Death of a Roman Warrior', circa 1800, 27 x 48.5cm. (Christie's) $3,085

A Wedgwood 'Fairyland' lustre vase and cover, 9¼in. high. (Christie's) $1,969

WEDGWOOD

Wedgwood Fairyland lustre footed bowl, 11in. diam. (Prudential Fine Art) $1,567

A creamware double rectangular tea caddy of Wedgwood/Whieldon type, circa 1760, 14.5cm. wide. (Christie's) $2,722

A Wedgwood black basalt encaustic-decorated potpourri vase, lid and pierced cover, circa 1820, 34cm. wide. (Christie's) $1,815

A Wedgwood & Bentley black basalt encaustic-decorated circular sugar bowl and cover, circa 1775, 11.5cm. diam. (Christie's) $2,904

Two Wedgwood black basalt miniature busts of Homer and Aristophanes, circa 1785, 11cm. and 10cm. high. (Christie's) $2,502

A Wedgwood solid pale-blue and white jasper cylindrical sugar bowl and cover, circa 1785, 10.5cm. diam. (Christie's) $673

A Wedgwood & Bentley creamware large flower pot and stand, circa 1775, the stand 27cm. diam. (Christie's) $1,633

Mid 19th century Wedgwood dipped lilac and white jasper centerpiece, 44.5cm. high. (Christie's) $3,657

A Wedgwood Fairyland lustre black-ground small globular jar and cover, circa 1925, 8.5cm. high. (Christie's) $2,359

A rare and small Whieldon
'pear' teapot and cover, 8.5cm.
high. (Phillips)
$11,408

A Staffordshire creamware
spirally molded wall-pocket
of Whieldon type, circa 1760,
21cm. high. (Christie's)
$871

A creamware globular tea-
pot and cover of Whieldon
type with vine-stock spout,
handle and finial, circa 1755,
11cm. high. (Christie's)
$871

A creamware plate of Whieldon
type, circa 1770, 24.5cm. diam.
(Christie's) $1,633

A Whieldon tortoiseshell
coffee pot and cover, of
baluster shape with domed
cover, circa 1760. (Phillips)
$8,010

A Staffordshire creamware
pierced oval stand of
Whieldon type, circa 1770,
24cm. wide. (Christie's)
$1,815

A creamware globular teapot
and cover of Whieldon type,
circa 1760, 9.5cm. high.
(Christie's) $1,597

An Astbury/Whieldon
glazed redware cylindrical
mug with loop handle,
9.5cm. high. (Phillips)
$1,503

A creamware miniature
globular teapot and cover
of Whieldon type, circa
1770, 8.5cm. high.
(Christie's) $1,361

WORCESTER

A large 'bow' vase, signed
John Stinton, 30.5cm. high,
shape no. 1428, date code
for 1908. (Phillips)
$4,342

Royal Worcester 'Sabrina'
porcelain circular dished
plate, signed R. Austin,
1929, 9.5in. diam. (Giles
Haywood) $76

A Grainger's Worcester
pedestal ewer with a painted
scene of swans, signed
indistinctly, 10in. high.
(Hetheringtons Nationwide)
$858

An ovoid vase, the body well
painted with two Highland
cattle, signed H. Stinton,
21cm. high, shape no. 1762,
date code for 1910. (Phillips)
$1,107

Royal Worcester Hadley-
style footed vase, designed
as a jardiniere, 1906, 5in.
high. (Giles Haywood)
$458

A Royal Worcester porcelain
jug (ice tusk), circa 1884,
approx. 12in. tall. (G. A. Key)
$548

Worcester porcelain jug, the
blush ivory ground with hand-
painted floral sprigs, circa
1902, 7in. high. (G. A. Key)
$346

One of a pair of Grainger Worcester
mugs with single spur handles,
titled below painted panels,
'Drawing Cover' and 'The Death',
11.5cm. high. (Phillips)
$12,606

A Dr. Wall Worcester quart
mug with strap handle,
circa 1770, 6.1/8in. high.
(Robt. W. Skinner Inc.)
$275

WORCESTER

A Worcester yellow-ground honeycomb molded oval dish, circa 1765, 30cm. wide. (Christie's) $23,100

An 18th century Worcester blue and white teapot and cover decorated in underglaze blue with peonies. (Dee & Watkinson) $388

A Chamberlains Worcester porcelain oval dish painted and gilded with 'Kylin' or 'Dragons in Compartments' pattern, 12½in. long, 9½in. wide. (Dacre, Son & Hartley) $1,122

A Worcester sparrow-beak cream jug of pear shape, painted with the 'Arcade' pattern, 10cm. high, circa 1765-70. (Phillips) $734

A Royal Worcester blue-ground three-piece garniture, decorated by Thomas Bott, the largest with TB monogram and 63, gilded by Josiah Davis, the largest 16in. high. (Christie's) $8,250

A Royal Worcester two-handled, footed bulbous vase, by Harry Davis, model no. 1428, puce mark, 1932, 12in. high. (Giles Haywood) $10,027

A Worcester blue-scale porcelain lobed circular plate, circa 1770, 19.5cm. diam. (Christie's) $1,361

One of a pair of ovoid ewer-shaped vases, signed A. Shuck, 24cm. high, shape no. 1944, date codes for 1912. (Phillips) $2,387

A Barr, Flight & Barr porcelain circular tureen and stand, the painted panel attributed to Thos. Baxter, 7in. high, 7½in. wide overall, circa 1810-15. (Dacre, Son & Hartley) $6,930

WORCESTER

Worcester porcelain teapot, printed in a blue and white pattern of fence and tram-line design, circa 1770, 5½in. high. (G. A. Key) $619

A Worcester shell-shaped pickle dish, circa 1755, 3.1/8in. wide. (Christie's) $831

A Worcester creamboat of 'Chelsea Ewer' shape, circa 1765, 6.5cm. high. (Phillips) $1,035

A Flight, Barr & Barr porcelain dessert plate with a central panel of painted shells, attributed to Smith, 8¼in. wide, circa 1813-19. (Dacre, Son & Hartley) $1,237

Royal Worcester china vase painted by Jas. Stinton, 5.75in. high, date code for 1909 and pattern no. 995. (Prudential Fine Art) $412

A Grainger's Worcester porcelain tankard with boldy gilded borders, scrolling and handle, 5¼in. high, circa 1812-20. (Dacre, Son & Hartley) $1,980

One of a pair of Worcester leaf dishes with green stalk handles, circa 1760, approx. 18cm. wide.(Christie's) $3,448

A Royal Worcester footed pot-pourri, model no. 1286, black mark, signed R. Lewis, 10in. high. (Giles Haywood) $611

A Worcester plate from The Duke of Gloucester Service, gold crescent mark, circa 1775, 22.5cm. diam. (Christie's) $23,595

WORCESTER

An early Worcester reeded
coffee cup with a scroll
handle, painted in Kakiemon
style, circa 1753-55.
(Phillips) $1,302

One of a pair of Worcester
Imari pattern leaf dishes,
painted with The Kemp-
thorne Pattern, circa 1770,
26.5cm. wide. (Christie's)
$816

An 18th century Worcester
porcelain teapot, the domed
lid with flower finial, 6in.
high. (Hobbs & Chambers)
$207

A Worcester faceted part tea and coffee service painted with bouquets and scattered
flowers and flower-sprays within gilt line rims, blue square seal marks, circa 1765,
the teapot and sugar bowl painted by a different hand. (Christie's) $6,897

A Royal Worcester two-handled
vase, the body painted by N.
Roberts, signed, blue painted
marks and date code for 1899,
no. 2007, 49cm. high.
(Christie's) $2,502

A Worcester fluted teabowl
and saucer, circa 1770.
(Phillips) $1,336

Royal Worcester two-handled
footed bulbous vase, signed W.
Hale, 1919, model no. 1428,
12in. high. (Giles Haywood)
$5,921

WORCESTER

An 18th century Worcester
blue and white butter tub,
cover and stand decorated
in underglaze blue with
roses and butterflies. (Dee
& Atkinson) $388

A Worcester faceted teapot,
cover and stand, circa 1765,
14cm. high. (Christie's)
$1,452

A Worcester blue-scale bowl
of Lady Mary Wortley
Montagu pattern, painted in
the atelier of James Giles,
circa 1770, 16.5cm. diam.
(Christie's) $998

A Grainger, Lee & Co. Worcester tea service, painted in bright Imari style with panels
of fences and foliage on blue and red grounds with zig-zag bands and flowerheads,
pattern no. 575, some pieces with script marks. (Phillips) $1,503

A Royal Worcester two-handled
footed bulbous vase, by John
Stinton, model no. 1428, puce
mark, 1930, 12in. high. (Giles
Haywood) $8,404

A Flight, Barr & Barr porcelain
dessert dish with paintings of
flowers and butterflies, attributed to Henry Stinton, circa 1825,
10in. wide. (Dacre, Son & Hartley)
$4,290

A Worcester teapot and cover,
circa 1758, 12.5cm. high.
(Phillips) $2,171

WORCESTER

One of a pair of Worcester blue-scale tapering hexagonal vases and covers, circa 1768, 28cm. and 29.5cm. high. (Christie's) $23,595

An 18th century Worcester porcelain dish decorated with a fable painting by Duvivier, 9½in. wide. (G. A. Key) $858

One of two Worcester porcelain mugs each with strap handle, open crescent mark to base, 3½in. high, circa 1760. (Lalonde Fine Art) $396

An early Worcester cream jug of pear shape with large sparrow-beak lip and scroll handle, 7cm. high, circa 1752-53. (Phillips) $3,438

One of a pair of Royal Worcester vases, date code for 1914, 10½in. high. (Reeds Rains) $599

Royal Worcester flower bowl, shape no. 1713, green circle and crown mark, date code 1900, 9in. high. (Peter Wilson) $680

A Worcester 'blind earl' sweetmeat dish, painted in deep underglaze blue and with scattered insects, 15cm. long, crescent mark, circa 1765. (Phillips) $3,915

A Grainger's Worcester two-handled pedestal vase with landscaped decoration, signed J. Stinton, 11in. high. (Hetheringtons Nationwide) $1,155

Royal Worcester plate, signed James Stinton, puce mark, 1922, 10in. diam. (Giles Haywood) $248

BRACKET CLOCKS

An 18th century mahogany bracket clock, the arched brass dial signed Sidney Smith, Sedgley, 48cm. high. (Phillips) $2,184

A Regency 8-day striking twin fusee bracket clock in figured mahogany case, signed on dial Loof of Tunbridge Wells. (J. M. Welch & Son) $787

A 19th century mahogany and brass mounted bracket clock, the bell topped case with carrying handle, 39cm. high. (Phillips) $1,596

Mid 19th century George II ebony quarter-repeating bracket clock, signed Rich'd. Gregg, London, 13in. high. (Christie's) $5,280

A Victorian walnut bracket clock, the case in Gothic style, 2ft.2in. high. (Phillips) $660

Georgian style inlaid mahogany mantel or bracket clock with 8-day striking movement, the dial inscribed Finnigans Ltd., Manchester, 12½in. high. (Capes Dunn) $465

A George III mahogany bracket timepiece, signed in the arch Perigal, Coventry Street, London, 26cm. high. (Phillips) $1,764

A Victorian mahogany chiming bracket clock with chime/silent and selection of 8-bell or Westminster chime, 26in. high. (Christie's) $2,816

A George III mahogany bracket clock, the circular enamel dial signed Biddell, London, 53cm. high. (Phillips) $2,352

BRACKET CLOCKS

An early George III faded mahogany striking bracket clock, the dial signed Henry Sanderson, 18in. high. (Christie's) $5,808

A 19th century bracket clock with 8-day movement, 29½in. high. (Dacre, Son & Hartley) $1,312

A George III ebonized striking bracket clock for the Spanish market by Higgs y Diego Evans, 18¼in. high. (Christie's) $3,085

A Regency Gothic mahogany bracket clock, the painted dial signed Manners & Sons, Stamford, 21½in. high. (Christie's) $1,542

A Queen Anne ebonized bracket clock, the 6¼in. sq. dial signed James Tunn, London, 15in. high. (Christie's) $2,722

Late 19th century mahogany 8-day domed bracket clock with silvered dial, 12in. high. (Giles Haywood) $393

A Charles II ebonized striking bracket clock with 6¾in. sq. dial, backplate signed Nathaniel Hodges, 13¾in. high. (Christie's) $5,808

A Charles II ebonized turn-table bracket clock, by E. Bird, London, 19in. high. (Christie's) $11,797

A William III ebonized striking bracket clock with gilt metal repousse basket top, dial signed Cha. Greeton, 14½in. high. (Christie's) $4,537

BRACKET CLOCKS

An early Georgian ebonized bracket timepiece with gilt brass handle, the backplate signed Dan. Quare, London, 12¾in. high. (Christie's) $5,082

An early George III dark japanned musical chiming bracket clock for the Turkish market, dial signed Edward Pistor, London, 23½in. high. (Christie's) $5,808

A George III mahogany striking bracket clock, dial signed Devereux Bowly, London, 20in. high. (Christie's) $5,445

A George II fruitwood striking miniature bracket clock with carrying handle, the backplate signed Wm. Hughes, 10in. high. (Christie's) $8,712

A Charles II ebonized striking bracket clock, dial signed J. Windmills, London, 14¼in. high. (Christie's) $8,167

A George II ebonized quarter striking bracket clock, the dial signed Jams. Snelling, London, 14¾in. high. (Christie's) $5,082

A Queen Anne ebony striking and quarter repeating bracket clock, signed Sam. Aldworth, 14in. high. (Christie's) $8,167

A George III mahogany striking bracket clock, signed Eardley Norton, London, 15¾in. high. (Christie's) $10,890

A Queen Anne kingwood striking bracket clock, the dial signed Cha. Gretton, 14in. high. (Christie's) $29,040

BRACKET CLOCKS

A George III satinwood bracket clock, the movement signed Tregent, Strand, London, 21in. high. (Christie's) $5,119

A 19th century mahogany cased 8-day bracket clock, the silvered dial signed James Doig of Edinburgh, 16in. high. (J. M. Welch & Son) $273

A Georgian green lacquered bracket clock, signed Stepn. Rimbault, London, 1ft.8in. high. (Phillips) $2,805

An early 18th century ebonized bracket clock with brass dial, by Thomas Gardner, London, 18½in. high. (Graves Son & Pilcher) $2,058

An 18th century C. European red lacquered quarter chiming bracket clock, the backplate signed Iohan Maurer in Prag, 57cm. high. (Phillips) $8,736

A Victorian mahogany bracket clock, the movement by Streeter & Co., 18 New Bond Street, London, 15in. wide, 29in. high. (Anderson & Garland) $1,770

A 19th century ebonized and brass mounted bracket clock, the silvered dial signed Payne, 163 New Bond St., London, 1ft.2½in. high. (Phillips) $1,650

Mid 18th century George II ebonized quarter-chiming bracket clock, signed B. Gray, London, 15½in. high. (Christie's) $8,250

A walnut chiming bracket clock, the three train fusee movement striking quarter hours on 8 bells or four gongs, 15in. high. (Christie's) $2,112

BRACKET CLOCKS

A George IV mahogany lyre-form musical bracket clock, signed Frodsham, London, 37in. high. (Christie's) $6,600

A William III quarter repeating ebony bracket clock, signed Claudius Du Chesne, Londini Fecit, 16½in. high. (Christie's) $19,694

A Georgian mahogany quarter chiming bracket clock, the painted dial signed Geo. Wilkins, Soho, 2ft.2in. high. (Phillips) $2,392

An 18th century ebony bracket clock, signed James Tregent, Leicester Square, London, 1ft.5½in. high. (Phillips) $4,125

A late 17th century ebony 'double six hour' grande sonnerie bracket clock, the 6½in. square dial now inscribed Tompion Londini, 35.5cm. high. (Phillips) $15,120

A Regency mahogany bracket clock, the arched brass dial signed Aynsth. & Jono. Thwaites, London, 1ft.6½in. high. (Phillips) $4,620

A Queen Anne ebonized bracket clock, the dial signed Dan. Quare, London, 20in. high. (Christie's) $15,427

A Victorian pollard oak Gothic Revival bracket clock, the dial signed Muller, Twickenham, 42in. high. (Reeds Rains) $1,169

A Victorian director's bracket clock with 8-day fusee movement chiming on eight bells, 30in. high. (Hy. Duke & Son) $2,700

CARRIAGE CLOCKS

A porcelain panelled carriage clock, the movement with the trademark of J. Dejardin, 7in. high. (Christie's) $4,180

A gilt brass porcelain mounted striking carriage clock with porcelain dial, stamp of Achille Brocot, 6¼in. high. (Christie's) $3,085

A lacquered brass carriage clock, signed on the dial in cyrillic, A. M. Geracimov, St. Petersburg, 8in. high. (Christie's) $1,320

A lacquered brass petite sonnerie carriage clock, with the trademark of Francois-Arsene Margaine, 7in. high. (Christie's) $1,650

A shagreen carriage clock of humpback form, dial signed Jump Paris 93 Mount Street (London), 7in. high. (Christie's) $1,542

A 19th century French brass carriage clock, the lever movement striking on a gong with alarm and bearing the Drocourt trademark, 16.5cm. high. (Phillips) $873

A gilt brass carriage clock with calendar and alarm, circa 1845, 7½in. high. (Christie's) $1,540

A brass calendar carriage timepiece, enamel dial with chapter disk above gilt mask, 4¾in. high. (Christie's) $363

A gilt brass and enamel striking carriage clock with uncut bimetallic balance to silvered lever platform, 5½in. high. (Christie's) $2,178

CARRIAGE CLOCKS

A gilt brass porcelain mounted striking carriage clock, the dial and side panels painted in the Sevres style, 5½in. high. (Christie's) $5,445

A gilt brass grande-sonnerie calendar carriage clock with uncut compensated balance to the silvered lever platform, stamp of Drocourt, 6½in. high. (Christie's) $6,352

A gilt brass carriage clock with engraved side panels, signed Paul Buhre, St. Petersburg, the movement by F.-A. Margaine, 7in. high. (Christie's) $3,300

A 19th century brass carriage clock with petit sonnerie and alarm movement, the enamel dial signed Dent, Paris, 4½in. high. (J. M. Welch & Son) $927

A miniature oval carriage timepiece with white enamel dial, 3in. high. (Christie's) $704

A grande sonnerie striking carriage clock; the white enamel dial signed A. Jackemann, Paris, 6in. high. (Christie's) $2,112

A 19th century French gilt brass and porcelain mounted carriage clock, 18cm. high. (Phillips) $3,528

A gilt brass carriage clock with gilt platform to lever escapement, 6¾in. high, including handle. (Christie's) $880

A gilt brass grande sonnerie carriage clock, 7½in. high, including handle. (Christie's) $1,430

CARRIAGE CLOCKS

A brass and glass panelled carriage clock, dial inscribed 'Aird & Thomson, Glasgow', 5½in. high. (G. A. Key) $595

A 19th century French gilt brass miniature carriage timepiece, the lever movement with enamel dial, 3¾in. high, together with a travelling case. (Phillips) $1,452

Large early English fusee carriage clock with silvered dial, by G. & W. Yonge, London, 5½in. high. (G. A. Key) $1,750

A gilt brass quarter striking carriage clock with uncut compensated balance to lever platform, 5in. high. (Christie's) $998

A 19th century French brass carriage clock, 7in. high, together with a leather travelling case. (Phillips) $825

An English petit sonnerie carriage clock with white enamel dial inscribed Lund & Blockley, 6in. high. (Graves Son & Pilcher) $3,401

A French gilt brass carriage clock, the dial and side panels decorated with scenes of young couples, 7in. high. (Phillips) $1,402

A 19th century French gilt brass and porcelain mounted grande sonnerie carriage clock, with trademark P.M., 18cm. high. (Phillips) $7,728

A 19th century French brass carriage clock, the lever movement striking on a gong, with push repeat and with the Margaine trademark on the backplate, 7¼in. high. (Phillips) $858

CARRIAGE CLOCKS

A French 19th century gilt brass carriage clock, the lever movement striking on a gong and bearing the Drocourt trademark, 7in. high. (Phillips) $1,402

A gilt brass striking carriage clock, the backplate stamped J. Klaftenburger, 5¼in. high. (Christie's) $3,085

A 19th century French miniature brass carriage time-piece, the lever movement bearing the Margaine trade-mark, 9.5cm. high. (Phillips) $672

An ornate gilt repeating carriage clock, signed Bolviller a Paris, 6¼in. high. (Christie's) $1,322

A quarter-repeating and cloisonne enamel carriage clock, 3in. high. (Christie's) $5,808

A gilt brass bottom-wind striking carriage clock with split bimetallic balance to silvered levered platform, dial signed Le Roy et fils (etc.), 5½in. high. (Christie's) $871

A 19th century French gilt brass grande sonnerie carriage clock, the lever movement striking on two gongs with push repeat, 20cm. high. (Phillips) $2,352

A petite-sonnerie repeating and alarm carriage clock, with Arabic numerals and signed A H Rodanet, Paris, 6in. high. (Christie's) $1,424

A 19th century French gilt brass carriage clock, the lever movement striking on a gong with push repeat, 19cm. high. (Phillips) $924

CLOCK SETS

A French gilt marble and gilt metal garniture, with matching three-arm candelabra, 18in. high. (Christie's) $1,980

A French veined marble garniture, 17in. high. (Christie's) $752

A good ormolu and porcelain garniture, 18in. high. (Christie's) $2,772

A French 19th century brass, enamel and porcelain mounted clock garniture, signed Lefranc, 1ft.3in. high, together with a pair of side urns. (Phillips) $2,722

Late 19th century gilt metal clock set of Renaissance style, the clock 28in. high, the candelabra 39½in. high. (Christie's) $3,630

An unusual 19th century enamelled and gilt brass 'Gothick' chamber clock and candle-sticks, clock 22in. high. (Christie's) $5,500

LANTERN CLOCKS

A brass lantern clock, the dial with brass chapter signed Wilmshurst, Odiham, 1ft.3in. high, together with an oak wall bracket. (Phillips) $1,732

A French brass lantern clock, the circular chased dial with enamel numerals, 41cm. high. (Phillips) $1,008

A brass lantern clock, 39.5cm. high (probably 17th century). (Phillips) $3,325

A George II small brass lantern clock with silent escapement, chapter ring signed John Fletcher, 9in. high.(Christie's) $1,633

A brass lantern clock, signed Chr. Gould, Londoni Fecit., late 17th century, 15in. high. (Christie's) $3,850

A Georgian brass lantern clock, made for the Turkish market, signed Jno. Parks, London, 1ft.2½in. high. (Phillips) $990

An early brass lantern clock, signed on the fret, Richard Beck, near Ye French Church, Londini, mid-17th century, 17½in. high. (Christie's) $5,060

A Georgian brass miniature lantern clock made for the Turkish market, signed Robt. Ward, London, 5½in. high. (Phillips) $2,145

A brass lantern clock with alarm, unsigned, 17th century, with restorations, 14½in. (Christie's) $2,860

LONGCASE CLOCKS

Late 19th century mahogany 8-day rack striking longcase clock, by Seddon & Moss. (Peter Wilson) $5,984

A William III walnut and marquetry longcase clock, the 12in. sq. dial signed John Marshall, 7ft.1in. high. (Christie's) $14,520

Scottish 19th century mahogany longcase clock by D. Robinson, Airdrie, 7ft. tall. (Chancellors Hollingsworths) $1,472

A George III mahogany musical longcase clock for the German market, the dial signed Jos. Herring, 8ft.11in.. high overall.(Christie's) $14,520

An 18th century walnut longcase clock, the 11in. square dial signed Jn⁰. Wise, London, 2.10m. high. (Phillips) $2,688

Late 18th century oak and walnut crossbanded longcase clock, by Thos. Shaw, Lancaster, 88in. high. (Prudential Fine Art) $825

Mid 17th century oak longcased 8-day clock, maker Wm. Webb, Wellington, 6ft.6in. high. (Giles Haywood) $1,312

A reproduction longcase clock. (Miller & Co.) $2,937

LONGCASE CLOCKS

A Georgian mahogany longcase clock, the dial with subsidiary seconds, 8ft. high. (Christie's) $5,082

Westminster and Whittington mahogany longcase clock with brass and silver dial. (Ball & Percival) $3,444

Early 19th century Federal painted tall-case clock, possibly Berks County, Penn., 96in. high. (Christie's) $2,530

A Federal mahogany inlaid tall case clock, Mass., circa 1790, 91in. high. (Robt. W. Skinner Inc.) $7,000

A George III mahogany regulator, the 10in. dial signed Holmes, London, 5ft.11½in. high. (Phillips) $9,075

A large Regina oak longcase 15½in. disc musical box clock, with eighty-six discs, 252cm. high, circa 1900. (Phillips) $5,760

A floral marquetry longcase clock, the dial signed Thos. Bradford, 6ft.6in. high. (Christie's) $12,100

A Georgian mahogany longcase clock, signed Williams, Preston, 7ft. 6½in. high. (Phillips) $4,290

LONGCASE CLOCKS

A George III mahogany longcase clock, the 13in. brass dial signed Samuel Young, Bonebury, 7ft.9in. high. (Phillips) $4,950

A small oak 30-hour striking longcase clock, the 11in. brass dial by Sam Hanley, circa 1750. (Peter Wilson) $1,539

A Georgian walnut and inlaid longcase clock, signed Jon. Sales, Dublin, 8ft. 5½in. high. (Phillips) $3,696

A George III mahogany longcase clock, the dial signed Chas. Cabrier, 7ft.11in. high. (Christie's) $7,260

A carved oak longcase clock, signed Edw. Whitehead, Wetherby, 86in. high. (Christie's) $1,056

A 19th century mahogany regulator, by Hepting, Stirling, 75in. high. (Reeds Rains) $1,068

An Arts & Crafts oak tallcase clock, by the Colonial Mfg. Co., Zeeland, Michigan, circa 1914, 84in. high. (Robt. W. Skinner Inc.) $2,000

An early 18th century walnut and panel marquetry longcase clock, the 11in. square brass dial signed Thos. Stubbs, London, 2.10m. high.(Phillips) $19,320

LONGCASE CLOCKS

A Regency mahogany longcase clock, the 12in. silvered dial signed Grant, London, 7ft. high. (Phillips) $6,270

An 18th century burr walnut longcase clock, the dial inscribed Robt. Maisley, London, 7ft. 6in. high. (Parsons, Welch & Cowell) $5,544

A Georgian mahogany musical quarter chiming longcase clock, signed J. Cooke, Cambridge, 8ft.2½in. high. (Phillips) $4,620

A longcase clock, by Tomlinson, London, with 8-day bell-striking movement, 76in. high. (Hy. Duke & Son) $2,430

A Black Forest organ clock, the 24-key movement with thirty-six wood pipes, eight-air barrel and painted dial, 97in. high. (Christie's) $3,564

An 18th century mahogany longcase clock, the 12in. brass dial signed Philip Lloyd, Bristol, 2.28m. high. (Phillips) $4,704

An oak longcase clock, the dial signed Creighton B-Mena No. 120, 91in. high. (Christie's) $880

An arabesque marquetry longcase clock, signed Rich. Colston, London, circa 1710, 7ft.4in. high. (Christie's) $11,550

LONGCASE CLOCKS

Late 18th century
30-hour oak long-
cased clock, maker
John Kent, Mon-
mouth, circa 1790.
(Giles Haywood)
$369

A Federal inlaid
mahogany tall
case clock, dial
signed by David
Wood, circa 1790,
90in. high.
(Christie's)
$33,000

A late Stuart walnut
and marquetry longcase
clock with 11in. sq.
dial, 7ft.0½in. high.
(Christie's)
$17,242

A Federal cherry
inlaid tall case clock,
E. New Hampshire,
circa 1800, 94in.
high. (Robt. W.
Skinner Inc.)
$7,000

A Federal mahogany
inlaid tall case clock,
by Samuel Foster,
New Hampshire, 1798,
86in. high. (Robt. W.
Skinner Inc.)
$14,000

A late 17th century
walnut and panel mar-
quetry longcase clock,
the 10in. brass dial
signed Bird, London,
6ft.8½in. high.
(Phillips)
$18,975

An L. & J. G. Stickley
tall case clock, signed
with red handcraft de-
cal, circa 1908, 81in.
high. (Robt. W.
Skinner Inc.)
$15,000

An 18th century oak
longcase clock with
brass and silvered dial,
maker J. Barrow,
London. (Dee &
Atkinson)
$1,620

LONGCASE CLOCKS

A George I month-going walnut longcase clock, the chapter ring signed John May, 100in. high. (Christie's) **$9,982**

A late Stuart walnut and marquetry longcase clock, the 10¾in. sq. dial signed Fromanteel, 7ft.11½in. high. (Christie's) **$23,595**

A George III mahogany longcase clock, dial signed Joseph Nardin, London, 6ft. high. (Christie's) **$5,082**

A Pennsylvania Chippendale inlaid walnut tallcase clock, 88in. high. (Christie's) **$4,400**

A Chippendale walnut tall case clock, dial signed by Johnson, London, case probably Penn., 1770-90, 92in. high. (Christie's) **$2,420**

A mahogany longcase sidereal regulator with break circuit work, signed Wm. Bond & Sons, Boston, circa 1858, 64½in. high. (Christie's) **$28,600**

An 18th century walnut month going longcase clock, the dial signed Christop Gould Londini fecit, 6ft.10in. high. (Phillips) **$5,775**

A Georgian mahogany quarter chiming longcase clock, the 12in. dial signed Wm. Haughton, London, 2.46m. high. (Phillips) **$6,720**

LONGCASE CLOCKS

Chippendale style mahogany eight-day longcase clock. (John Hogbin & Son) $3,690

A George II 8-day mahogany longcase clock, by Daniel Ray, Manningtree, 88in. high. (Lacy Scott) $4,125

Longcase clock with bombe marquetry case, enamel and brass dial. (Ball & Percival) $4,756

A painted pine tall case clock, by Silas Hoadley, Conn., circa 1825, 93½in. high. (Robt. W. Skinner Inc.) $9,000

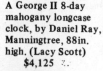

An early 18th century walnut and panel marquetry longcase clock, signed J. Windmills, London, 7ft.2in. high. (Phillips) $14,850

A mahogany longcase clock, the brass dial inscribed Maple & Co. Ltd., London, 7ft. 11in. high. (Parsons, Welch & Cowell) $1,142

A mahogany grand-daughter longcase clock with 7in. brass dial, 59½in. high. (Christie's) $2,816

A George III oak cased 8-day striking longcase clock, the dial signed J. Marr of Retford. (J. M. Welch & Son) $1,018

LONGCASE CLOCKS

Early 19th century painted and carved tallcase clock, Penn., 98in. high. (Christie's) $18,700

Early 19th century Lancashire mahogany longcase clock, 94½in. high. (Prudential Fine Art) $1,980

A Federal maple tall case clock, by Silas Hoadley, circa 1820, 81in. high. (Robt. W. Skinner Inc.) $1,800

A George II mahogany longcase clock, the dial signed Christo. Goddard, 8ft.5in. high. (Christie's) $4,719

A Pennsylvania Chippendale walnut tallcase clock, the dial signed C. Warner, 91in. high. (Christie's) $3,960

An 18th century Dutch oak longcase clock, signed De Wancker TotLoo, 98in. high. (Christie's) $1,362

Art Nouveau mahogany tall case clock, late 19th century, by Gerr Suss, Hamburg, 96½in. high. (Robt. W. Skinner. Inc.) $1,750

A mid Georgian mahogany longcase clock, inscribed Andrew Reed, London. (Locke & England) $3,586

Kneeling girl with clock, a bronze and ivory figure cast after a model by F. Preiss, 54.4cm. high. (Christie's) $14,071

A Sevres pattern gilt bronze mantel clock, the movement by Gasnier a Paris, circa 1875, 41cm. wide. (Christie's) $1,361

A Charles X ormolu mantel clock with circular dial signed 'Guyerde(?) aine Paris', 12in. wide. (Christie's) $1,102

A George III giltwood mantel clock, the associated George I watch movement by William Webster, 13in. high. (Christie's) $1,623

A George III ormolu mantel clock for the Oriental market, the dial signed W. Mahr, 19in. high. (Christie's) $7,260

A Charles X ormolu and malachite mantel clock, the dial flanked by the brothers Horatii taking their oath, after J-L David, 21½in. wide. (Christie's) $6,980

An Ato Art Deco table clock with a pair of bronze owls perched on top, 41.5cm. high. (Christie's) $811

An early Victorian maple wood lancet mantel timepiece, the dial with inscription Thos. Cole, London, 10in. high. (Christie's) $2,178

A Charles X ormolu and bronze mantel clock with silvered dial, 16in. high. (Christie's) $1,653

MANTEL CLOCKS

Late 19th century Sevres pattern pink-ground porcelain gilt bronze mounted mantel clock, 34cm. high. (Christie's) $1,285

A silvered bronze mantel clock, by Edgar Brandt, 30.6cm. high. (Christie's) $5,051

A Louis Philippe ormolu mantel clock, the silvered dial signed A. C. Decauville A Paris, 24½in. high. (Christie's) $2,204

An automaton clock in the form of a waterwheel in brickwork surround, 16in. high. (Christie's) $7,260

A French brass four-glass clock with perpetual calendar, the calendar dial signed Achille Brocot, 13in. high. (Christie's) $4,900

A Louis XVI ormolu and terracotta mantel clock, the dial signed Sotiau A Paris, with figures of Minerva and attendants, 18in. wide. (Christie's) $4,592

A Charles X ormolu mantel clock with enamel dial surmounted by a bust of Aristotle flanked by a cherub, 19½in. high. (Christie's) $1,652

A silvered bronze Art Deco table clock, signed R. Terras, 34.5cm. high. (Christie's) $1,623

A Charles X bronze and ormolu mantel clock with circular dial surmounted by Cato amidst the ruins of Carthage, 17½in. wide. (Christie's) $2,020

MANTEL CLOCKS

A Regency rosewood and brass inlaid mantel timepiece, the silvered dial signed Carpenter, London, 9½in. high. (Phillips) $3,135

A 19th century French ormolu and bronze mantel clock, the gilt dial with enamel numerals, 1ft.10in. high. (Phillips) $1,320

A 19th century French rosewood floral inlaid classical shaped 8-day mantel clock, 10in. high. (Giles Haywood) $278

An ormolu mantel clock of Louis XVI style, the dial signed Antide-Janvier a Paris in oval vase-shaped case, 20in. high. (Christie's) $1,468

'Inseparables', a Lalique square-shaped clock with blue and white painted dial, 11cm. high. (Christie's) $1,984

An ormolu mantel clock of rococo style, 29in. high, 19½in. wide. (Christie's) $2,020

A 19th century mahogany and brass inlaid mantel clock, the circular painted dial signed Condliff, Liverpool, 35cm.high. (Phillips) $1,176

A Continental spelter mystery timepiece on a rectangular base, 32cm. high. (Phillips) $638

An Austrian silver plated quarter chiming mantel clock, signed Carl Wolfe in Wien, 9½in. high. (Phillips) $693

MANTEL CLOCKS

A 19th century French ormolu and porcelain mantel clock, 1ft.3in. high. (Phillips) $1,188

An enamelled silver grande sonnerie world time table clock, signed Patek Philippe & Co., Geneve, 7½in. diam. (Christie's) $38,500

A Paris (Jacob Petit) blue-ground clockcase and stand, the movement by Hrr. Marc a Paris, circa 1835, 34cm. high. (Christie's) $871

A 19th century gilt bronze mantel timepiece, the silvered dial signed for Hunt & Roskell, London, 1ft.7¼in. high. (Phillips) $4,950

An ormolu mantel clock with enamel dial and drum-shaped case, 12in. wide. (Christie's) $580

An Empire ormolu and bronze mantel clock of lyre shape supported upon seated griffins, 10½in. high. (Christie's) $1,562

A Regency mahogany and brass inlaid mantel time-piece, the circular enamel dial signed Scott, Horl^r to H.R.H. The Duke of Kent, 674, 26cm. high. (Phillips) $806

An automaton clock in the form of a ship's bridge, 12½in. high. (Christie's) $3,465

A Regency mahogany and brass inlaid mantel timepiece with circular enamel dial (damaged), 9½in. high. (Phillips) $429

MANTEL CLOCKS

A George III ormolu mounted timepiece clock, by James Tregent, London, in the style of M. Boulton, 12½in. high. (Christie's) $11,797

A 19th century French ormolu and porcelain mantel clock, the square dial signed Klaftenburger, London, together with a giltwood base, 46cm. high. (Phillips) $873

An Austrian 19th century silver and enamel timepiece, with polychrome champleve dial, 18cm. high. (Phillips) $1,596

A 19th century black slate mantel timepiece, signed Payne, 163 New Bond Street, 22cm. high. (Phillips) $429

A Black Forest trumpeter clock in walnut case, 39in. high. (Christie's) $3,385

A late 19th century walnut mantel clock, the dial signed Chas. Frodsham, Clock-maker to the Queen, No. 2057, 30cm. high. (Phillips) $1,260

An Arts & Crafts mahogany mantel clock with bevelled glass, circa 1900, 12in. high. (Robt. W. Skinner Inc.) $500

A Federal mahogany pillar and scroll clock, by E. Terry & Sons, Conn., circa 1820, 29in. high. (Robt. W. Skinner Inc.) $1,500

Sterling silver 8-day travelling clock, Swiss movement 'Black Starr & Frost, New York', 4 x 2in. (Giles Haywood) $229

MANTEL CLOCKS

A German gilt metal monstrance clock, the reverse with astrolabic dial, movement late 19th century, 18in. high. (Christie's) $17,242

A mid 19th century French ormolu and Sevres panel mantel clock, under glass dome, 18in. high. (G. A. Key) $840

A Charles X vase-shaped mantel clock with enamel dial and swan-neck handles, 13in. high. (Christie's) $1,377

A 19th century French brass mantel clock, the enamel dial signed for Payne, Tunbridge Wells, 1ft.8in. high. (Phillips) $2,062

A French champleve enamel four glass clock, the 8-day movement striking on bell, 13in. high. (Christie's) $968

A Victorian rosewood four-glass mantel clock, the backplate signed French Royal Exchange, London, 9½in. high. (Christie's) $2,722

A 19th century French brass and porcelain mantel clock, 36cm. high. (Phillips) $2,856

A modern Swiss singing bird box in engine-turned lacquered brass case, surmounted by a French 8-day alarm clock, 6in. high, with travelling case. (Christie's) $2,138

A Charles X ormolu mantel clock with circular dial and striking movement in a foliate drum case, 19in. high. (Christie's) $1,469

MANTEL CLOCKS

A travelling clock in scroll and flower embossed silver case, by Charles James Fox, London, 1899, 3¼in. overall. (Dreweatt Neate) $710

A Victorian lacquered brass mantel clock with French movement by F. Martie, 16in. high, 22in. wide. (Capes Dunn) $751

A French ormolu and Sevres style panel clock, signed on the dial Lagarde A Paris, 49cm. high. (Wellington Salerooms) $4,368

A large Victorian chiming mantel clock with brass and silver dial, 28in. high. (Ball & Percival) $1,584

A French four-glass clock, the dial with enamelled swags above a mercury double chamber pendulum, the top and base of onyx, 27cm. high. (David Lay) $864

A Swiss travelling clock, the enamel face inscribed 'Goldsmiths and Silversmiths Co. Ltd.', London import marks for 1913, 2½ x 1¼in. wide. (Dreweatt Neate) $1,122

Late 18th century George III gilt and cut glass mounted floral painted quarter-chiming musical bracket clock for the Turkish market, signed Benj. Barber, London, 37½in. high. (Christie's) $52,800

A French ormolu 8-day mantel clock with porcelain dial, circa 1870, 17in. high, on serpentine shaped base with glass dome. (Lacy Scott) $594

Victorian 'ginger bread' framed shelf clock with an Ansonia Clock Co. striking movement. (G. A. Key) $112

MANTEL CLOCKS

A Regency white marble and gilt bronze mantel timepiece, the gilt dial signed Viner, London, 8in. high. (Phillips) $742

An Empire ormolu mounted clock, the dial within the wheel of Diana's chariot, 21¾in. wide. (Christie's) $2,349

A 19th century French ormolu and porcelain mantel clock, the dial signed for F. Armstrong & Bros., Paris, 1ft.6½in. high. (Phillips) $858

A Charles X ormolu and porcelain clock, the movement signed Le Roy, Paris 1102, 16in. high. (Christie's) $1,370

An Arts & Crafts square oak mantel clock, by Seth Thomas Clock Co., 20th century, 12½in. high, 10½in. wide. (Robt. W. Skinner Inc.) $1,200

Mid 19th century rosewood mantel clock with carrying case, signed James Murray, Royal Exchange London, 12in. high. (Christie's) $5,280

A brass Eureka mantel timepiece, the enamel dial inscribed S. Fisher Ltd., 1ft.1in. high, under a damaged glass shade. (Phillips) $660

A 19th century French ormolu and porcelain mantel clock, the enamel dial signed Vieyres & Repignon a Paris, 11in. high. (Phillips) $990

A Charles X ormolu and bronze mantel clock with silvered dial, 15in. high. (Christie's) $2,153

MANTEL CLOCKS

An ormolu mounted scarlet boulle bracket clock, dial signed V. Courtecuisse & Cie Lille, 45in. high. (Christie's) $3,122

An Empire ormolu mantel clock, the movement signed James McCabe, London 2133, 12½in. high. (Christie's) $2,937

Late 19th century enamelled silver gilt Renaissance style table clock, the case by H. Bohm, Vienna, 7½in. high. (Christie's) $1,320

An oval four-glass lacquered brass 8-day striking mantel clock with enamel dial, 9½in. tall. (J. M. Welch & Son) $393

A Louis Philippe ormolu, bronze and white marble mantel clock, with enamel circlet dial, 14in. high. (Christie's) $1,272

An ormolu mounted scarlet boulle bracket clock, the glazed dial with Roman enamel numerals, 48in. high. (Christie's) $4,307

A contre-partie polychrome boulle bracket clock, the enamel face signed Gille L'Aine a Paris, basically 18th century, 31in. high. (Christie's) $2,937

A mantel clock in gilt metal case decorated with champleve enamelled panels of scarlet, green and blue flowers on a pale blue ground, 2½in. (Dreweatt Neate) $205

A 19th century French ormolu mantel clock, the circular chased dial signed Hy. Marc a Paris, 41cm. high. (Phillips) $1,344

MANTEL CLOCKS

A 19th century French ormolu and porcelain mantel clock, the decorated dial signed for Miller & Co., Bristol, 43cm. high. (Phillips) $873

A 19th century French Empire style 8-day striking mantel clock, 17in. high. (J. M. Welch & Son) $561

An alabaster and gilt pillar/vase clock with central milk-glass dial, 12in. tall, circa 1900. (J. M. Welch & Son) $228

A gilt brass calendar strut clock attributed to Thos. Cole, London, the backplate signed Hunt & Roskell, London, 5½in. high. (Christie's) $2,359

A 19th century tortoiseshell and cut brass inlaid bracket clock, signed Lepeltier a Paris, 2ft.2½in. high. (Phillips) $1,567

A 19th century rosewood cased four-glass mantel clock, dial signed French Royal Exchange, London, 9¼ x 6¼in. (J. M. Welch & Son) $3,444

A 19th century French ormolu mantel clock, the case in the form of a lyre, 38cm. high, on an oval ebonized stand under a glass shade. (Phillips) $974

An early 19th century time-piece inkstand, the movement with engine-turned gilt face by Edward Lock, 19cm. high, 18cm. wide. (David Lay) $594

A Louis XV style red boulle bracket clock with two-train movement by Gay Vicarino & Co., Paris, 44cm. high. (Osmond Tricks) $785

WALL CLOCKS

A French Louis XVI 3-month duration console clock, signed on a porcelain plaque Nicolas Texier a Philippeville, 23½in. high. (Christie's) $7,524

A George III brass wall clock, the dial signed Edwd. Pashier, London, 1ft.6½in. high. (Phillips) $2,310

A French bracket wall clock, the white enamelled dial signed Causard Horloger Du Roy, Paris, the back plate stamped Vincenti, Paris. (Wellington Salerooms) $3,696

A 19th century carved mahogany Vienna wall clock, 4ft.9in. high. (Giles Haywood) $1,098

A musical picture clock with figures on a river bank with the clock face in church tower, 29½ x 34½in. overall. (Christie's) $1,960

A musical 19th century German carved wood wall clock, 6ft.11in. high. (Phillips) $11,220

Early 19th century Federal mahogany giltwood and eglomise banjo clock, 3.3½in. long. (Christie's) $1,760

Early 19th century inlaid mahogany clock with brass bezel and convex 10in. dial. (Reeds Rains) $701

Late 19th century softwood German wall clock, the white enamel dial with 8-day movement, 13in. high. (Peter Wilson) $680

WALL CLOCKS

A 19th century mahogany wall timepiece, the brass dial signed Mattw. & Thos. Dutton, London, 2ft.2½in. high. (Phillips)
$4,125

An 18th century striking Act of Parliament clock, signed Ino. Wilson, Peterborough, 56½in. high. (Christie's)
$1,881

A 19th century 8-day rosewood and oak cased wall clock with painted metal dial. (J. M. Welch & Son)
$155

An ormolu and bronze clock with glazed enamel dial, indistinctly signed ... Armentieres, 32½in. high. (Christie's)
$2,204

Mid 19th century wall clock in circular mahogany case, the enamel dial inscribed Ed. Russell, Foulsham. (G. A. Key) $313

A Federal gilt and eglomise girandole clock, by Lemuel Curtis, Concord, Mass., circa 1816, 46in. high. (Christie's)
$13,200

A George III giltwood cartel clock with associated silvered dial signed Wm. Linderby, London, 34in. high. (Christie's) $4,989

A Regency mahogany wall regulator, the movement of two week duration, 65in. high. (Christie's)
$5,020

An early 19th century French brass octagonal cased portable or hanging clock, the movement signed Du Louier a Rouen. (Parsons, Welch & Cowell) $420

WATCHES

A gold keyless openface free sprung fusee lever watch with winding indicator, signed Barraud & Lunds, London, 1893, 51mm. diam. (Christie's) $1,870

A gold hunter-cased lever watch, signed Barraud & Lunds, London, 1882, 50mm. diam. (Christie's) $770

A gold minute repeating keyless lever chronograph, signed Breguet No. 1310, 56mm. diam. (Phillips) $9,072

A gold floral enamel dress watch, signed L. Gallopin & Co., Suc'rs to Henry Capt, Geneva, 44mm. diam. (Christie's) $1,980

A gold openface chronograph, signed Vacheron & Constantin, Geneve, with an 18kt. gold fob, 51mm. diam. (Christie's) $1,980

An enamelled gold pendant watch and chain, signed Ed. Koehn, Geneva, retailed by J. E. Caldwell & Co., Phila., 29mm. diam. (Christie's) $1,100

A gold pair case verge watch, signed Wm. Robertson, London, 1793, together with an 18kt. gold chain, 52mm. diam. (Christie's) $1,320

A platinum openface split-second chronograph, signed Patek Philippe & Co., 47mm. diam. (Christie's) $6,050

An enamelled gold openface dress watch of Napoleonic interest, signed Movado, the 18kt. gold case with London import mark 1910, 47mm. diam. (Christie's) $3,080

WATCHES

A finely enamelled gold open-face dress watch, signed Vacheron & Constantin, 47mm. diam. (Christie's) $3,300

An 18kt. gold hunter-cased minute-repeating chrono-graph, signed Albert H. Potter & Co., Geneva, 52mm. diam. (Christie's) $10,450

Early 19th century gold verge watch with retrograde second hand , probably Swiss, 55mm. diam. (Christie's) $2,090

An 18kt. chased gold hunter-cased lever watch, signed Longines, with damascened nickel movement jewelled to the third wheel, 52mm. diam. (Christie's) $1,540

A gold openface medical chronograph, signed Ulysse Nardin, Locle & Geneve, 55mm. diam. (Christie's) $2,200

A gold openface lever watch, signed Jules Jurgensen, with-in a plain 18kt. gold case, 51mm. diam. (Christie's) $2,420

An 18kt. gold minute repeating keyless lever watch, the movement signed James Murray, London, 1882, 51mm. diam. (Phillips) $1,596

A silver pair cased verge stop watch, the movement with pierced cock signed Wm. Graham, London, No. 11437, the cases marked London, 1797. (Phillips) $352

A gold box hinge hunter-cased watch, by American Waltham Watch Co., within an engraved 14kt. gold box hinged case, 55mm. diam. (Christie's) $1,100

WATCHES

A gold openface fusee lever watch, signed J. R. Arnold, Chas. Frodsham, London, 1853, 55mm. diam. (Christie's) $1,210

An 18kt. gold openface dress watch, signed Patek Philippe & Co., with nickel 18-jewel movement and silvered dial, 45mm. diam. (Christie's) $825

A large gold openface lever watch, signed Chronometro Gondolo, by Patek Philippe & Cie, 56mm. diam. (Christie's) $1,760

A keyless gold openface minute-repeating watch with perpetual retrograde calendar, signed on the case Eugene Lecoultre, 54mm. diam. (Christie's) $9,900

An engraved gold openface lever watch, signed Lucien Dubois, Locle, 48mm. diam. (Christie's) $1,210

An 18kt. gold openface minute-repeating split-second chronograph with box and certificate, signed Jules Jurgensen, Copenhagen, 55mm. diam. (Christie's) $19,800

An engraved gold hunter-cased pocket chronometer, signed on the cuvette Constantaras Freres, Constantinople, 55mm. diam. (Christie's) $1,320

A Swiss silver Masonic keyless lever watch, the triangular case with mother-of-pearl dial, 60mm. high. (Phillips) $1,428

An openface floral enamel silver gilt centre seconds watch for the Chinese Market, signed Bovet, Fleurier, 55mm. diam. (Christie's) $3,300

WATCHES

Early 19th century silver openface clock watch, Swiss, the cuvette signed Breguet & Fils, the top plate signed Japy, 58mm. diam. (Christie's) $1,650

A gold openface lever watch, signed Paul Ditisheim, La Chaux-De-Fonds, 56mm. diam. (Christie's) $2,420

An 18th century gold and enamel pair cased watch, signed Geo. Phi. Strigel, London, 1770, 48mm. diam. (Phillips) $3,192

An 18kt. gold openface minute-repeating watch, signed Patek Philippe & Cie, 47mm. diam. (Christie's) $7,150

A verge watch, quarter-repeating on two visible bells, the gilt movement signed Georg Schmit, Neustadt, 56mm. diam. (Christie's) $2,200

An 18kt. gold openface quarter-repeating ruby cylinder watch, signed Ph. Fazy, dated 1816, probably Geneva, 52mm. diam. (Christie's) $935

A gilt metal and tortoiseshell pair cased quarter repeating verge watch made for the Turkish market, signed Geo. Prior, London, 62mm. diam. (Phillips) $1,344

A platinum dress watch with integral stand, retailed by Bucherer, Lucerne, 42mm. wide. (Christie's) $990

An enamelled gold convertible cased cylinder watch, signed J. FS. Bautte & Co., Geneve, with gilt cylinder movement jewelled to the third wheel, 36mm. diam. (Christie's) $2,860

A gold openface chronograph, Swiss, retailed by Tiffany & Co., New York, signed Tiffany, 53mm. diam. (Christie's) $990

A Swiss gold minute repeating grande sonnerie keyless lever clock watch, the cuvette signed for Breguet No. 4722, 57mm. diam. (Phillips) $38,640

A Swiss gold openface watch, signed with Patent No. 98234, the 18kt. gold case, London, 1925, 51mm. diam. (Christie's) $935

A small engraved gold pocket chronometer, signed.Couvoisier & Comp'e, Chaux-De-Fonds, 46mm. diam. (Christie's) $660

An 18kt. gold openface chronograph, signed Patek Philippe & Co., Geneve, with nickel 23-jewel movement, 48mm. diam. (Christie's) $3,300

A floral enamel silver gilt centre seconds watch for the Chinese Market, Swiss, mid 19th century, 57mm. diam. (Christie's) $3,300

A platinum openface dress watch, signed Patek Philippe & Co., Geneva, on movement and case, with original box and guarantee certificate, 44mm. diam. (Christie's) $2,640

A platinum openface dress watch, signed Patek Philippe & Co., Geneva, with nickel 18-jewel lever movement, 44mm. diam. (Christie's) $1,870

A 14kt. rose gold openface dress watch and chain, signed Vacheron & Constantin, Geneve, with 17-jewel nickel lever movement, 42mm. diam. (Christie's) $1,540

WATCHES

An 18kt. gold openface minute-repeating split-second chronograph, Swiss, retailed by Tiffany & Co., 54mm. diam. (Christie's) $6,600

Mid 19th century gold openface pivoted detent chronometer for the American market, Swiss, the dial signed William F. Ladd, 46mm. diam. (Christie's) $550

A gold openface free sprung fusee lever watch with winding indicator, signed Aldred & Son, Yarmouth, the 18kt. gold case, London, 1891, 53mm. diam. (Christie's) $1,320

A Continental silver pair cased verge watch, signed Blanc Pere & Fils, Geneve, the silver champleve dial signed P. B., London, 50mm. diam. (Phillips) $806

A gold openface Masonic watch, with nickel 19-jewel movement, signed Dudley Watch Co., Lancaster, Pa., 45mm. diam. (Christie's) $1,650

An enamelled gilt metal verge watch, signed Gregson A Paris, with white enamel dial, 53mm. diam. (Christie's) $935

A gold openface split second chronograph, signed C. H. Meylan, Brassus, 48mm. diam. (Christie's) $825

A platinum openface dress watch, signed Patek Philippe & Cie, Geneve, on movement and case, 44mm. diam. (Christie's) $1,760

An 18kt. gold openface dress watch, signed Patek Philippe & Co., Geneve, with nickel 18-jewel cal. 17-170 lever movement, 44mm. diam. (Christie's) $2,420

WRISTWATCHES

A stainless steel and gold self-winding wristwatch with center seconds, signed Rolex Oyster Perpetual. (Christie's) $1,320

A 14kt. gold curvex wristwatch, signed Gruen, with curved cushion shaped 17-jewel movement, (Christie's) $1,100

A 14kt. gold self-winding wristwatch with center seconds, signed Rolex Oyster Perpetual, with a 14kt. gold bracelet. (Christie's) $2,090

An 18kt. gold wristwatch, signed Patek Philippe & Co., retailed by Cartier. (Christie's) $3,850

A lady's stainless steel wristwatch with calendar, signed Patek Philippe & Co., Geneva, Nautilus model. (Christie's) $1,210

A gold self-winding wristwatch with center seconds, signed Omega Seamaster, the leather strap with 14kt. gold buckle. (Christie's) $330

An early waterproof wristwatch, signed Rolex, within a silver case hinged to outer protective silver case. (Christie's) $1,650

A 14kt. gold curvex wristwatch, signed Gruen Watch Co., with curved nickel 17-jewel movement. (Christie's) $2,200

A thin 18kt. gold wristwatch, signed Vacheron & Constantin, with nickel 17-jewel movement, the leather strap with 18kt. gold buckle. (Christie's) $1,430

WRISTWATCHES

A stainless steel self-winding wristwatch with center seconds, signed Rolex Oyster Perpetual, with steel bracelet. (Christie's) $462

An 18kt. gold self-winding wristwatch with perpetual calendar, signed Patek Philippe & Co. (Christie's) $13,750

A stainless steel self-winding wristwatch with center seconds, signed Rolex Oyster Perpetual. (Christie's) $825

An 18kt. white gold minute repeating wristwatch, signed Vacheron & Constantin, Geneva. (Christie's) $60,500

A gold wristwatch, signed Movado, with nickel 17 jewel movement, within a circular 14kt. gold case with unusual lugs. (Christie's) $935

A gold self-winding wristwatch with center seconds, signed Rolex Oyster Perpetual, the leather strap with 14kt. gold buckle. (Christie's) $1,980

A gold self-winding wristwatch, signed Patek Philippe & Co., within a signed 18kt. gold waterproof case. (Christie's) $2,640

An 18kt. gold wristwatch, retailed by Cartier, the movement signed Jaeger Lecoultre, with oblong duoplan nickel movement. (Christie's) $6,050

An 18kt. gold wristwatch, signed Vacheron & Constantin with nickel 17-jewel P 453/3B movement, signed on movement and case. (Christie's) $2,200

WRISTWATCHES

An 18kt. thin white gold wristwatch, signed Patek Philippe & Co., the nickel 18-jewel movement with Geneva Observatory seal. (Christie's) $1,980

An 18kt. white gold timezone wristwatch, signed Patek Philippe & Co., Geneva, with nickel 18-jewel cal. 27-HS 400 movement. (Christie's) $9,350

A platinum wristwatch, signed Audemars Piguet, on the movement and case, inscribed and dated 1926 in the interior. (Christie's) $6,600

An 18kt. gold self-winding wristwatch with center seconds, signed Rolex Oyster Perpetual, with gold bracelet. (Christie's) $1,430

An 18kt. rose gold world time wristwatch, signed Patek Philippe & Co., Geneva, with nickel movement jewelled through the center. (Christie's) $35,200

A stainless steel and gold self-winding wristwatch with center seconds, signed Rolex Oyster Perpetual. (Christie's) $528

A stainless steel wristwatch, signed Patek Philippe & Co., with shaped oblong 18-jewel nickel lever movement. (Christie's) $1,430

A stainless steel wrist chronograph, signed Longines, within a waterproof stainless steel case. (Christie's) $660

A gold wristwatch, signed International Watch Co., Schaffhausen, with leather strap with 14kt. gold buckle and a spare crystal. (Christie's) $1,650

WRISTWATCHES

An 18kt. gold bracelet watch, signed Vacheron & Constantin, on movement, case and bracelet. (Christie's) $2,420

A stainless steel self-winding wristwatch with center seconds, signed Rolex Oyster Perpetual, Submariner. (Christie's) $770

An enamelled gold wristwatch, retailed by Cartier, the movement signed European Watch & Clock Co. (Christie's) $9,900

A stainless steel self-winding wristwatch with center seconds, signed Rolex Oyster Perpetual, Explorer, with Oyster crown and steel bracelet. (Christie's) $462

A stainless steel chronograph, signed Longines, with lever movement. (Christie's) $220

An 18kt. gold self-winding wristwatch, signed Rolex Oyster Perpetual Day Date, with 18kt. gold bracelet. (Christie's) $3,300

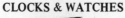

A steel duoplan wristwatch, signed Jaeger, with oblong nickel lever movement, the white dial signed Cartier. (Christie's) $1,980

A stainless steel and gold self-winding wristwatch with center seconds, signed Rolex Oyster Perpetual, with 14kt. gold and stainless steel bracelet. (Christie's) $1,980

A wristwatch, signed Rolex Prince, the 9kt. gold case bearing Glasgow import mark for 1930. (Christie's) $3,850

WRISTWATCHES

An 18kt. white gold and hard-stone skeletonized wristwatch, signed Chopard, Geneve, with original leather strap and 18kt. white gold buckle. (Christie's) $7,150

A platinum wristwatch, signed Patek Philippe & Co., Geneva, signed on movement and case. (Christie's) $7,150

A stainless steel wristwatch, signed Patek Philippe & Co., Geneve, with nickel 18-jewel movement. (Christie's) $1,320

A large silver and stainless steel aviator's hour angle watch, to the designs of Charles A. Lindbergh, by Longines. (Christie's) $7,700

A lady's 18kt. gold self-winding wristwatch, signed Rolex Perpetual Super Precision, signed on movement and case. (Christie's) $1,320

A gold self-winding wrist-watch with calendar, signed Universal, Geneva, within an 18kt. gold case. (Christie's) $605

A gold and stainless steel self-winding wristwatch with center seconds, signed Rolex Oyster Perpetual, with original guarantee certificate. (Christie's) $1,430

A gold and stainless steel wristwatch with calendar, signed Patek Philippe & Co., Geneva, Nautilus model with reeded black dial. (Christie's) $3,850

An 18kt. gold wristwatch with center seconds, signed Audemars Piguet, with nickel 20-jewel movement with gold train. (Christie's) $2,420

WRISTWATCHES

An 18kt. gold skeletonized wristwatch, signed Vacheron & Constantin, with signed 18kt. gold buckle to leather strap. (Christie's)
$4,950

An 18kt. gold shaped oblong wristwatch, signed Patek Philippe, signed on movement and case. (Christie's)
$4,950

A platinum wristwatch, signed Patek Philippe & Co., with nickel 18-jewel movement, signed on movement and case. (Christie's) $4,950

A steel wrist chronograph, signed Breguet, and another signed Henry K. Tournheim-Tourneau, without calendar. (Christie's) $1,760

An 18kt. gold wristwatch, signed Patek Philippe & Co., Geneva, with circular nickel movement jewelled to the center. (Christie's)
$3,080

A gold wristwatch with calendar, signed Movado, within a reeded 14kt. gold case, and a self-winding 14kt. gold wristwatch, signed Bulova. (Christie's)
$990

An 18kt. gold wristwatch, signed Patek Philippe & Co., with nickel 18-jewel lever movement. (Christie's)
$1,650

A stainless steel and gold self-winding center seconds wristwatch with calendar, signed Rolex Oyster Perpetual. (Christie's) $777

An 18kt. thin gold wrist-watch, signed Patek Philippe, with nickel 18-jewel cal. 10-200 movement. (Christie's)
$1,320

A pair of 19th century brass candlesticks, each with urn-turned drip-pan, 6¾in. high. (Christie's) $308

An Arthur Stone decorated copper bowl, Mass., circa 1910, stamped with Stone logo, 5¼in. diam. (Robt. W. Skinner Inc.) $5,040

One of a pair of George III brass and blacked steel basket grates, 40½in. wide, 34in. high. (Christie's) $17,930

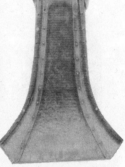

A late 19th century ship's brass plaque, enamelled with H.M.S. Centurion Comm[n] 1895-98, 14in. diam. (Christie's) $258

An Arts & Crafts hammered copper fireplace hood, circa 1910, 43in. high, 12½in. wide at top, 36in. wide at bottom. (Robt. W. Skinner Inc.) $900

A Victorian copper oval jelly mold, orb and scepter mark, 5.5in. high. (Woolley & Wallis) $140

Early 20th century hammered copper lamp base with mother-of-pearl mountings, 13in. high. (Robt. W. Skinner Inc.) $400

Early 20th century brass bottle bar with 'optic' taps, overall length 37in. (Christie's) $715

A brass electric bridge search-light with polished mirror reflector, 9in. diam., and two brass deck lamps and reflectors. (Christie's) $924

A late Victorian brass coal box with domed lid and pierced finial, 17in. wide. (Christie's) $551

A brass pen tray in the form of a roaring hippopotamus with hinged back, 12½in. wide. (Christie's) $5,808

A circular copper jelly mold with a swirl top, 5.5in. (Woolley & Wallis) $148

A copper and brass diver's helmet, date 8.29.41, with clamp screws, valves, plate glass windows and guards, 20in. high. (Christie's) $2,032

A copper and brass masthead lamp with spirit lamp and molded glass lens, 23½in. high, and another lamp labelled Toplight. (Christie's) $332

An enamelled hammered copper humidor, by R. Cauman, Boston, circa 1925, 6½in. high. (Robt. W. Skinner Inc.) $425

A pair of brass candlesticks, one with a caryatid shaft, the other with Atlantes shaft, 11in. high. (Christie's) $587

Four 19th century brass chambersticks, 9½in. and 4½in. high. (Robt. W. Skinner Inc.) $350

Pair of Federal brass andirons, probably Boston, circa 1810, 18in. high. (Robt. W. Skinner Inc.) $700

A fine pair of 20th century brass candlesticks, 8½in. high. (Robt. W. Skinner Inc.) $375

A hammered copper wine pitcher, no. 80, by the Stickley Bros., circa 1905, 15in. high. (Robt. W. Skinner Inc.) $150

Pair of knife blade andirons, America, circa 1780, 25½in. high. (Robt. W. Skinner Inc.) $800

A hammered brass umbrella stand, possibly Belgium circa 1900-20, 24in. high. (Robt. W. Skinner Inc.) $650

Pair of relief decorated copper plaques, signed by Raymond Averill Porter, 1912 and 1913, 10½ x 9½in. (Robt. W. Skinner Inc.) $600

One of a pair of brass candlesticks, each with cylindrical candlecup 7½in. high. (Christie's) $175

A bronze mounted copper diver's helmet, overall height 20in, maker's plate of 'Siebe Gorman & Co. Ltd., Submarine Engineers, London'. (Wallis & Wallis) $1,200

Pair of Georgian brass door stops, the molded bases with weighted iron insets, 13¾in. high. (Woolley & Wallis) $736

An Onondaga Metal Shop hammered copper and repousse wall plaque, circa 1905, 20in. diam. (Robt. W. Skinner Inc.) $5,500

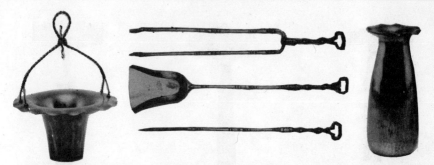

A Roycroft copper and brass wash handled basket, East Aurora, N.Y., circa 1920, 9in. diam. (Robt. W. Skinner Inc.) $100

A set of three George III brass fire-irons with shaped ring handles and baluster shafts, 24in. long. (Christie's) $1,960

A Karl Kipp copper vase, model no. 218, East Aurora, N.Y., circa 1919, 6½in. high. (Robt. W. Skinner Inc.) $275

A triangular hammered copper umbrella stand, with single panel of stylized poppies, circa 1900, 23in. high. (Robt. W. Skinner Inc.) $425

Set of brass postage scales and full set of weights. (McKenna's) $473

A hammered copper chamber-stick, by Gustav Stickley, circa 1913, 9¼in. high. (Robt. W. Skinner Inc.) $700

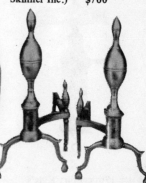

A pair of brass dome-base candle-sticks, each with ring-turned cylindrical candlecup, 9in. high. (Christie's) $715

A hammered copper jar with enamelled cover, Boston or Worcester, Mass., circa 1915, 4½in. diam. (Robt. W. Skinner Inc.) $400

A pair of Federal brass andirons and matching fire tools, New York, 1800-25, andirons 20in. high. (Christie's) $1,980

CORKSCREWS

A Dutch silver corkscrew by J. J. Koen of Amsterdam, 3¼in. high. (Christie's) $305

A Dutch silver and mother-of-pearl corkscrew, apparently unmarked, circa 1780, 3¼in. high. (Christie's) $825

A Dutch silver and mother-of-pearl corkscrew, circa 1800, maker's mark apparently DP with vase of flowers between, 3¼in. high. (Christie's) $1,100

A 19th century Dutch silver corkscrew, the platform handle with the cast figures of a man in 18th century dress and two rearing horses, 4in. high. (Christie's) $880

A Dutch silver corkscrew, by Josephius Servatius Anderlee, Amsterdam, 1785, 3½in. high. (Christie's) $770

A Dutch silver corkscrew, struck with date letter for 1908, 4in. high. (Christie's) $935

Early 19th century King's screw double action corkscrew, with turned bone handle and helical worm, nickel side handle. (Christie's) $462

A George III silver corkscrew, by Thos. Willmore, 1798, 3¾in. high, the second of silver and mother-of-pearl, late 18th century, 3¾in. high. (Christie's) $1,320

Hull's 'Royal Club' side lever corkscrew, with helical worm. (Christie's) $880

Early 19th century Thomason-type double action corkscrew with open frame, turned bone handle and helical worm. (Christie's) $528

Early 19th century Thomason-type double action corkscrew, with horn handle. (Christie's) $550

Early 19th century Thomason-type double action corkscrew, with turned bone handle and helical worm. (Christie's) $825

A Dutch silver and mother-of-pearl corkscrew, struck with indistinct maker's mark, circa 1780, 3.1/8in. high. (Christie's) $880

A Dutch silver corkscrew, by Johannes Van Geelen, Gouda, 1799, the handle cast in the form of a lion passant on a scroll base, 3¾in. high. (Christie's) $1,320

A Dutch silver corkscrew, by L. Olfers, Groningen, the handle cast as a galloping horse on a scroll base, 3¾in. high. (Christie's) $935

A George II silver combination corkscrew and nutmeg grater, apparently unmarked, circa 1750, 3½in. long. (Christie's) $1,540

Late 19th century silver 'lady's legs' folding corkscrew, probably American, marked Sterling, height closed 2in. high. (Christie's) $418

A 19th century Dutch silver corkscrew, the curled plat-form handle with the cast figure of a cow, 3½in. high. (Christie's) $605

A Dutch silver corkscrew, circa 1760, unmarked, 3½in. high. (Christie's) $520

Early 19th century Thomason-type double action corkscrew, with turned bone handle. (Christie's) $1,760

A Dutch silver corkscrew, struck with date letter for 1895, 4in. high. (Christie's) $880

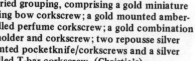

Two horn and two tusk-handled corkscrews, comprising a frame corkscrew; another with Williamson's type bell cap; an antler-handled example with grape-vine chased silver mount and another antler-handled example carved with a bulldog's face silver cap. (Christie's) $1,760

A varied grouping, comprising a gold miniature golding bow corkscrew; a gold mounted amber-handled perfume corkscrew; a gold combination keyholder and corkscrew; two repousse silver mounted pocketknife/corkscrews and a silver handled T-bar corkscrew. (Christie's) $2,200

An English gold roundlet corkscrew, by J. C. Vickery, London, 1912, 9kt., 3½in. long closed, gross weight 1oz. 5dwt. (Christie's) $495

A cast iron bar corkscrew, black painted with gold decoration, origin unknown. (Christie's) $1,100

A German 'folding lady' corkscrew, circa 1900, height closed 2.5/8in. (Christie's) $605

Late 18th century silver corkscrew by Cocks & Bettridge of Birmingham, 3in. high. (Christie's) $255

Early 19th century variant of Thomason's double action corkscrew with elliptical brass turning handle and helical worm. (Christie's) $1,540

A Dutch silver and mother-of-pearl corkscrew, apparently unmarked, circa 1775, 3in. high. (Christie's) $770

Nine, 19th/20th century, silver mounted corkscrews. (Christie's) $1,430

Three German 'lady's legs' folding corkscrews, the celluloid legs clothed in variously striped and colored stockings and high lace-up boots, average height 2¾in. (Christie's) $605

'Amor', a German figural folding corkscrew, formed as a Bakelite soldier and his lady, circa 1900, height closed 2¾in. (Christie's) $572

A rotary eclipse bar corkscrew, in brass, with steel helical worm and wood side handle. (Christie's) $770

Late 19th century American silver mounted and mother-of-pearl corkscrew, stamped Sterling, 4¼in. wide. (Christie's) $528

A late 18th century open robe of chine silk with linen lined bodice, the matching petticoat altered and accompanying stomacher. (Phillips) $6,048

An early 19th century Turkish coat woven with rows of florets in red, green and yellow silks on an ivory ground and trimmed with blue braid, lined. (Phillips) $75

An early 17th century purse of red silk with gold thread embroidery and having applied seed pearls, garnets and sequins, lined. (Phillips) $1,344

A late 18th century gentleman's waistcoat, the ivory silk fronts embroidered in pastel silk threads with sprays of spring flowers. (Phillips) $159

A pair of mid 19th century North American Eastern Woodlands Indian gloves of light brown leather, lined, probably Cree. (Phillips) $235

The Court dress of King Otto of the Hellenes, circa 1835. (Christie's) $14,437

A pair of mid 19th century ivory silk stockings, initialled 'AB' numbered 36, the instep decorated with an inset of Brussels needlepoint lace. (Phillips) $854

A 19th century Chinese robe of midnight-blue silk embroidered in colored silks. (Phillips) $486

A mid 18th century open robe of calimanco, the bodice part lined in linen and with front lacing. (Phillips) $504

A gown of red cotton printed overall with multi- colored cones, scrolls and floral motifs, circa 1870's. (Phillips) $504

An early 19th century Chinese robe of K'o-ssu woven mainly in green, blue and white silks and gold thread, lined. (Phillips) $1,980

A late 19th century bridal veil of tamboured net designed with flower sprays and sprigs, 2 x 2m. (Phillips) $320

An Indonesian shawl of cotton Ikat woven mainly in madder and indigo, 2.32 x 1.28m., Sumba. (Phillips) $259

A pair of late 19th century American Woodlands Indian gauntlets of brown leather, probably Cree. (Phillips) $672

A 19th century Chinese vest of midnight blue silk, embroidered in pekin knot and satin stitch, lined. (Phillips) $828

A deshabille of pale pink crepe de chine trimmed and inset with lace, circa 1900. (Christie's) $385

Two early 20th century Chinese summer gauze robes, one with dragon and cloud motif, the other with goldfish and seaweed motif. (Robt. W. Skinner Inc.) $525

An evening dress of ivory silk with yellow and black stripes, by Vincent Lachartroulle, 8 Rue Auber, Paris, circa 1900. (Christie's) $1,155

Early 20th century German bisque bathing belle with painted facial feature and auburn wig held in a net cap, 3in. high. (Lawrence Fine Art) $469

A composition shoulder headed doll, by Joel Ellis of the Cooperative Doll Co., 11in. high. (Christie's) $326

Early 20th century German bisque bathing belle, lying propped on her elbows and one leg raised, in original pink net costume. (Lawrence Fine Art) $509

A terracotta headed creche figure modelled as a Turk with moustache and pigtail, painted wooden hands and feet, 19in. high. (Christie's) $610

A pair of advertising dolls modelled as the 'Bisto Kids', designed by Will Owen, 11in. high, circa 1948. (Christie's) $386

A composition character headed doll modelled as Lord Kitchener, in original clothes with Sam Browne hat and puttees, 19in. high. (Christie's) $305

A German bisque head doll, marked 283/297, Max Handwerck, 24¾in. high. (Geering & Colyer) $468

A bisque headed doll's house doll modelled as a man with cloth body and bisque hands, 6in. high. (Christie's) $235

A German bisque head doll, marked Heubach-Koppelsdorf, 250-4, 25¾in. high. (Geering & Colyer) $468

Early 20th century German bisque bathing belle, resting on one hand, the other raised shielding her eyes, 3½in. high. (Lawrence Fine Art) $587

A composition mask faced googlie eyed doll, with smiling watermelon mouth, wearing spotted dress, 10½in. high. (Christie's) $610

A composition headed Motschmann type baby doll with dark inset eyes, painted curls and floating hands and feet, 8in. high, circa 1850. (Christie's) $689

A 'Chad Valley' boxed set of Snow White and the Seven Dwarfs in Original clothes, Snow White with painted pressed felt face, jointed velvet body, the blue velvet bodice with pale blue and pink slashed sleeves and short cape, 17in. high, the Dwarfs 9½in. high. (Christie's) $5,291

A composition mask faced googlie eyed doll, with smiling watermelon mouth, wearing pinafore and bonnet, 9in. high. (Christie's) $345

A French bisque headed doll with cork pate, the leather shoes impressed with a number 11, a bee and a Paris Depose, 25in. high. (Ambrose) $2,430

A Hebe bisque headed doll, marks indistinct, with open mouth and upper teeth, sleeping blue eyes and long fair plaited hair, 24in. high. (Lawrence Fine Art) $332

A painted head doll with blue eyes, the felt body in original, clothes, 16in. high, marked Lenci, circa 1930. (Christie's) $202

A painted cloth character doll with blue shaded eyes, ginger wool wig and jointed legs, 18in. high, with Deans Rag Book Co. Ltd. circa 1926. (Christie's) $330

A bisque headed character child doll, marked 231 DRMR 248 FANY A2/0M, 14in. high. (Christie's) $3,993

An 18th century group of Italian creche figures, six average height 9in., four average height 11½in., and two at 14½in. (Robt. W. Skinner Inc.) $3,700

A papier mache mask faced doll with turquoise blue eyes, the cloth and wood body in original Central European costume, 15½ in. high, circa 1860. (Christie's) $330

Two all bisque doll's house dolls with fixed blue eyes, blonde wigs and molded socks and shoes in original national costume, 4in. high. (Christie's) $183

A bisque headed child doll with fixed brown eyes and blonde wig, 10in. high, marked 1079 DEP S&H. (Christie's) $312

A bisque headed clockwork Bebe Premier Pas with kid upper legs and blonde wig, 17½in. high, by Jules Nicholas Steiner, circa 1890. (Christie's) $1,837

A painted wooden child doll the jointed wooden body (one foot missing) 17in. high, probably by Schilling. (Christie's) $330

A bisque headed child doll with closed mouth, fixed blue eyes, blonde wig and composition body, 7in. high, marked 16. (Christie's) $183

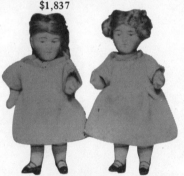

A pair of all bisque doll's house dolls with blue painted eyes, 5in. high, marked 1503 and 1603 on the legs, by Kestner, circa 1910. (Christie's) $238

A pair of all bisque doll's house dolls modelled as roguish girls, jointed at neck, shoulder and hip, 3½in. high. (Christie's) $762

One of two bisque headed doll's house dolls with blue sleeping eyes, one with brown wig, 5½in. high, one marked Halbig K*R 13. (Christie's) $477

An all bisque doll's house doll, marked 253 12 on the head and body, 5¼in. high, and an all bisque standing character boy, 3¼in. high. (Christie's) $163

A bisque figure of a seated fat baby, marked 95 and the Heubach square mark, stamped in green 68, 5in. high, together with two child dolls. (Christie's) $170

Heubach Koppelsdorf bisque headed doll, 20½in. high. (Hobbs & Chambers) $385

Bisque headed German doll marked 'Mignon', 22in. high. (Warren & Wignall Ltd.) $440

A Simon & Halbig bisque headed Jutta character doll, impressed 'Jutta 1914 12', circa 1920, 21in. high. (Hobbs & Chambers) $704

A bisque headed bebe with fixed blue yeux fibres and pierced ears, 15in. high, impressed 6 body stamped Jumeau Medaille d'or Paris. (Christie's) $1,928

A bisque figure of a seated naked woman with molded black bobbed hair, 3in. high. (Christie's) $163

A bisque headed character doll with closed mouth, blue painted eyes, blonde wig and jointed composition body, 18in. high, marked K*R 114.46. (Christie's) $4,041

Pedigree Coronation doll in original clothes, 14in. high. (Giles Haywood) $36

Set of six late 19th century all bisque dolls, German, mounted in candy box, inscribed on cover 'found in the nursery of a ruined old chateau — Verdun, France — 1917', 4in. high. (Robt. W. Skinner Inc.) $650

A bisque headed doll's house doll modelled as a man with full beard and hair, 6½in. high. (Christie's) $344

Charlotte Norris, a wax-over-composition headed doll with smiling mouth, the stuffed body with pink kid arms, 23in. high, 1840-45. (Christie's) $514

A bisque group of two googly-eyed figures in original hats, by William Goebel, 3½in. high. (Christie's) $508

A bisque headed doll jointed at neck, shoulder, thigh and knee, 7in. high, marked 199 2/0, also a doll's house doll, 5in. high. (Christie's) $275

A cloth character doll, the head in five sections, 16in. high, by Kathe Kruse, and The Katy Kruse dolly book, published 1927. (Christie's) $1,745

A pair of poured wax portrait dolls, modelled as Edward VII and Queen Alexandra, 21in. high, by Pierotti. (Christie's) $1,837

A bisque headed doll, impressed SFBJ 236 Paris 12, with composition toddler body, circa 1910, 24in. high. (Hobbs & Chambers) $960

A bisque headed doll's house doll modelled as a man, 6½in. high. (Christie's) $326

A bisque figure of a chubby baby, impressed No. 9902, 4½in. high, and a bisque figure of a baby playing with his toes, 5½in. long, impressed Gebrüder Heubach. (Christie's) $635

A bisque headed doll's house doll modelled as a man with a black-painted moustache and hair, 7in. high. (Christie's) $217

Mid 19th century Austro-Hungarian jewelled and enamelled silver gilt and metal theatrical axe and shield, Vienna, the axe 38½in. long, the shield 20in. diam. (Christie's) $44,000

A 19th century enamel box, in South Staffordshire style, 7¼in. long. (Christie's) $1,100

An 18th century German enamel box with French reeded silver mounts, 8cm. wide. (Phillips) $1,586

A 19th century Limoges polychrome enamel plaque, in the 16th century style, after Pierre Reymong, 7.1/8 x 5.1/8in. (Christie's) $990

A South German double-ended enamel snuff box of waisted form, circa 1740, 2.5/8in. high. (Christie's) $3,920

A German rectangular enamel snuff box painted in colors with battle scenes from the Seven Years' War, circa 1760, 3in. wide. (Christie's) $5,445

A George III enamel patch box, South Staffordshire, circa 1770, 1.5/8in. wide. (Christie's) $2,420

Mid 19th century Chinese enamelled filigree fan, 7½in. long, together with a small pierced ivory brise fan. (Christie's) $770

An Austrian enamelled Art Nouveau cigarette case, in the style of Alphonse Mucha, circa 1900. (Phillips) $1,137

A South Staffordshire George III enamel bonbonniere, circa 1770, 3in. long. (Christie's) $4,180

A George III enamel bottle ticket, Birmingham or South Staffordshire, circa 1770, 3in. long. (Christie's) $264

An Arts & Crafts period enamelled plaque depicting a galley, 14in. wide. (Christie's) $295

A 19th century French enamel plaque of Eve, signed L. Penet, in ebonized frame, 39 x 27cm. (Christie's) $2,388

A 19th century cloisonne vase decorated with birds and flowers, 21in. high, damaged. (Lots Road Chelsea Auction Galleries) $2,560

An Austrian enamelled cigarette case, the cover depicting a Caucasian warrior. (Phillips) $1,050

A South Staffordshire oval enamel patch box, transfer-printed and painted on the cover with Bristol Hot Wells, circa 1800, 1¾in. long. (Christie's) $544

Mid 19th century Limoges polychrome enamel triptych, in the Nazarene Style, 22.1/8in. high, 19.3/8in. wide when open. (Christie's) $1,980

An enamel wine funnel, South Staffordshire, circa 1770, 4¼in. long. (Christie's) $1,980

A late 18th century fan, the leaf an etching in brown of heraldic devices, with ivory sticks, 25cm. long. (Phillips) $518

A French fan with carved, pierced, painted and gilt ivory sticks decorated with mother-of-pearl, circa 1760, 28cm. long. (Phillips) $2,430

A Chinese fan of carved and pierced ivory, circa 1760, 25.5cm. long. (Phillips) $680

A fan with plain ivory sticks and 18kt. gold loop at pivot, the leaf of Brussels bobbin and needlepoint applique, circa 1890, 27cm. long. (Phillips) $680

A Chinese telescopic fan with black and gilt lacquer sticks, circa 1840, 26cm. long extended, in original box. (Phillips)
$615

A Chinese silver gilt filigree fan with mainly blue and green enamel decoration, circa 1830, 19.5cm. long. (Phillips) $907

A late 19th century fan with ivory sticks, the leaf of Brussels point de gaze, 35cm. long, in original box inscribed J. Duvelleroy, London. (Phillips) $684

A French fan, the ivory sticks decorated with chinoiserie, circa 1760, 28cm. long. (Phillips) $648

A French fan with gilded ivory sticks and ivory silk leaf painted with lovers at an altar, circa 1770, 28cm. long. (Phillips) $405

A gilded horn brise fan with pique work, painted with figures on a quay overlooking a bay, circa 1810, 16cm long. (Phillips) $324

A fan with carved, pierced, silvered and gilt mother-of-pearl sticks and the chicken-skin leaf painted and gilded, circa 1760, 30cm. long, probably German. (Phillips) $777

A Chinese fan with carved and pierced shaped sticks of tortoiseshell, mother-of-pearl, stained and unstained ivory and metal filigree with enamel decoration, circa 1840, 28cm. long, in box. (Phillips) $777

A Chinese cabriolet fan with black, pink, silver and gilt lacquer sticks, circa 1830, 28.5cm. long, in original box with label printed in Spanish. (Phillips) $1,053

A fan with carved, pierced, silvered and gilt mother-of-pearl sticks and an 18th century pastiche, signed Donzel, circa 1870, in a shaped, glazed case. (Phillips) $2,268

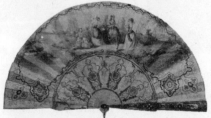

A 19th century painted fan, the guards inlaid with green enamel, porcelain plaques, semi-precious stones and pearls, probably French, 11¼in. long. (Christie's) $880

A French fan, the carved, pierced and painted ivory sticks decorated with red and green florets, circa 1760, 26cm. long, and a shaped case. (Phillips) $1,053

BEDS

A Gustav Stickley spindle-sided baby's crib, no. 919, circa 1907, 56½in. long. (Robt. W. Skinner Inc.) $1,400

Early 18th century Spanish or Venetian parcel gilt and polychrome hanging cradle of navette form, 49½in. wide. (Christie's) $3,674

Mission oak double bed with exposed tenons, circa 1907, 58½in. wide. (Robt. W. Skinner Inc.) $2,500

An Empire grain painted tall post bed, possibly Mahantango Valley, Penn., circa 1825, 51in. wide. (Robt. W. Skinner Inc.) $2,800

A German figured walnut single bedstead on turned tapering legs and bun feet, 74in. long, 34in. wide. (Christie's) $1,070

A four-poster bedstead decorated with leafage, six drawing curtains, 97in. high. (Lawrence Fine Art) $2,286

A mahogany four-poster bedstead, labelled Heal & Son, Makers of Bedsteads and Bedding, London W, 74in. wide, 92in. high. (Christie's) $5,808

Late 18th/early 19th century pine deception bedstead, Penn., in the form of a slant-front desk with four sham graduated long drawers, the back enclosing a hinged bedstead, 48in. high, 93in. long. (Christie's) $880

A Federal carved mahogany four-post tester bedstead, probably Mass., 1800-20, 66in. wide. (Christie's) $12,100

BEDS

A mahogany four-post bed with blind-fret carved canopy, hung with aquamarine watered silk, 54½in. wide, 97in. high. (Christie's) $6,582

An L. & J. G. Stickley slatted double-bed, signed with red (Handcraft) decal, 58in. wide. (Robt. W. Skinner Inc.) $10,000

A French Louis XV style walnut and carved bedstead, 48in. wide. (J. M. Welch & Son) $243

A Federal figured maple and ebonized high-post bedstead, Mass., 1810-20, 59in. wide. (Christie's) $1,430

An Empire mahogany and ormolu mounted Lit en Bateau with cushion and bolsters. (Phillips) $5,460

A Chippendale mahogany tall post bed, Goddard-Townsend School, Rhode Island, circa 1770, 54in. wide, 86in. high. (Robt. W. Skinner Inc.) $7,000

A 19th century Italian blue-painted and parcel gilt four-post double bedstead, 71in. wide, 103in. high. (Christie's) $1,996

A Federal carved and inlaid walnut field bedstead, New England, 1800-20, 57in. wide. (Christie's) $7,150

One of a pair of mahogany Mission oak beds, possibly Roycroft, circa 1912, 42in. wide. (Robt. W. Skinner Inc.) $650

BOOKCASES

A Gustav Stickley double-door bookcase, no. 719, circa 1912, 60in. wide. (Robt. W. Skinner Inc.) $3,600

A Gustav Stickley V-top bookrack, signed with red decal in a box, 1902-04, 31in. wide, 31in. high. (Robt. W. Skinner Inc.) $1,400

A Sidney Barnsley walnut bookcase on two stepped trestle ends, 106.8cm. wide. (Christie's) $11,781

A mahogany breakfront library bookcase with four astragal glazed doors enclosing adjustable shelves, 8ft.2in. wide. (Parsons, Welch & Cowell) $5,376

Victorian, American walnut bookcase, the top section with two glazed doors, 3ft. 9in. wide. (G. A. Key) $885

An L. & J. G. Stickley two-door bookcase, no. 654, circa 1910, 50in. wide. (Robt. W. Skinner Inc.) $3,000

A two-door bookcase, with mitred mullions, by Gustav Stickley, circa 1902-03, 35½in. wide. (Robt. W. Skinner Inc.)$6,000

A George III mahogany break-front bookcase with two pairs of geometrically glazed cup-board doors, 116in. wide. (Christie's) $34,485

A mahogany bookcase on plinth base, partly late 18th century, 60½in. wide. (Christie's) $12,705

BOOKCASES

A Regency mahogany dwarf bookcase on ormolu paw feet, 46in. wide. (Christie's) $14,767

George III mahogany breakfront bookcase having double-opening glazed doors, 7ft. wide. (Giles Haywood) $7,258

One of a pair of Regency brass inlaid mahogany dwarf bookcases, the sides with lion-mask and ring handles, 33½in. wide. (Christie's) $53,163

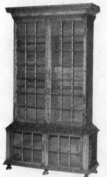

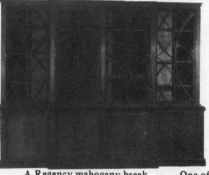

An oak book-press of the Pepys model, on bun feet, 57in. wide, 96½in. high. (Christie's) $7,009

A Regency mahogany breakfront bookcase with partly replaced molded cornice, 122in. wide. (Christie's) $16,736

One of a pair of Regency mahogany bookcases with ebony stringing and later scrolled broken pediments, 52¼in. wide. (Christie's) $21,780

A mahogany bookcase with three glazed cupboard doors and three panelled cupboard doors with plinth base, 83in. wide. (Christie's) $3,406

A Regency brass inlaid and mounted mahogany breakfront open bookcase with Gothic pierced galleried top, 94in. wide. (Christie's) $98,450

A mahogany bookcase with molded arcaded cornice above three glazed cupboard doors, 54½in. wide. (Christie's) $3,610

BOOKCASES

A Regency mahogany bookcase, double glazed doors with brass strip and trellis fronts. (Locke & England) $1,304

A Georgian carved mahogany breakfront library bookcase with four glazed astragal doors, 2.50m. wide. (Phillips) $31,160

A French inspired walnut bookcase, upper section with three velvet-lined shelves, 49in. wide. (Locke & England) $4,401

A Gustav Stickley two-door bookcase, no. 718, signed with large red decal, circa 1904-05, 54in. wide. (Robt. W. Skinner Inc.) $3,600

An Arts & Crafts oak bookcase, the cupboard doors with copper hinges, 101.3cm. wide. (Christie's) $613

A Regency rosewood dwarf bookcase with later rectangular verde antico marble top, 49in. wide. (Christie's) $1,353

L. & J. G. Stickley single door bookcase with keyed tenons, no. 641, circa 1906, 36in. wide. (Robt. W. Skinner Inc.) $2,400

A Regency mahogany bookcase in the Gothic style, 132¾in. wide. (Christie's) $20,619

An ormolu mounted tulipwood bibliotheque in the Transitional style, 30in. wide. (Christie's) $3,306

BOOKCASES

A mid Victorian walnut bookcase with three glazed and three panelled doors, 89in. wide. (Christie's) $7,260

An early George III mahogany breakfront bookcase with scrolling pediment, 85½in. wide. (Christie's) $124,740

A George IV mahogany bookcase with undulating cornice flanking a broken scrolled pediment, 66in. wide. (Christie's) $14,520

A Gustav Stickley two-door bookcase with keyed tenons, no. 716, 42½in. high. (Robt. W. Skinner Inc.) $2,500

A 19th century Continental breakfront heavily carved bookcase, 10ft. wide. (Giles Haywood) $4,202

A late Victorian walnut library bookcase, by Maple & Co., 183cm. wide. (Osmond Tricks) $1,650

A George III mahogany bookcase with a pair of geometrically glazed cupboard doors, 52in. wide. (Christie's) $12,342

A George III mahogany breakfront bookcase with two pairs of geometrically glazed doors, 82in. wide. (Christie's) $16,137

One of a pair of Regency simulated rosewood and parcel gilt bookcases, 71½in. wide, 111in. high. (Christie's) $133,650

BOOKCASES

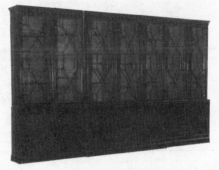

A Victorian mahogany glazed bookcase, 3ft.9in. wide. (Giles Haywood) $2,387

A mahogany breakfront bookcase, 182in. wide, 101in. high. (Christie's) $10,463

A Regency mahogany bookcase with waved top and sides, 36in. wide. (Christie's) $1,793

George IV mahogany breakfront library bookcase with four panel glazed, folding doors enclosing adjustable shelves, 113in. wide. (Prudential Fine Art) $6,930

A grain painted wall shelf with scalloped sides, New England, circa 1840, 25½in. wide. (Robt. W. Skinner Inc.) $1,600

An early 19th century mahogany breakfront library bookcase, 8ft.8in. wide. (Phillips) $9,828

An early 19th century figured mahogany bookcase, 158 x 208cm. high. (Wellington Salerooms) $7,728

A George III mahogany double breakfront library bookcase, 220in. wide. (Christie's) $17,930

Late 19th century satin walnut bookcase cupboard with two-door glazed and leaded upper section, 41in. wide.. (J. M. Welch & Son) $537

BUREAU BOOKCASES

A George III mahogany bureau bookcase, with four graduated drawers. (Phillips)
$3,280

A Chippendale mahogany desk and bookcase with four graduated long drawers, on ball-and-claw feet, 94in. high. (Christie's) $3,850

A George III satinwood secretaire cabinet of Sheraton style, the solid cylinder enclosing a fitted interior, 34½in. wide. (Christie's) $19,057

A Chippendale walnut desk and bookcase with four graduated long drawers, on ogee bracket feet, 85in. high. (Christie's) $5,500

A mahogany bureau bookcase, with fitted interior above four long drawers, 83in. high. (Lawrence Fine Art) $3,950

A George III mahogany and inlaid bureau bookcase with single astragal glazed door, 33in. wide. (Dacre, Son & Hartley) $3,772

A Georgian oak bureau bookcase, with two panel doors, bureau with fitted interior and four drawers, 81in. high. (Lawrence Fine Art) $3,118

A small Chippendale mahogany desk bookcase, Mass., circa 1780, 34in. wide. (Robt. W. Skinner Inc.) $14,000

A walnut veneered bureau bookcase, the drawers oak-lined. 31in. wide. (Woolley & Wallis) $3,240

BUREAU BOOKCASES

A William and Mary period walnut bureau bookcase, on bun feet, 3ft.6in. wide. (Jacobs & Hunt) $51,330

A walnut bureau cabinet with a pair of bevelled glazed cupboard doors enclosing a partly fitted interior with two candle slides, 39¼in. wide. (Christie's) $6,864

A mid Georgian red walnut bureau cabinet, the cupboard doors enclosing a partly fitted interior with candle slides, 41in. wide. (Christie's) $16,335

A tiger marked walnut veneered bureau cabinet, basically 18th century, 3ft.7½in. wide. (Woolley & Wallis) $6,480

A Chippendale mahogany desk and bookcase, possibly Charleston, S. Carolina, 1760-90, 53in. wide, 109in. high. (Christie's) $242,000

A Queen Anne walnut bureau cabinet with two arched later glazed cupboard doors enclosing shelves, 31in. wide. (Christie's) $47,256

A George III mahogany slope front bureau beneath a later but matching bookcase, 99cm. wide. (David Lay) $2,340

A William and Mary walnut bureau cabinet, the sloping flap enclosing a fitted interior, 42in. wide. (Christie's) $16,236

A William and Mary stained burr-elm bureau cabinet with molded double-domed cornice, on later turned oak feet, 43½in. wide. (Christie's) $49,225

BUREAU BOOKCASES

Late 18th century mahogany bureau bookcase with fitted interior, 84in. high, (some restoration). (Brown & Merry) $5,278

A George I walnut bureau cabinet with arched broken pediment, 40in. wide. (Christie's) $35,442

A late Victorian mahogany and inlaid bureau bookcase. (Hobbs Parker) $1,628

A Georgian mahogany, satin-wood crossbanded and inlaid bureau bookcase, 4ft. wide. (Phillips) $5,642

A George III mahogany bureau/cabinet in two parts, circa 1775, 7ft.6in. high, 4ft.4in. wide. (Ambrose) $6,120

A walnut bureau bookcase with molded cornice above a pair of glazed cupboard doors, 35¾in. wide. (Christie's) $14,602

A George I walnut bureau cabinet on bracket feet, 41½in. wide, 82in. high. (Christie's) $24,948

A George I walnut bureau bookcase with two candle slides, 3ft.4in. wide. (Prudential Fine Art) $9,020

A late 18th/early 19th century Dutch walnut and floral marquetry bureau cabinet in three parts, 1.39m. wide. (Phillips) $17,220

BUREAUX

A Chippendale mahogany
slant top desk, the fall-front
reveals a fitted interior, Mass.,
circa 1780, 40in. wide. (Robt.
W. Skinner Inc.)
$5,500

A Georgian mahogany
bureau. (Hobbs Parker)
$1,120

An oak bureau, the hinged
writing fall disclosing a fitted
interior, on bracket feet, 3ft.
wide. (Prudential Fine Art)
$1,377

An 18th century George II
mahogany fall-front bureau.
(Warren & Wignall Ltd.)
$1,000

A George III mahogany
bureau, the sloping lid
enclosing a fitted interior,
37in. wide. (Christie's)
$3,247

An early Georgian walnut
bureau, banded with elm,
the sloping flap enclosing a
fitted interior and well,
36½in. wide. (Christie's)
$9,735

An early Georgian walnut
bureau, the sloping flap
enclosing a fitted interior
including a well, 39½in. wide.
(Christie's) $9,345

A Chippendale mahogany
block-front slant top desk
with fitted interior, Salem,
Mass., 1760-90, 43½in. wide.
(Christie's) $22,000

A Georgian mahogany
bureau. (Hobbs Parker)
$2,000

BUREAUX

An 18th century oak bureau. (Hobbs Parker) $1,088

Georgian mahogany fall-front bureau with fitted interior. (Ball & Percival) $4,756

An Edwardian mahogany fall-front bureau with rose-wood crossbandings, 2ft.6in. wide. (G. A. Key) $460

An 18th century Colonial padoukwood bureau, 3ft. 1½in. wide. (Phillips) $6,916

A George III fruitwood bureau, the flap top opening to reveal serpentine interior, 96cm. wide. (Lacy Scott) $4,732

A laburnum bureau, the cross-banded sloping flap with fitted oak interior, the whole inlaid with a chevron pattern, 38in. wide. (Christie's) $5,907

A figured mahogany bureau on bracket feet with fitted interior. (Broader & Spencer) $2,268

A Chippendale tiger maple slant lid desk, the fall-front reveals a stepped interior, New England, circa 1780, 36in. wide. (Robt. W. Skinner Inc.) $4,500

A Chippendale mahogany slant lid serpentine desk, Mass., circa 1780, 41½in. wide. (Robt. W. Skinner Inc.) $7,500

BUREAUX

An early 18th century walnut, crossbanded and featherstrung bureau, the sloping fall enclosing a fitted interior, 87cm. wide. (Phillips) $4,100

A Chippendale maple slant top desk, the fall-front opening to reveal a fitted interior, circa 1790, 36in. wide. (Robt. W. Skinner Inc.) $1,600

A Chippendale birch reverse-serpentine front desk, Mass., 1765-85, 42½in. wide. (Christie's) $10,450

George I walnut feather crossbanded fall-front bureau with fitted interior, circa 1720, 30in. wide. (Giles Haywood) $8,200

A Chippendale mahogany slant-front desk with fitted interior, N.Y., 1760-90, 44¼in. wide. (Christie's) $4,400

A Chippendale walnut slant-front desk with fitted interior, Penn., 1760-80, 41in. wide. (Christie's) $3,300

A Federal inlaid mahogany cylinder-top desk with fitted interior, Baltimore, 1790-1810, 41in. wide. (Christie's) $14,300

A Chippendale carved figured maple slant front desk, Rhode Island, 1760-80, 38in. wide. (Christie's) $12,650

A Queen Anne walnut bureau, the crossbanded sloping flap enclosing a fitted interior, 36½in. wide. (Christie's) $18,040

BUREAUX

A George III mahogany bureau with sloping lid enclosing an interior of serpentine drawers and pigeonholes, 42¾in. wide. (Christie's) $3,608

A George III mahogany bureau, the sloping flap enclosing a fitted interior, 41in. wide. (Christie's) $2,164

A George I walnut bureau with crossbanded sloping flap enclosing a fitted interior, 34in. wide. (Christie's) $15,334

A George I walnut bureau inlaid with chequered lines, the slant lid enclosing a fitted interior, 41½in. wide. (Christie's) $20,493

Early 19th century walnut and herringbone banded bureau on bun feet, 40in. wide. (Prudential Fine Art) $6,156

An oyster-veneered laburnum bureau, the sloping lid enclosing a fitted interior with a well and central door, 31¾in. wide. (Christie's) $7,484

A George II burr-yewwood bureau, the sloping fall enclosing an oak fitted and graduated interior, 88cm. wide. (Phillips) $9,020

A Queen Anne maple desk on frame, the fall-front opens to interior of four drawers and valanced compartments, 24in. wide, circa 1760. (Robt. W. Skinner Inc.) $2,700

A Georgian mahogany bureau with four tapered drawers and octagonal brass handles, 36in. wide. (Jacobs & Hunt) $2,080

BUREAUX

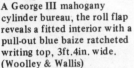

A George III mahogany cylinder bureau, the roll flap reveals a fitted interior with a pull-out blue baize ratcheted writing top, 3ft.4in. wide. (Woolley & Wallis) $11,550

An early Georgian burr-yew and burr-walnut bureau, the sloping flap enclosing a fitted interior, 39in. wide. (Christie's) $5,082

An Edwardian mahogany and marquetry inlaid cylinder front bureau with fitted interior, 32in. wide. (J. M. Welch & Son) $672

Late 19th century ormolu mounted marquetry and trellis parquetry bureau a cylindre with musical trophy, 44in. wide. (Reeds Rains) $5,010

A mid 19th century Danish oak bureau cabinet. (Miller & Co.) $2,640

A George I burr-walnut bureau with hinged flap enclosing a fitted interior, 41¾in. wide. (Christie's) $6,855

An inlaid pollard oak writing bureau with fitted interior, on bracket feet, 3ft. wide. (Ball & Percival) $4,136

A Chippendale walnut desk, the hinged lid with molded bookrest opening to a fitted interior, probably Virginia, 1760-80, 36in. wide. (Christie's) $6,050

A mid Georgian walnut bureau inlaid with boxwood lines, the sloping flap enclosing a fitted interior, 34¼in. wide. (Christie's) $6,897

CABINETS

One of a pair of 19th century Continental serpentine-fronted walnut inlaid and crossbanded side cabinets, 26in. wide. (Giles Haywood) $3,533

One of a pair of mid 19th century satinwood, seaweed marquetry and ebonised credenzas, 172cm. wide. (Wellington Salerooms) $13,440

Late 19th century lacquer cabinet formed in four sections, 216 x 135 x 44cm. (Christie's) $70,400

A Regency ebonised, parcel gilt and Chinese lacquer dwarf cabinet with bowed breakfront black and yellow marble top, 68½in. wide. (Christie's) $48,114

An Edwardian mahogany and marquetry inlaid side cabinet with carved and glazed door, 23in. wide. (J. M. Welch & Son) $364

A mid 19th century burr-walnut, kingwood crossbanded and satinwood inlaid side cabinet with bow-fronted central section, 69in. wide. (Dacre, Son & Hartley) $5,445

An Arts & Crafts oak cabinet with repousse hammered copper panels, circa 1900, 31¾in. wide. (Robt. W. Skinner Inc.) $1,000

Mid 19th century burr-walnut marquetry inlaid and crossbanaded credenza with ormolu mounts, 75in. wide. (J. M. Welch & Son) $2,542

A 19th century Oriental side cabinet with mother-of-pearl inlaid panels. (McKenna's) $1,092

CABINETS

A giltmetal mounted ebony and scarlet boulle side cabinet with later black-painted top, 50in. wide. (Christie's) $2,178

Late 17th century style oak and fruitwood panelled two-door cupboard, 48in. wide. (J. M. Welch & Son) $912

A 19th century French style ebony veneered side cabinet with cast gilt brass mounts, 4ft. wide. (Woolley & Wallis) $992

Burr-walnut, rosewood and marquetry gilt metal mounted breakfront side cabinet, 45¾in. wide. (Prudential Fine Art) $3,840

One of a pair of late 19th century ormolu mounted ebonized side cabinets, 28½in. wide. (Christie's) $4,537

A Regency parcel gilt and rosewood side cabinet with eared white marble top with concave sides, 38½in. wide. (Christie's) $19,602

Edwardian inlaid mahogany music cabinet with four drawers and open shelf. (Lots Road Chelsea Auction Galleries) $495

A late 17th/early 18th century japanned and decorated cabinet on carved and silvered stand, 1.18m. wide, 1.65m. high. (Phillips) $9,840

One of a pair of Japanese lacquer cabinets on stands, decorated in gilt on red and black, 19in. wide. (Parsons, Welch & Cowell) $1,377

CABINETS

Late 16th century Spanish walnut and red-painted cabinet with two frieze drawers, 48in. wide. (Christie's) $34,903

A Regency rosewood and parcel gilt dwarf cabinet with eared rectangular white marble top, 51in. wide. (Christie's) $14,256

One of two Regency brass inlaid and parcel gilt rosewood side cabinets with verde antico marble tops, one 37in. wide, the other 45in. wide. (Christie's) $19,602

A Regency ormolu mounted rosewood and ebonized side cabinet, 29in. wide. (Christie's) $37,411

A Chinese Export black lacquer cabinet-on-stand, mid 19th century, 41in. wide. (Christie's) $7,172

A 19th century French design mahogany breakfront side cabinet on bun turned feet, 3ft.10in. wide. (Woolley & Wallis) $3,300

A William IV parcel gilt painted and oak cabinet-on-stand, painted with the arms of the Duke of Westminster, 43in. wide. (Christie's) $15,262

A mid Victorian ormolu mounted ebony breakfront side cabinet, 85½in. wide. (Christie's) $7,623

A Flemish ivory inlaid ebony and tortoiseshell cabinet-on-stand, the cabinet 17th century, 40in. wide. (Christie's) $4,776

CABINETS

A Flemish walnut, tortoiseshell and ebonized cabinet-on-stand, 30¼in. wide. (Christie's) $2,571

A Regency rosewood side cabinet, the doors with panels of pleated red silk, 43in. wide. (Christie's) $3,427

Late 17th century Flemish ebony cabinet-on-stand with hinged top, the interior painted in the style of Keirincx, 30¾in. wide. (Christie's) $8,266

A figured walnut veneered cabinet-on-chest, the drawers with brass swanneck handles, 3ft.2in. wide. (Woolley & Wallis) $4,860

A Regency rosewood and parcel gilt side cabinet in the Southill manner, 59½in. wide. (Christie's) $44,550

A mid Victorian walnut marquetry side cabinet with shaped, foliate edged backplate, 29½in. wide. (Christie's) $1,837

A 19th century satinwood cabinet in the French style, crossbanded with kingwood, 2ft.9in. wide. (Warners Wm. H. Brown) $4,800

A 19th century serpentined boulle dwarf corner cabinet, brass inlaid into red tortoiseshell, 2ft.6in. wide. (Lots Road Chelsea Auction Galleries) $1,252

A mid Victorian tulipwood, ebony and marquetry side cabinet with later eared serpentine top, 44½in. wide. (Christie's) $3,490

CABINETS

A George III mahogany
cabinet-on-stand, the
panelled doors enclosing
seven various-sized drawers,
32in. wide. (Christie's)
$5,379

A Regency rosewood and
parcel gilt side cabinet,
42¾in. wide. (Christie's)
$26,730

A 19th century Spanish marquetry cabinet-on-stand, the
interior with twenty-two
various sized panelled doors,
49.1/8in. wide. (Christie's)
$6,980

One of a pair of mid Victorian
figured walnut and marquetry
side cabinets, 31½in. wide.
(Christie's) $3,267

A Regency mahogany and
ebony strung D-shaped
side cabinet with a reeded
edge, 1.45m. (Phillips)
$7,872

A side cabinet, the chromium
plated metal frame supporting
two walnut shelves, 125cm.
wide. (Christie's) $360

One of a pair of Regency
pollard oak side cabinets,
attributed to G. Bullock,
53½in. wide. (Christie's)
$392,040

One of a pair of George IV
mahogany side cabinets,
the doors filled with ormolu
trellis and pleated faded pale
green silk, 22in. wide.
(Christie's) $6,813

A Regency mahogany break-
front side cabinet with
molded top and three
panelled doors, 63in. wide.
(Christie's) $1,793

CANTERBURYS

A Regency mahogany canterbury with carrying handle and one division with spindle uprights, 18in. wide. (Christie's) $4,123

A Victorian carved mahogany canterbury. (Hobbs Parker) $841

A mahogany canterbury with concave rectangular top and three pierced divisions, 18½in. wide. (Christie's) $2,032

A 19th century mahogany canterbury on turned legs with brass castors, 1ft.9in. wide. (Hobbs & Chambers) $957

A 19th century canterbury with spiral turned uprights and shaped lower drawer, 22in. wide. (Lots Road Chelsea Auction Galleries) $512

A Victorian mahogany trolley with canterbury beneath, approx. 2ft. x 1ft.6in. (G. A. Key) $177

A rosewood canterbury with X-shaped divisions centered by roundels, 20in. wide. (Christie's) $2,868

An early Victorian mahogany canterbury on tapering legs. (David Lay) $805

A Regency mahogany canterbury with three divisions on spindle supports, 18¾in. wide. (Christie's) $1,984

CANTERBURYS

Mid 19th century figured walnut music canterbury with ebony inlay and one short drawer, 25in. wide. (Lalonde Fine Art) $528

Mid 19th century rosewood canterbury on china castors. (Brown & Merry) $1,092

A Victorian carved mahogany canterbury. (Hobbs Parker) $604

An early Victorian rosewood veneered canterbury on turned legs. (David Lay) $1,074

A 19th century walnut canterbury on barley-twist supports, 26in. wide. (Locke & England) $1,222

An early Victorian walnut canterbury of three divisions, 23½in. wide. (Locke & England) $978

A mahogany canterbury with ring turned uprights and slatted sides on tapering legs and brass feet, 17¾in. wide. (Christie's) $1,524

A Regency mahogany canterbury with four pierced divisions and a frieze drawer, 19in. wide. (Christie's) $2,868

A Regency mahogany canterbury with slatted divided top, the base with a drawer, 20½in. wide. (Christie's) $4,477

DINING CHAIRS

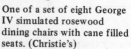

One of a set of eight George IV simulated rosewood dining chairs with cane filled seats. (Christie's) $8,068

Two of a set of five rosewood mahogany and marquetry inlaid occasional chairs, circa 1900. (J. M. Welch & Son) $1,271

One of a set of six mid Victorian rosewood shaped back standard chairs with drop-in seats. (Hetheringtons Nationwide) $1,840

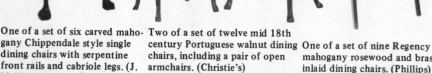

One of a set of six carved mahogany Chippendale style single dining chairs with serpentine front rails and cabriole legs. (J. M. Welch & Son) $1,107

Two of a set of twelve mid 18th century Portuguese walnut dining chairs, including a pair of open armchairs. (Christie's) $14,685

One of a set of nine Regency mahogany rosewood and brass inlaid dining chairs. (Phillips) $12,740

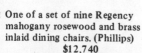

One of a set of twelve Regency mahogany dining chairs in the manner of Gillows. (Christie's) $33,858

Two of a set of six Federal painted fancy chairs, N.Y., 1800-15, 33¾in. high. (Christie's) $3,850

A rush-seated oak sidechair, by Joseph P. McHugh & Co., N.Y., circa 1900, 36in. high. (Robt. W. Skinner Inc.) $300

DINING CHAIRS

One of a pair of mid
Victorian oak hall chairs,
the arched back carved
with a crest and the date
1873. (Christie's)
$1,270

Two of a matching set of eight
Hepplewhite style dining chairs
with tapestry upholstered seats.
(J. M. Welch & Son)
$3,772

One of a set of six stencilled
green-painted side chairs,
probably New York, circa
1820, 33¼in. high.
(Christie's) $2,860

One of a set of six Queen
Anne cedar side chairs,
Bermuda, 1730-40, 41in.
high. (Christie's)
$28,600

One of a set of eight George
III mahogany dining chairs,
including a pair of open armchairs. (Christie's)
$38,665

Mid 18th century Chinese
carved padoukwood side
chair. (Phillips)
$10,920

A Chippendale cherrywood
side chair with a square slip
seat, Mass,, 1780-1800,
38in. high. (Christie's)
$715

Two of a set of eight William IV
mahogany dining chairs, the
Trafalgar seats covered in floral
needlework tapestry. (Capes
Dunn) $3,043

A Queen Anne maple side
chair with rush seat, 41in.
high. (Christie's)
$495

DINING CHAIRS

One of a pair of Chippendale period carved mahogany dining chairs with slip-in seats. (Phillips) $1,230

One of a set of twelve Regency simulated rosewood and parcel gilt dining chairs comprising six armchairs and six side chairs. (Christie's) $28,512

One of a set of six George III mahogany dining chairs with bowed padded seats. (Christie's) $7,530

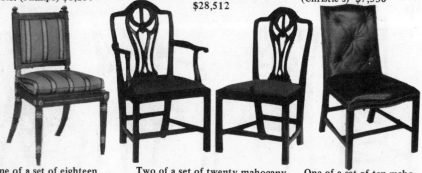

One of a set of eighteen Regency oak and parcel gilt dining chairs, attributed to George Bullock, 19in. wide, 34¾in. high. (Christie's) $142,560

Two of a set of twenty mahogany dining chairs of George III style, including two armchairs and five side chairs of late 18th century date, one labelled Coutts & Findlater Ltd., Sunderland. (Christie's) $13,530

One of a set of ten mahogany dining chairs of George III style including a pair of open armchairs. (Christie's) $10,463

One of a set of four Regency blue-painted and parcel gilt side chairs with cane-filled backs and seats with squabs. (Christie's) $2,359

Two of a set of six Sheraton design mahogany dining chairs including one carver. (Worsfolds) $3,198

One of a set of six Louis Philippe walnut dining chairs, each with cartouche-shaped back and bowed cane-filled seat. (Christie's) $1,194

DINING CHAIRS

A George III mahogany dining chair with padded seat on molded square legs. (Christie's) $681

Two of a set of six Regency mahogany dining chairs with drop-in seats, on sabre supports. (Prudential Fine Art) $4,428

One of a set of four mahogany dining chairs, each with a serpentine toprail. (Christie's) $18,150

One of a set of six Louis Philippe carved giltwood and gesso salon chairs in the manner of Fournier. (Phillips) $8,200

Two of a set of twelve Regency mahogany dining chairs in the style of Gillows. (Christie's) $30,294

One of a set of eight George III mahogany dining chairs, including one armchair, on square tapering legs. (Christie's) $6,096

One of a set of seven Regency mahogany dining chairs including an open armchair, with drop-in seats. (Christie's) $3,066

Two of a set of twelve George III carved mahogany dining chairs, including a pair of elbow chairs, in the Hepplewhite taste. (Phillips) $24,600

One of a set of seven mahogany dining chairs including one armchair of Regency style, early 19th century. (Christie's) $2,755

DINING CHAIRS

One of a set of eight mahogany dining chairs including a pair of open armchairs with pierced ladder-backs. (Christie's) $8,167

Two of a set of five Gustav Stickley dining chairs with rush seats, circa 1907, 37in. high. (Robt. W. Skinner Inc.) $1,700

One of a set of four 18th century mahogany dining chairs. (Warren & Wignall Ltd.) $1,200

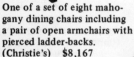
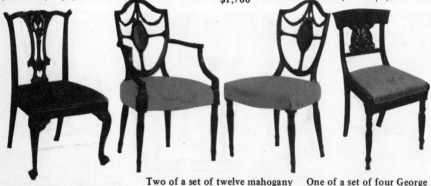

One of a set of four George III mahogany dining chairs including an open armchair. (Christie's) $8,712

Two of a set of twelve mahogany dining chairs, including a pair of open armchairs, the calico covered seats on turned fluted tapering legs. (Christie's) $10,527

One of a set of four George IV mahogany dining chairs with bowed tablet toprails and drop-in seats. (Christie's) $1,255

One of a set of ten George III mahogany dining chairs with tablet toprails and molded X-shaped splats. (Christie's) $8,553

Two of a set of seven late Georgian mahogany framed dining chairs, including two carvers. (Prudential Fine Art) $1,467

One of a set of ten Regency green-painted and parcel gilt dining chairs. (Christie's) $24,948

DINING CHAIRS

One of a set of eight mid
Georgian mahogany hall
chairs with cartouche-shaped
solid backs. (Christie's)
$10,692

Two of a set of six 20th century
Adirondack splint seat chairs,
one armchair and five sidechairs,
38in. high. (Robt. W. Skinner
Inc.) $475

One of a pair of George III
mahogany side chairs with
oval padded backs and
bowed seats. (Christie's)
$811

One of a set of ten Regency
ebonised dining chairs with
solid tablet toprails carved
with rosettes. (Christie's)
$7,260

One of a set of four George
III mahogany dining chairs
and a similar open armchair.
(Christie's) $3,968

One of a set of six George
III mahogany dining chairs
with pierced shield-shape
backs, bowed padded seats
and square tapering legs.
(Christie's) $4,356

One of a set of four Regency
brass inlaid simulated rosewood dining chairs with
drop-in and cane-filled seats.
(Christie's) $1,804

Two of a set of eight mahogany
inlaid chairs, Edwardian.
(Warren & Wignall Ltd.)
$3,040

One of a set of four Regency
brass mounted simulated
rosewood dining chairs on
sabre legs. (Christie's)
$1,443

EASY CHAIRS

One of a set of four mid 19th century giltwood fauteuils of Louis XVI style. (Christie's) $2,178

One of a pair of Regency mahogany wing armchairs, upholstered in hide. (Christie's) $7,260

A mid Victorian ebonized oak open armchair by J. Kendell & Co., the back and seat with squabs. (Christie's) $816

A George III mahogany wing armchair upholstered in pale blue repp. (Christie's) $3,406

A late Regency mahogany hall porter's chair with arched hooded back and seat covered in brown leather, 61½in. high. (Christie's) $4,303

A George III white and green-painted bergere with padded back, sides and seat covered in pale green cloth. (Christie's) $980

A mahogany armchair of George III style, the padded serpentine back, arms and seat upholstered in floral repp. (Christie's) $541

Late 19th century wing easy chair with reclining action. (Lots Road Chelsea Auction Galleries) $810

A walnut fauteuil, the cartouche-shaped back and bowed seat upholstered in gros and petit-point needlework. (Christie's) $1,775

One of a pair of George III parcel gilt and cream painted open armchairs with bowed seats. (Christie's) $5,379

A Louis XVI stained beechwood fauteuil with oval padded back and bowed seat covered in foliate repp. (Christie's) $1,194

One of a pair of Hepplewhite carved mahogany elbow chairs in the French taste with serpentine stuffover seats. (Phillips) $9,512

A Regency mahogany bergere chair with caned back and seat. (Woolley & Wallis) $1,101

An early Victorian oak open armchair attributed to A. W. N. Pugin, the back and seat upholstered in contemporary foliate cut velvet. (Christie's) $8,910

An early George III mahogany open armchair with padded back and seat upholstered in pink and brown cut velvet. (Christie's) $24,948

A George III giltwood open armchair arributed to Thos. Chippendale. (Christie's) $3,029

A George III mahogany library armchair, the padded back and seat covered in red leather. (Christie's) $8,606

One of a pair of giltwood fauteuils of Louis XVI style. (Christie's) $1,542

EASY CHAIRS

A Chippendale mahogany
easy chair, Penn., 1780-
1800, 47¾in. high.
(Christie's) $8,800

A Victorian walnut framed
sewing chair on cabriole
legs. (G. A. Key) $619

A Chippendale upholstered
wing chair, New England,
circa 1810, 45¾in. high.
(Robt. W. Skinner Inc.)
$1,800

A Federal inlaid mahogany
lolling chair with serpentine
front, possibly Portsmouth,
New Hampshire, 1800-10,
43in. high. (Christie's)
$11,000

Part of a late-19th century
suite of furniture of Louis XV
style, comprising a canape and
four fauteuils, labelled E. G.
Gaze Meubles Anciens Dorures,
Rue Charles V. No. 8 Paris, the
canape 86in. wide. (Christie's)
$14,520

A Federal mahogany lolling
chair, Mass., circa 1815,
44in. high. (Robt. W.
Skinner Inc.) $5,500

One of a pair of George II mahogany
side chairs upholstered in gros and
petitpoint needlework, the needlework early 18th century. (Christie's)
$44,550

One of a pair of upholstered
easy armchairs by Howard &
Sons. (Christie's)
$3,306

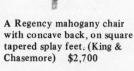

A Regency mahogany chair
with concave back, on square
tapered splay feet. (King &
Chasemore) $2,700

EASY CHAIRS

One of a pair of early Victorian rosewood open armchairs with cartouche-shaped buttoned padded backs and serpentine seats. (Christie's) $11,654

A Victorian carved walnut nuring chair, upholstered in velvet. (King & Chasemore) $468

A Country Federal child's mahogany wing chair, New England, circa 1770, 30¼in. high. (Robt. W. Skinner Inc.) $5,500

Mid 18th century walnut wing armchair with high arched back, outscrolled arms and squab cushion. (Christie's) $5,062

One of a pair of walnut bergeres upholstered in green velvet, on molded cabriole legs and scrolled toes. (Christie's) $1,633

A Queen Anne walnut easy chair on cabriole legs with pointed slipper feet, N.Y., 1735-55. (Christie's) $22,000

One of a set of three mahogany open armchairs of Louis XV style, upholstered in strawberry damask. (Christie's) $9,020

Victorian button-back armchair upholstered in champagne velvet dralon.) (County Group) $283

A gentleman's 19th century wing armchair upholstered in floral tapestry, on cabriole supports with claw and ball feet. (Greenslade & Co.) $516

EASY CHAIRS

One of a pair of giltwood fauteuils of Louis XVI style, upholstered in floral tapestry. (Christie's) $1,996

A wing armchair with shaped back on stretcher base. (Lots Road Chelsea Auction Galleries) $388

One of a set of six Louis XVI carved beechwood fauteuils en cabriolet with stuffover bowed seats. (Phillips) $15,580

A George III cream painted and parcel gilt open armchair with oval padded back and serpentine seat. (Christie's) $2,330

An early George III walnut wing armchair with padded back, bowed seat with a squab cushion. (Christie's) $12,474

One of a set of eight George III giltwood open armchairs with heart-shaped backs and serpentine seats. (Christie's) $44,550

One of a pair of George III mahogany library armchairs, the padded backs, arms and seats covered in close-nailed beige velvet. (Christie's) $9,801

Victorian spoon-back and buttoned chair in walnut frame, upholstered in green and gold cut-patterned velvet. (County Group) $442

A Louis XVI carved giltwood bergere with arched upholstered panel back and padded scroll arm supports with stuffover serpentine seat. (Phillips) $951

EASY CHAIRS

Mid 18th century giltwood fauteuil with padded cartouche-shaped back and serpentine feet. (Christie's) $918

One of a pair of mahogany open armchairs of George III design, covered in light cream damask. (Christie's) $5,808

A Louis XV giltwood fauteuil, the cartouche-shaped padded back and bowed seat covered in embroidered silk. (Christie's) $1,561

A Louis XV walnut fauteuil with cartouche-shaped back and bowed seat. (Christie's) $2,204

A mahogany framed tub-shaped low seat chair with stuffed overseat. (County Group) $83

A Louis XVI giltwood fauteuil with padded oval back and circular seat covered in green damask. (Christie's) $2,020

A Regency mahogany bergere with rectangular padded back, arm-rests and seat, the sides filled with split cane. (Christie's) $4,719

One of a matched pair of Louis XV fauteuils with cartouche-shaped padded backs and seats upholstered in salmon repp. (Christie's) $2,388

A Regency mahogany library armchair, the cane filled back and seat with red leather squab cushions. (Christie's) $3,406

ELBOW CHAIRS

One of a set of ten George III painted open armchairs, the padded and caned seats with pink and ivory striped silk squab cushions. (Christie's) $17,820

One of a pair of Regency mahogany open armchairs with blue brocade covered drop-in seats, (Christie's) $4,123

A Regency mahogany reading chair with horseshoe-shaped toprail and vertical bar splats. (Christie's) $3,207

One of a set of eight Regency mahogany dining chairs, including two elbow chairs, with stuffover seats. (Phillips) $7,872

Early 20th century wicker arm rocker, 31in. wide. (Robt. W. Skinner Inc.) $200

One of a pair of 19th century hardwood elbow chairs with marble inset panel splats and cane seats, (Phillips) $3,116

One of a set of twelve Spanish walnut open arm-chairs, seven upholstered in distressed gilt leather, five in cream cotton. (Christie's) $8,450

A Gustav Stickley spindle-sided cube chair, no. 391, circa 1907, 26in. wide. (Robt. W. Skinner Inc.) $16,000

One of a pair of Charles X gilt metal mounted mahogany side chairs with padded drop-in seats. (Christie's) $2,204

ELBOW CHAIRS

A Regency mahogany library armchair with cane-filled back and seat with yellow repp squab cushion. (Christie's) $1,533

A George II mahogany elbow chair on cabriole legs with trifid pad feet. (Phillips) $1,804

One of a pair of Regency blue-painted and parcel gilt armchairs with padded arm rests and seats, both stamped T. Gray. (Christie's) $19,057

A Chippendale carved mahogany elbow chair with slip-in gros point needlework seat and arm supports. (Phillips) $1,804

A Gustav Stickley bent arm spindle Morris chair, circa 1907, with spring cushion seat. (Robt. W. Skinner Inc.) $1,300

A Regency cream and parcel gilt open armchair with cane-filled seat and sabre legs. (Christie's) $902

One of a set of five Regency green-painted and parcel gilt open armchairs, the caned seats with yellow silk squab cushions. (Christie's) $23,166

A Gustav Stickley bird's-eye maple wide slat cube chair, circa 1903-04, no. 328. (Robt. W. Skinner Inc.) $3,000

A mahogany open armchair of George II style, with padded drop-in seat. (Christie's) $3,448

ELBOW CHAIRS

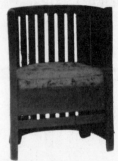

A Victorian woven canework rocking armchair. (Osmond Tricks) $198

A wicker patio chair designed by Terence Conran. (Christie's) $134

A Plail Bros. barrel-back armchair, Wayland, N.Y., circa 1910, 33in. high. (Robt. W. Skinner Inc.) $900

A George III carved mahogany elbow chair in the Hepplewhite taste with serpentine stuffover seat. (Phillips) $2,460

One of a pair of Venetian silver and brown-painted grotto chairs, each with a mussel shell-shaped back, dolphin arms and clam shell-shaped seat on carved base with pearls. (Christie's) $5,482

A Regency mahogany library bergere with cane back, sides and seat with cushions. (Phillips) $2,132

A Queen Anne mahogany armchair, Mass., circa 1750, 42in. high. (Robt. W. Skinner Inc.) $60,000

An adjustable back armchair, attributed to J. Young & Co., circa 1910, 31½in. wide. (Robt. W. Skinner Inc.) $800

A Chippendale maple corner chair, the square slip seat above a deep double-ogee-shaped skirt, 1760-80. (Christie's) $3,850

ELBOW CHAIRS

George IV mahogany elbow chair with carved back rail and center splat. (J. M. Welch & Son) $524

A leather upholstered dining armchair, by Gustav Stickley, circa 1910, no. 355A, 36¼in. high. (Robt. W. Skinner Inc.) $1,800

One of a set of eight well matched early 19th century Macclesfield dining chairs with rush seats. (Brown & Merry) $5,005

An oak and oak veneered armchair with scenic inlay, circa 1910, unsigned, 37in. high. (Robt. W. Skinner Inc.) $1,400

A mahogany Hepplewhite style chair with tapered legs and splayed feet. (Hetheringtons Nationwide) $480

George III oak corner chair with cabriole front leg and pad foot. (Brown & Merry) $1,055

A George II white-painted and parcel gilt open elbow chair in the manner of Thos. Chippendale. (Christie's) $1,452

Plail Bros. barrel-back rocker, with spring cushion seat, N.Y., circa 1910, 31½in. high. (Robt. W. Skinner Inc.) $325

One of a set of ten hand-carved mahogany chairs, the seats with brown leather style covers. (Lots Road Chelsea Auction Galleries) $1,452

ELBOW CHAIRS

One of a pair of Empire mahogany fauteuils with scrolled padded backs and bowed seats upholstered in green silk. (Christie's) $3,306

An L. & J. G. Stickley adjustable back flat armchair, no. 412, circa 1909, 35in. wide. (Robt. W. Skinner Inc.) $2,700

One of a set of eight George III mahogany dining chairs, including a pair of open armchairs. (Christie's) $7,216

One of a set of eight early Victorian rosewood open armchairs of George II style. (Christie's) $15,240

A Gustav Stickley slat-sided cube chair, no. 331, circa 1910, 25¼in. wide. (Robt. W. Skinner Inc.) $5,250

One of a pair of oak framed ecclesiastical chairs. (Lots Road Chelsea Auction Galleries) $501

A Regency ebonized bergere with deep curved toprail and upholstered back and seat covered in pale green leather. (Christie's) $13,365

A Gustav Stickley oak 'Eastwood' chair with original rope support for seat, circa 1902. (Robt. W. Skinner Inc.) $28,000

One of a set of twelve parcel gilt and black-painted open armchairs of Regency style with cane-filled backs and seats, redecorated. (Christie's) $25,256

ELBOW CHAIRS

A George III mahogany
open armchair, the padded
drop-in seat covered in
needlework. (Christie's)
$1,172

A late Louis XVI beechwood
fauteuil bureau with circular
caned seat, stamped I. B.
Lelarge. (Christie's)
$4,592

One of a pair of Spanish
walnut armchairs with
close-nailed rectangular
leather backs and seats.
(Christie's) $2,020

One of a pair of George III
mahogany open armchairs
with oval padded backs
and bowed seats upholstered
in green repp. (Christie's)
$11,583

One of a set of ten Regency
carved mahogany dining
chairs on sabre legs, including
two armchairs. (Phillips)
$5,904

One of a pair of Regency
mahogany armchairs, the
arms with turned supports
and padded seats. (Christie's)
$4,690

Late 18th century blue-
painted and parcel gilt
fauteuil, possibly Scandinavian. (Christie's)
$4,776

William IV mahogany
framed library armchair,
with leatherette cushions.
(Lots Road Chelsea Auction
Galleries) $567

A Regency mahogany arm-
chair with cane-filled back
and seat with red leather
squab cushion. (Christie's)
$1,262

CHESTS OF DRAWERS

An early Georgian walnut
and elm chest with two short
and three graduated long
drawers on later bun feet,
36½in. wide. (Christie's)
$1,262

A George II mahogany chest
with rectangular top and
brushing slide, 28½in. wide.
(Christie's) $8,068

An early Georgian burr-yew
chest with two short and
four graduated long drawers,
43in. wide. (Christie's)
$8,167

A Gustav Stickley chest-of-
drawers, no. 901, with
wooden pulls, circa 1907,
37in. wide. (Robt. W.
Skinner Inc.) $1,300

A George III mahogany
chest with molded
rectangular top, on
bracket feet, 38in. wide.
(Christie's) $1,996

A Chippendale curly maple
chest-of-drawers, probably
New Hampshire, 1775-1810,
39in. wide. (Christie's)
$6,600

A Charles II oak chest-of-
drawers with oyster walnut
veneered front, 3ft.3in.
wide. (Woolley & Wallis)
$2,268

A George I walnut chest with
crossbanded and quartered
chamfered top, 35in. wide.
(Christie's) $5,737

A Regency mahogany bow-
fronted chest, the top crossbanded with satinwood, 36in.
wide. (Christie's)
$4,329

CHESTS OF DRAWERS

A George III Cuban mahogany chest, the drawers oak lined, 32in. wide. (Woolley & Wallis) $1,536

A Country Federal maple painted four-drawer chest, possibly Maine, circa 1800, 38¾in. wide. (Robt. W. Skinner Inc.) $3,700

A George III mahogany chest with crossbanded molded serpentine top, 39in. wide. (Christie's) $10,463

A Chippendale poplar blanket chest, New England, circa 1780, 37¾in. wide. (Robt. W. Skinner Inc.) $950

An early 18th century walnut veneered crossbanded and featherstrung chest, fitted with a slide, 81cm. (Phillips) $5,904

A Chippendale curly maple five-drawer chest, New England, circa 1780, 37¼in. wide. (Robt. W. Skinner Inc.) $1,000

A George III mahogany chest with serpentine top and leather-lined dressing slide, 37in. wide. (Christie's) $9,922

A Gustav Stickley nine-drawer tall chest, no. 913, circa 1907, 36in. wide, 50in. high. (Robt. W. Skinner Inc.) $4,000

A Federal mahogany and mahogany veneer bowfront bureau, possibly Penn., circa 1815, 41½in. wide. (Robt. W. Skinner Inc.) $850

CHESTS-OF-DRAWERS

George II mahogany chest with brushing slide above two short and three graduated long drawers, 36½in. wide. (Reeds Rains) $2,087

A Chippendale mahogany chest-of-drawers, Penn., circa 1780, 38in. wide. (Robt. W. Skinner Inc.) $3,500

A mahogany bowfront chest-of-drawers with ivory inset escutcheons. (Broader & Spencer) $1,263

A Country Chippendale tiger maple blanket chest, New England, circa 1760, 37¾in. wide. (Robt. W. Skinner Inc.) $9,500

A Queen Anne painted maple tall chest on a tall bracket base, New England, circa 1750, 36in. wide. (Robt. W. Skinner Inc.) $6,500

A Chippendale tiger maple tall chest on bracket feet, replaced brasses, New England, circa 1790, 38½in. wide. (Robt. W. Skinner Inc.) $5,500

A grain painted pine five-drawer chest, New England, circa 1780, 37¾in. wide. (Robt. W. Skinner Inc.) $6,000

A Chippendale cherry and pine four-drawer bureau on ogee bracket feet, Conn., circa 1780, 39½in. wide. (Robt. W. Skinner Inc.) $4,250

A Queen Anne painted pine two-drawer blanket box, the lift-lid above three false drawers and two working drawers, probably Mass., circa 1750, 38¾in. wide. (Robt. W. Skinner Inc.) $2,400

CHESTS-OF-DRAWERS

A George III mahogany bow-front chest with four long graduated drawers, on French bracket feet, 3ft.1in. wide. (Lalonde Fine Art) $858

Early 19th century mahogany chest-of-drawers, having oval burr walnut inset with rosewood crossbanding, 3ft.5in. wide. (Lawrences) $1,428

Early 19th century oak square fronted chest of four long graduated drawers, 32in. wide. (J. M. Welch & Son) $470

A George III mahogany chest of two short over three long graduated drawers on shaped bracket feet, 36in. wide. (Hy. Duke & Son) $1,116

A George II mahogany chest crossbanded with rosewood, 37in. wide. (Christie's) $8,606

A 19th century mahogany square-front chest of three graduated drawers, 21in. wide. (J. M. Welch & Son) $520

An early 18th century mahogany chest of four long graduated drawers. (Hobbs Parker) $2,608

A Chippendale maple tall chest-of-drawers with original pulls, circa 1780, 36in. wide. (Robt. W. Skinner Inc.) $6,500

A small Georgian mahogany chest of four long drawers. (Hobbs Parker) $1,897

CHESTS-ON-CHESTS

An early 18th century walnut chest on chest, three short and three long boxwood strung drawers with three graduated drawers, 102cm. (Phillips) $5,576

A George I walnut tallboy, fitted with three short and six long drawers, original brass handles, on bracket feet, 74in. high. (Dreweatt Neate) $12,852

A George I burr-walnut secretaire tallboy crossbanded and inlaid with chevron bands, 42¼in. wide. (Christie's) $29,535

A mahogany veneered tallboy chest on bracket feet, 3ft.7in. wide. (Woolley & Wallis) $2,430

The John Mills family Chippendale cherrywood chest-on-chest, by Major Dunlap, New Hampshire, circa 1780, 41½in. wide. (Christie's) $66,000

A Queen Anne maple chest-on-chest, in two sections, New Hampshire, 1740-70, 41in. wide. (Christie's) $14,300

A George III mahogany tallboy with two short and six graduated long drawers, 40in. wide. (Christie's) $7,876

A mahogany bowfront chest-on-chest on splay feet, 3ft.6in. wide. (Lots Road Chelsea Auction Galleries) $2,720

An early 18th century walnut chest on chest, three short and seven long drawers, on bracket feet, 194 x 106cm. (Phillips) $4,900

CHESTS-ON-CHESTS

George I figured walnut tallboy, in two sections, 3ft.6in. wide. (Prudential Fine Art) $6,560

A George II walnut chest-on-chest, molded cornice and three short drawers, over six long drawers, 69¾in. high. (Robt. W. Skinner Inc.) $6,750

A George I walnut tallboy on bracket feet, 42in. wide, 69in. high. (Christie's) $11,048

A Chippendale maple chest-on-chest, Mass., circa 1780, 38in. wide. (Robt. W. Skinner Inc.) $8,750

A George I walnut tallboy chest, with three short and six long drawers, on shaped bracket feet, 5ft.9in. x 3ft.8in. (Phillips) $10,850

A George I walnut tallboy with molded cavetto cornice, 43in. wide. (Christie's) $12,705

An early George III carved mahogany tallboy chest on bracket feet, 1.14m. wide. (Phillips) $5,248

Early 18th century walnut chest on bracket feet, 28in. wide. (Chancellors Hollingsworths) $2,755

A George III mahogany chest-on-chest with two short and six long drawers. (Chancellors Hollingsworths) $2,004

CHESTS-ON-STANDS

Black lacquer bowfront chest with chinoiserie decoration, 2ft. wide. (Warners Wm. H. Brown) $960

Spanish Colonial painted chest-on-stand, Mexican/New Mexican, 38in. wide. (Robt. W. Skinner Inc.) $1,800

A walnut chest-on-stand with brass escutcheons and handles, 98cm. wide. (Dee & Atkinson) $2,025

A William and Mary walnut chest on later stand, crossbanded and herringbone inlaid with walnut and rosewood, 102cm. wide. (Lacy Scott) $2,275

An Ernest Gimson walnut bureau cabinet on stand, circa 1906, 99.5cm. wide. (Christie's) $16,830

William and Mary design walnut veneered chest-on-stand, the drawers with brass drop handles. (Worsfolds) $1,280

An early 19th century Chinese Export dark green and gilt lacquer coffer-on-stand, 31½in. wide. (Christie's) $2,330

A Queen Anne carved maple high chest-of-drawers, in two sections, New England, 1750-60, 39in. wide. (Christie's) $20,900

An early George III mahogany chest-on-stand, the sides with carrying handles, 30¾in. wide. (Christie's) $9,075

CHESTS-ON-STANDS

A Queen Anne cherry high-
boy on four cabriole legs,
Conn., circa 1770, 37¼in.
wide. (Robt. W. Skinner Inc.)
$11,500

A Queen Anne walnut chest-
on-stand, the drawers fitted
with pierced brass handles,
40in. wide. (Chancellors
Hollingsworths)
$2,754

Mid 19th century North
Italian ebony and ivory inlaid
cabinet-on-stand, 58¼in. wide.
(Christie's) $27,412

A Queen Anne curly maple
bonnet top highboy, New
England, circa 1770, 36¾in.
wide. (Robt. W. Skinner
Inc.) $3,500

A walnut chest-on-stand
with molded quartered top,
basically early 18th century,
40in. wide. (Christie's)
$2,345

A walnut and mulberry inlaid
chest-on-stand, circa 1770.
(McKenna's) $13,650

Late 17th century oak chest-
on-stand with four long
graduated drawers with brass
furniture, 3ft.2in. wide.
(Hobbs & Chambers)
$1,750

An early Georgian figured
and pollard oak chest-on-
stand, 43in. wide. (Christie's)
$7,398

A William and Mary oyster-
veneered walnut marquetry
cabinet-on-stand, 51in. wide.
(Christie's) $19,602

CHIFFONIERS

Victorian mahogany chiffonier with serpentine front, 41in. wide. (County Group) $183

A Regency mahogany chiffonier inlaid with ebonized lines, 26¾in. wide. (Christie's) $5,231

A Regency brown-painted chiffonier, decorated with yellow lines, 34¼in. wide. (Christie's) $2,689

Early Victorian figured mahogany chiffonier with raised and carved back, 36in. wide. (J. M. Welch & Son) $590

A Regency mahogany chiffonier the top surface crossbanded with rosewood, 33in. wide. (Lacy Scott) $1,732

A late Regency rosewood chiffonier, the recessed panelled doors filled with gilt trellis and backed with green watered silk, 40in. wide. (Christie's) $2,178

A Regency mahogany dwarf chiffonier on short square section tapering legs, 67cm. wide, 150cm. high. (David Lay) $3,150

One of a pair of Regency rosewood chiffoniers with brass galleries and mirrored doors, 47in. wide. (Worsfolds) $6,552

A Victorian mahogany and ebony banded chiffonier with galleried and mirrored upper section, 48in. wide. (J. M. Welch & Son) $759

COMMODES & POT CUPBOARDS

One of a pair of painted bedside tables with concave-fronted rectangular tops, 22¼in. wide. (Christie's) $7,128

A Louis XVI mahogany and brass mounted oval pot cupboard with marble top and dummy drawer door, 1ft6½in. high. (Phillips) $2,625

A mahogany bowfronted bedside cupboard with three-quarter galleried top, stamped Gillows, Lancaster, 15¾in. wide. (Christie's) $1,548

One of a pair of late 18th/early 19th century Italian walnut bedside commodes, 16¼in. wide. (Christie's) $5,482

A set of Regency mahogany bedside steps with three red leather-lined treads, the top hinged, the middle sliding, previously fitted with a commode, 20½in. wide. (Christie's) $1,645

One of a pair of French mid 19th century mahogany bedside cabinets, 20¾in. wide. (Christie's) $2,937

George III inlaid feathered mahogany commode fitted with two dummy drawers and cupboard under, 23in. wide. (Lalonde Fine Art) $363

A Georgian mahogany tray-top commode cupboard, 31in. high, 22in. square. (J. M. Welch & Son) $330

Early 19th century Shaker pine commode with hinged slant lid opening to reveal a shelf interior, 18in. wide. (Robt. W. Skinner Inc.) $4,500

COMMODE CHESTS

A South Italian walnut and
marquetry commode with
four graduated long drawers,
73in. wide. (Christie's)
$5,143

A George III painted
commode, the top with
concave sides, 47¾in. wide.
(Christie's) $23,166

Early 18th century German
gilt metal mounted kingwood
commode, 46in. wide.
(Christie's) $6,429

A George III ormolu mounted
black and gold lacquer commode with serpentine top,
36in. wide. (Christie's)
$33,473

A gilt metal mounted mar-
quetry commode, the waved
crossbanded quartered top
inlaid with a songbird amid a
cornucopia of flowers, 31½in.
wide. (Christie's) $1,745

Hepplewhite style commode
in flame figured mahogany
framed in burr-walnut
with boxwood and ebony
stringing, 3ft. wide. (Capes
Dunn) $1,074

A French provincial oak
commode with serpentine
top and three long drawers,
51½in. wide. (Christie's)
$5,143

A serpentine fronted three-
drawer walnut commode of
early Georgian design, 3ft.6in.
wide. (Lots Road Chelsea
Auction Galleries)
$15,200

A George III mahogany
commode with chamfered
serpentine top, the top
drawer fitted with a leather-
lined slide, 38in. wide.
(Christie's) $11,420

COMMODE CHESTS

A Regency kingwood commode, the brass bound bowfronted top crossbanded with strapwork, 46½in. wide. (Christie's) $7,348

A George III satinwood commode banded with mahogany, the four doors with rosewood banded oval centers, 54in. wide. (Christie's) $24,948

Mid 18th century Dutch kingwood and tulipwood commode, 53in. wide. (Christie's) $4,592

Late 18th century North Italian walnut and parquetry commode, 50½in. wide. (Christie's) $6,265

Mid 18th century fruitwood commode with mottled later marble slab, probably German, 32½in. wide. (Christie's) $1,928

One of a pair of early George III mahogany serpentine commodes, in the style of Thos. Chippendale, 51¼in. wide. (Christie's) $196,020

Mid 18th century Swedish ormolu mounted kingwood bombe commode by C. G. Wilkom, 42½in. wide. (Christie's) $7,715

Late 18th century Italian neoclassic inlaid walnut commode, 53in. wide. (Christie's) $7,150

A mahogany commode with eared serpentine rectangular top and two short and three long graduated drawers, 51in. wide. (Christie's) $29,535

CORNER CUPBOARDS

A Federal poplar corner
cupboard, with glazed door
opening to three shelves,
1800-20, 41½in. wide.
(Christie's) $1,870

One of a pair of directoire
fruitwood corner cabinets
with mottled black marble
tops, 30½in. wide.
(Christie's) $2,755

A mahogany corner cupboard
with glazed door enclosing
two shelves. (Worsfolds)
$1,920

George III mahogany bow-
fronted corner wall cup-
board, 27½in. wide.
(Prudential Fine Art)
$1,458

A Federal pine and poplar
corner cupboard, in two
sections, 1800-20, 53in.
wide. (Christie's)
$4,400

Georgian bowfronted oak
and crossbanded two-door
hanging corner cupboard,
37in. high, 28in. wide.
(J. M. Welch & Son)
$590

Early 20th century Sheraton
design standing corner cabinet,
3ft.6in. wide. (Lalonde Fine
Art) $1,320

A Chippendale red-painted
corner cupboard, on ogee
bracket feet, 88in. high.
(Christie's) $3,300

A painted and decorated
Mahantongo Valley corner
cupboard, Penn., circa 1825,
50in. wide. (Robt. W. Skinner
Inc.) $15,000

CORNER CUPBOARDS

A satinwood standing corner cupboard, the panelled doors painted in the classical style of Kauffman, 80cm. wide, 196cm. high. (David Lay) $1,440

An 18th century black lacquered two-door hanging corner cupboard, 21in. wide. (G. A. Key) $511

A painted pine Federal corner cupboard, America or England, circa 1800, 49in. wide. (Robt. W. Skinner Inc.) $3,000

Late Georgian mahogany bowfronted corner cabinet inlaid with boxwood lines, 2ft.6in. wide. (Lots Road Chelsea Auction Galleries) $972

A mahogany bowfronted corner display cabinet, 22in. wide. (Giles Haywood) $561

A 19th century pine hanging corner cupboard, the door with rat-tailed hinges, 49in. high, 40in. wide. (Christie's) $2,090

A Federal cherry corner cupboard, possibly Penn., circa 1820, 50in. wide. (Robt. W. Skinner Inc.) $2,200

One of a pair of 18th century South German walnut corner cabinets with bowed panel doors, 42in. wide. (Christie's) $4,283

A Federal pine corner cupboard, New England, mid-19th century, with molded cornice, 90in. high. (Christie's) $3,520

CUPBOARDS

A George II mahogany cabinet with a pair of arched doors, 50in. wide. (Christie's) $235,386

A poplar hanging cupboard, Ephrata, Penn., 1743-60, 18½in. wide, 24½in. high. (Christie's) $990

Early 17th century German oak cupboard fitted with four panelled doors, 51¼in. wide. (Christie's) $5,511

A Federal blue-painted cupboard with two glazed doors, possibly N. Jersey, 1775-1810, 50in. wide. (Christie's) $7,150

An 18th century Chippendale pine step-back cupboard in two sections, Penn., 73½in. wide. (Christie's) $13,200

A painted pine stepback cupboard, Virginia, circa 1840, 38in. wide. (Robt. W. Skinner Inc.) $2,000

A Country poplar cupboard, red-brown grain painted to simulate mahogany, Penn., circa 1825, 55in. wide. (Robt. W. Skinner Inc.) $6,000

A 17th century oak spice cupboard fitted with twenty-three drawers. (Lawrence Butler & Co.) $4,100

A Country Federal pine stepback cupboard, circa 1800, 50in. wide. (Robt. W. Skinner Inc.) $800

CUPBOARDS

A painted and grained pine Empire cupboard, New England, circa 1830, 18¼in. deep. (Robt. W. Skinner Inc.) $900

Mid/late 18th century Chippendale poplar hanging cupboard, Penn., 36½in. high, 27in. wide. (Christie's) $1,045

An 18th century carved pine buffet, Canada, 58in. wide. (Robt. W. Skinner Inc.) $1,000

Federal pine cupboard, possibly Penn., circa 1820, 42½in. wide. (Robt. W. Skinner Inc.) $2,400

A 17th century Flemish carved oak side cupboard, 4ft.4in. wide. (Phillips) $3,822

A Shaker painted pine and poplar cupboard, possibly N.Y., circa 1830, 28in. wide, 86¾in. high. (Robt. W. Skinner Inc.) $3,500

Early 19th century sponge-decorated step-back cupboard in two sections, Penn.; 56in. wide. (Christie's) $12,650

Chinese objets d'art display cabinet, circa 1890-1900. (Locke & England) $7,172

A Country Federal cupboard, Penn., circa 1820, 48in. wide, 86½in. high. (Robt. W. Skinner Inc.) $1,200

DAVENPORTS

George IV mahogany davenport, the sliding top section with three-quarter pierced brass gallery, 20in. wide. (Christie's) $2,990

Victorian burr-walnut harlequin davenport with sliding desk top internally lined with satinwood, 24in. wide. (Giles Haywood) $1,435

A George IV rosewood davenport with sliding top and lined writing surface, 22in. (Christie's) $2,153

A Regency mahogany davenport, writing slope enclosing two short drawers and pen drawer, and with pull out writing slide and four drawers, 50cm. wide. (Phillips) $4,592

A Wheeler & Wilson type S. Davis & Co. walnut 'Davenport' treadle sewing machine, serial no. 21535, 96cm. high, 63cm. wide, circa 1870. (Phillips) $2,080

A mid Victorian amboyna and ebony davenport, the cupboard doors enclosing a fitted interior, 22in. wide. (Christie's) $1,452

A Victorian rosewood davenport, with fitted side cupboard enclosing four trays and pull-out hinged drawer, 26in. wide. (Lalonde Fine Art) $1,188

Mid Victorian figured walnut davenport with serpentine front and raised stationery box with hinged lid, 21in. wide. (Lalonde Fine Art) $1,650

A Victorian burr walnut davenport, inlaid with marquetry and geometric boxwood lines, 23¼in. (Christie's) $4,525

DAVENPORTS

A late Victorian rosewood davenport, inlaid with ivory marquetry and geometric lines. (Christie's)$1,821

An early Victorian calamander davenport with pierced scrolling three-quarter gallery and leather-lined sloping top, 21in. wide. (Christie's) $2,178

A Victorian walnut davenport. (Hobbs Parker) $1,191

A mid Victorian ebony and amboyna davenport with sloping lid and tambour, 23½in. wide. (Christie's) $1,561

A Regency mahogany and ebony banded davenport, the fall-front writing section with brass galleried rail, 16½in. wide. (J. M. Welch & Son) $9,900

A Regency burr-yew davenport with pierced gothic brass gallery and leather-lined sloping top, 20¼in. wide. (Christie's) $3,066

A George IV mahogany davenport by Gillows of Lancaster, with gilt metal three-quarter gallery and red leather-lined sloping flap, 20¼in. wide. (Christie's) $8,140

A William IV burr-yew davenport with three-quarter spindle gallery and green leather-lined sloping flap, 20½in. wide. (Christie's) $11,228

An early Victorian walnut davenport with three-quarter gallery, sloping flap enclosing a fitted interior, stamped Johnstone & Jeanes, London 11544, 23¼in. wide. (Christie's) $3,308

DISPLAY CABINETS

A Dutch mahogany and marquetry display cabinet on square tapering legs and bun feet, 41in. wide. (Christie's) $4,776

A mid Victorian ormolu mounted and walnut side cabinet, 62in. wide. (Christie's) $2,571

An 18th/19th century Dutch oak display cabinet with bombe base, 7ft. wide. (Prudential Fine Art) $4,785

A Limbert single door china cabinet, no. 1347, Grand Rapids, Michigan, circa 1907, 34¼in. wide. (Robt. W. Skinner Inc.) $1,900

A Dutch marquetry display cabinet with molded arched cornice, a glazed door and sides enclosing scalloped shelves, 34¾in. wide. (Christie's) $1,762

A satinwood display cabinet with crossbanded, herringbone and line inlay in various woods, 3ft.4in. wide. (Warners Wm. H. Brown) $3,120

One of a pair of mid 19th century brass mounted and kingwood side cabinets, 42½in. wide. (Christie's) $2,904

Edwardian carved mahogany display cabinet with demilune display shelf, 30in. wide. (Giles Haywood) $1,196

Mission oak two-door china closet, no. 2017, circa 1910, 46½in. wide. (Robt. W. Skinner Inc.) $350

DISPLAY CABINETS

Sheraton Revival mahogany glazed china cabinet, 3ft. wide. (G. A. Key)
$726

A brass mounted ebonized vitrine cabinet with simulated green marble top, 48in. wide. (Christie's)
$816

An Edwardian mahogany china cabinet on tapering rectangular legs with spade feet, 3ft. wide. (G. A. Key)
$654

One of a pair of black and gold lacquer display cabinets of drum-shape, 30in. wide, 63½in. high. (Christie's) $2,886

An early Victorian display cabinet on cabriole legs with eagle's claw and ball feet, 64in. wide. (Christie's)
$5,737

One of a pair of William IV rosewood display cabinets, 25½in. wide. (Christie's)
$12,342

A William IV faded rosewood glazed display cabinet with mirrored and shelved superstructure, 30in. wide. (J. M. Welch & Son) $2,805

A mahogany display cabinet in the Arts & Crafts style, 53in. wide. (Prudential Fine Art) $777

American Dutch-style bombe-fronted walnut and oak glazed display cabinet, 6ft. wide, 7ft. 6in. high. (Giles Haywood)
$1,640

DRESSERS

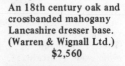

A mid Georgian oak dresser, the waved frieze with three drawers on square tapering legs, 78½in. wide. (Christie's) $3,427

An 18th century oak and crossbanded mahogany Lancashire dresser base. (Warren & Wignall Ltd.) $2,560

A George III oak and fruit-wood dresser on ogee bracket feet, 64½in. wide, 77in. high. (Christie's) $21,384

An 18th century oak dresser with two shelves, the base with four drawers, on turned supports, 63in. wide, 76in. high. (Lacy Scott) $3,960

An early 18th century brown oak dresser with wavy frieze. (John Hogbin & Son) $5,330

A painted pine step-back cupboard, the top section with two open shelves, possibly Canada, circa 1800, 59¾in. wide. (Robt. W. Skinner Inc.) $4,750

An 18th century oak dresser with three brass handled drawers, 185cm. wide. (Dee & Atkinson) $3,645

An oak enclosed dresser base fitted with two drawers and two panelled cupboards, 56in. wide. (J. M. Welch & Son) $577

A George III oak dresser fitted with three drawers and shaped apron, 73in. wide. (J. M. Welch & Son) $3,444

DRESSERS

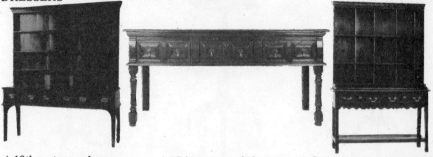

A 19th century mahogany
crossbanded oak dresser with
raised plate rack, 5ft.9in. wide.
(Lalonde Fine Art)$1,085

A 17th century oak dresser
base on turned legs, 68in.
wide. (Parsons, Welch &
Cowell) $4,200

A Georgian oak and elm dresser
with plate rack, 4ft.2in. wide.
(Lots Road Chelsea Auction
Galleries) $2,821

An 18th century oak dresser,
150cm. wide, 200cm. high.
(David Lay) $4,654

Late 18th century George III
oak dresser, 8ft. wide, 6ft.6in.
high. (Ambrose) $2,970

An early 18th century oak
dresser, the delft rack with
molded top and shelves,
65in. wide. (Dacre, Son &
Hartley) $11,550

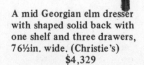

An 18th century and later
oak dresser on bracket feet,
57½in. wide. (Christie's)
$5,097

A mid Georgian elm dresser
with shaped solid back with
one shelf and three drawers,
76½in. wide. (Christie's)
$4,329

A late George III fruitwood
dresser and shelves, 54in.
wide. (Hy. Duke & Son)
$3,780

DUMB WAITERS

A mid Georgian mahogany dumb-waiter with three graduating tiers, 43½in. high. (Christie's) $3,448

A Regency mahogany two-tier dumb-waiter on arched tapering tripartite base, 38in. high. (Christie's) $2,151

Three-tier mahogany circular dumb-waiter, designed in the Georgian Chippendale mold. (G. A. Key) $825

One of a pair of Georgian mahogany dumb waiters, each with three graduated tiers, 19 x 23½in. in diam. (Prudential Fine Art) $7,955

A Sheraton period two tier mahogany dumb waiter, the two tiers with hinged flaps, 37in. high. (Prudential Fine Art) $1,387

A mid 19th century mahogany circular three tier dumb waiter, with three molded swept feet. (Peter Wilson) $1,852

An early George III mahogany three-tier dumb waiter, the graduated trays revolving on turned waisted spiral cut stems, 24in. diam. (Woolley & Wallis) $2,475

A George III style mahogany dumb-waiter with triple rimmed circular molded tiers, 46in. high. (Christie's) $968

A George III mahogany three-tier folding dumb waiter with sabre legs and brass castors, 177 x 71cm. (Phillips) $1,680

KNEEHOLE DESKS

A Regency mahogany partner's desk with rounded rectangular leather-lined top, 67in. wide. (Christie's) $4,356

An early John Makepeace, Andaman padouk and leather-covered desk, by M. Doughty, D. Pearson and A. Freeman, 199cm. wide, and a chair. (Christie's) $3,247

A mahogany kneehole desk with leather-lined top and nine drawers, 53in. wide. (Christie's) $1,804

A William III walnut and featherstrung kneehole bureau on later bun feet. (Phillips) $13,940

A George I walnut, crossbanded and featherstrung kneehole desk, on bracket feet, 76cm. wide. (Phillips) $6,560

A mid Georgian walnut kneehole desk on bracket feet, 34in. wide. (Christie's) $2,722

George I walnut feather crossbanded kneehole desk, circa 1720, 32in. wide. (Giles Haywood) $8,610

A Victorian figured walnut kneehole writing desk with brass gallery, 4ft.6in. wide. (Prudential Fine Art) $3,444

A Regency mahogany pedestal desk with leather-lined top, 62in. wide. (Christie's) $3,227

KNEEHOLE DESKS

A small Regency mahogany partner's desk with leather-lined top, 54in. wide. (Christie's) $3,267

A desk, the top suspended on tubular steel U-shaped supports, with cantilever chair, desk 164.4cm. wide. (Christie's) $1,262

A William IV walnut pedestal desk with serpentine leather-lined top and two frieze drawers, 63½in. wide. (Christie's) $12,117

A Regency rosewood partner's desk with knob handles and original William IV locks. (James Norwich Auctions)$17,136

A French Art Deco beechwood writing desk on trestle ends, 105.4cm. wide. (Christie's) $992

A Cotswold School oak kneehole desk and armchair, desk 152cm. wide. (Christie's) $631

An early Gustav Stickley flat-top, kneehole desk, circa 1902-03, 54in. wide. (Robt. W. Skinner Inc.) $1,400

A mahogany veneered writing desk, designed by Frank L. Wright, produced by Heritage-Henredon Furniture Co., circa 1955, 52in. wide. (Robt. W. Skinner Inc.)$1,100

KNEEHOLE DESKS

An early Victorian oak and burr-walnut partner's desk of Gothic style, 84in. wide. (Christie's) $7,260

A mid Victorian bird's-eye maple ebonized partner's desk, 75in. wide. (Christie's) $11,726

A partner's mahogany desk with inset leather writing surface, circa 1900, 84 x 60in. (J. M. Welch & Son) $5,376

A shaped front oak pedestal desk with tooled leather top and nine drawers below, circa 1900, 48in. wide. (J. M. Welch & Son) $852

Satin walnut pedestal desk with nine drawers, circa 1900, 36in. wide. (J. M. Welch & Son) $742

An oak 'Shannon' roll-top pedestal desk with fitted interior and ten drawers below, 53½in. wide, circa 1900. (J. M. Welch & Son) $951

A partner's mahogany desk on plinth base with carrying handles, 61½in. wide. (Christie's) $6,897

A Chippendale-design mahogany pedestal desk with scale-carved border and blind-fret decoration to drawer fronts, 4ft. wide. (Prudential Fine Art) $4,200

KNEEHOLE DESKS

A George III mahogany pedestal desk with leather-lined top, fitted with three frieze drawers, 44in. wide. (Christie's) $16,038

A George II ormolu mounted mahogany and parcel gilt kneehole desk attributed to John Boson, 55¾in. wide. (Christie's) $240,570

A Louis XIV boulle and rosewood bureau mazarin, the top inlaid in pewter with scrolling foliage and strapwork, 45in. wide. (Christie's) $11,940

An early Georgian walnut kneehole coffer with leather-lined top, 35in. wide. (Christie's) $4,633

A Regency mahogany cylinder desk with stencilled label 'A. Ardley & Son Office Fitters, 11 Great St, 27 Wormwood Street', 46in. wide. (Christie's) $4,329

A George II red walnut kneehole desk with narrow folding leather-lined top, 37in. wide. (Christie's) $4,811

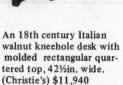

A George I walnut kneehole desk with crossbanded top, 49½in. wide. (Christie's) $42,768

An early Victorian burr-yew kneehole desk, 48in. wide. (Christie's) $3,448

An 18th century Italian walnut kneehole desk with molded rectangular quartered top, 42½in. wide. (Christie's) $11,940

LOWBOYS

An early Georgian oak low boy with mahogany crossbandings, with one frieze drawer above two short drawers, 33in. high. (Lawrence Fine Art) $2,910

A walnut side table with three drawers on cabriole legs and pad-feet, 30½in. wide. (Christie's) $2,402

A George II walnut lowboy fitted with three drawers with original handles, on cabriole legs, 35¾in x 20¼in. (Dreweatt Neate) $10,584

A Dutch oak lowboy, fitted with two short and one long drawer , on cabriole legs, 28½in., part 18th century. (Christie's) $1,265

An 18th century rectangular mahogany lowboy, the three cockbeaded drawers with brass bail handles, 32in. wide. (Parsons, Welch & Cowell) $5,880

A mid Georgian mahogany side table on cabriole legs and pad feet, 29¼in. wide. (Christie's) $1,460

A walnut lowboy with two short and one long drawer on cabriole legs and pad feet, 28½in. wide. (Christie's) $3,066

An 18th century oak lowboy with drawers, shaped frieze, cabriole legs and pad feet, 2ft6in. wide. (Phillips) $1,215

A George I walnut lowboy, the quartered top crossbanded in ash, with three drawers, brass handles, shaped apron on cabriole legs, 29in x 18in. (Dreweatt Neate) $7,182

SCREENS

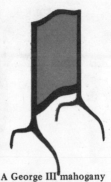

A scarlet and gold lacquer six-leaf screen decorated in black and gilt, each leaf 21¾in. wide, 97in. high. (Christie's) $26,730

A George III mahogany fire-screen with arched glazed sliding panel, 19¼in. wide. (Christie's) $466

An inlaid oak three-panelled screen, designed by Harvey Ellis for Gustav Stickley, circa 1903-04, 66¾in. high, each panel 20in. wide. (Robt. W. Skinner Inc.) $18,000

A four-leaf screen covered in Brussels verdure tapestry, the tapestry 17th century, each leaf 84½ x 25½in. (Christie's) $11,022

Regency carved giltwood ornate three-fold fire-screen, upper section with ten mirrored glass panels, 3ft.6in. wide. (Giles Haywood) $902

A mid 18th century firescreen panel worked in tent stitch with mainly red and blue wools and ivory silk, 61 x 45cm. (Phillips) $1,344

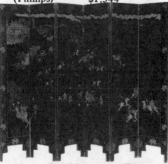

A Regency painted three-leaf screen, decorated with panels of chinoiserie landscapes with courtly figures, each panel 63½ x 24½in. (Christie's) $13,365

An early Victorian rosewood fire-screen with glazed panel, 29in. wide. (Christie's) $573

An early 19th century Chinese coromandel lacquer six-leaf screen, each leaf 80½ x 17½in. (Christie's) $3,267

SCREENS

An early Gustav Stickley leather fire-screen, 1902, 35in. high, 31in. wide. (Robt. W. Skinner Inc.) $2,000

An early George III walnut polescreen, the adjustable panel with gros and petit-point needlework, 51in. high. (Christie's) $3,741

Early 19th century Chinese five-leaf black and gold lacquer screen, each leaf 83½ x 21½in. (Christie's) $8,068

A painted leather three-leaf screen, decorated overall with an English rustic scene, 36 x 48in. (Christie's) $726

Parcel gilt and gesso pole screen on tripod base with silk embroidered panel, 53in. high. (Worsfolds) $574

A late Victorian scrapwork four-leaf screen with colored figures and scenes, each leaf 66½ x 22¼in. (Christie's) $1,452

A Dutch leather four-leaf screen painted with exotic birds, shrubs and vases of flowers and fruit on a gilt ground, the leather 18th century, each leaf 20 x 74¾in. (Christie's) $2,722

A Regency mahogany fire-screen with sliding panel and pilaster uprights, 25in. high. (Christie's) $448

A late Victorian ebonized, parcel gilt and scrapwork three-leaf screen, each leaf 70 x 23¾in. (Christie's) $2,541

SCREENS

A 19th century two-leaf screen depicting a scene with Europeans watching dancers and musicians on stage, each panel approx. 60 x 83cm. (Christie's) $3,553

A mid Georgian mahogany polescreen with needlework panel, 54½in. high. (Christie's) $896

An 18th century Chinese scarlet and gilt lacquer eight-leaf screen, each leaf 85½ x 21¾in. (Christie's) $18,826

A wood and copper phone screen, circa 1910, 12in. high, 13in. wide. (Robt. W. Skinner Inc.) $125

A mid-Victorian rosewood cheval firescreen, the panel with a petit-point vase of flowers and fruit, on scrolled legs carved with foliage, 25¾in. wide, 46½in. high. (Christie's) $827

A wrought-iron and pierced copper fire-screen, circa 1900, 34½in. wide. (Robt. W. Skinner Inc.) $300

A 19th century Chinese lacquer and hardstone eight-leaf screen, each panel 91 x 21¾in. (Christie's) $17,451

A mahogany polescreen with petit-point floral panel on a dark brown ground, on claw feet, 23in. wide. (Christie's) $617

A 19th century six-leaf screen depicting pine groves in Kano style, each panel approx. 152 x 61cm. (Christie's) $3,553

SECRETAIRES

George III Provincial oak and crossbanded mahogany secretaire cabinet on bracket feet, 3ft.6in. wide. (Hobbs & Chambers) $2,187

A Federal mahogany veneered inlaid secretary/desk, Mass., circa 1800, 38in. wide. (Robt. W. Skinner Inc.) $2,750

A George II period red walnut secretaire tallboy chest on ogee bracket feet, 3ft.8½in. wide. (Geering & Colyer) $3,150

A French style mahogany marquetry inlaid escritoire having brass gallery over fall-front enclosing fitted interior, 2ft.7in. wide. (Lawrences) $3,731

Early 19th century faded mahogany veneered secretaire with fitted interior, 31in. wide. (Woolley & Wallis) $1,360

A Queen Anne figured walnut secretaire on later bun feet, 43¼in. wide, 66¾in. high. (Christie's) $26,730

An inlaid oak secretary, designed by Harvey Ellis for Gustav Stickley, circa 1903-04, 42in. wide. (Robt. W. Skinner Inc.) $93,000

Late 17th century period Export lacquer escritorio or writing cabinet, 89 x 49 x 65cm. high, the George I stand 18th century, 76.5cm. high. (Christie's) $12,320

A Queen Anne walnut cabinet-on-chest, the glazed doors enclosing a fitted interior with eleven various-sized drawers, 44in. wide. (Christie's) $17,820

SECRETAIRE BOOKCASES

A 19th century inlaid mahogany secretaire bookcase with glazed upper section, 3ft.4in. wide. (Hobbs & Chambers) $4,025

A George III satinwood cabinet with gothic arched cornice, 48¼in. wide. (Christie's) $6,275

A George III mahogany secretaire cabinet with molded cornice, 43½in. wide. (Christie's) $5,297

A Georgian mahogany secretaire bookcase. (Hobbs Parker) $1,600

Late 19th century French ormolu mounted kingwood and rosewood vitrine with secretaire-a-abattant, 33in. wide. (Graves Son & Pilcher) $10,203

A Queen Anne walnut and featherstrung double dome secretaire cabinet on chest, 1.05m. wide. (Phillips) $15,580

A George III mahogany secretaire cabinet with a pair of Gothic glazed cupboard doors, 43in. wide. (Christie's) $8,712

A Regency rosewood, tulipwood crossbanded and strung secretaire dwarf bookcase, 78cm. wide. (Phillips) $6,560

A Regency mahogany cabinet with a pair of geometrically glazed doors enclosing shelves, 40in. wide. (Christie's) $3,944

SECRETAIRE BOOKCASES

A George III mahogany secretaire cabinet, 49in. wide, 101in. high. (Christie's) $13,447

A William IV mahogany secretaire bookcase, the upper section fitted with adjustable shelves, 4ft.1in. wide. (Prudential Fine Art) $1,968

A Regency mahogany secretaire cabinet on partly replaced bracket feet, 46½in. wide. (Christie's) $2,151

A George I cream lacquer secretaire cabinet with bow-shaped molded cornice, 43¾in. wide, 86½in. high. (Christie's) $427,680

Mid 19th century classical mahogany veneered desk and bookcase, mid-Atlantic States, 88in. high. (Christie's) $1,045

An early 18th century walnut and featherstrung double dome secretaire cabinet on chest, 1.09m. wide. (Phillips) $19,680

A George III mahogany secretaire cabinet, the base with a leather-lined secretaire drawer, 43in. wide. (Christie's) $9,861

An early 19th century mahogany secretaire bookcase, the two doors with satinwood strung astragals, 51in. wide. (Parsons, Welch & Cowell) $2,772

A late 18th century mahogany secretaire bookcase on swept bracket feet, 118cm. wide. (Wellington Salerooms) $6,048

SETTEES & COUCHES

One of a pair of early Victorian rosewood sofas, the molded shaped backs and bowed seats with buttoned upholstery, 96in. wide. (Christie's) $15,240

A Regency ivory and green-painted beech-wood daybed upholstered in crimson damask on fluted sabre legs, 87in. wide. (Christie's) $3,811

Mid 19th century walnut frame three-seater settee covered in button down embossed velvet fabric. (Locke & England) $815

A George III cream-painted and parcel gilt sofa, the padded back, arms and seat with spirally-turned spreading arm supports, 77in. wide. (Christie's) $2,178

An early Gustav Stickley settle with arched slats, 1901-03, 60in. wide. (Robt. W. Skinner Inc.) $27,000

A Regency oak and parcel gilt sofa, attributed to George Bullock, 61½in. wide. (Christie's) $106,920

A Regency parcel gilt and ebonized sofa, the padded back, arms and bowed seat with squab cushions, 72in. wide. (Christie's) $1,415

A Regency cream-painted sofa with rectangular button back, sides and squab covered in brown silk, 76in. wide. (Christie's) $2,706

SETTEES & COUCHES

An early Victorian oak daybed in the Gothic style, the padded seat covered in green leather, 77in. wide. (Christie's) $3,993

A Louis XV parcel gilt and gray-painted canape, with waved upholstered back and seat, 77in. wide. (Christie's) $4,408

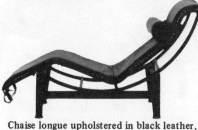

Chaise longue upholstered in black leather, designed by Le Corbusier, 1926. (Lots Road Chelsea Auction Galleries) $496

A mid Victorian walnut sofa, the padded back, outscrolled arms, back and seat upholstered in buttoned slate-blue velvet, on cabriole legs, 80in. wide. (Christie's) $1,815

An Empire bird's eye maple sofa with panelled back, padded arms and seat covered in white calico, 76in. wide. (Christie's) $3,426

A walnut sofa of William and Mary style with padded back, outscrolled arms and seat upholstered with fragments of 17th century tapestry, 82in. wide. (Christie's) $9,801

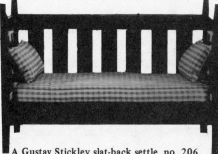

A Gustav Stickley slat-back settle, no. 206, circa 1904-06, 60in. wide. (Robt. W. Skinner Inc.) $15,000

A mid Victorian walnut sofa, the buttoned back upholstered in celadon green velvet with deep fringe, 78in. wide. (Christie's) $2,204

SETTEES & COUCHES

A George II giltwood sofa with arched rectangular padded back, armrests and seat
covered in bottle-green velvet, 106½in. wide.
(Christie's) $14,245

A painted and stencil decorated settee, Penn.,
circa 1830, with J. Swint Chairmaker stamped
on base, 76¼in. long. (Robt. W. Skinner Inc.)
$2,000

Early 18th century Dutch green painted hall
bench, 72in. wide. (Christie's) $8,811

A mahogany sofa with slightly arched back and
serpentine seat upholstered in russet velvet,
76in. wide. (Christie's) $902

An Art Nouveau mahogany and marquetry
settle on three arched trestle supports,
circa 1890, 185cm. wide. (Christie's)
                    $1,514

A Gustav Stickley tall spindleback settee, no.
286, signed with decal, circa 1906, 48in. wide.
(Robt. W. Skinner Inc.) $36,000

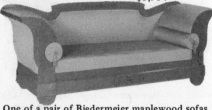

One of a pair of Biedermeier maplewood sofas
with double scrolling padded backs, arms and
seats, 101in. wide. (Christie's) $16,643

A painted and decorated settee, the rolled
crest rail above three slats and twelve spindles,
Penn., circa 1825, 76in. long. (Robt. W.
Skinner Inc.) $2,750

SETTEES & COUCHES

A Victorian walnut conversational sofa upholstered in figured damask, on scrolling feet, 50in. wide. $1,262
(Christie's)

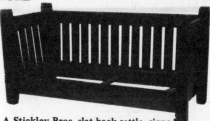

A Stickley Bros. slat-back settle, signed with paper label, Quaint, circa 1910, 72in. wide. (Robt. W. Skinner Inc.) $4,500

A Victorian carved mahogany shaped settee with button back, 80in. wide. (J. M. Welch & Son) $1,246

Part of a Victorian carved walnut three-piece suite. (Hobbs Parker) $1,310

A 19th century pine settle with backrest, the seat with three drawers under, 74in. wide. (Greenslade & Co.) $729

An oak bench, the padded back and squab cushion covered in tapestry, on turned legs and molded stretchers, 57½in. wide. (Christie's) $1,070

William IV double scroll-ended mahogany framed shaped settee with rising back rail and four small turned legs, 75in. long. (J. M. Welch & Son) $571

A Victorian walnut sofa, the seat and padded arms upholstered in moquette, raised on scrolling legs, 74in. wide, complete with easy chair. (Anderson & Garland) $2,478

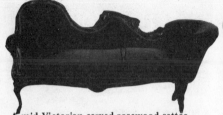

A mid Victorian carved rosewood settee with serpentine front and cabriole legs, 78in. wide. (Dacre, Son & Hartley) $1,558

A George III white painted and parcel gilt sofa with rounded arched back, sides, seat and squab covered in green repp on turned tapering fluted legs, 98½in. wide. (Christie's) $2,330

Part of a cream-painted and parcel gilt suite of Louis XVI style, comprising a pair of chaises, a pair of fauteuils and a canape, the canape 56in. wide. (Christie's) $2,722

A George III carved mahogany twin chairback settee in the Chinese and Gothic Chippendale taste. (Phillips) $13,940

A George III parcel gilt and cream painted sofa, the waved back and serpentine seat lacking upholstery, 84in. wide. (Christie's) $4,123

A Gustav Stickley bird's-eye maple wide slat settee, no. 214, circa 1903-04, 50¼in. wide. (Robt. W. Skinner Inc.) $4,000

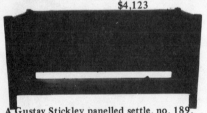

A Gustav Stickley panelled settle, no. 189, signed with large red decal with signature in a box, 1901-03, 84in. long. (Robt. W. Skinner Inc.) $6,250

A stencilled green-painted triple chair-back settee, probably New York, circa 1820, 74¼in. long. (Christie's) $2,860

SETTEES & COUCHES

A mid Victorian walnut sofa with arched deep buttoned back, curved sides and serpentine seat covered in bottle green velvet, 79½in. wide. (Christie's) $2,178

A Regency simulated rosewood and parcel gilt quadruple chairback settee, the seat covered in white calico, 71in. wide. (Christie's) $2,178

A walnut three-seater settee in the George II style, having triple carved vase splat and shaped arms, 62in. long. (Chancellors Hollingsworths) $640

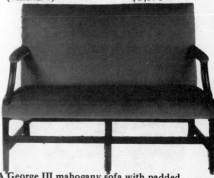

A George III mahogany sofa with padded rectangular back and seat with square legs and plain stretchers, 49in. wide. $2,541 (Christie's)

A Biedermeier walnut sofa with arched padded back, scrolling arms and seat covered in striped silk with two bolsters, 62½in. wide. (Christie's) $4,592

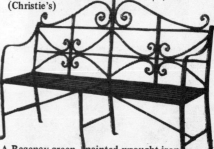

A Regency green-painted wrought-iron garden seat with scrolling pierced back and pierced seat, 66in. wide. (Christie's) $3,630

A 'lip' sofa, after a design by Salvador Dali, upholstered in red nylon stretch fabric. (Christie's) $1,894

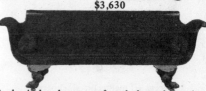

A classical mahogany sofa upholstered in red woven horsehair bordered with brass nails, attributed to Duncan Phyfe, N.Y., circa 1816, 94in. wide. (Christie's) $18,700

SIDEBOARDS

A Federal inlaid mahogany sideboard, the serpentine top edged with line inlay, 72¾in. wide. Mass., 1790-1815. (Christie's) $16,500

A George III mahogany veneered bowfronted sideboard, crossbanded in rosewood and inlaid stringing, 5ft. wide. (Woolley & Wallis) $6,642

A George III mahogany sideboard with D-shaped top crossbanded with satinwood, 47½in. wide. (Graves Son & Pilcher) $8,592

A Limbert sideboard with arched mirrored backboard with corbel detail, Michigan, circa 1910, 47¾in. wide. (Robt. W. Skinner Inc.) $1,200

A George III mahogany sideboard with bowed breakfront top and a frieze drawer, 71in. wide. (Christie's) $7,530

A mid Victorian pollard oak sideboard with arched mirror backplate, 102in. wide. (Christie's) $2,755

SIDEBOARDS

An eight-legged sideboard, model no. 961, plate rail with V-board panelled back, by Gustav Stickley, circa 1902-04, 70in. wide. (Robt. W. Skinner Inc.) $3,750

A Federal inlaid mahogany sideboard with serpentine front, Baltimore, 1790-1810, 72in. wide. (Christie's) $41,800

A Gustav Stickley oak sideboard with open plate rack, circa 1905-06, 49in. wide. (Robt. W. Skinner Inc.) $1,300

A Limbert mirrored sideboard, no. 1453 3/4, circa 1910, 48in. wide. (Robt. W. Skinner Inc.) $475

A 19th century brass bound military unit, 6ft.10in. wide. (Geering & Colyer) $1,890

A George III mahogany and inlaid sideboard of concave outline with crossbanded top containing a short central and two deep drawers in the arched apron, 185cm. wide. (Phillips) $4,756

SIDEBOARDS

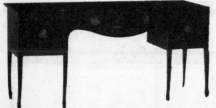

A George III mahogany sideboard with waved serpentine top, possibly Scottish, 83½in. wide. (Christie's) $18,150

A Sheraton breakfront mahogany inlaid and crossbanded sideboard, 183cm. wide. (Dee & Atkinson) $2,880

A George III mahogany sideboard, the breakfront bowed top crossbanded with satinwood, 71¾in. wide. (Christie's) $5,412

A Stickley Bros. sideboard, Grand Rapids, Michigan, 1912, 60in. wide. (Robt. W. Skinner Inc.) $425

George III mahogany bowfronted kneehole sideboard fitted with center drawer flanked by cellarette, small cupboard and one larger cupboard with four sliding trays. (Prudential Fine Art) $6,232

Regency mahogany bowfronted sideboard with ebony and satinwood stringing, 72in. wide. (Worsfolds) $1,428

Early 19th century sideboard on turned legs with central drawer, cellarette drawer and cupboard, 5ft. wide. (Lots Road Chelsea Auction Galleries) $1,263

A George III mahogany bowfronted sideboard crossbanded in satinwood, 77in. wide. (Christie's) $5,808

SIDEBOARDS

A George III Scottish mahogany sideboard, the eared rectangular superstructure formerly with a gallery and with bowed tambour doors, 71¾in. wide. (Christie's) $3,968

A Federal inlaid mahogany sideboard with bowed serpentine top, Mass., 1790-1810, 72¾in. wide. (Christie's) $6,600

A George III mahogany sideboard with triple-bowed top, 90¼in. wide. (Christie's) $4,719

A George III mahogany sideboard with bow-fronted top and frieze drawer above an arched recess, 69½in. wide. (Christie's) $11,583

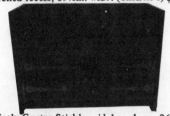

Early Gustav Stickley sideboard, no. 967, with long copper strap hardware and square copper pulls, 60in. wide. (Robt. W. Skinner Inc.) $9,500

Antique inlaid mahogany sideboard. (John Hogbin & Son) $2,050

A Regency mahogany veneered breakfront sideboard, banded in satinwood with stringing, 6ft. wide. (Woolley & Wallis) $2,880

A George III mahogany sideboard with D-shaped top with a frieze drawer and arched recess, 71in. wide. (Christie's) $6,494

STANDS

A three-tiered muffin stand, by Charles Rohlfs, Buffalo, N.Y., 1907, 34in. high. (Robt. W. Skinner Inc.) $1,300

An 18th century Japanese sword stand, for court tachi, 26in. high. (Robt. W. Skinner Inc.) $700

A mahogany three-tier etagere with rectangular top and square supports, 18½in. wide. (Christie's) $1,258

An Art Nouveau oak hall stand with circular mirror, stylish hooks and embossed copper panels, 36in. wide. (Lots Road Chelsea Auction Galleries) $567

Regency dark mahogany small fly press with two small drawers to the front, on squat circular feet. (G. A. Key) $875

An Italian walnut pedestal with shaped rectangular top on a bombe support, 50¼in. high. (Christie's) $2,020

A Regency brass and rosewood etagere with four rectangular trays, 16½in. wide, 39½in. high. (Christie's) $13,783

A cane-sided plant stand, pro-bably Limbert, circa 1910, 23in. high, the top 16in. sq. (Robt. W. Skinner Inc.) $475

A magazine stand with cut-outs, Michigan, 1910, 20in. wide. (Robt. W. Skinner Inc.) $700

STANDS

An Edwardian mahogany and inlaid pedestal jardiniere with liner. (J. M. Welch & Son) $380

A set of George III mahogany library steps with molded handrail and leather-lined treads, 104in. high. (Christie's) $6,891

A rosewood grained one-drawer poplar stand, American, circa 1830, top 21 x 16in. (Robt. W. Skinner Inc.) $6,250

An L. & J. G. Stickley slat-sided magazine rack, no. 46, circa 1910, signed with decal, 42in. high. (Robt. W. Skinner Inc.) $2,100

A Regency mahogany teapoy with folding top enclosing a divided interior, 26¾in. wide. (Christie's) $9,768

Early 20th century Mission oak magazine stand with cut out arched sides, 49in. high. (Robt. W. Skinner Inc.) $500

A Federal tiger maple candle-stand, New England, circa 1810, top 17 x 17½in. (Robt. W. Skinner Inc.) $1,300

A Gustav Stickley slat-sided folio stand, no. 551, 1902-03, 40½in. high, 29½in. wide. (Robt. W. Skinner Inc.) $3,000

A drink stand, by L. & J. G. Stickley, no. 587, circa 1912, 16in. sq. (Robt. W. Skinner Inc.) $650

STANDS

A Regency mahogany three-tier etagere with circular shelves and ring-turned supports, 14in. diam. (Christie's) $1,548

An 18th century spinning wheel with turned wood spindles. (J. M. Welch & Son) $262

A Country Federal birch candlestand, possibly New Hampshire, circa 1810, 27¼in. high. (Robt. W. Skinner Inc.) $325

A Regency mahogany torchere, fitted for electricity, 54in. high. (Christie's) $13,365

A Regency ebony and oak open display stand, attributed to George Bullock, 80in. wide, 82½in. high. (Christie's) $187,110

An early Victorian oak reading stand with rectangular easel-supported top, 19in. wide. (Christie's) $2,359

An L. & J. G. Stickley magazine rack, no. 45, circa 1912, 44½in. high. (Robt. W. Skinner Inc.) $1,300

A fine pair of George III giltwood torcheres, 49in. high. (Christie's) $40,986

A painted Country candlestand, circa 1810, 26¼in. high, 17in. diam. (Robt. W. Skinner Inc.) $1,800

STANDS

A Regency mahogany double music stand with candleholders, 108cm. high. (Osmond Tricks) $5,115

Country Federal tiger maple one-drawer stand, New England, circa 1810, top 19¾ x 20in. (Robt. W. Skinner Inc.) $7,200

Late Regency rosewood brass inlaid teapoy with sarcophagus shaped top, 17in. wide. (Lalonde Fine Art) $2,310

A carved wood hallstand depicting bear and cubs. (Ball & Percival) $5,808

A marquetry panelled oak smoking rack, possibly Stickley Bros., Michigan, circa 1910, style no. 264-100, 22in. high, 24in. wide. (Robt. W. Skinner Inc.) $130

A black and gold-painted umbrella stand with scrolling foliate sides, 32in. wide. (Christie's) $902

A Chippendale walnut dish-top stand, Phila., 1770-90, 20¾in. diam. (Christie's) $8,250

A matched pair of Italian giltwood torcheres with circular platforms, 49½in. high. (Christie's) $1,653

An ebonized hardwood Oriental jardiniere stand with inset rouge marble top. (Peter Wilson) $550

A Gustav Stickley upholstered
footstool with tacked leather
surface, no. 300, circa 1905,
20½in. wide. (Robt. W.
Skinner Inc.) $1,600

A Gustav Stickley mahogany
footstool, no. 302, signed
with red decal, 1905-05,
4½in. high. (Robt. W. Skinner
Inc.) $900

A Queen Anne walnut stool
with a slip-in gros point
needlework seat, on cabriole
legs. (Phillips) $2,975

A George III mahogany stool,
the seat covered in close-nailed
green cloth with crewelwork
flowers, on cabriole legs, 23½in.
wide, 17in. high.
(Christie's) $8,140

An oak stool of William and
Mary style with machined
tapestry circular seat and turned scrolled legs, 19in. wide.
(Christie's) $1,050

Victorian rosewood stool on
cabriole legs with scroll
feet and brass castors, 18in.
square. (Peter Wilson)
                $372

A George III mahogany
stool with drop-in seat
covered in blue and red
floral needlework, 19in.
wide. (Christie's)
        $3,544

A leather upholstered footstool, no. 300, by Gustav
Stickley, 20in. wide, circa
1905. (Robt. W. Skinner
Inc.) $950

A 19th century Continental
carved giltwood rectangular
stool covered in floral material.
(Peter Wilson) $915

STOOLS

A George I walnut stool with close-nailed rectangular padded seat, on claw-and-ball feet, 19½in. wide. (Christie's) $3,291

A Gustav Stickley footstool with notched feet, style no. 726, circa 1902-04, 12¼in. wide. (Robt. W. Skinner Inc.) $700

A Victorian walnut dressing stool, the upholstered seat with shell carved serpentine apron. (David Lay) $540

A walnut stool with concave waisted padded drop-in seat on cabriole legs, 26½in. wide. (Christie's) $2,336

A William and Mary walnut stool with square padded top covered in floral needlework, 15½in. square. (Christie's) $2,468

An unusual mahogany stool, the rectangular gros and petit point needlework drop-in seat, on cabriole legs and paw-feet, 19in. wide. (Christie's) $1,028

A 19th century mahogany dressing stool in George I style, with upholstered serpentine seat on four cabriole legs. (David Lay) $432

An early Victorian oak stool in the Gothic style, with padded seat covered in close-nailed green leather, 51in. wide. (Christie's) $8,712

Late 17th century oak joint stool. (Brown & Merry) $1,274

STOOLS

One of a pair of early 19th century late Federal mahogany footstools, 12¾in. long. (Christie's) $7,700

An early Victorian oak hall stool the octagonal arms with scrolled ends and solid seat, 25in. wide. (Christie's) $1,452

A Regency oak footstool, attributed to George Bullock, with padded seat covered in white-striped blue silk, 13½in. square. (Christie's) $22,275

One of a pair of North Italian giltwood rococo stools, the serpentine seats upholstered with maroon velvet with silver thread borders, 23in. wide. (Christie's) $28,473

One of a pair of giltwood fender stools of William and Mary style, 72in. wide. (Christie's) $6,133

A Regency rosewood piano stool with adjustable padded seat, 14in. wide. (Christie's) $1,742

A George I walnut stool, the top upholstered in gros and petit-point floral needlework, on square cabriole legs, 26in. wide. (Christie's) $15,752

A George II mahogany stool, the padded seat covered in yellow velvet, 24in. wide. (Christie's) $3,993

A tabouret with cut corners, by L. & J. G. Stickley, no. 560, circa 1912, 16in. wide. (Robt. W. Skinner Inc.) $750

STOOLS

A Regency oak window-seat, attributed to George Bullock, the solid seat with squab cushion, 38in. wide. (Christie's)
$67,716

A Regency mahogany gout stool with buttoned brown leather upholstery, 26¼in. wide. (Christie's)
$1,936

A Gustav Stickley piano bench, no. 217, plank sides with D-shaped handles, circa 1907, 36in. long. (Robt. W. Skinner Inc.) $800

A walnut stool, the padded seat covered in floral needlework on turned baluster legs, with scrolled feet, 17¾in. wide. (Christie's) $3,385

A Regency pollard oak, oak and holly commode stool, by George Bullock, 22in. wide. (Christie's)
$2,904

One of a pair of Regency oak and ebonized stools attributed to George Bullock, 24½in. wide. (Christie's)
$37,411

Mid 19th century rosewood stool, the padded seat covered in floral needlepoint, 17¼in. wide. (Christie's)
$902

Early 20th century octagonal oak garden seat, unsigned, 16in. diam. (Robt. W. Skinner Inc.) $425

One of a pair of giltwood stools of Louis XVI style with padded seats, 21in. wide. (Christie's)
$1,469

SUITES

Part of a suite of George II ebonized and parcel gilt seat furniture with velvet upholstered rectangular padded backs and seats on foliate cabriole legs and claw feet, comprising six side chairs, an armchair and two sofas, the sofas 69in. long. (Christie's) $77,330

Early 20th century Plail & Co., barrel-back settee and matching armchairs, 46¼in. long. (Robt. W. Skinner Inc.) $4,800

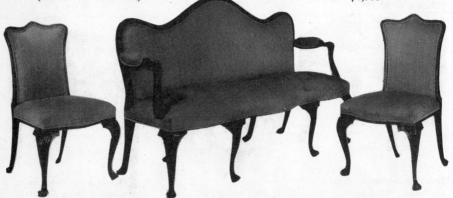

Part of a suite of George III mahogany seat furniture comprising eight side chairs, each with arched rectangular back and serpentine seat covered in pink striped material with plain molded frames, the sofa 77in. long. (Christie's) $18,315

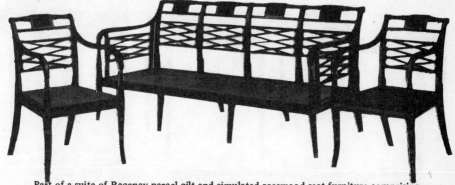

Part of a suite of Regency parcel gilt and simulated rosewood seat furniture comprising a set of six open armchairs, four with red velvet covered squab cushions, two chairs and the settee with blue velvet covered squabs, the settee 76¾in. long. (Christie's)
$22,385

A suite of George III mahogany seat furniture, now parcel gilt and cream painted, comprising five open armchairs and a sofa, the sofa 60½in. wide. (Christie's)
$88,605

An Edwardian mahogany and boxwood strung five-piece salon suite. (Phillips) $2,002

CARD & TEA TABLES

A George III satinwood card table on square tapering legs and spade feet, 35½in. wide. (Christie's) $3,993

A Federal inlaid mahogany card table with D-shaped top, Mass., 1790-1810, 34in. wide. (Christie's) $4,400

A Federal mahogany inlaid card table, probably Mass., circa 1790, 35in. wide. (Robt. W. Skinner Inc.) $2,750

A George III mahogany tea table, the serpentine twin-flap top with carved border on chamfered molded square legs, 36in. wide. (Christie's) $2,541

A George II mahogany demi-lune tea table with single gate action. (Locke & England) $1,059

A mid Georgian mahogany card table, the eared rectangular twin-flap top with guinea wells, 29½in. wide. (Christie's) $2,722

An early George III mahogany card table, the top with candle sconces, 35in. wide. (Christie's) $18,040

A Federal inlaid mahogany card table on five square tapering legs, New England, 1800-20, 32.7/8in. wide. (Christie's) $715

A mid Victorian gilt metal mounted mahogany and amboyna card table with leather-lined eared shape rectangular top, 35in. wide. (Christie's) $4,408

CARD & TEA TABLES

A Regency mahogany tea table with crossbanded D-shaped top, 39in. wide. (Christie's) $1,443

A Queen Anne figured maple octagonal tilt-top tea table, Conn., 1730-40, 33in. wide, 26in. high. (Christie's) $19,800

One of a matched pair of George III mahogany card tables, one with chamfered folding baize-lined top, the other a tea table, one 39½in. wide, the other 19in. wide. (Christie's) $8,910

A mid Georgian mahogany card table with hinged top enclosing a baize-lined interior, possibly American, 35¾in. wide. (Christie's) $3,630

A Chinese Export black and gilt lacquer tea table with triple-flap top, early 19th century, 30in. wide. (Christie's) $3,085

One of a pair of George III figured mahogany card tables, the D-shaped tops crossbanded and lined with baize, each 36in. wide. (Christie's) $17,138

A George III mahogany card table with baize-lined serpentine top, 35½in. wide. (Christie's) $2,345

A George III mahogany inlaid and crossbanded D-shaped card table with fold-over top, 36in. wide. (Dacre, Son & Hartley) $1,394

A William and Mary walnut card table with crossbanded folding suede-lined top, 33½in. wide, 30¼in. high. (Christie's) $13,365

CARD & TEA TABLES

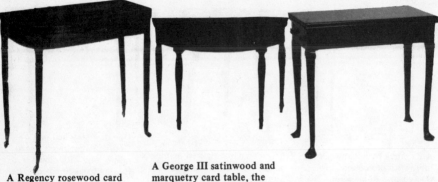

A Regency rosewood card table inlaid with boxwood dots in a burr-yew band, 33¾in. wide. (Christie's) $2,330

A George III satinwood and marquetry card table, the baize-lined D-shaped top crossbanded with rosewood, 42¼in. wide. (Christie's) $8,910

Late Georgian mahogany fold-over tea table, 30in. square, open. (J. M. Welch & Son) $1,180

A Regency pollard oak tea table with folding top, 36in. wide. (Christie's) $1,298

A Federal inlaid mahogany card table, Mass., 1800-15, 34in. wide. (Christie's) $1,320

Regency mahogany fold-over pedestal tea table. (Biddle & Webb) $749

An early 19th century D-end mahogany fold-over card table on turned and tapered legs, 36in. square. (J. M. Welch & Son) $328

A Country Chippendale maple tea table, New England, circa 1780, 33½in. wide. (Robt. W. Skinner Inc.) $850

An 18th century demi-lune mahogany card table, 36in. wide. (Warren & Wignall Ltd.) $1,088

CARD & TEA TABLES

A Federal carved mahogany card table, attributed to Henry Connelly, circa 1810, 36in. wide. (Christie's) $2,640

A William IV mahogany fold-over card table on scrolled feet, 36in. wide. (J. M. Welch & Son) $590

An early Victorian figured mahogany fold-over card table on slender turned legs, 36in. square. (J. M. Welch & Son) $623

A Federal inlaid mahogany card table on four tapering legs, Baltimore, 1790-1810, 36¼in. diam. (Christie's) $3,850

A Chippendale birch tea table, the serpentine tip top on a vase and ring turned post and tripod cabriole leg base, circa 1780, 37in. wide. (Robt. W. Skinner Inc.) $800

A Regency rosewood card table with swivelling baize-lined top inlaid with a band of pollard oak and ebony, 36¼in. wide. (Christie's) $3,630

A Regency kingwood card table with baize-lined crossbanded rectangular top, 36in. wide. (Christie's) $1,815

A mid Georgian mahogany card table, the eared top with counter wells and a frieze drawer, 24½in. wide. (Christie's) $9,323

A George II mahogany card table with folding top, 32¾in. wide. (Christie's) $3,227

CENTER TABLES

An Italian giltwood and pietra dura center table, ink label beneath stretcher 'Monsieur R. O. Milne Florence 18.4.99', 26¾in. wide. (Christie's)
$6,171

A Regency rosewood center table by Gillows, with tip-up top on spreading hexagonal stem and concave sided triangular base, 54½in. diam. (Christie's)
$23,166

A tortoiseshell, walnut and parcel gilt center table, the crossbanded top bordered with ivory, 33in. wide. (Christie's)
$11,583

Early 19th century Italian scagliola circular table top on a mahogany tripartite pedestal, 34½in. diam. (Christie's)
$11,583

A George IV pollard oak center table with circular top, 47½in. diam. (Christie's)
$3,993

A Napoleon III ormolu mounted Sevres pattern porcelain and mahogany center table, 33in. diam. (Christie's) $11,940

A Morris & Co. walnut center table, 69cm. diam. (Christie's) $811

A Salvatore Meli ceramic and glass center table, 120.5cm. wide. (Christie's)
$11,726

A mid Victorian oak and parcel gilt center table 30½in. diam. (Christie's)
$6,534

CENTER TABLES

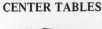

An early 18th century oak center table on tapering cabriole legs and pad feet, the gallery initialled 'W', 29½in. wide. (Christie's) $1,353

An early Victorian rosewood center table with well figured circular tip-up top, 48in. diam. (Christie's) $5,020

One of two ormolu mounted kingwood and parquetry center tables of Louis XVI style, 37in. wide and 39¼in. wide. (Christie's) $6,429

A walnut center table with circular top and scrolling supports, 25½in. diam. (Christie's) $2,204

A mid Victorian rosewood center table on spirally-turned twin column end-standards, 45¾in. wide. (Christie's) $1,633

An early Victorian pollard oak center table with an Italian circular specimen marble top, 22¼in. diam. (Christie's) $1,713

A Dutch mahogany and ebony oval center table on square tapering legs headed by rosettes, on ball feet, 36in. wide. (Christie's) $1,837

A mahogany center table with circular specimen marble top, 19½in. diam. (Christie's) $1,815

An early Victorian ebonized and parcel gilt center table with Italian scagliola top, 36¼in. diam. (Christie's) $14,256

FURNITURE

A gilt and cream-painted center table with brass bound rectangular scagliola top, 51½in. wide. (Christie's) $8,553

A Regency pollard oak center table, attributed to George Bullock, with octagonal tip-up top, 53½in. diam. (Christie's) $35,442

One of a pair of George IV mahogany center tables with slightly later rounded rectangular tops, 67in. wide. (Christie's) $26,730

An early Victorian figured walnut center table with tip-up top, 57½in. wide. (Christie's) $1,996

A mid Victorian ormolu mounted marquetry center table with shaped oval top, 58in. wide. (Christie's) $4,356

An early Victorian mahogany circular snap-top table, 100cm. diam. (David Lay) $984

A Victorian walnut center table, the rectangular top with burr-walnut banding, 75 x 117cm. (David Lay) $805

A Regency rosewood and parcel gilt center table with molded circular tip-up top, 53½in. diam. (Christie's) $29,040

A George IV rosewood veneered center table with D-ends, 65 x 134cm. (David Lay) $1,350

CENTER TABLES

A Victorian figured walnut
center table with double
serpentine shaped top, circa
1880, 47in. long. (Peter
Wilson) $1,654

Mid 19th century drawingroom
center table in veneered figured
walnut with oval tilt-top, 5ft.
long. (Lalonde Fine Art)
$792

A giltwood and specimen
marble center table on
entwined dolphin supports,
47½in. wide. (Christie's)
$21,659

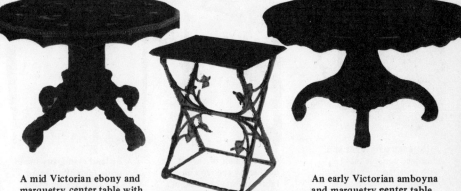

A mid Victorian ebony and
marquetry center table with
sixteen-sided tip-up top,
46½in. wide. (Christie's)
$5,143

A mid Victorian wrought-
brass center table, the black
slate top inlaid with gothic
brass strapwork enamelled
in green, red and blue, 30in.
wide. (Christie's) $6,352

An early Victorian amboyna
and marquetry center table
in the style of E. H. Baldock,
54in. diam. (Christie's)
$9,075

Victorian oval top walnut
center table on carved and
turned stretcher supports,
circa 1880. (Brown &
Merry) $1,274

A Regency brass inlaid rosewood center table, the two
frieze drawers with lion-mask
handles, 41in. wide.
(Christie's) $11,814

An early Victorian oak and·
walnut center table in the
manner of A. W. N. Pugin,
59½in. wide. (Christie's)
$1,837

CONSOLE TABLES

Mid 18th century rococo turquoise-painted and parcel gilt console table, possibly Genoese, 43in. wide. (Christie's) $12,859

One of a pair of oyster-veneered walnut and cream-painted console tables with crossbanded serpentine tops, 69½in. wide. (Christie's) $4,041

Early 19th century white-painted and gilded pier table with eared rectangular black marble top, 41in. wide, 33in. high. (Christie's)$37,422

A Regency parcel gilt and ebonized console table with mottled rounded rectangular black marble top, 39in. wide. (Christie's) $4,636

One of a pair of carved mahogany rococo console tables of bracket design, 98cm. wide. (Phillips) $18,040

A Federal mahogany inlaid console table, Baltimore, circa 1800, 37½in. wide. (Robt. W. Skinner Inc.) $8,500

One of a pair of William IV mahogany and bronze corner console tables with mottled green scagliola tops, 28in. wide. (Christie's) $3,586

One of a 19th century pair of black and gilt japanned and parcel gilt console tables of early Georgian style, 57in. wide. (Christie's) $4,537

One of a pair of early 19th century mahogany pier tables each with black marble top, 19in. wide. (Christie's)$16,038

CONSOLE TABLES

An Empire mahogany console table with gray marble top and frieze drawer, 28½in. wide. (Christie's) $1,469

A Regency parcel gilt and rosewood console table with white marble top, 47¾in. wide. (Christie's) $2,689

One of a pair of Empire mahogany marble-top pier tables, probably Boston, circa 1830, 49in. wide. (Christie's) $4,400

A Louis XV oak console table with shaped veined gray marble top, 35in. wide. (Christie's) $4,041

A Louis XVI console table with a 'D' shaped marble top, 3ft.4¾in. wide. (Phillips) $7,700

A pine console table with rectangular white marble top, now painted to simulate verde antico, 32in. wide. (Christie's) $8,712

A Regency mahogany console table with molded black mottled green marble top, with mirror glazed back, 35½in. wide. (Christie's) $6,314

Mid 18th century German giltwood console table with gray marble eared serpentine top, 37in. wide. (Christie's) $20,207

One of a pair of Empire mahogany veneer marble-top pier tables, attributed to the shop of Duncan Phyfe, N.Y., 1834-40, 41½in. wide. (Christie's) $24,200

DINING TABLES

A Regency mahogany and satinwood breakfast table with tip-up top, 59in. wide. (Christie's) $16,137

A Queen Anne maple dining table with oval drop-leaf top, Rhode Island, circa 1760, 50in. wide open. (Robt. W. Skinner Inc.) $7,500

A Queen Anne mahogany drop-leaf dining table, New England, 1750-70, 50in. deep with leaves open. (Christie's) $8,800

A George III mahogany library table with leather-lined circular top and four frieze drawers and four false drawers, 47in. diam. (Christie's)
$13,365

A Federal painted maple dining table with rounded drop leaves, New England, circa 1800, 42in. wide. (Robt. W. Skinner Inc.) $4,000

One of a pair of George IV rosewood breakfast tables with circular tip-up tops, 47½in. diam. (Christie's) $14,256

A Regency mahogany breakfast table with rounded rectangular tip-up top, 53¼in. wide. (Christie's)
$3,630

A rosewood dining table of circular form, carved collar decoration to column. (McKenna's) $1,456

Early 19th century faded mahogany tip-top pedestal dining table, 56 x 46in. (J. M. Welch & Son)
$541

DINING TABLES

A George IV mahogany breakfast table with cross-banded circular top, 54in. wide. (Christie's)
$6,855

A George II period mahogany oval top drop-leaf dining table, 5ft.4in. by 6ft. opened. (Geering & Colyer)
$8,280

A Regency rosewood break-fast table with circular tip-up top, 53¾in. diam. (Christie's) $6,237

A George IV oval mahogany snap top breakfast table on a ring turned bulbous column and quadruple scrolled supports, 4ft.6in. x 4ft. (Prudential Fine Art)
$1,650

A Regency rosewood circular breakfast table on platform base with three brass lion paw feet, 120cm. diam. (Osmond Tricks) $1,870

Round pedestal base dining table, Hastings Co., Michigan, circa 1915, signed with decal on pedestal top, 54in. diam. (Robt. W. Skinner Inc.)
$1,200

A Regency mahogany break-fast table with tip-up top, 56in. wide. (Christie's)
$2,525

A dining table, the five legs joined by flared stretchers, by Gustav Stickley, circa 1905-07, 54in. diam. (Robt. W. Skinner Inc.)
$6,800

A Victorian burr-walnut and marquetry inlaid oval pedestal 'loo' table, 50 x 40in. (J. M. Welch & Son)
$592

DRESSING TABLES

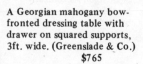

An Arts & Crafts dressing table by George Walton, 134.2cm. wide. (Christie's) $992

A Chippendale tiger maple dressing table on cabriole legs, probably Penn., circa 1780, 33¾in. wide. (Robt. W. Skinner Inc.)$20,000

A Georgian mahogany bow-fronted dressing table with drawer on squared supports, 3ft. wide. (Greenslade & Co.) $765

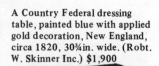

An early George III mahogany dressing table, the well fitted interior with sliding easel mirror, 24½in. wide. (Christie's) $16,929

A 19th century inlaid mahogany kneehole dressing table with lift-up top enclosing a fitted interior, 4ft.1in. wide. (Hobbs & Chambers) $1,072

A Country Federal dressing table, painted blue with applied gold decoration, New England, circa 1820, 30¾in. wide. (Robt. W. Skinner Inc.) $1,900

A Federal painted dressing table, New England, circa 1820, 35in. wide. (Robt. W. Skinner Inc.) $1,800

A George III satinwood, tulipwood crossbanded and marquetry serpentine dressing table in the French taste, 69cm. wide. (Phillips) $5,740

A George III satinwood and marquetry dressing table in the manner of John Cobb, 27½in. wide. (Christie's) $27,730

DRESSING TABLES

A George III mahogany and satinwood dressing table, adjustable mirror, and false drawer, 49½in. open. (Dreweatt Neate) $2,835

Late George III figured mahogany kneehole dressing table with end fold-over flaps concealing lidded and other compartments, 3ft.3in. wide. (Lalonde Fine Art) $1,402

Part of an Edwardian mahogany three-piece bedroom suite, the dressing table with swing mirror, label Warings, London. (Peter Wilson) $2,728

A George II oak dressing table, circa 1740, raised on cabriole legs ending in trifid feet, 29½ in. high. (Robt. W. Skinner. Inc.) $1,100

A Scandinavian mahogany and parcel-gilt dressing-table with bronzed dolphin supports and two convex drawers flanked by two small drawers, early 19th century, 54½in. high. (Christie's) $5,291

Part of an Art Deco Macassar ebony bedroom suite, the dressing table 47in. across. (Christie's) $3,207

A George III satinwood and ebony inlaid dressing table, circa 1785, top enclosing mirror and compartments, 34in. high. (Robt. W. Skinner. Inc.) $2,750

A George IV mahogany dressing table by Gillows of Lancaster, 50¾in. wide. (Christie's) $3,944

A George III satinwood and rosewood banded table , after a design by Thomas Sheraton, 30in. wide. (Christie's) $6,771

DROP-LEAF TABLES

Mid 18th century Chippendale drop-leaf table, 3ft.4in. x 5ft.3in. (Woolley & Wallis) $2,560

A Classical Revival mahogany table, possibly New York, circa 1830, 50in. wide, open. (Robt. W. Skinner Inc.) $1,300

A drop-leaf table, by Gustav Stickley, no. 638, circa 1912, 42in. long, 40in. wide, open. (Robt. W. Skinner Inc.) $2,800

A late Regency mahogany pedestal two-flap table with four hipped splay supports and brass claw feet and castors. (Greenslade & Co.) $712

A mid Georgian mahogany drop-leaf table with twin-flap top, on cabriole legs, 48in. wide. (Christie's) $3,993

A Queen Anne mahogany drop-leaf table, Newport, 1740-60, 47.7/8in. wide. (Christie's) $4,950

A Queen Anne maple and birch drop-leaf table, New England, circa 1760, 39¼in. wide. (Robt. W. Skinner Inc.) $1,000

An oak drop-leaf table, no. 638, by Gustav Stickley, circa 1906, 42in. long extended. (Robt. W. Skinner Inc.) $2,100

A Chippendale cherrywood drop-leaf table, with wavy stretchers, Conn., 1760-80 (Christie's) $1,980

GATELEG TABLES

A William and Mary walnut gateleg table, probably New England, circa 1740, 56in. wide. (Robt. W. Skinner Inc.) $3,700

A small 18th century oval oak gateleg table, 3ft.7in. long. (Greenslade & Co.) $302

George II mahogany drop-leaf gateleg table with rectangular top, 55in. long open. (Abridge Auctions) $1,000

Early 18th century oak , oval top, gateleg table with solid shaped ends, 52in. wide extended. (Abridge Auctions) $1,750

A Gateleg table with oval twin-flap top and molded channelled trestle ends, basically 17th century, 46in. wide. (Christie's) $2,141

An oak gateleg table with oval twin-flap top on ring-turned legs and molded stretchers, basically 17th century, 36½in. wide. (Christie's) $1,460

A figured walnut inlaid Sutherland table with four turned columns and turned gatelegs with porcelain castors, 35in. wide. (Peter Wilson) $915

A William and Mary maple gateleg table with oval drop-leaf top, New England, circa 1740, 41in. long, 51in. wide. (Robt. W. Skinner Inc.) $2,500

Victorian figured walnut oval Sutherland table on turned end pedestals, 42 x 35in. (J. M. Welch & Son) $453

LARGE TABLES

A Jacobean draw-leaf table, having planked and clamped top, supported on trestle ends, the draw-leaf top extending to 16ft. (Locke & England) $3,260

A Regency mahogany extending dining table with rounded rectangular end-sections and concertina action, 53 x 88½in. including two extra leaves. (Christie's) $12,210

A George III mahogany two-pillar dining table, the rounded oblong top with thumb mold edge, 5ft.6in. x 3ft.11in. (Hobbs & Chambers) $2,681

A Regency mahogany patent extending dining table with D-shaped folding top, including three extra leaves, 2.83 x 1.30m. extended. (Phillips) $9,020

A mid Georgian walnut supper table with twin-flap top, club legs and pad feet, 54in. wide, open. (Christie's) $3,608

A mahogany twin-pedestal D-end dining table, including two extra leaves, 1.37 x 3.01m. extended. (Phillips)$13,940

Late 19th century Regency style mahogany D-end dining table having inlaid ebony and sycamore stringing, 6ft.6in. long. (Giles Haywood) $792

A dining table, centre section 4ft. x 4ft., and two D-end tables, 4ft. x 2ft. making one table 8ft. x 4ft. (J. M. Welch & Son) $1,312

LARGE TABLES

A 1930's Art Deco mahogany octagonal topped dining table supported on eight carved legs with mask decoration and honeycombed stretcher, 78in. x 55in. (J. M. Welch & Son) $1,260

Early 19th century Shaker tiger maple and cherry trestle base dining table, Canterbury, New England, 71¼in. wide. (Robt. W. Skinner Inc.) $86,000

A Georgian style two-pedestal oval dining table with center leaf, 86 x 36in., circa 1900. (J. M. Welch & Son) $1,246

A late George III D-end mahogany dining table with gateleg center section on fourteen square channelled tapering legs, stamped R. Bradley, Warrington, 43 x 102in. (Christie's) $6,776

One of a pair of mahogany serving tables with molded shaped tops and recessed concave stepped fluted and beaded friezes, 66in. wide. (Christie's) $8,606

A mid Victorian mahogany D-end dining table. (Miller & Co.) $2,774

A Country maple and pine painted harvest table, New England, circa 1800, 72in. long. (Robt. W. Skinner Inc.) $2,800

A mahogany D-ended dining table (converted to accommodate two center leaves), circa 1800, 89 x 48in. (J. M. Welch & Son) $1,489

OCCASIONAL TABLES

A George III scarlet japanned tripod table with chinoiserie tip-up top, 30in. diam. (Christie's) $1,394

A kingwood and marquetry petit table of Louis XV style, the top inlaid with a hunting scene, 17in. wide. (Christie's) $1,179

A mahogany tripod table with serpentine tip-up top and spirally ribbed ring-turned pedestal on arched tripod base, 21½in. diam. (Christie's) $8,019

A mahogany tripod table with circular tip-up pie-crust top, 32in. diam. (Christie's) $1,793

An early Victorian low table with out-curved foliate border and gadrooned frieze, 29½in. wide. (Christie's) $6,454

A Sheraton period mahogany crossbanded and strung drum top table, 60cm. diam. (Phillips) $9,512

A mahogany tripod table with circular tip-up top, 27¾in. diam. (Christie's) $2,345

An ormolu mounted mahogany and parquetry gueridon in the manner of Weisweiler, 18in. diam. (Christie's) $2,204

One of a pair of Regency brass inlaid rosewood tripod tables, 18in. wide, 28in. high. (Christie's) $19,723

OCCASIONAL TABLES

An early George III maho-
gany occasional or wine
table with a circular snap-
top, 52cm. diam. (Phillips)
$1,640

George III mahogany
pedestal reading table with
adjustable slope, 24in. wide.
(Prudential Fine Art)
$2,460

An early Victorian oak
occasional table in the style
of A. W. N. Pugin, with octagonal parquetry top, 20¼in.
wide. (Christie's)
$1,452

A gilt metal mounted mahogany gueridon in the style of
Weisweiler, stamped Wright
and Mansfield, 27¼in. diam.
(Christie's) $6,980

A mahogany silver table
with serpentine top on
molded cabriole legs,
33in. wide. (Christie's)
$18,711

A Regency mahogany cheese
table with divided bowed
rectangular top, 22in. wide.
(Christie's) $1,804

A Regency rosewood and
mahogany small table in
the manner of G. Bullock,
22in. wide. (Christie's)
$4,356

One of a pair of silver
mounted and malachite
gueridons in the style of
Weisweiler, possibly Russian,
15¾in. diam. (Christie's)
$44,088

A gilt metal mounted burr-
walnut jardiniere on cabriole
legs, 22½in. wide. (Christie's)
$907

OCCASIONAL TABLES

A Gustav Stickley hexagonal leather-top table, no. 624, circa 1910-12, 48in. diam. (Robt. W. Skinner Inc.) $7,000

A Georgian mahogany pie-crust tip-top pedestal table, 24in. diam. (J. M. Welch & Son) $790

William and Mary cherry and pine hutch table, Hudson River Valley, circa 1750, 44in. diam. (Robt. W. Skinner Inc.) $6,400

A painted birch and pine one-drawer stand, possibly Maine, circa 1810, top 24¼ x 19in. (Robt. W. Skinner Inc.) $4,000

A Regency mahogany drum table with leather-lined circular top and four frieze drawers, 37in. diam. (Christie's) $8,659

An Edwardian mahogany nest of three oval tables on sabre legs. (David Lay) $519

An occasional table, no. 609, by Gustav Stickley, circa 1904-05, unsigned, 36in. diam. (Robt. W. Skinner Inc.) $900

A Regency mahogany tripod table with circular tip-up top, 16½in. wide. (Christie's) $1,713

A Country Queen Anne maple tavern table, the oval overhanging top on shaped skirt and block-turned tapering legs, circa 1740, 33in. wide. (Robt. W. Skinner Inc.) $8,500

OCCASIONAL TABLES

An 18th century maple tavern table with breadboard ends, New England, the top 40 x 24½in. (Robt. W. Skinner Inc.) $2,700

A George III mahogany breakfast table on baluster turned shaft and ribbed splayed legs, 43in. wide. (Christie's) $1,435

A Limbert oval occasional table, style no. 146, circa 1907, 36in. long. (Robt. W. Skinner Inc.) $2,200

A Gustav Stickley round leather-top table, no. 645, circa 1907, 36in. diam. (Robt. W. Skinner Inc.) $2,100

Set of four mahogany quartetto tables. (Worsfolds) $1,344

An occasional table with cut corners, possibly early Gustav Stickley, circa 1902-04, 29in. high. (Robt. W. Skinner Inc.) $1,100

A painted 'Windsor' tavern table, possibly Rhode Island, circa 1780, 28in. wide. (Robt. W. Skinner Inc.) $6,000

A George III mahogany tripod table, the later octagonal top with pierced border, 10½in. wide. (Christie's) $2,868

A Limbert oval table with cut-out sides, Grand Rapids, Michigan, circa 1907, no. 146, 45in. long. (Robt. W. Skinner Inc.) $1,200

A George III satinwood Pembroke table with twin-flap top, 37½in. wide, open. (Christie's) $9,845

A George III satinwood and burr-yew Pembroke table with twin-flap top, 46in. wide. (Christie's) $11,583

A mahogany Pembroke table with twin-flap top and one frieze drawer on cabriole legs, 34¼in. wide, open. (Christie's) $1,262

A George III mahogany, tulipwood crossbanded and boxwood strung oval Pembroke table, 79cm. x 1m. (Phillips)$3,608

An Hepplewhite period carved mahogany and tulipwood crossbanded Pembroke table with hinged top, 91.5 x 46cm. extended. (Phillips) $22,140

Early 19th century mahogany Pembroke table on four slender turned legs, 36in. square. (J. M. Welch & Son) $250

A George III tulipwood Pembroke table, the oval twin-flap top banded in ebony, 40in. wide. (Christie's) $13,227

A Chippendale mahogany Pembroke table, possibly Penn., circa 1780, the shaped top with serpentine leaves, 31in. wide. (Robt. W. Skinner Inc.) $1,300

A George III mahogany Pembroke table in the French taste with twin-flap serpentine top, 38½in. wide. (Christie's) $9,438

PEMBROKE TABLES

A Regency mahogany
Pembroke table in the manner
of Gillows, on ribbed tapering
legs, 42in. wide. (Christie's)
$1,344

A Federal mahogany inlaid
Pembroke table with D-shaped
leaves, probably New York,
circa 1800, 39¾in. wide open.
(Robt. W. Skinner Inc.)
$3,500

Late George III mahogany
Sheraton design ovoid top
Pembroke table, 33in. wide.
(Locke & England)
$1,059

A George III mahogany
inlaid and oval Pembroke
table with hinged top,
86 x 108cm. extended.
(Phillips) $1,804

An early George III mahogany
Pembroke table with rectangu-
lar twin-flap top, 33¼in. wide.
(Christie's) $1,633

A George III mahogany
Pembroke table with twin-
flap top and frieze drawer,
42in. wide, open. (Christie's)
$1,161

A Georgian mahogany
Pembroke table on square
tapering fluted supports and
castors, 2ft.4in. wide.
(Greensalde & Co.)
$534

A George III satinwood
Pembroke table with a
frieze drawer, 39¼in. wide.
(Christie's) $5,379

A well figured mahogany
Pembroke table banded in
satinwood, above square
tapering legs to brass castors,
31in. long. (Woolley & Wallis)
$1,980

A George I gilt gesso side table with rectangular verde antico marble top, 35½in. wide. (Christie's) $8,019

A mid Georgian mahogany side table with single-flap top, 34in. wide. (Christie's) $998

One of a pair of George III satinwood and marquetry side tables with D-shaped tops crossbanded in rosewood, 54½in. wide. (Christie's) $33,858

A George II mahogany side table with frieze drawer, on club legs and pad feet, 27¼in. wide. (Christie's) $2,525

Regency painted pine side table fitted with a frieze drawer, 30in. wide. (Prudential Fine Art) $1,840

One of a pair of George III mahogany side tables, each with serpentine top and plain frieze, 28in. wide. (Christie's) $19,602

A George I walnut side table, the quartered top crossbanded with burr-walnut, 30¾in. wide. (Christie's) $14,256

A George III mahogany side table with serpentine top and one frieze drawer, 28in. wide. (Christie's) $7,260

Mid 18th century Venetian pine side table with molded serpentine top, 35in. wide. (Christie's) $1,745

SIDE TABLES

A George III sycamore, marquetry and gilt gesso elliptical side table, 1.23m. wide. (Phillips) $11,480

A George III mahogany side table in the manner of Thos. Chippendale, 46½in. wide. (Christie's) $21,384

A George III satinwood, marquetry and giltwood elliptical side table in the manner of Wm. Moore of Dublin, 1.23m. wide. (Phillips) $9,512

A rosewood side table with rectangular specimen marble top with three-quarter brass gallery, 45½in. wide. (Christie's) $7,623

A Regency mahogany and fruitwood side table, 27in. wide. (Christie's) $2,722

One of a pair of Italian giltwood side tables, each with a serpentine eared green marble top, 59½in. wide. (Christie's) $18,370

An early Georgian walnut side table with later veneered rectangular top, 32in. wide. (Christie's) $5,412

An Italian gray-painted side table with molded rectangular mottled yellow and pink marble slab, 39½in. wide. (Christie's) $4,408

An early Georgian oak side table on scrolling lappeted cabriole legs and hoof feet, 34in. wide. (Christie's) $6,133

SIDE TABLES

An English mahogany veneered serpentine front serving table, 4ft.9in. wide, together with a pair of matching pedestals, 3ft. 9in. high, circa 1780. (Woolley & Wallis) $5,120

A mahogany side table, the rounded rectangular top with inset mottled green marble and one frieze drawer, 11¾in. wide. (Christie's)$1,082

One of a pair of George III mahogany side tables, each with a serpentine top, 64½in. wide. (Christie's) $35,640

A mahogany serving table with rectangular top and bowfronted centre, 84in. wide. (Christie's) $3,247

One of a pair of Regency mahogany side tables, comprising a card table and a tea table, 36in. wide. (Christie's) $10,399

A George III mahogany satin-wood and yew side table, the crossbanded D-shaped top inlaid with a batswing motif, 70in. wide. (Christie's) $5,412

A mahogany veneered side table, designed by Frank L. Wright, circa 1955, 21½in. wide, red decal on back. (Robt. W. Skinner Inc.) $800

A 19th century Irish carved mahogany hall or side table, the apron carved in relief with a mask, 1.80m. wide. (Phillips) $6,232

One of a pair of French style ormolu mounted small tables, by Donald Ross of Denmark Hill, circa 1870, tops 16 x 13½in. (Graves Son & Pilcher) $6,802

SIDE TABLES

A library table with one drawer, by L. & J. G. Stickley, signed with Handcraft label, 42in. wide. (Robt. W. Skinner Inc.) $950

A George III mahogany serving table with crossbanded serpentine top on molded tapering legs, 57in. wide. (Christie's) $5,445

A George III giltwood side table with associated specimen marble top, 49¼in. wide. (Christie's) $19,690

One of a pair of black and gold japanned side tables of Regency style with D-shaped tops, 61in. wide. (Christie's) $6,897

A Regency mahogany bedside table with rounded rectangular twin-flap top, 29½in. wide. (Christie's) $1,082

A George III mahogany serving table with molded rectangular top and blind-fret frieze on chamfered square legs, 71½in. wide. (Christie's) $6,237

A Regency style walnut and marquetry side table with single frieze drawer. (Hetheringtons Nationwide) $1,600

An early Victorian giltwood and composition side table with shaped serpentine molded green marble top, 81in. wide. (Christie's) $6,352

A Country Federal grain painted maple tray table, possibly New Hampshire, circa 1820, top 17 x 16½in. (Robt. W. Skinner Inc.) $3,250

SOFA TABLES

A Regency rosewood sofa
table with twin-flap top
crossbanded with yew-wood
and zebrawood, 59¾in. wide,
open. (Christie's)
$12,474

Regency rosewood brass inlaid
sofa table with plate glass top,
34in. wide. (Prudential Fine
Art) $1,539

A Regency rosewood and
satinwood sofa table with
rounded rectangular twin-
flap top, 60½in. wide, open.
(Christie's) $5,051

A William IV rosewood sofa
table fitted with two short
frieze and two dummy
drawers. (Lots Road Chelsea
Auction Galleries)
$1,662

A Regency rosewood and
boxwood strung sofa
table with hinged top,
1.50m. x 53cm. extended.
(Phillips) $7,380

Late Regency rosewood
veneered sofa table with
twin-flap top with inlaid
brass marquetry and
stringing, 3ft.1in. wide.
(Woolley & Wallis)
$3,240

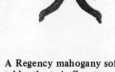

A Regency mahogany sofa
table, the twin-flap top
crossbanded in rosewood,
62½in. wide. (Christie's)
$5,808

A Regency mahogany sofa
table, the twin-flap top
crossbanded with rosewood,
57¾in. wide. (Christie's)
$3,066

A Regency rosewood sofa
table, the twin-flap top
with canted corners and
two frieze drawers, 58.5/8in.
wide. (Christie's)
$3,048

SOFA TABLES

A Regency brass inlaid rosewood sofa table, 60¼in.
wide, open. (Christie's)
$60,588

Late Regency figured mahogany sofa table with rosewood
crossbanding and line inlay,
4ft.11in. fully extended.
(Lalonde Fine Art) $825

A Regency mahogany sofa
table with twin-flap top and
two frieze drawers, 61in.
wide, open. (Christie's)
$3,484

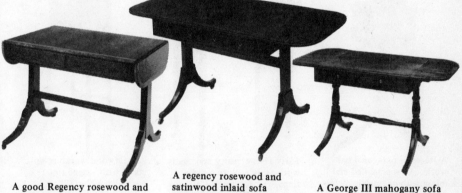

A good Regency rosewood and
maple banded sofa table, the
rounded rectangular top over
two frieze drawers, 128cm.
(Phillips) $6,888

A regency rosewood and
satinwood inlaid sofa
table, with two drawers,
142cm x 63cm. (Phillips)
$13,125

A George III mahogany sofa
table with twin-flap top and
two frieze drawers, 52in.
wide, open. (Christie's)
$4,690

A 19th century Dutch mar-
quetry sofa table, 23½ x
52in. extended. (J. M. Welch
& Son) $1,444

A mahogany sofa table with
drop leaves, 23in. long
extending to 46in. (County
Group) $651

A 19th century walnut crossbanded sofa table with two
drawers on stretcher frame
and brass capped feet and
castors. (Jacobs & Hunt)
$4,956

WORKBOXES & GAMES TABLES

An early 19th century figured mahogany pedestal work box with fold-over top, drawer and work-basket, 20 x 14½in. (J. M. Welch & Son) $656

A painted satinwood work table with pleated silk basket, 22in. wide. (Christie's) $1,984

A 19th century walnut work table with shaped hinged top, on four fluted baluster supports. (David Lay) $450

A Regency octagonal oak workbox crossbanded and inlaid with geometric mahogany and satinwood lozenges, 15½in. wide, 31in. high. (Christie's) $1,179

Early 19th century mahogany work table with two drop-flaps, end drawer and dummy drawer, 2ft.4in. wide. (Lots Road Chelsea Auction Galleries) $560

A satinwood workbox-on-stand with hinged top enclosing a blue silk padded interior above a sliding well, labelled John Bagshaw & Sons, Liverpool, 11¾in. wide. (Christie's) $689

A Country Federal inlaid cherry work table, New England, circa 1800, top 20 x 19¼in. (Robt. W. Skinner Inc.) $3,500

A Victorian burr walnut inlaid work table with rising top, drawer and slide (writing slope missing), 24in. wide. (King & Chasemore) $1,044

A George III oak work table with twin-flap top crossbanded with rosewood, 29in. wide. (Christie's) $2,689

WORKBOXES & GAMES TABLES

Federal mahogany and mahogany veneer and satinwood work table, circa 1820, 18¼ in. wide. (Robt. W. Skinner Inc.) $2,600

An early 19th century Chinese lacquer work table with hinged top and fitted interior, 25in. wide. (Robt. W. Skinner Inc.) $2,300

A Chinese Export lacquer games table with eared triple-flap top, 32½in. wide. (Christie's) $2,886

Mid 19th century giltwood and composition games table with square pietra dura top inlaid with chess squares, 21in. wide. (Christie's) $2,178

A Country Federal maple and pine painted and grained two-drawer work table, possibly Mass., circa 1820, top 19 x 17½in. (Robt. W. Skinner Inc.) $14,000

A mid Victorian parcel gilt, painted and sycamore work table with hinged top, 19½in. wide. (Christie's) $1,633

A work table with original 'vinegar painted' ochre decoration, New England, circa 1830, 21in. wide. (Robt. W. Skinner Inc.) $2,000

A Regency faded mahogany and rosewood work-table, the rounded rectangular top with two frieze drawers, 20in. wide. (Christie's) $3,608

A cherry and tiger maple work table, the bottom drawer fitted with bag frame, St. Louis, circa 1830, 26in. wide. (Robt. W. Skinner Inc.) $1,400

WRITING TABLES & DESKS

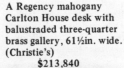

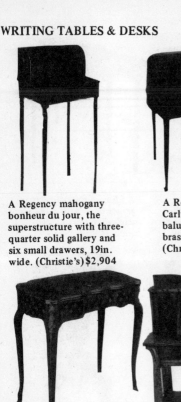

A Regency mahogany
bonheur du jour, the
superstructure with three-
quarter solid gallery and
six small drawers, 19in.
wide. (Christie's) $2,904

A Regency mahogany
Carlton House desk with
balustraded three-quarter
brass gallery, 61½in. wide.
(Christie's)
$213,840

A Regency rosewood cylinder
bureau crossbanded and inlaid with boxwood lines, 25¾in.
wide. (Christie's)
$8,910

A Louis Philippe burr-walnut
and tulipwood table a ecrire
with brass bound top, 31½in.
wide. (Christie's)
$3,674

Shop-O'-The-Crafters slant
front desk, Ohio, circa 1906,
style no. 279, signed with
paper label, 42in. wide. (Robt.
W. Skinner Inc.) $450

A parcel gilt walnut and marquetry bureau mazarin with
folding rectangular top,
41½in. wide. (Christie's)
$9,185

A gilt metal mounted mahogany bureau a cylindre on
fluted turned tapering legs,
30in. wide. (Christie's)
$4,041

An ormolu mounted kingwood
bureau plat of Regency style
with leather-lined top, 69in.
wide. (Christie's)
$10,890

One of a pair of George III
satinwood cheveret tables,
one 20in. wide, 44½in. high,
the other 19¼in. wide,
44¼in. high. (Christie's)
$10,692

WRITING TABLES & DESKS

An L. & J. G. Stickley flat top writing desk, circa 1905, 40in. wide. (Robt. W. Skinner Inc.) $550

A Regency mahogany library table, the frieze with two drawers, 46½in. wide. (Christie's) $2,868

A lady's Edwardian inlaid rosewood desk, the back fitted with two mirror panels. (Chancellors Hollingsworths) $810

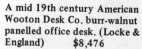

A Gustav Stickley flat-top writing desk, style no. 720, signed with red decal, circa 1907, 38¼in. wide. (Robt. W. Skinner Inc.) $1,100

An ormolu mounted kingwood and marquetry double-sided bureau of Louis XV style, 51in. wide. (Christie's) $12,705

A mid 19th century American Wooton Desk Co. burr-walnut panelled office desk. (Locke & England) $8,476

An L. & J. G. Stickley drop-front writing desk, no. 613, writing surface with fitted interior, circa 1910, 32in. wide. (Robt. W. Skinner Inc.) $650

Partner's Victorian mahogany table with leather-lined writing surface, 4ft. 6in. x 3ft.6in. (Lots Road Chelsea Auction Galleries) $1,148

An Italian bureau base inlaid with Renaissance style decoration and ivory panels. (Lots Road Chelsea Auction Galleries) $1,023

WRITING TABLES & DESKS

A brass-mounted mahogany writing-table with rectangular leather-lined top and frieze drawer on turned tapering legs, 31in. wide. (Christie's) $2,645

Victorian mahogany library table with shaped end supports and turned center stretcher, 48 x 26in. (J. M. Welch & Son) $852

Lady's Regency rosewood writing/work table with five small drawers with workbox slide under. (Worsfolds) $1,848

A Transitional style tulipwood and ormolu mounted desk, inlaid with boxwood and ebony lines, of bowed form, 36in. (Christie's) $1,468

A 20th century mahogany Carlton House desk with leather inset writing slide, 41in. wide. (Peter Wilson) $1,036

A Kingwood and tulipwood bureau-de-dame of bombe shape, sloping flap enclosing a fitted interior, 30½in. wide. (Christie's) $4,070

A school master's grain painted pine desk with slant lift lid, New England, 1830, 3ft. wide. (Robt. W. Skinner Inc.) $750

An inlaid oak drop-front desk, designed by Harvey Ellis for Gustav Stickley, 1903-04, style no. 706, 30in. wide. (Robt. W. Skinner Inc.) $20,000

An Edwardian mahogany Carlton House writing table on square tapering legs, 45in. wide. (Parsons, Welch & Cowell) $3,528

WRITING TABLES & DESKS

Mid 19th century mahogany library writing table, 58in. long. (Peter Wilson) $1,337

A 19th century French walnut and parcel gilt library table, 135cm. wide. (Wellington Salerooms) $7,056

An Edwardian mahogany inlaid kidney-shaped pedestal writing desk, 4ft. wide. (King & Chasemore) $2,700

A Gustav Stickley desk, no. 721, circa 1912, 29in. high. (Robt. W. Skinner Inc.) $425

A rosewood bonheur-du-jour, the rectangular top with leather-lined panel and pierced three-quarter gallery, with three drawers, 46in. high. (Christie's) $4,884

A 19th century inlaid walnut amboyna and ebonized writing desk with hinged stationery compartment, 26½in. wide. (Reeds Rains) $1,235

An Edwardian mahogany writing table, interior fitted with a rising stationery rack and drawers, 26in. high. (Christie's) $3,866

A William IV mahogany writing table with inset top on turned and reeded supports, 3ft.3in. x 3ft.6in. (Prudential Fine Art) $6,600

A Sheraton Revival rosewood and marquetry small cylinder desk, 28in. wide. (Dreweatt Neate) $2,232

WRITING TABLES & DESKS

A George III mahogany
writing table, now with
Regency leather-lined top,
60in. wide. (Christie's)
$74,844

A black and gold lacquer
Carlton House desk deco-
rated with chinoiserie panels
of flowers, landscapes and
figures, 59½in. wide.
(Christie's) $4,510

A Regency mahogany
writing table with rectangular
leather-lined top, 45in. wide.
(Christie's) $5,737

A Victorian walnut bonheur
du jour decorated with
ormolu handles and mounts.
(Lots Road Chelsea Auction
Galleries) $2,754

An ormolu mounted king-
wood and tulipwood
bonheur-du-jour, 28in. wide.
(Christie's) $5,082

A late Victorian ormolu
mounted ebonized bonheur-
du-jour mounted with
Sevres style plaques, 43in.
wide. (Christie's)
$1,452

A brass mounted mahogany
writing desk with a tambour
roll-top, 26½in. wide.
(Christie's) $2,204

A George III mahogany
writing table with leather-
lined top and arched
secretaire drawer, 50½in.
wide. (Christie's)
$8,068

A satinwood veneered bonheur
du jour, Maple & Co. trade
label, 28.5in. wide. (Woolley &
Wallis) $1,620

WRITING TABLES & DESKS

An ormolu mounted mahogany and marquetry bureau plat in the manner of B.V.R.B., stamped G. Durand, 45½in. wide. (Christie's) $4,592

An early George III mahogany architect's table with rectangular easel-supported top, 39¼in. wide. (Christie's) $9,801

A Regency mahogany writing table in the manner of Gillows, with eared leather-lined top and three frieze drawers, 48in. wide. (Christie's) $40,986

A Carlo Bugatti ebonized and rosewood lady's writing desk with pewter and ivory inlay, 75.5cm. wide. (Christie's) $6,314

A Dutch ebonized and lacquer writing table, the top with inset panel of courtly figures boating in a water landscape, 34½in. wide. (Christie's) $4,225

A German oak green stained writing desk in the style of C. A. Voysey, 110.5cm. wide. (Christie's) $5,772

A Regency rosewood bonheur du jour, the open superstructure with shelves and two cupboards, 34½in. wide. (Christie's) $5,445

A Louis XVI ormolu mounted bureau a cylindre with three-quarter galleried white marble top and three drawers above a panelled cylinder, 49¾in. wide. (Christie's) $11,022

A late Victorian satinwood bonheur-du-jour on square tapering legs, 33¾in. wide. (Christie's) $3,993

TRUNKS & COFFERS

Late 18th/early 19th century painted pine blanket chest, Penn., 50in. wide. (Christie's) $3,300

Late 16th century Momoyama period coffer with domed hinged lid, 79 x 44 x 53.8cm. (Christie's) $6,688

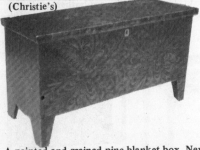

A painted and grained pine blanket box, New England, circa 1810. (Robt. W. Skinner. Inc.) $1,300

A 17th century oak coffer with a rectangular cover over a lunette frieze and a triple panelled front, on stile supports, 44in. wide. (Hy. Duke & Son) $810

An oak and poplar chest with drawer, probably Conn., 1690-1710, 48½in. wide. (Christie's) $20,900

A 17th century gilt metal kingwood coffre fort with oyster-veneered top and fallflap, possibly Flemish, 15½in. wide. (Christie's) $1,557

A painted pine blanket chest, New England, circa 1800, 43in. wide. (Robt. W. Skinner Inc.) $1,700

Late 18th century Mediterranean ivory inlaid olivewood coffer, 67in. wide. (Christie's) $3,306

TRUNKS & COFFERS

A vinegar painted blanket box, probably New England, circa 1830, 39in. wide. (Robt. W. Skinner Inc.) $1,100

A carved and grain painted blanket chest, America, circa 1820, 44in. wide. (Robt. W. Skinner Inc.) $4,000

A grain painted blanket box, the molded lift-top on dovetailed base and cut-out bracket feet, Conn., circa 1850, 40½in. wide. (Robt. W. Skinner Inc.) $650

A painted and decorated pine blanket chest, Schoharie County, N.Y., circa 1810, 40¾in. wide. (Robt. W. Skinner Inc.) $8,500

A 19th century yellow grain-painted miniature blanket chest on French feet, 14in. high, 22in. wide, 12¾in. deep. (Christie's) $1,760

A mid-Victorian walnut Ottoman, rectangular top and bracket feet, 33in. wide. (Christie's) $1,964

Mid 17th century Flemish oak coffer, the interior fitted with a well, the coffered front inlaid with ivory and ebony, 52½in. wide. (Christie's) $1,561

Early 19th century North African ivory and hardwood inlaid walnut chest, 40½in. wide. (Christie's) $2,020

TRUNKS & COFFERS

A painted and decorated rectangular box, fabric lined, America, circa 1830, 30in. long. (Robt. W. Skinner Inc.) $2,750

Late 17th century Italian walnut cassone, heavily carved to front and sides, 85in. long. (Brown & Merry) $3,185

Late 18th/early 19th century Chippendale tiger maple two drawer blanket chest, New England, 38¾in. wide. (Christie's) $2,640

A Federal painted poplar blanket chest, probably Penn., 1800-30, 50in. wide. (Christie's) $6,600

An experimental Gustav Stickley cedar-lined chest, circa 1901-02, 27¾in. wide. (Robt. W. Skinner. Inc.) $9,000

A red-painted two drawer blanket chest, labelled by F. W. Spooner Vermont, 1836, 42in. wide. (Christie's) $660

A putty painted pine blanket chest, New England, circa 1820, 38½in. wide. (Robt. W. Skinner. Inc.) $8,500

An oak coffer, panelled rising lid, with panelled and carved front, 56in. wide. (Locke & England) $1,059

TRUNKS & COFFERS

Early 19th century grain painted blanket box, New England, 38¼in. wide. (Robt. W. Skinner Inc.) $750

A George III crossbanded oak mule chest with plain top, panelled sides, arched panelled front and two drawers, on bracket feet, 4ft.1in. wide. (Hobbs & Chambers) $825

An eagle-painted pine blanket chest, possibly Hanover area, York County, Penn., circa 1808, 52in. wide. (Christie's) $8,800

A painted blanket chest, Pennsylvania, dated 1760, 21in. high, 51½in. wide, 24½in. deep. (Christie's) $385

An oak coffer with panelled rising top, front and sides, inlaid with lozenge and star motifs, 3ft.9in. wide. (Geering & Colyer) $961

A 19th century painted pine and poplar dower chest, Penn., 48in. wide. (Robt. W. Skinner Inc.) $6,000

Early 17th century Italian oak bridal chest with walnut facings and colored marble inlays. (Worsfolds) $2,624

Early 19th century grain painted pine six board chest with hinged lid, probably New England, 47¾in. wide. (Robt. W. Skinner Inc.) $1,800

WARDROBES & ARMOIRES

Mid 18th century Tyrolean cream and black-painted armoire on later bun feet, 55in. wide, 73½in. high. (Christie's) $4,592

Late 18th century Dutch brass mounted mahogany armoire, 74in. wide. (Christie's) $16,533

A George IV mahogany wardrobe on bun feet, 85½in. high, 55in. wide. (Christie's) $2,151

An Arts & Crafts breakfront oak wardrobe by George Walton, 230.2cm. wide. (Christie's) $6,855

An early 19th century gentleman's mahogany wardrobe, the gilded Nelson mask handles celebrating The Battle of Trafalgar 1805, 122cm. wide. (Wellington Salerooms) $2,016

An English Arts & Crafts walnut combination wardrobe with ebony crossbanding, 66in. wide. (Reeds Rains) $567

An Arts & Crafts walnut wardrobe by Cope & Collinson, 188cm. wide. (David Lay) $1,890

A George III gentleman's mahogany linen press, 49 x 85in. high. (Lacy Scott) $2,062

A maple and walnut kas, in two sections, N.Y., or N. Jersey, 1750-1800, 72in. wide. (Christie's) $4,400

WARDROBES & ARMOIRES

A Louis XV oak armoire with foliate overhanging cornice, minor restoration, 64in. wide. (Christie's) $3,916

Late 18th century Dutch walnut kas on turned onion feet, 67in. wide. (Christie's) $1,533

A 19th century mahogany and marquetry linen press on splay bracket feet, 42in. wide. (Parsons, Welch & Cowell) $3,360

A Gustav Stickley two-door wardrobe, no. 920, 1904-06, 33in. wide. (Robt. W. Skinner Inc.) $3,100

An 18th century William and Mary walnut schrank, Penn., 74¼in. wide. (Christie's) $7,700

A George III mahogany clothes press, the base with two short and one long drawer, 53in. wide. (Christie's) $3,406

A Regency satinwood clothes press, the base with two short and two graduated long drawers, 50½in. wide. (Christie's) $16,736

An early George III mahogany clothes press on panelled bracket feet, 49½in. wide, 79in. high. (Christie's) $6,494

A French 18th century Provincial chestnut armoire with a pair of arched triple fielded panel doors, 59½in. wide. (Christie's) $7,398

WASHSTANDS

A 19th century enclosed washstand with lift-top revealing a rising mirror. (Lots Road Chelsea Auction Galleries) $968

George III mahogany corner wash-stand with fitted shelf, additional shelf beneath having central drawer, 3ft3in. high. (Phillips) $520

A late 18th century mahogany washstand with side carrying handles, 45cm. wide. (Wellington Salerooms) $1,344

A mid Georgian mahogany washstand on turned supports, 31in. high. (Christie's) $973

An early 19th century mahogany enclosed washstand, 30in. high. (Dreweatt Neate) $1,302

A 19th century painted pine washstand, painted old pink over other colors, America, 15½in. wide. (Robt. W. Skinner Inc.) $800

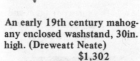

A painted and decorated washstand, New England, circa 1830, 15¼in. wide. (Robt. W. Skinner Inc.) $300

An Empire rosewood washstand, the molded rectangular top with three recesses, 42in. wide. (Christie's) $1,958

Classical Revival mahogany washstand, probably Boston, circa 1815, 18¼in. diam. (Robt. W. Skinner Inc.) $3,600

WHATNOTS

A Regency mahogany three-
tier whatnot, 16in. wide.
(Christie's) $1,623

A Victorian mahogany three-
tier carved and turned buffet.
(J. M. Welch & Son)
$516

A Regency mahogany whatnot
with four rectangular shelves,
20in. wide. (Christie's)
$1,839

A Regency rosewood and
brass etagere with four
rectangular tiers, the top
with pierced gallery, 39¼in.
high. (Christie's)
$14,245

A Victorian walnut and marquetry four-tier corner whatnot on turned supports. (J.
M. Welch & Son) $511

A Regency mahogany what-
not with two tiers, ring-
turned supports and two
drawers, 24in. wide.
(Christie's) $2,525

A Regency mahogany
whatnot with four rectan-
gular tiers, 19in. wide.
(Christie's) $2,525

A grain painted pine and
poplar etagere, New England,
circa 1820, 35½in. wide.
(Robt. W. Skinner Inc.)
$450

A Regency mahogany what-
not with three shelves, 16in.
wide. (Christie's)
$1,262

WINE COOLERS

Late 18th century George III mahogany cellaret, the sides with brass carrying handles, 17¾in. wide. (Christie's) $4,950

An Irish George III mahogany wine waiter of rectangular shape with divided and undulating galleried top, 26in. wide. (Christie's) $13,783

Late 18th century George III brass bound mahogany cellaret, the hinged top enclosing a lead-lined fitted interior, 18½in. wide. (Christie's) $4,400

A George III mahogany and brass bound octagonal cellaret with hinged top, 46cm. wide. (Phillips) $3,936

A Regency mahogany sarcophagus cellaret with revolving panelled doors enclosing a fitted interior for six bottles, 33in. wide. (Christie's) $5,020

A mahogany cellaret, the waved body with detachable tin-liner, 15in. wide. (Christie's) $1,262

A satinwood cellaret crossbanded with tulipwood and inlaid with burr-walnut ovals, 20in. wide. (Christie's) $3,048

A George IV mahogany wine cooler of sarcophagus shape with stepped hinged top enclosing a lead-lined interior, 28in. wide. (Christie's) $1,645

A Georgian mahogany wine cooler with brass carrying handles. (McKenna's) $1,729

WINE COOLERS

A Regency mahogany wine cooler of sarcophagus shape with lead-lined interior, 31¾in. wide. (Christie's) $10,399

A George III mahogany brass bound hexagonal cellaret, 15in. wide, 27½in. high. (Graves Son & Pilcher) $2,058

An early 19th century mahogany cellaret with lead lining and set on four bun feet, 79 x 47cm. (Wellington Salerooms) $2,184

A George III mahogany cellaret with octagonal hinged top enclosing a later divided interior, 19in. wide. (Christie's) $2,904

A George IV mahogany cellaret with lead-lined interior, 34in. wide. (Christie's) $2,345

A George III brass bound mahogany cellaret with a lead-lined interior, 19in. wide. (Christie's) $3,968

A George III brass bound mahogany wine cooler, the tapering oval body with scrolling handles, 28½in. wide. (Christie's) $5,033

A George IV mahogany sarcophagus cellaret with hinged lid, lead-lined interior and Bramah lock, 33in. wide. (Christie's) $1,533

A George III mahogany wine cooler, the oval lid enclosing a detachable tin liner, 26in. wide. (Christie's) $8,269

GLASS

BEAKERS

Mid 19th century Bohemian engraved cylindrical beaker with scenes and quotes from The Lord's Prayer, 5½in. high. (Christie's) $550

Late 18th/early 19th century engraved Masonic toasting glass, 4¾in. high. (Christie's) $1,760

A Venetian Zwischengoldglas beaker with panelled sides and a scene of The Last Supper, after da Vinci, 3¾in. high. (Christie's) $1,320

BOTTLES

Early 18th century sealed wine bottle of olive-green tint and onion shape, 18cm. high. (Christie's) $787

A sealed wine bottle of upright form and olive-green tint, the body with a seal inscribed M Stripp/Lyskerd, circa 1745, 23.5cm. high. (Christie's) $275

A 19th century brownish green carboy with gilt scrolled label for Acet Distill, 11½in. high. (Christie's) $360

An early sealed wine bottle in dark green glass, bearing a seal 'Thos. Abbott 1728', 19.5cm. high. (Phillips) $1,375

A Nuremburg engraved serving bottle, the neck with foliate and scrolling floral foliage bands, circa 1700, 25cm. high. (Christie's) $1,535

A sealed wine bottle of upright form and olive-green tint, dated 1747, 21.5cm. high. (Christie's) $511

BOWLS

A cut glass punch bowl with Van Dyke edge above a band of diamonds, 16½in. diam. (Christie's) $1,100

A Victorian vaseline glass bowl with an off-white exterior and pink interior, approx. 9in. wide. (G. A. Key) $61

Galle Cameo glass bowl, wide raised rim on shallow round bowl, 'Galle' signature, diam. 6in. (Robt. W. Skinner Inc.) $550

An Irish cut turnover fruit bowl, circa 1800, 36cm. wide. (Christie's) $2,520

Late 19th century Bohemian rose bowl on stand, 16½in. high. (Peter Wilson) $1,231

A Venetian deep bowl, on a radially ribbed spreading foot, second half of the 15th century. (Christie's) $1,980

Early 19th century Cork Glass Co. engraved finger bowl, 13cm. diam. (Christie's) $1,082

One of two Daum Cameo glass rosebowls, crimped ruffled rim decorated with cameo-cut sprays of violets, signed 'Daum/Nancy', diam. 7in. (Robt. W. Skinner Inc.) $800

A Schwarzlot decorated armorial deep bowl in the manner of Preissler, Bohemia or Saxony, circa 1736, 25cm. diam. (Christie's) $5,513

BOWLS

Art glass bowl, attributed to
Victor Durand, diam. 4¾in.
(Robt. W. Skinner Inc.)
$100

A Lalique opalescent bowl,
the blue opalescent glass
molded with a frieze of
budgerigars, 24cm. diam.
(Christie's) $2,886

One of a pair of 'Lynn' finger
bowls and one stand, the
bowl 12cm. diam., the stand
15.5cm. diam., circa 1775.
(Christie's) $393

Late 19th century Venetian
pedestal bowl in blotched
pink and opaque white and
clear aventurine glass, 10½in.
high. (Lalonde Fine Art)
$297

Two of ten George III glass
wine rinsers, circa 1810,
5in. diam. (Christie's)
$660

An Irish cut oval turnover
fruit bowl, circa 1800, 28cm.
wide. (Christie's)
$720

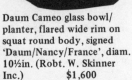

Daum Cameo glass bowl/
planter, flared wide rim on
squat round body, signed
'Daum/Nancy/France', diam.
10½in. (Robt. W. Skinner
Inc.) $1,600

Steuben centerpiece bowl
with adjusting holder, diam.
12in. (Robt. W. Skinner Inc.)
$475

'Lys', a Lalique opalescent
bowl molded with four
lily flowers, 24cm. diam.
(Christie's) $902

CANDLESTICKS

A pedestal stemmed candlestick with detachable waxpan, circa 1750, 25cm. high. (Christie's) $720

A pair of Charles X gilt metal and cut glass candlesticks and a dressing table mirror en suite, the candlesticks 6¾in. high, the mirror 13¼in. high. (Christie's) $2,153

One of a pair of harlequin cut glass twin branch wall lights, 30in. high. (Christie's) $2,151

A pedestal stemmed candlestick and a detachable waxpan, 18th century, 25cm. high. (Christie's) $864

A fine pair of gilt metal and Bohemian glass candlesticks, mid 19th century, 15in. high. (Christie's) $7,832

A pedestal stemmed candlestick, the cylindrical nozzle with everted rim, mid 18th century, 19.5cm. high. (Christie's) $360

One of a pair of Venetian glass table lustres, 38.5cm. high. (Phillips) $1,050

An opaque twist taperstick, the slender nozzle with everted rim, circa 1765, 18.5cm. high. (Christie's) $3,938

One of a pair of Regency ormolu and cut glass twin-light candelabra with flaming finials, 16in. high. (Christie's) $3,029

DECANTERS

Two George III glass decanters, classic-shaped with panel-cut shoulders and bases, circa 1800, 9.7/8in. high and 8½in. high. (Christie's) $605

A George III glass decanter, Indian club-shaped with wide neck, circa 1790, overall height 29cm. (Christie's) $935

A Victorian decanter stand with three oval glass decanters, one in green, one in ruby and one in clear glass, by Elkington & Co., 12in. high. (Christie's) $915

A Venini 'Vetro pesante inciso' decanter and stopper designed by Paolo Venini, circa 1957, 18.5cm. high. (Christie's) $1,232

An Archimede Seguso 'Compisizione Piume' carafe, circa 1960, 29cm. high. (Christie's) $7,920

A Venini 'Vetro pesante inciso' decanter and stopper, 27.5cm. high. (Christie's) $1,046

A Venini 'Vetro pesante inciso' carafe, dark brown cased in clear glass, circa 1957, 25.5cm. high. (Christie's) $1,232

A pair of Georgian mallet-shaped decanters facet cut with bull's eye stoppers, 27cm. high, and another matching, 28.5cm. high. (Osmond Tricks) $445

A 'Lynn' decanter of club shape with horizontally ribbed sides and kick-in base, circa 1775, 23.5cm. high. (Christie's) $945

DISHES

Tiffany glass Floriform dish, gold iridescent bowl form with scalloped and crimped irregular rim, marked 'L.C.T', diam. 4½in. (Robt. W. Skinner Inc.) $175

A 17th century Venetian diamond engraved tazza, 20cm. diam. (Christie's) $3,544

North Country machine-pressed milk glass oval butter dish cover on wood plinth, 2.5in. (Giles Haywood) $19

A 'Non-Such' blue glass dish, by Isaac Jacobs, circa 1805, 18.5cm. diam. (Christie's) $3,544

An opaque twist sweetmeat glass, the double ogee bowl with everted dentil rim, circa 1765, 9.5cm. high. (Christie's) $511

Mid 19th century cobalt blue blown glass cuspidor, American, 5in. high, 9in. diam. (Robt. W. Skinner Inc.) $250

A North Country pressed crystal shaped dish designed as a basket with cane handle, circa 1900, 4in. high. (Giles Haywood) $22

One of a pair of Charles X ormolu and cut glass sweetmeat dishes with ring finials, the dishes supported by mermaids and tritons, 20in. high. (Christie's) $8,223

A Schneider cameo glass dish of circular shape, 39cm. diam., signed 'Charder' for Charles Schneider. (Phillips) $528

DRINKING SETS

An Art Deco glass decanter set, the decanter 20.5cm. high and six octagonal glasses, 6.5cm. high. (Phillips)
$774

Early 19th century glass liqueur set, in a mahogany fitted chest, probably French, chest 11in. long. (Christie's)
$935

A WMF Art Deco molded glass liqueur set on a stand with molded handle. (Woolley & Wallis)
$247

Two Lalique clear glass decanters and stoppers, the spherical bodies molded with fine vertical ribbing and twenty glasses en suite. (Christie's) $801

Four liqueur drinking glasses, on tall flaring stems with various sized bowls, possibly Austrian, each 6½in. high. (Christie's) $1,279

An Art Deco decanter and glasses, the decanter 22.5cm. high and six liqueur glasses 5cm. high (one glass chipped). (Phillips)
$264

GOBLETS

Mid 18th century Newcastle engraved composite stemmed goblet on a folded conical foot, 16.5cm. high. (Christie's) $511

Late 19th century Venetian goblet vase in nacreous marbled pink and amber, and clear aventurine glass, 12½in. high. (Lalonde Fine Art) $280

An engraved Bohemian goblet and cover, 38.5cm. high. (Phillips) $1,680

A baluster goblet with a round funnel bowl, the solid lower part with a tear, circa 1710, 16.5cm. high. (Christie's) $945

One of three large Vedar glass goblets, the bowls enamel painted with continuous frieze of naked females and peacocks, 7½in. high, signed XVII. (Christie's) $1,248

Mid 18th century engraved composite stemmed goblet with bell bowl, 21.5cm. high. (Christie's) $2,559

A color twist goblet with an ogee bowl, circa 1765, 19.5cm. high. (Christie's) $3,544

A James Powell flower form goblet, milky vaseline glass, the flower form bowl with frilly rim, 30cm. high. (Christie's) $1,178

Mid 18th century Newcastle light baluster engraved goblet, the bell bowl with a border of laub-und-Bandelwerk, 17cm. high. (Christie's) $590

GOBLETS

A heavy baluster goblet, the ovoid bowl drawn from a stem terminating in an angular knop, circa 1710, 17.5cm. high. (Christie's) $2,165

A 19th century crystal glass, the hollow bulbous knopped stem containing a Swingewood opal cat and three amethyst mice, circa 1890, 5in. high. (Giles Haywood) $343

An ale glass, the slender funnel bowl with crisp wrythen molded lower part, circa 1730, 15cm. high. (Christie's) $630

An Almeric Walter pate-de-verre goblet, designed by Henri Berge, 6¼in. high. (Anderson & Garland) $1,595

A James Powell goblet, milky vaseline glass, 21cm. high. (Christie's) $420

An Absolon rummer of emerald-green tint, the ovoid bowl decorated in gilt with a sailing ship heightened in black, circa 1800, 12cm. high. (Christie's) $905

A baluster goblet with bell bowl, the stem with two true baluster sections, circa 1710, 17.5cm. high. (Christie's) $472

Late 17th century Netherlands green tinted roemer, the stem applied with raspberry prunts, 15cm. high. (Christie's) $1,279

An engraved pedestal stemmed goblet with round funnel bowl, circa 1750, 17.5cm. high. (Christie's) $905

GOBLETS

A pedestal stemmed goblet with straight-sided funnel bowl, circa 1750, 16cm. high. (Christie's) $630

An emerald green incised twist goblet with cup-shaped bowl, circa 1765, 14cm. high. (Christie's) $2,362

A facet stemmed engraved goblet with funnel bowl, circa 1785, 19.5cm. high. (Christie's) $511

One of three large Vedar goblets, the bowls enamel painted with continuous frieze of dancing putti, 7½in. high, signed Vedar XIII, XX, VIII. (Christie's) $1,245

A German Royal armorial goblet and a cover, the glass possibly Thuringia, the engraving Potsdam, 1720-25, 32cm. high overall. (Christie's) $3,150

One of a pair of Venetian ruby glass goblets with panels of The Road to Calvary, 9in. high. (Christie's) $605

A baluster goblet with straight-sided funnel bowl, circa 1715, 16.5cm. high. (Christie's) $393

A gilt decorated emerald green goblet with cup-shaped bowl, circa 1765, 14cm. high. (Christie's) $1,673

A mammoth baluster goblet, the funnel bowl with a solid lower part, circa 1710, 30.5cm. high. (Christie's) $3,544

GOBLETS

A baluster goblet with round funnel bowl on a small knop, on a conical folded foot, 20cm. high. (Phillips) $668

Late 19th century Venetian goblet in pale pink and clear aventurine glass, 15½in. high. (Lalonde Fine Art) $396

A baluster goblet, the round funnel bowl with a tear to the solid lower part, circa 1715, 15.5cm. high. (Christie's) $393

A baluster goblet, the bell bowl supported on an annulated knop above a true baluster stem and short plain section, circa 1715, 21cm. high. (Christie's) $748

A Bohemian engraved amber flash goblet, the flared fluted bowl on a fluted knopped stem, circa 1840, 26cm. high. (Christie's) $984

A baluster toastmaster's glass, the funnel bowl set on an inverted baluster stem enclosing a tear, circa 1710, 12cm. high. (Christie's) $630

A 'single flint' goblet, the straight-sided funnel bowl with a solid lower part, circa 1700, 18cm. high. (Christie's) $984

A 19th century crystal glass, the hollow bulbous knopped stem containing a black Swingewood cockerel and hen, circa 1890, 5in. high. (Giles Haywood) $229

A plain stemmed goblet, the bucket bowl inscribed Success to Sir Francis Knollys, circa 1760, 19.5cm. high. (Christie's) $590

JUGS

An ovoid glass claret jug with a star design, the plain mount with bracket handle, 7¾in. high. (Christie's) $144

An Elton squat globular jug with elongated spout, 16.5cm. high. (Osmond Tricks) $187

A Hukin & Heath EPNS mounted large cut glass claret jug, 12in. high. (Hetheringtons Nationwide) $304

D. Christian cameo glass pitcher, shaped upright pouring lip and applied handle on slender cylindrical form, signature 'D. Christian/Meisenthal/Loth', height 10¼in. (Robt. W. Skinner Inc.) $1,400

An early serving bottle, the compressed globular body with a kick-in base, circa 1700, 14.5cm. high. (Christie's) $1,530

A hand cut crystal tall pitcher with notched handle, circa 1890. (Du Mouchelles) $300

A Continental silver mounted ewer, the silver cap with embossed fruit decoration, on a lead crystal base, 10in. high. (Hetheringtons Nationwide) $152

An Elton jug with bifurcated spout and handle above, 18cm. high. (Osmond Tricks) $504

A 19th century Arts & Crafts period claret jug, by Heath & Middleton, Birmingham, 1893. (Peter Wilson) $422

A clear and frosted glass oval tray with DT monogram mark, for Dorothy Thorpe, 25¼ x 17¾in. (Christie's) $495

Early 18th century posset jar and cover, 21.5cm. high. (Christie's) $2,756

Lalique opaque blue stained glass circular inkwell molded with four mermaids, 6¼in. diam. (Reeds Rains) $868

A Bohemian pewter and porcelain mounted ruby overlay tankard and cover, engraved in the manner of Pfhol, circa 1860, 25cm. high. (Christie's) $708

A pair of 19th century glass specie jars enamelled in white on the inside and enamelled colors with the Royal Arms, 18.1/8in. high. (Christie's) $844

A cranberry triple trumpet-shaped three-branch blown glass epergne on circular crimped base. (Hetheringtons Nationwide) $448

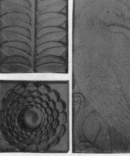

A St. Louis patterned concentric millefiori wafer-stand, 3.3/8in. high. (Christie's) $715

Three of eight Lalique satin glass panels, three rectangular and five of square shape, one panel signed R. Lalique. (Christie's) $1,804

An English cameo glass biscuit barrel with plated mount, swing handle and cover, 17cm. diam. (Phillips) $1,337

A Victorian glass epergne, opaline and green tinted decoration, 23in. high. (Peter Wilson) $457

A Lalique glass inkwell. (Hobbs Parker) $1,890

A flask of flattened oviform shape, the sides with a band of trailed loop ornament above 'nipt diamond waies', circa 1695, 13.5cm. high.(Christie's) $945

A Lalique clear and frosted glass presse-papier, the plaque intaglio molded with the figure of St. Christopher carrying the infant Christ, 4½in. high. (Christie's) $712

A pair of Nancy pate de verre bookends fashioned as dolphins, signed X Momillon, 6½in. high. (Lots Road Chelsea Auction Galleries) $4,550

An Art Deco glass cocktail shaker with silver mounts, Birmingham, 1936, 8in. high. (Dreweatt Neate) $748

A Millville steel die sailing boat mantel ornament, attributed to Michael Kane, 5½in. high. (Christie's) $1,210

A pair of early 19th century urn-shaped honey jars with domed covers and cut knop finials, 12in. high, overall. (Anderson & Garland) $566

Two of six 19th century cut glass stirrup cups, four 6¼in. high, the other two 7in. high. (Christie's) $550

A Baccarat flat bouquet
weight, 3in. diam. (Christie's)
$13,200

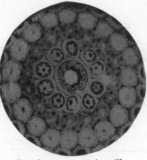

A Bacchus concentric millefiori paperweight, the dark
green central cane encircled
by five rows of canes in red,
white and blue, 8.5cm. diam.
(Phillips) $751

A Baccarat close concentric
millefiori mushroom weight
on a star-cut base, 3.1/8in.
diam. (Christie's)
$1,870

A Baccarat faceted blue-flash
patterned millefiori weight,
3.1/8in. diam. (Christie's)
$3,080

A Millville rose pedestal weight,
the flower with numerous bright
yellow petals, 3¾in. high.
(Christie's) $1,320

A Baccarat faceted pink-ground
sulphide weight, the crystallo-
ceramie portrait of St. Joseph,
named below, 2.5/8in. diam.
(Christie's) $440

A St. Louis faceted blue-berry
weight, 2½in. diam.
(Christie's) $2,090

A Clichy close millefiori small
paperweight, the canes including a pink and a white rose,
5.2cm. diam. (Phillips)
$1,085

A Baccarat faceted concentric
millefiori mushroom paperweight, 7.5cm. diam.
(Phillips) $1,586

A Baccarat millefiori paperweight, one cane dated B.
1847, 7.5cm. diam. (Phillips)
$1,135

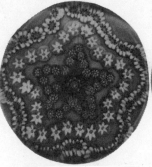

A Clichy pink-ground patterned concentric millefiori
weight, 3.1/8in. diam.
(Christie's) $2,420

A Mount Washington magnum
pink rose weight, 4in. diam.
(Christie's) $4,400

A French (unknown factory)
strawberry weight, 3.1/8in.
diam. (Christie's)
$3,850

An Almaric Walter pate-de-
verre paperweight designed
by H. Berge, 8cm. high.
(Christie's) $15,334

A St. Louis double clematis
paperweight, the two rows of
pink striated petals with yellow
match-head stamen, on a green
leafy stalk, 6.4cm. diam.
(Phillips) $764

A Baccarat patterned millefiori white carpet-ground
weight, 3in. diam. (Christie's)
$6,050

A St. Louis blue dahlia
weight on a star-cut base,
2¾in. diam. (Christie's)
$1,650

A Clichy triple-color swirl
paperweight, 7.4cm. diam.
(Phillips) $1,536

PAPERWEIGHTS

A St. Louis purple dahlia weight on a star-cut base, 2¾in. diam. (Christie's) $2,860

A Clichy faceted pink double-overlay concentric millefiori mushroom weight on a strawberry-cut base, 3.1/8in. diam. (Christie's) $5,500

A Clichy close concentric millefiori weight, 2.1/8in. diam. (Christie's) $3,520

A Sandwich blue poinsettia weight, the pale-blue flower with twelve petals, 2½in. diam. (Christie's) $550

An Almaric Walter pate-de-verre paperweight, the blue glass molded as a bird, 12cm. high. (Christie's) $902

A Baccarat garlanded butterfly weight, on a star-cut base, 3.1/8in. diam. (Christie's) $2,420

A St. Louis concentric mille-fiori paperweight, one cane dated SL 1848, 6.8cm. diam. (Phillips) $2,254

A Gillinder flower weight, 2.7/8in. diam. (Christie's) $935

A St. Louis amber flash garlanded sulphide weight, the portrait of the young Victoria in profile, 2½in. diam. (Christie's) $1,430

PAPERWEIGHTS

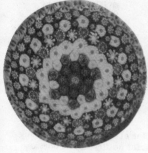

A Clichy close concentric millefiori weight, 2.7/8in. diam. (Christie's) $3,520

A Baccarat faceted green-ground sulphide huntsman weight, 3.3/8in. diam. (Christie's) $1,760

A St. Louis faceted upright bouquet weight, 2¾in. diam. (Christie's) $2,420

A Baccarat blue pompom and bud weight, 3.1/8in. diam. (Christie's) $13,200

A sulphide paperweight, the lobed globular surmount inset with a crystallo-ceramie bust of Voltaire, 12.5cm. diam., possibly reduced. (Phillips) $501

A Clichy faceted patterned millefiori weight, 3in. diam. (Christie's) $1,320

A Baccarat faceted sulphide huntsman paperweight, 8.5cm. diam. (Phillips) $918

A St. Louis crown weight, 2¾in. diam. (Christie's) $2,090

A St. Louis concentric mille-fiori mushroom paperweight, the base star cut, 7.5cm. diam. (Phillips) $1,169

SCENT BOTTLES

Daum Cameo and enamelled glass perfume bottle with conforming stopper, signature 'Daum/Nancy', height 4½in. (Robt. W. Skinner Inc.) $1,400

A cameo citrine-ground silver mounted scent bottle, the silver with maker's mark JNM, London, 1884, 14.5cm. long. (Christie's) $472

One of a pair of blue tapering scent bottles and stoppers, gilt in the atelier of James Giles, circa 1760, in a contemporary Birmingham gilt metal filigree case, circa 1760, the case 5cm. high. (Christie's) $1,673

An opaque scent bottle of pear shape, one side inscribed I*E:CAY, Newcastle-upon-Tyne, circa 1785, 8.5cm. long. (Christie's) $196

A facet cut green scent bottle, stopper and gold screw cover, gilt in the atelier of James Giles, circa 1765, 6cm. long. (Christie's) $1,673

A crystal perfume bottle/ink well with matching stopper, 3.5in. high. (Giles Haywood) $28

A cameo scent-bottle and stopper of tapering form with waisted neck, circa 1880, 14.5cm. high. (Christie's) $900

A Webb cameo glass scent phial with Tiffany white metal hinged cap, 6½in. high. (Christie's) $748

An opaque white scent bottle of tear-drop form, gilt in the atelier of James Giles, circa 1770, 8cm. long. (Christie's) $826

SCENT BOTTLES

A cameo silver gilt mounted scent bottle and screw cover, maker's mark for Sampson Mordan, London, 1884, 15cm. long. (Christie's) $354

An English cameo scent bottle, in the form of a swan's head, marked Birmingham ·1888, 16cm. (Phillips) $1,732

Coralene decorated perfume bottle with matching beaded stopper, height 6¾in. (Robt. W. Skinner Inc.) $250

An opaque scent bottle of flattened pear shape, one side inscribed A*B 1780, Newcastle-upon-Tyne, 7.5cm. long. (Christie's) $630

An Apsley Pellatt cut-glass sulphide scent bottle and stopper, 5.3/8in. high. (Christie's) $1,100

A gilt decorated blue scent bottle and stopper, decoration in the atelier of James Giles, circa 1765, 18cm high. (Christie's) $1,620

Continental amber glass, shaped perfume bottle with matching stopper, 6in. high. (Giles Haywood) $28

A Lalique scent bottle and stopper, the clear glass impressed and molded with stylized marguerites, 13.2cm. high. (Christie's) $324

A bottle-shaped cut crystal perfume bottle and matching stopper, with silver spoon and silver rim, hallmarked Sheffield, 1912, 4in. high. (Giles Haywood) $61

STAINED GLASS

A 16th century Flemish stained glass panel of the parable of Dives and Lazarus, 23.5 x 17.5cm. (Christie's) $1,194

A set of four late 18th or early 19th century English painted glass panels of female allegories of Justice, Faith, Hope and Charity, probably by Thos. Jarvis, after Sir J. Reynolds, each panel 72 x 40cm. (Christie's) $3,490

One of a pair of 18th century English oval stained glass armorial panels, 46 x 34.5cm. (Christie's) $734

A large 19th century English stained glass panel showing a lady in Renaissance costume at the prie-dieu, 100 x 55cm. (Christie's) $826

An Art Deco leaded stained glass panel by Jacques Gruber, 70.2cm. wide, 50.3cm. high. (Christie's) $5,772

A large rectangular glass panel by John Hutton, sand blasted and wheel engraved with Perseus before the Three Graces, 206.5 x 97cm. (Christie's) $2,706

A leaded and stained glass panel by George Walton, after a design by Charles Rennie Mackintosh, 133.6cm. high, 91.4cm. wide. (Christie's) $1,082

A 17th century French rectangular stained glass panel centered with an oval of the martyrdom of St. Stephen, 46.5 x 59cm. (Christie's) $918

A large 19th century English stained glass panel of Mary Queen of Scots, 151 x 80cm. (Christie's) $1,837

TUMBLERS

A Charpentier engraved cylindrical tumbler with a recumbent sheep, a dog, hat and crook, circa 1820, 9cm. high. (Christie's) $756

One of a pair of 'Lynn' flared tumblers with horizontally ribbed sides, circa 1775, 11.5cm. high. (Christie's) $315

A Bohemian 'Zwischengoldglas' fluted tumbler, initialled 'IHS', circa 1730, 8cm. high. (Christie's) $1,530

Possibly late 18th century Central European enamelled 'Jagd' tumbler, 16.5cm. high. (Christie's) $6,694

A lower Austrian 'Zwischengold' tumbler by Johann Mildner, the cylindrical body set with a double-walled medallion, circa 1788, 8.5cm. high. (Christie's) $1,530

An Austrian 'Zwischengold' Armorial tumbler by Johann Mildner, set with a double walled medallion, circa 1794, 12cm. high. (Christie's) $5,760

A Baccarat double medal cylindrical tumbler with cut foot and sunray base, 10.5cm. high. (Christie's) $1,378

A gilt decorated blue tumbler from the atelier of James Giles, circa 1765, 10.5cm. high. (Christie's) $1,338

A Charpentier dated cylindrical tumbler engraved with Cupid standing beside an urn, circa 1823, 9cm. high. (Christie's) $905

VASES

A Gabriel Argy-Rousseau
pate-de-verre vase, 12cm.
high. (Christie's)
$3,427

'Beliers', a Lalique vase
with two handles molded
as rams, 19cm. high.
(Christie's) $902

'Languedoc', a Lalique vase,
the body deeply molded
with bands of stylized
leaves, 22.6cm. high.
(Christie's) $2,164

A Stourbridge cameo glass
vase, the mid-blue ground
overlaid in white and carved
all-over with trailing wall-
flowers, 12cm. high.
(Phillips) $1,169

A James Powell vase, milky
vaseline glass, the flattened
bulbous base pinched into
four arms supporting a floppy
quatrefoil rim, 16.5cm. high.
(Christie's) $673

A Gabriel Argy-Rousseau pate-
de-verre vase, the body molded with tall stemmed plants
with hanging red pods, 6in.
high. (Christie's) $3,207

A miniature Daum enamelled
and acid etched vase enamelled with Sweet Violets, 4.3cm.
high. (Christie's) $793

Mid 19th century decalcomania
slender oviform vase and a
ball cover, the vase 40.5cm.
high. (Christie's)
$1,575

A Seguso 'valva' vase designed
by Flavio Poli, gray cased in
amethyst colored glass, circa
1958, 15cm. high. (Christie's)
$4,400

A Daum double-overlay carved vase of flattened globular shape, 11.5cm. high. (Christie's) $1,172

A Venini vase designed by Ludovico de Santillana, the gray glass with irregular applied white drips, circa 1962, 20.5cm. high. (Christie's) $352

'Caudebec', a Lalique vase with two semi-circular handles, 14.5cm. high. (Christie's) $902

An Orrefors cylindrical flared vase designed by Simon Gate, wheel engraved with naked maidens on classical columns, 17.5cm. high. (Christie's) $865

A pair of Lithyalin vases, in sealing wax red glass, with trumpet necks and circular feet, 23cm. high. (Phillips) $1,085

A Venini 'vaso a Canne', flaring cylindrical shape with waved rim, circa 1950, 22cm. high. (Christie's) $3,168

A Gabriel Argy-Rousseau pate-de-verre vase, the body molded with black spiders spinning their webs amongst leaves, 4¾in. high. (Christie's) $5,702

A Louis XVI ormolu mounted blue glass vase and cover, 11in. high. (Christie's) $459

A Daum enamelled and acid etched vase of rounded cube form, 11.5cm. high. (Christie's) $2,345

VASES

A large Galle carved and acid etched double-overlay 'vase aux ombelles', with cameo signature Galle, 63.5cm. high. (Christie's) $5,412

A Daum Art Deco acid etched vase, bell-shaped, 28cm. high. (Christie's) $992

A Venini cylindrical vase, composed of three equal cylinders of purple, amber and smoke-gray glass, 24cm. high. (Christie's) $1,353

'Martins Pecheurs', a black Lalique vase, with impressed signature R. Lalique, 23.5cm. high. (Christie's) $8,659

A Lalique vase, the milky opaque glass molded with intertwined brambles, 23cm. high. (Christie's) $793

A Daum acid textured two-handled vase, engraved signature Daum Nancy with the Cross of Lorraine, France, 25.5cm. high. (Christie's) $1,443

A Venini 'vetro a Granulari' vase, designed by Carlo Scarpa, circa 1951, 20cm. high. (Christie's) $12,320

'Albert', a Lalique vase, the topaz glass with two handles molded as eagles' heads, 17.3cm. high. (Christie's) $1,713

'Bacchantes', a Lalique opalescent glass vase molded in relief with naked female dancing figures, 24.5cm. high. (Christie's) $13,530

A Daum vase, circular base and waisted cylindrical shape with flared rim, 35.1cm. high. (Christie's) $1,172

A Venini vase designed by Fulvio Bianconi, concave lozenge shape internally decorated with a 'tartan' pattern, 27.5cm. high. (Christie's) $98,560

A Daum enamelled and acid etched vase, enamelled Daum Nancy with Cross of Lorraine, 21.6cm. high. (Christie's) $1,262

A Daum Art Deco acid etched vase, oviform with tall neck, 29cm. high. (Christie's) $1,533

'Coqs et Plumes', a Lalique flaring cylindrical vase, 15.5cm. high. (Christie's) $865

A Lalique vase, the satin finished glass molded with marguerites, highlighted with amber staining, 20.5cm. high. (Christie's) $902

A Daum Art Deco acid etched vase, the smoky-blue glass deeply etched with oval and circular panels, 33.5cm. high. (Christie's) $2,345

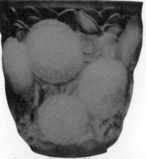

'Oran', a large Lalique opalescent glass vase molded in relief with flowerheads and foliage, 26cm. high. (Christie's) $7,216

A Galle cameo baluster vase, the amber and milky white glass overlaid in purple, carved with fuschia, 16cm. high. (Christie's) $902

VASES

A large Barovier & Toso patchwork vase, the white and mauve glass forming a checker-pattern overall, 44.5cm. high. (Christie's) $3,608

'Rampillon', an opalescent Lalique vase, 12.6cm. high. (Christie's) $613

A tall Daum carved and acid etched mold-blown vase, baluster shape, engraved with the Cross of Lorraine, 44cm. high. (Christie's) $4,329

A Gabriel Argy-Rousseau pate-de-verre vase of swollen cylindrical shape, 9.5cm. high. (Christie's) $2,525

An Archimede Seguso vase, tomato-red cased with clear glass and with gold foil inclusions, circa 1960, 37cm. high. (Christie's) $1,760

A Loetz oviform vase, the body with four dimples, 25.4cm. high. (Christie's) $1,353

A Venini vase designed by Fulvio Bianconi, 1949, 21cm. high. (Christie's) $7,040

A 19th century Viennese rock crystal and enamel vase in the form of a fish, the cover surmounted by an enamelled figure of Neptune, 31cm. high. (Phillips) $14,670

An ormolu mounted cut glass vase of slightly tapering form with waved top and ram mask handles, 14in. high. (Christie's) $551

VASES

A Galle carved acid etched
triple overlay landscape
vase, 50.5cm. high.
(Christie's) $10,824

'Danaides', a Lalique vase
molded with six nude
maidens pouring water from
urns, 18.3cm. high.
(Christie's) $2,525

A carved double-overlay
cameo vase, bearing an
incised Galle chinoiserie
signature, 25cm. high.
(Christie's) $3,608

A Lalique clear glass stained
vase molded with grass-
hoppers on blades of grass
with blue and lime-green
staining, 27.4cm. high.
(Christie's) $4,690

A Venini vase designed by
Fulvio Bianconi, circa
1950, 32cm. high.
(Christie's)
$11,440

A Venini vase designed by
Thomas Stearns, asym-
metric bubble shape, circa
1962, 25cm. high.
(Christie's) $7,392

A Galle carved and acid
etched double-overlay
landscape vase, 29cm. high.
(Christie's) $8,659

'Violettes', a Lalique vase,
the satin finished opalescent
glass partially blue stained
and molded with eight overlapping leaves, 15.7cm. high.
(Christie's) $1,443

A vase attributed to Ferro
Lazzarini and the design
to Flavio Poli, circa 1960,
32cm. high. (Christie's)
$1,584

WINE GLASSES

A 'Newcastle' baluster wine glass on a wide conical foot, 19.2cm. high. (Phillips) $701

Late 18th/early 19th century green pedestal stemmed wine flute, 15.5cm. high. (Christie's) $1,986

A baluster wine glass, the bell bowl with a tear to the lower part, circa 1720, 15.5cm. high. (Christie's) $590

An engraved composite stemmed wine glass of drawn trumpet shape, circa 1750, 17.5cm. high. (Christie's) $826

A baluster dram glass with short round funnel bowl on a bladed knop containing a tear, 10.7cm. high. (Phillips) $217

A quadruple knopped opaque twist wine glass, the bell bowl supported on a double series opaque twist stem with four knops, circa 1770, 17cm. high. (Christie's) $551

A George III wine glass, the plain stem with single series opaque twist, with saucer-top bowl, circa 1760, 6½in. high. (Christie's) $242

A colored wine glass of blue/ green tint, the double ogee bowl supported on a plain stem and foot, circa 1765, 15cm. high. (Christie's) $1,378

A baluster cordial glass, the trumpet bowl with solid base containing a tear, 16.5cm. high. (Phillips) $567

WINE GLASSES

A George III wine glass with facet cut stem and tapering bowl, circa 1775, 6.1/8in. high. (Christie's) $220

A baluster wine glass, the funnel bowl with solid base on conical folded foot, 16.5cm. high. (Phillips) $400

Mid 18th century pale-green tinted wine glass for the European market, 16cm. high. (Christie's) $315

An opaque twist champagne glass, the double ogee bowl with everted rim, circa 1765, 18cm. high. (Christie's) $1,476

A George III wine glass, the plain stem with double series opaque twist, part-fluted tapering bowl, circa 1760, 5.3/8in. high. (Christie's) $264

A baluster toastmaster's glass on a conical firing foot, 13.5cm. high. (Phillips) $217

A Beilby opaque twist wine glass, the funnel bowl enamelled in white with floral swags pendant from the rim, circa 1770, 15.5cm. high. (Christie's) $1,870

Late 18th/early 19th century colored wine glass of dark blue/green tint with bucket shaped bowl, 15cm. high. (Christie's) $295

A 'Lynn' opaque twist wine glass on a conical foot, circa 1770, 14.5cm. high. (Christie's) $826

A large oblong gold snuff-box, the plaque early 18th century, the box 19th century, 3½in. long. (Christie's) $24,288

A Swiss oval gold snuff-box, the medallion painted with a warrior courting his lady, Geneva, circa 1800, maker's initials AI crowned, 2¾in. long. (Christie's) $11,132

A French oblong gold snuff-box, the cover with initials RH in monogram, by Veuve Blerzy, Paris, 1809-19, 3¼in. long. (Christie's) $5,667

A Swiss bombe oblong gold snuff box, probably by Joli & Chenevard, Geneva, circa 1830, 2¾in. long. (Christie's) $5,544

A French gold mounted onyx and enamel scent bottle of amphora form, circa 1870, 3¼in. high. (Christie's) $2,673

An Austrian narrow oval gold and enamel snuff box, circa 1780, 2¾in. long. (Christie's) $7,128

An Irish octagonal gold Freedom Box, maker's initials IK incuse probably for James Kennedy, Dublin, 1798, 22ct. in case, 3.5/8in. long. (Christie's) $16,830

An important Louis XV rect-angular gold snuff-box with diagonal bands of flowers, by Jean-Baptiste Bertin, Paris, 1749-50, 3in. long. (Christie's) $36,432

A fine Swiss gold and enamel card case, one side painted with a gallant taking leave of his loved one, circa 1830, 3¾in. long. (Christie's) $5,667

A German gold snuff box, the cover signed Gaab, Augsburg, circa 1755. (Christie's) $7,920

A Louis XV narrow rectangular gold snuff box, by Germain Chaye, Paris, 1765, with the poincons of J. J. Prevost, in case, 3in. long. (Christie's) $5,940

A French oblong gold snuff box, by Jean-Baptiste Fossin, with Paris gold standard mark and excise mark for 1819-38, 3.1/8in. long. (Christie's) $8,910

A Swiss gold and enamel snuff box of lobed oval form, the hinged cover painted en grisaille with a musical trophy, circa 1820, 3½in. long. (Christie's) $8,019

A gold etui case, the body chased with flowers and bearing the Royal cypher. (Wellington Salerooms) $8,064

A Swiss oval gold and enamel snuff box, the hinged cover painted en grisaille with an allegorical trophy of the sciences, circa 1820, 2.7/8in. long. (Christie's) $8,019

A Swiss oblong gold snuff box champleve enamelled in black, probably by G. L. Malacreda, Geneva, circa 1830, 2¾in. long. (Christie's) $4,752

An Irish circular gold Freedom Box, maker's initials IK incuse probably for James Kennedy, Dublin, 1798, 22ct. in case, 2¾in. diam. (Christie's) $7,524

A French oblong gold snuff box, the cover painted on enamel with a portrait of George Annesley, 3in. long. (Christie's) $8,910

Late 19th century four-case roironuri inro, 8.5cm. high, with an attached ojime with fish, squid and seaweed in Hiramakie. (Christie's) $3,520

A 19th century three-case Kinji inro, signed Tatsuke Takamasu. (Christie's) $4,114

A 19th century four-case inro, signed Nikkosai, 8.5cm. long. (Christie's) $3,366

Late 19th century lozenge-shaped inro, signed on a mother-of-pearl tablet Yasuyuki, 9cm. long. (Christie's) $5,610

A 19th century five-case roironuri inro, 10cm. high, with an attached agate ojime. (Christie's) $5,632

Early 19th century five-case fundame inro, signed Kaji-kawa saku with red tsuba seal, 9.2cm. high, and an ivory ojime of a monkey. (Christie's) $1,230

A 19th century three-case inro, signed Tojo saku, with an attached coral ojime, 7cm. long. (Christie's) $13,090

Early 19th century three-case circular inro, signed Kanshosai, with a silvered-metal ojime, 8.3cm. diam. (Christie's) $3,179

A 19th century five-case inro, signed Jokasai, with an attached soft metal ojime, 9.4cm. long. (Christie's) $7,106

A 19th century sleeve inro with attached soft-metal ojime and a wood and ivory netsuke, the inro 10.2cm. long, the netsuke 4.2cm. high. (Christie's) $6,545

An 18th century four-case inro, signed Gyokumin, with an attached agate ojime and a kagamibuta with ivory bowl and shibuichi disc, inro 7.7cm. high, netsuke 4.5cm. diam. (Christie's) $1,230

A 19th century four-case inro, signed Shokasai, with an attached gold stone ojime, 8.7cm. long. (Christie's) $2,431

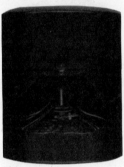

Late 18th/early 19th century four-case nashiji inro, unsigned. (Christie's) $4,114

A 19th century four-case inro, signed Kajikawa saku, 8.3cm. long. (Christie's) $1,683

A 19th century four-case inro decorated in gold taka-makie and inlaid with coral, amber, metal and other materials, 7.2cm. long. (Christie's) $2,431

A 19th century four-case inro, signed Shokasai, 8.5cm. high. (Christie's) $1,936

A 19th century three-case inro, unsigned, with an attached coral ojime, 7cm. long. (Christie's) $2,805

Early 19th century three-case silver lined iron inro, signed Toshinaga, the iron ojime with a silver frog, 5.7cm. long. (Christie's) $2,431

An 18th century brass way-wiser dial, signed Made by Tho. Wright Infrumt maker to ye Prince of Wales, 6¼in. diam. (Christie's)
$865

A Grover & Baker hand sewing machine, serial no. 441414, brass disk and gilt lining, on mahogany base, circa 1873. (Phillips) $1,840

A small circular brass sextant, signed Thos. Harris & Son, London. (Greenslade & Co.)
$267

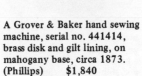

A late 19th century oxidized brass surveying aneroid barometer, by Pidduck & Sons, Hanley, 6in. diam. (Christie's)
$211

A 19th century brass compound binocular microscope signed Ross, London, No. 4119, in mahogany case, 20¾in. high. (Christie's) $968

A brass stamp box by W. Avery & Son, 2½in. high. (Christie's) $396

A brass cased dip-circle by F. E. Becker & Co., on adjustable stand, 10¾in. high. (Christie's) $528

A polished teak and brass ship's wheel of eight spokes, inscribed William Cory & Son Ltd., overall diam. 54in. (Christie's) $776

A Country painted globe, New England, circa 1810, 15in. diam., 37in. high. (Robt. W. Skinner Inc.)
$5,500

A late 18th century demonstration apparatus, signed Fraser, Instrument Maker to his Majesty, London, 12¼in. wide. (Christie's) $528

A Melloni's thermopile by Griffin & Tatlock Ltd., with telescopic stand and the associated tangent galvanometer, 9in. high. (Christie's) $158

A wood and brass magic lantern with brass bound lens and chimney with a slide holder and a small quantity of slides in wood box. (Christie's) $277

An 18th century silver and silver gilt equinoctial automatic dial, unsigned, but of the Johan Willebrand type. (Christie's) $3,520

An Italian brass ship's pedestal telegraph with enamelled dial, lever and pointer, two lamps and chain drive, 42in. high. (Christie's) $1,108

An early 19th century universal equinoctial ring dial, unsigned, 6in. diam. (Christie's) $1,496

A Betts's portable terrestrial globe arranged so as to fold like an umbrella, 15in. diam. (Christie's) $563

A Kriegsmarine micrometer sextant, signed C. Plath, Hamburg, No. 21536, with certificate dated 21.XI.42, 6½in. index arm radius, in wooden box, 12½in. wide. (Christie's) $295

A mid 19th century brass propeller pitchometer signed Edwin Craven, Maker, Hull, 16.3/8in. long, with brass carrying handle. (Christie's) $462

A two-day marine chronometer in two-tier glazed mahogany box, the 4½in. silvered dial with Arabic numerals, signed Thomas Mercer, No. 28271, in travelling box. (Christie's) $776

A set of early Victorian mahogany jockey scales with ivory plaque De Grave & Co., Makers, London, 39in. wide. (Christie's) $4,329

A 19th century single cupping set by J. Laundy, with lacquered brass syringe and shaped glass cup, the case 5in. wide. (Christie's) $422

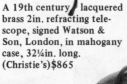

A 17th century brass sector, unsigned, 18in. long. (Christie's) $1,936

A 19th century lacquered brass 2in. refracting telescope, signed Watson & Son, London, in mahogany case, 32¼in. long. (Christie's)$865

A wax model of the human head showing the nerves, arteries, veins and muscles, in an ebonized and glazed case, 9¾in. high, by Lehrmittelwerke, Berlin. (Christie's) $302

A 19th century lacquered brass drum pattern French cross, trade label for J. & W. E. Archbutt, in mahogany case, 6¾in. wide. (Christie's) $211

A pair of early Victorian terrestrial and celestial globes, by Malby & Son, London, dated 1850. (Lacy Scott) $2,227

A 19th century bone saw and three dental elevators. (Christie's) $153

A brass transit theodolite by Cooke Troughton & Simms Ltd., London, in mahogany case, 5¼in. wide. (Christie's) $616

A collapsible A. H. Baird patent stereoscope with a quantity of stereocards in wood box. (Christie's) $396

A mid 18th century brass theodolite, by Benjamin Cole, the telescope 15¾in. long. (Christie's) $2,464

A 17th century fruitwood nocturnal, unsigned, main plate 4.1/8in. diam., index arm length 7.3/8in. (Christie's) $2,956

The 'Improved Phantasmagoria Lantern, by Carpenter & Westley, with patent argand solar lamp with a quantity of lantern slides. (Christie's) $369

An early 19th century lacquered brass azimuth sighting instrument, signed Narrien, London, 9½in. wide. (Christie's) $2,164

A 19th century gilt Sheffield two-draw monocular, signed Watkins & Hill, 2.1/8in. diam. (Christie's) $246

A 19th century mahogany inclined plane, with arc engraved 0°-40°, 27¾in. wide. (Christie's) $126

A sextant by Lilley & Son, London, in wooden case. (Greenslade & Co.) $551

One of a pair of William IV terrestrial and celestial globes by W. Harris, dated 1836, 40in. high, 22in. diam. (Christie's) $26,730

A late 18th century 'Ladder Scale', the 1oz. and 2oz. beams stamped De Grave & Co. London, 16.1/8in. wide. (Christie's) $811

A French terrestrial globe signed J. Forest, on ebonized base, 23in. high. (Christie's) $734

Early 19th century lacquered brass universal equinoctial ring dial, signed Dollond, London, in original fishskin covered case, 9½in. diam. (Christie's) $5,772

A mid 19th century lacquered brass theodolite by Troughton & Simms, 11½in. wide. (Christie's) $1,262

A late 19th century desk calendar compendium, 3¼in. diam. (Christie's) $270

A 19th century brass double-rack action twin cylinder vacuum pump, unsigned, 14in. high. (Christie's) $992

A brass vacuum pump of small size, unsigned, with tall jar and a lacquered brass vacuum chamber with cap and glass insulated ball and hook, 6in. high. (Christie's) $234

A Wimshurst pattern plate machine by Philip Harris Ltd., Birmingham, 21.5/8in. wide, and a pair of brass and ebonite discharge forks. (Christie's) $811

Late 19th century sectional model of the eye, the plaster body decorated in colors and with glass lenses, 6¾in. high. (Christie's) $541

A lacquered brass 3in. refracting telescope signed Watson & Son, London, 45¼in. long. (Christie's) $757

A mid Victorian terrestrial globe by Thos. Malby & Son, 19in. high. (Christie's) $2,345

A 17th century silver perpetual calendar, unsigned, with suspension loop, 1in. diam. (Christie's) $902

A lacquered and oxidized brass compound monocular microscope, by W. Watson & Sons Ltd., London, and other items in a mahogany case, 13in. high. (Christie's) $505

One of a pair of mid 18th century terrestrial and celestial table globes with Latin inscription, 17in. wide, 19in. high. (Christie's) $13,365

A Pascal's apparatus, unsigned, 14in. wide, with three different shaped glass vessels mounted in brass collars to fit the limb. (Christie's) $811

Late 18th century lacquered brass compound monocular microscope, unsigned, 8¾in. long. (Christie's) $3,247

A 19th century cupping set by Weiss, London, with two glass cups in plush lined fitted case, 5½in. long. (Christie's) $432

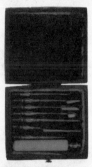

A two-day marine chronometer, the 4in. dial signed Kelvin Bottomley & Baird Ltd., Glasgow, and numbered 9550, in a brass bound mahogany box. (Phillips) $1,567

A late 19th century oxidized and lacquered brass simple theodolite, signed on the plate R. W. Street & Co., in mahogany case, 15¾in. wide. (Christie's) $577

A late 18th century pocket dental scaling kit, with mirror in a shagreen case, 2¼in. wide. (Christie's) $286

A demonstration refractometer, unsigned, with a set of twelve lenses. (Christie's) $360

Early 19th century planetary motion compendium, unsigned, in a fitted mahogany case, 13.7/8in. wide. (Christie's) $2,164

A George II glass celestial globe by Thomas Heath, 15in. diam., engraved by John Cowley. (Christie's) $66,748

A sheet brass letter balance signed Parnell, London and inscribed Hall's Patent, 5¼in. wide. (Christie's) $234

A black enamelled and lacquered brass Grand Theodolite by T. Cooke & Sons, 16in. high. (Christie's) $2,345

A 19th century Norrenberg's polariscope, unsigned, with mirrors and calibrated scales. (Christie's) $631

A 19th century German
diptych dial signed J.
Kleininger on the compass
rose, 3.1/8in. long.
(Christie's) $342

A deflection magnetometer
on mahogany base with
adjustable feet, 13in. high.
(Christie's) $938

A lacquered brass aneroid
barometer signed J. Gold-
schmid, Zurich, 3in.
diam. (Christie's)
            $541

A 'Geryk' vacuum pump, 23in.
high, a Callendar's apparatus by
Griffin & George Ltd. on a
stand and a compression/expan-
sion demonstration apparatus.
(Christie's) $216

An early 19th century lacquered brass and mahogany
vacuum pump, 18¾in. long,
with an extensive collection
of accessories. (Christie's)
            $8,298

A late Victorian terrestrial
table globe with turned
walnut shaft, 17½in. high.
(Christie's) $396

A 19th century lacquered brass
compound monocular micro-
scope, the base signed Ross,
London, No. 3354, with a few
accessories, 13¾in. high.
(Christie's) $902

A 19th century brass theo-
dolite, signed by Troughton
& Simms, 9½in. high.
(Christie's) $811

A 19th century amputation
saw by Weiss, with anti-clog
teeth and ebony handle,
15½in. long. (Christie's)
            $144

An iron trivet, posnet and toaster. (Christie's) $121

A 17th century Spanish iron strongbox with hinged top, the sides with carrying handles, 20½ in. wide. (Christie's) $1,460

Late 19th/early 20th century painted and gilded tin and wrought-iron wall mounted trade sign, American or English, 42½in. high, 39in. wide. (Christie's) $4,180

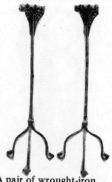

A pair of ebonized torcheres with iron nozzles and circular drip-pans, 58½in. high. (Christie's) $3,674

A Regency black-painted and cast iron basket grate in the manner of George Bullock, 31in. wide. (Christie's) $4,719

A pair of wrought-iron torcheres with circular foliate platforms, 55in. high. (Christie's) $2,388

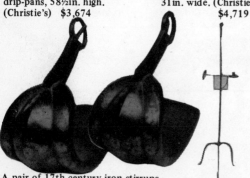
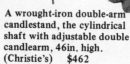

A pair of 17th century iron stirrups finely inlaid in silver hirazogan with a chrysanthemum and water design (kikusui), each signed Kashu ju Morisada saku. (Christie's) $1,589

A wrought-iron double-arm candlestand, the cylindrical shaft with adjustable double candlearm, 46in. high. (Christie's) $462

A pair of mid 19th century American painted cast iron dressing glasses, 21in. high. (Christie's) $770

An 18th century wrought iron bound salt bucket with swing handle, 7¼in. diam. (Christie's) $203

A rare Eley percussion cap measure, 4¾in., cast 'W & C Eley London', with solid steel nipples graded in sizes 4-24 with military cap at top. (Wallis & Wallis) $297

A polished steel grate of George III style, the pierced frieze filled with key-pattern, 32½in. wide, 35in. high. (Christie's) $2,468

One of six pairs of wrought and cast iron andirons. (Christie's) $550

An impressive iron 17th century 'Armada' chest, 37 x 19 x 20in. (Wallis & Wallis) $3,052

19th century white painted iron stickstand modelled as a boy holding a serpent, 2ft.10in. high. (Lots Road Chelsea Auction Galleries) $400

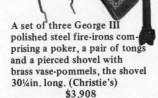

A white metal and polished steel basket grate of serpentine form, 21in. wide, 21in. high. (Christie's) $3,702

A set of three George III polished steel fire-irons comprising a poker, a pair of tongs and a pierced shovel with brass vase-pommels, the shovel 30¼in. long. (Christie's) $3,908

A George III polished steel basket grate, 33in. wide. (Christie's) $3,247

A 19th century German miniature ivory tankard with silvered metal mounts, 10.5cm. high. (Christie's) $3,674

Late 18th century ivory Kitsune mask, 3.5cm. high. (Christie's) $345

A 19th century carved ivory bust of a bishop in the Gothic style, on silver metal base with lion supports at each corner, 16cm. high. (Phillips) $896

Late 19th century ivory carving of a farmer holding a birdcage, 33cm. high. (Christie's) $2,640

An 18th century ivory work-box of octagonal form, 22.5cm. wide. (Phillips) $684

Late 19th century ivory carving of a hunter, signed Kozan saku, 22cm. high. (Christie's) $792

A pair of curved ivory elephant tusks on ebonized bases, 6ft. high, overall. (Prudential Fine Art) $2,788

Late 19th century boxwood, rootwood and ivory group of doves attending their young, signed Mitsuhiro, 49cm. high. (Christie's) $18,700

An ivory carving of a sennin, eyes inset in dark horn, stylized seal mark, 20.5cm. high. (Christie's) $935

IVORY

A 19th century ivory
okimono of a farmer with
a fox and a hare, dressed
as humans, 6cm. high.
(Christie's) $748

A 19th century ivory mask
of a Buaku, signed Ryuraku,
3.8cm. high, (age cracks).
(Christie's) $566

A 19th century German carved
ivory lidded tankard with caryatid handle, 13¾in. high.
(Capes Dunn) $8,055

Late 19th century ivory
carving of a scholar, signed
Akira, 26cm. high.
(Christie's) $704

A pair of Chinese 19th century ivory
handscreens with ivory handles hung
with ornaments and silk tassels, 13½in.
long, contained in a fitted brocade
case. (Christie's) $1,870

Late 19th century ivory
carving of a kannon, signed
Masayuki, 33cm. high, wood
stand. (Christie's)
$4,114

A 19th century Dieppe
ivory tazza, by E. Blard,
17.5cm. high. (Christie's)
$2,204

A 19th century Japanese
ivory group on wood stand,
signed, 8¾in. high. (Capes
Dunn) $841

A 19th century Japanese
ivory tusk vase, 12in. high,
with a lobed wooden base
and wood stand, 23in. high
overall. (Capes Dunn)
$501

Late 19th century Uncle Sam animated ivory cane, when button on hat is pressed his jaw drops, America, 35in. long. (Robt. W. Skinner Inc.) $1,400

A Napoleonic prisoner-of-war period bone-ivory games box, raised on four cabriole legs, 8½in. wide. (Christie's) $1,386

Late 19th century ivory carving of a fisherman, signed Shizuhisa, 29cm. high. (Christie's) $968

A carved ivory figure of a young woman, signed Gogyoku saku, Meiji period, 32.2cm. high. (Christie's) $1,589

Late 19th century stained ivory group of four children playing beside a drum, 21cm. high. (Christie's) $2,618

Mid 14th century Flemish or German carved ivory relief, 6½ x 3.5/8in. (Christie's) $14,300

Late 19th century carved ivory okimono group of a fisherman and a boy assistant, signed Ogawa Munekata, 13cm. high. (Christie's) $1,496

Pair of 19th century carved ivory figures of a swain and his lass, 14cm. high. (Phillips) $1,793

A 19th century Dieppe ivory tazza, its stem carved with a classical female figure, 18cm. high. (Christie's) $2,020

A 19th century carved ivory figure of a cherub playing a flute, 33cm. overall. (Phillips) $1,630

A 19th century walrus tusk modelled in the form of a cribbage board, 11¼in. long. (Christie's) $517

Late 19th century carving of a kannon standing beside a seated attendant holding a koro, signed Ryushin, 32cm. high. (Christie's) $2,992

A 19th century German ivory flagon carved in relief with scenes of Scipio, 53cm. high. (Phillips) $14,670

Late 19th century ivory and wood group of a scholar with children, 16cm. high. (Christie's) $2,992

Late 19th century carved sectional ivory okimono of a man and a small boy, signed Munehisa, 15.5cm. high. (Christie's) $1,589

Late 19th century carved sectional ivory okimono of a street vendor, signed Munehisa, 15.8cm. high. (Christie's) $654

Late 19th century ivory vase and cover inlaid in shibayama style, signed Gyokiukendo san, 20cm. high. (Christie's) $5,610

Late 19th century ivory carving of an itinerant basket seller, signed Hododa, 35.3cm. high. (Christie's) $4,114

A 20th century sterling silver and opal pin, 1¾in. diam. (Robt. W. Skinner Inc.) $325

Four 19th century onyx cameos, probably Italian, one signed L. Rosi, oval 1-1½in. high. (Christie's) $1,210

A Victorian mourning brooch centred by a woven hair panel within a half pearl surround, and with a foliate scroll gold border. (Lawrence Fine Art) $473

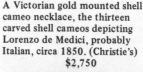

An oval carved shell cameo with a profile of a classical maiden in 9kt. gold openwork brooch mount. (Prudential Fine Art) $189

A Victorian gold mounted shell cameo necklace, the thirteen carved shell cameos depicting Lorenzo de Medici, probably Italian, circa 1850. (Christie's) $2,750

An antique pink topaz and cannetille gold necklace and earrings, in a fitted case from Hunt & Roskell, late Storr & Mortimer. (Lawrence Fine Art) $6,788

An Arts & Crafts oval white metal brooch designed by Arthur Gaskin, 4.5cm. long. (Christie's) $1,082

An 18kt. gold, diamond and baroque pearl floral spray brooch. (Hobbs & Chambers) $2,640

A diamond pendant brooch with detachable brooch pin and pendant ring. (Lawrence Fine Art) $7,405

JEWELRY

An Arts & Crafts bangle bracelet with mounted opals and diamonds, stamped 'Peacock', 2½in. diam., circa 1910. (Robt. W. Skinner Inc.)
$2,600

Pair of 20th century enamelled sterling silver pins, hallmarked and stamped J.F., 1¼in. diam. (Robt. W. Skinner Inc.)
$125

A pair of reverse intaglio cufflinks, in 18kt. gold mounts with corded borders. (Lawrence Fine Art) $1,892

A plique-a-jour pendant with pearl drop and sterling silver chain, circa 1910, 15in. long. (Robt. W. Skinner Inc.)
$350

A Victorian pietra dura and gold pendant and earrings, in a fitted case. (Lawrence Fine Art)
$1,810

A Gabriel Argy-Rousseau pate-de-verre oval pendant, 6.5cm. diam. (Christie's)
$1,623

A Swiss enamel brooch, the rectangular panel painted in colors with Madonna and Child with the infant St. John after Raphael. (Lawrence Fine Art) $740

A Guild of Handicrafts Ltd. silver and enamel brooch designed by C. R. Ashbee, London hallmarks for 1907, 7.8cm. long. (Christie's)
$16,236

A diamond roundel brooch with fourteen brilliant cut diamonds in an open circle. (Lawrence Fine Art)
$1,604

A plique-a-jour pin with fresh-water pearls, probably French, circa 1910, marked 800, 1½in. long. (Robt. W. Skinner Inc.) $200

9kt. gold and plique-a-jour Art Nouveau wing brooch in Egyptian style, 4¼in. wide, maker's mark HL conjoined. (Capes Dunn) $547

A Russian diamond, sapphire, ruby and plique-a-jour enamel moth brooch, St. Petersburg maker's mark JV. (Lawrence Fine Art) $16,661

An early George III moss agate and garnet ring on a gold shank with memorial inscription and dated 1765. (Lawrence Fine Art) $514

A 19th century sapphire and diamond frog brooch, set in silver and gold. (Dreweatt Neate) $6,358

An emerald and diamond cluster ring, in a basket mount on a plain gold shank. (Lawrence Fine Art) $1,357

An oval diamond set gold mounted shell cameo brooch, 1¾in. high. (Christie's) $2,860

Zuni silver and turquoise bracelet, openwork silver cuff, 3¼in. diam. (Robt. W. Skinner Inc.) $650

A 19th century oval gold mounted onyx cameo pendant brooch, the frame set with pearls and with black enamel ropework, 2½in. high. (Christie's) $1,650

An old cut diamond and pearl three stone ring, center stone approx. 1.65ct. (Dreweatt Neate) $3,459

A Murrle Bennett gold wirework oval brooch, with opal matrix and four seed pearls, stamped MB monogram and 15kt. on the pin, circa 1900. (Christie's) $336

A diamond bracelet composed of 17 graduated stones in a half-hoop gold setting. (Morphets) $2,537

A diamond solitaire ring, the stone weighing 4.23ct, claw set on an18kt. gold shank. (Lawrence Fine Art) $7,816

An opal and diamond bangle with nine oval cabochon opals divided by pairs of old cut diamonds on a hinged 15kt. gold band. (Lawrence Fine Art) $1,604

A diamond set bound scroll double dress clip set in white gold, combining to form a brooch with white metal conversion. (Dreweatt Neate) $2,150

A 15kt. gold and enamelled ceremonial coat-of-arms pendant, made by Spencer of London. (Dreweatt Neate) $299

Victorian gold, diamond and turquoise ring. (Hobbs & Chambers) $464

A 19th century large sapphire cluster ring set in silver and gold with leaf pierced scrolling shoulders. (Dreweatt Neate) $1,271

A 19th century oval gold mounted shell cameo brooch, probably Italian, 2½in. high. (Christie's) $1,650

Zuni silver and turquoise bracelet, large single stone carved in the form of a leaf, 3in. diam. (Robt. W. Skinner Inc.) $375

A gold mounted pink coral carved brooch, the openwork scrolling foliage frame set with four small diamonds, 2¼in. high. (Christie's) $1,760

An 18kt. gold bracelet set with eight sapphires alternating with seven diamonds. (Worsfolds) $504

A double trapezoid shaped amethyst brooch bordered by small rose cut diamonds, calibre jet and seed pearls. (Dreweatt Neate) $897

A diamond and half pearl ring, all claw set on a gold shank. (Lawrence Fine Art) $678

LAMPS

One of a pair of oak and leaded glass wall lanterns, circa 1910, 23in. long. (Robt. W. Skinner Inc.) $1,100

A hammered copper and mica table lamp, circa 1910, 14¾in. high. (Robt. W. Skinner Inc.) $1,400

A conch shell and hammered copper table lamp, designed by E. E. Burton, California, circa 1910, 24in. high. (Robt. W. Skinner Inc.) $3,400

A Bradley & Hubbard table lamp with gold iridescent shade, Mass., circa 1910, 15in. high. (Robt. W. Skinner Inc.) $700

Pair of 19th century gilt metal cherub lamps with hexagonal shades, 14in. high. (Lots Road Chelsea Auction Galleries). $384

A Tiffany Studio lamp with green-blue Favrile glass molded as a scarab, N.Y., circa 1902, 8½in. high. (Robt. W. Skinner Inc.) $3,000

A Le Verre Francais acid etched table lamp with three-pronged wrought-iron mount, 42.2cm. high. (Christie's) $2,886

A Handel adjustable desk lamp, with green glass shade, circa 1920, 12¾in. high. (Robt. W. Skinner Inc.) $750

A Satsuma pottery gilt bronze mounted oil lamp base, 12in. high. (Reeds Rains) $668

An Art Deco frosted glass lamp painted in colors with banding and linear decoration, 31cm. high. (Phillips) $563

A hammered copper table lamp with mica shade, Old Mission Kopperkraft, San Francisco, circa 1910, 13¾in. high, 15in. diam. (Robt. W. Skinner Inc.) $2,700

A Degue Art Deco glass lamp, 35cm. high. (Phillips) $352

A Daum enamelled and acid etched landscape table lamp with wrought-iron mounts, 48.5cm. high. (Christie's) $5,231

A pair of Regency bronzed and ormolu lamps, fitted for electricity, 30¾in. high, 13in. diam. (Christie's) $28,512

A Tiffany Studios enamelled copper electric lamp base, circa 1900, 15in. high. (Robt. W. Skinner Inc.) $3,700

Muller Freres cameo glass illuminated column table lamp and mushroom shaped shade, 23in. high. (Prudential Fine Art) $825

A copper and leaded glass piano lamp, cone-shaped slag glass shade, incised mark 'KK', 13¾in. high. (Robt. W. Skinner Inc.) $400

A copper and amber glass lantern, style no. 324, by Gustav Stickley, circa 1906, 15in. high, globe 5¼in. diam. (Robt. W. Skinner Inc.) $7,500

MARBLE

A 19th century French marble bust of Psyche, by Albert Carrier-Belleuse, 60cm. high. (Christie's) $4,592

An early 20th century Italian white marble statue of a female nude, by Alfredo Pina, 81cm. high. (Christie's) $15,427

A 19th century marble bust of 'Jeunefille', probably Flora, by Albert Carrier-Belleuse, 62cm. high. (Christie's) $6,429

A marble bust of Prince Albert, in Classical drapes, signed on the reverse W. Theed, 1857, 35cm. high overall. (Phillips) $2,526

A 19th century Italian marble figure of a Bacchante, in the style of Bartolini, 85cm. long. (Christie's) $8,266

A 19th century marble head of Aphrodite, after the Antique, 49cm. high. (Christie's) $3,448

A 19th century Italian neo-classical bust of a classical lady, in the manner of Canova, 47cm. high. (Christie's) $5,445

A pair of early 19th century Venetian colored marble busts of a Blackamoor boy and girl, 55cm. high. (Christie's) $8,266

A 19th century marble figure of the Apollino, on oval gray marble base, 62cm. high. (Phillips) $847

A 19th century Italian marble figure of Apollo Belvedere, 127cm. high. (Christie's) $10,890

A marble stele, possibly Roman period from Sicily, 21cm. high. (Phillips) $492

A 19th century marble figure of a girl, by Joseph Gott, 31cm. high. (Christie's) $1,452

A 19th century marble group of Apollo and Daphne, incised P. Barranti, Firenze, 117cm. high. (Phillips) $1,141

A 19th century American marble group of two children asleep on a mattress, by Wm. Rinehart, 37 x 90 x 48cm. (Christie's) $68,970

A 19th century English marble figure of Venus and Cupid, by Joseph Gott, 124cm. high, on a marble pedestal 110cm. high. (Christie's) $30,855

A 19th century English marble bust of a gentleman wearing a toga, by Theed, 71cm. high. (Christie's) $918

One of a pair of 19th century mottled pink marble urns, 30in. high. (Christie's) $6,429

A 19th century Italian marble neo-classical bust of a vestal, after Canova, 50cm. high. (Christie's) $7,260

An early 19th century Irish
marble bust of Angelica
Catalani, by Thos. Kirk,
1824, 79cm. high.
(Christie's) $8,167

An Italian sienna marble
miniature sarcophagus, the
lid with scrolling ends, 8in.
wide. (Christie's)
$1,996

White marble bust of a young
woman in 19th century dress
and Neapolitan bonnet, on
socle, 31in. high. (Lots Road
Chelsea Auction Galleries)
$1,670

A 19th century French
marble figure of a nymph,
by Jean Baptiste Carpeaux,
95cm. high. (Christie's)
$7,482

A pair of 19th century polychrome
marble busts of a blackamoor and
his wife, 62cm. and 60cm. high.
(Christie's) $8,860

A 19th century English marble
figure of Ino teaching Bacchus
to dance, by Joseph Gott,
145cm. high, on a veined marble pedestal 110cm. high.
(Christie's) $344,850

A mid 19th century Swedish
marble statue of a nymph
stepping forward to bathe,
by J. Lundberg, after J. N.
Bisstrom, 153cm. high.
(Christie's)
$13,777

A Roman marble relief of
Eros, 20 x 30cm., 2nd-3rd
century A.D. (Phillips)
$728

A 19th century English
marble figure of Susannah,
by Joseph Gott, 120cm. high,
supported on an original
pedestal 110cm. high.
(Christie's) $87,120

A 19th century English marble bust of General George Guy Carlton L'Estrange, by Wm. Theed, 1853, 70cm. high. (Christie's) $1,815

A 19th century Italian marble figure of a child pulling a thorn from a spaniel's foot, by G. M. Benzoni, 1846, 80cm. high, standing on marble column, 110cm. high. (Christie's) $15,752

A 19th century English marble bust of King Arthur, by Charles Francis Fuller, 68cm. high. (Christie's) $2,559

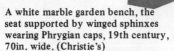

A 19th century Italian marble figure of Venus De'Medici, 102cm. high. (Christie's) $3,306

A white marble garden bench, the seat supported by winged sphinxes wearing Phrygian caps, 19th century, 70in. wide. (Christie's) $14,256

A 19th century white marble figure of a barefoot peasant girl on a gray marble plinth, 22in. high. (Lots Road Chelsea Auction Galleries) $340

A neo-classical marble bust of Napoleon, 59cm. high. (Phillips) $1,956

A pair of 19th century Florentine marble figures of Love Found and Love Abandoned, by Pasquale Romanelli, 1876 and 1877, 160cm. and 155cm. high, the plinths 60cm high. (Christie's) $78,760

A 20th century English marble bust of Pharaoh's Daughter, by John Adams-Acton, 1904, 69cm. high. (Christie's) $7,876

A burr-yew wood miniature chest inlaid with lines, on bracket feet, 11in. wide. (Christie's) $4,633

A 19th century miniature wallpapered bandbox, American, 4½in. high. (Robt. W. Skinner Inc.) $325

A 19th century miniature, Empire mahogany veneer chest-of-drawers, New England, 15in. wide. (Robt. W. Skinner Inc.) $600

A 19th century painted miniature ladder-back arm-chair, American. (Robt. W. Skinner Inc.) $225

A William and Mary walnut oyster veneer and cross-banded chest of small size. (Phillips) $3,280

A 19th century miniature tilt-top tea table, 13in. high. (Robt. W. Skinner Inc.) $275

A Victorian mahogany and marquetry banded miniature chest of five drawers, 14in. wide. (J. M. Welch & Son) $330

A mid Georgian walnut miniature chest, the base with one long drawer on bracket feet, 13½in. wide. (Christie's) $2,141

A 19th century miniature, Empire mahogany and painted chest-of-drawers, American, 19½in. wide. (Robt. W. Skinner Inc.) $800

A Regency giltwood convex mirror with eagle cresting and molded berried apron, 40 x 23¾in. (Christie's) $4,356

Shop-O'-The Crafters mahogany wall mirror, Ohio, 1910, 27½in. high, 30½in. wide. (Robt. W. Skinner Inc.) $750

Early 19th century kingwood and tulipwood cheval mirror with rectangular plate, 66 x 25½in. (Christie's) $5,878

Late 17th century beadwork mirror with four ladies surrounded by exotic animals, flowers and insects, 30 x 26in., English. (Christie's) $3,272

A mirror clock with polychrome stencilled eglomise tablet framing the painted iron dial, circa 1825, 31in. long. (Robt. W. Skinner Inc.) $1,500

A painted and carved Federal courting mirror, painted in old red and black with yellow ochre, circa 1820, 12in. high. (Robt. W. Skinner Inc.) $4,750

A table top mirror on shoe foot base, by Gustav Stickley, circa 1910, 21¼in. high. (Robt. W. Skinner Inc.) $800

A William and Mary looking glass, walnut burl veneer, 1690-1700, 28½in. high. (Robt. W. Skinner Inc.) $2,000

A scarlet japanned toilet mirror, the serpentine base with five drawers, 16in. wide. (Christie's) $627

A George III giltwood pier glass by Thos. Chippendale Snr. or Jnr., 127½ x 64¼in. (Christie's) $40,986

A Regency giltwood over-mantel with verre eglomise panel painted with a rustic scene, 55in. wide. (Christie's) $2,541

A George III giltwood mirror with shaped rectangular plate, 40 x 21½in. (Christie's) $4,690

A WMF electroplated pewter mirror, stamped marks B 2/0 GK H, 40cm. high. (Christie's) $757

A William and Mary walnut and rolled paper mirror, 31½ x 28½in. (Christie's) $17,820

A George III giltwood mirror with later shaped rectangular plate and pierced gothic sur-round, 64 x 34½in. (Christie's) $10,335

A Regency carved giltwood convex mirror, bearing a label T. Rushworth & Son, 1.77m. x 1.06m. (Phillips) $5,248

A walnut and gilt metal mirror with convex molded surround, 41 x 27½in. (Christie's) $1,745

A giltwood mirror of rococo style. 45 x 31in. (Christie's) $1,452

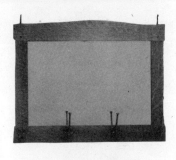

A giltwood mirror with shaped rectangular plate in a rockwork frame, 37¾ x 20¼in. (Christie's) $1,443

A Gustav Stickley hall mirror, style no. 66, circa 1905-06, 28in. high, 36in. wide. (Robt. W. Skinner Inc.) $1,200

One of a pair of Queen Anne gilt gesso girandoles, 37 x 22¼in. (Christie's) $53,460

Late 18th century Louis XV parcel gilt and cream-painted mirror, 57 x 39½in. (Christie's) $4,592

Late 17th/early 18th century Flemish ebony, tortoiseshell and ivory mirror, 27½ x 24½in. (Christie's) $3,306

A George III giltwood mirror with later rectangular plate and mirrored slips with beaded frame, 55 x 25in. (Christie's) $3,765

A WMF polished pewter mirror, the frame cast with a partly draped maiden, stamped marks, 28.9cm. high. (Christie's) $1,443

A George III giltwood over-mantel, 88 x 71in. (Christie's) $46,332

An early Georgian walnut toilet mirror with shaped plate, on later bun feet, 16½in. wide. (Christie's) $1,353

A giltwood mirror, the
moulded frame with pierced
foliate and C-scroll cresting
and apron, 42½ x 22in.
(Christie's) $896

A George I giltwood mirror,
the bevelled oval plate bordered with egg-and-dart
ornament, 38 x 25½in.
(Christie's) $21,384

A giltwood pier glass with
divided shaped plate, 105½
x 59in. (Christie's)
$4,408

A mid Georgian walnut and
parcel gilt mirror with later
rectangular plate and eared
foliate surround, 50 x 27in.
(Christie's) $9,861

A Queen Anne marginal wall
mirror with arched bevelled
plate and divided frame giltwood surround, 92 x 64cm.
(Phillips) $10,660

A mid Georgian walnut and
parcel gilt mirror with
bevelled rectangular plate,
53½ x 26in. (Christie's)
$6,352

A Chippendale period carved
giltwood wall mirror, 1.1m. x
53cm. (Phillips)
$10,660

A George I walnut toilet
mirror, the base with three
short drawers and a con-
cave long drawer, 17in.
wide. (Christie's)
$2,151

Late 18th century brass
mounted, mahogany and
parcel gilt cheval mirror,
probably German, 77½ x
46½in. (Christie's)
$5,143

One of a pair of George III giltwood mirrors by Thos. Chippendale Snr. or Jnr., 77½ x 46½in. (Christie's) $392,040

A giltwood mirror, the rock-work cresting supporting a stylized pagoda with a Chinese man, 55 x 38in. (Christie's) $1,623

One of a pair of George II giltwood mirrors, 56 x 35½in. (Christie's) $53,460

An early George III mahogany and parcel gilt fret carved wall mirror, 1.30m. x 67cm. (Phillips) $9,020

A WMF Secessionist electro-plated mirror, 34cm. high. (Christie's) $1,353

A walnut and parcel gilt mirror of George I style, 60 x 34in. (Christie's) $1,623

An early Georgian walnut mirror with shaped rectangular divided bevelled plate, 31½ x 15¼in. (Christie's) $1,118

A George III giltwood mirror with later oval plate and fluted surround, 44½ x 32in. (Christie's) $2,494

A Queen Anne black and gold japanned toilet mirror, the base with three short and two serpentine long drawers, 17¾in. wide. (Christie's) $1,075

Late 18th century, possibly German, giltwood mirror, 49 x 29in. (Christie's) $6,980

A 19th century Federal giltwood girandole mirror, 54½in. high, 40in. wide. (Christie's) $7,700

A Regency giltwood convex mirror, the circular plate with ebonized surround, 43 x 26in. (Christie's) $1,613

A Regency giltwood mirror with rectangular plate, the frieze with verre eglomise panel, 38½ x 22½in. (Christie's) $1,270

A Regency giltwood convex mirror with ebonized fluted slip, 25½in. diam. (Christie's) $907

A George II giltwood mirror, previously with candle branches, 50¾ x 30¾in. (Christie's) $11,583

One of a pair of George III giltwood mirrors with oval plates, 48 x 30in. (Christie's) $51,678

A Regency colonial calamanderwood toilet mirror, 28in. wide. (Christie's) $1,905

A George III giltwood mirror with later pear-shaped divided plate, 61 x 32½in. (Christie's) $12,474

A Regency giltwood convex
mirror with candle branches,
35 x 25in. (Christie's)
$1,542

A giltwood mirror with
rectangular bevelled plate,
53 x 43in. (Christie's)
$1,724

One of a pair of giltwood
mirrors with oval plates, 62
x 31½in. (Christie's)
$3,227

A silver gilt dressing table
mirror, in the Charles II
style, the reverse engraved
Mappin & Webb, 24in. high.
(Christie's) $7,128

A George I giltwood mirror
with rectangular plate and
channelled frame, 40¼ x
29in. (Christie's)
$1,633

A giltwood Italian mirror
with rectangular plate,
92 x 47in. (Christie's)
$4,041

A Chippendale period carved
giltwood cartouche-shaped
mirror, 1.7m. x 60cm.
(Phillips) $8,200

An Austrian shaped rectangu-
silver dressing table mirror,
maker's mark M & K, Vienna,
1846, 26½in. high, weight of
frame 40oz. (Christie's)
$8,910

One of a pair of early George
III giltwood mirrors, 90 x 44in.
(Christie's) $60,588

One of a pair of gilt metal twin-light wall-lights, 13½in. high. (Christie's) $1,194

A Russian papier mache box realistically painted with a scene of two fishermen on a riverbank, signed and dated. 19 x 17.5cm. (Phillips) $423

A 19th century leather, metalwork and agate tobacco pouch, kagamibuta netsuke and ojime, the netsuke signed Naohiro, 15cm. wide and 5.4cm. diam. (Christie's) $3,532

'The Tap Dancer', a life-size metal figure of a young negro, 185cm. high. (Christie's) $3,608

John Speede 'The Countie Pallatine of Lancaster', hand-colored engraved map with English text on the reverse, circa 1676, 15 x 20in. (Capes Dunn) $268

Mid 19th century North Italian parcel gilt and painted sedan chair, 30½in. wide, 69in. high. (Christie's) $14,696

The Glasgow Herald £650 Golf Tournament at Gleneagles Open to the World's Players May 1920, poster 40 x 30in. (Onslow's) $93

A Victorian child's sledge, painted red on shaped metal runners. (Lots Road Chelsea Auction Galleries) $486

A Victorian glass dome containing a collection of foreign stuffed birds. (G. A. Key) $115

MISCELLANEOUS

Pacific Northwest Coast Attu circular basket with cover, 4in. high. (Christie's) $1,980

An American 19th century papercut picture, depicting two eagles with flags, 5¾ x 7½in. (Christie's) $1,100

A 19th century pouch 8 x 7.5cm, with a boxwood seated baku netsuke, signed Gyokumin, 4.6cm. long. (Christie's) $5,205

A black and white poster, advertising 'Kathleen Mavourneen', Theatre Stamford, 1871. (James Norwich Auctions) $21

Christopher Saxton and Philip Lea 'The County Palatine of Lancaster', engraved and hand- colored map and Lancaster town map with castle, circa 1693, 15½ x 18½in. (Capes Dunn) $268

A lead winged cherub with dolphin fountain, 26in. high. (Lots Road Chelsea Auction Galleries) $992

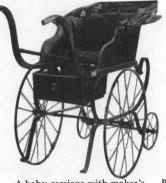

A 19th century Palekh School icon, depicting St. Roman in a wooded landscape, by Ovchinnikov, 17.5 x 11cm. (Phillips) $2,934

A baby carriage with maker's name plate attached, A. Mitchell, Margate, height to hood 31in. (Worsfolds) $537

Poster for George Humphrey's bookstore, by M. Louise Stowell, 1896, 11 x 15½in. (Robt. W. Skinner Inc.) $300

Victorian gilded metal watch stand designed as a mother-of-pearl bird-bath. (Giles Haywood) $98

Papier mache and lacquered vesta box with striker to the base, late 19th century period, Continental. (G. A. Key) $262

A Hepple & Co. malachite fish pattern jug, 7in. high. (Anderson & Garland) $106

An Empire gilt metal frame, with molded acanthus leaf and Vitruvian scroll border and pierced olive leaf cresting, 12 x 8¼in. (Christie's) $2,153

A fine pair of gilt metal and malachite candlesticks with vase-shaped nozzles, 6¾in. high. (Christie's) $2,755

A Norwich General firemark, Policy No. 7522, 1799-1802, made of lead. (James Norwich Auctions) $248

A late 19th century French plaster bust of 'L'Espiegle', signed on the shoulder J. B. Carpeaux, 51cm. high. (Christie's) $2,571

A micro-mosaic panel of the Colosseum, signed G. Rinaldi, 59 x 77cm. (Phillips) $34,230

An Egyptian mummified hawk, 22cm. long, Late Dynastic Period. (Phillips) $473

An alabaster peep egg with three scenes of the Crystal Palace, 4½in. high. (Christie's) $175

Stone fountain base, 3ft. 6in. diam. (Lots Road Chelsea Auction Galleries) $448

A 19th century stag-antler pipe-case and tobacco box, signed Seiryu, 20.2cm. and 9.5cm. (Christie's) $8,365

Late 17th/early 18th century gentleman's green velvet undress hat embroidered in silver and gold thread, 8½in. (Hy. Duke & Son) $1,440

A rock crystal relief plaque depicting the life of Christ, in the Gothic style, 5¼ x 3½in., mounted in a leather case. (Christie's) $1,430

A Russian icon: The Mother of God Vladimirskaya, Moscow 1861, maker's mark cyrillic I.A., 31 x 27cm. (Lawrence Fine Art) $1,337

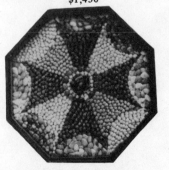

A late 19th century French original plaster half length portrait of Mme. La Baronne Cecile Demarcay, signed J. B. Carpeaux, 80cm. high. (Christie's) $29,392

One of three 19th century shell pictures in octagonal wooden frames, 11in. wide. (Lots Road Chelsea Auction Galleries) $480

One of a pair of gilt metal sconces of 17th century design, 15in. high. (Christie's) $642

A 19th century tin and alloy inkwell depicting 'Mr Punch', 3in. wide. (Giles Haywood) $82

A 19th century sailor's woolwork ship picture in original mahogany veneered frame, 39.5 x 61cm. (David Lay) $1,404

Late 19th century red lacquered mask of a Karasu Tengu, signed Somin, 5cm. high. (Christie's) $2,442

A large Maori nephrite adze head of rounded rectangular form, 17cm. long. (Phillips) $582

Isaac Taylor III, a family conversation group, silhouette painted on glass, 12.5/8in. high. (Christie's) $1,425

A Maori bone comb, 12.7cm. high. (Phillips) $254

A Solomon Islands shell ornament, Kap Kap, the tridacna clam shell base with turtle shell disc attached, 11.7cm. diam. (Phillips) $691

A pale celadon jade carving of a Maiden Immortal standing beside a deer, 8½in. high, carved giltwood stand. (Christie's) $4,620

A model of a horse-drawn gypsy caravan, the interior furnished in traditional manner, 20½in. long, excluding shafts. (Lawrence Fine Art) $372

One of a pair of 19th century lacquered coasters, 5½in. diam. (Hobbs & Chambers) $525

A 19th century sedan chair, the interior with buttoned and studded leather, complete with carrying bars. (Jacobs & Hunt) $3,894

A Davidson jade green square shaped Tutankhamen bowl, circa 1923, 6in. sq. (Anderson & Garland) $77

Late 19th century American Toleware painted and stencilled chocolate pot, 8½in. high. (Christie's) $1,100

Augustin Edouart, a full-length group silhouette of the Lambe family, Hogarth frame, 12in. high. (Christie's) $1,514

Mid 19th century Chinese Export lacquer tea caddy of quatre-foil shape, 10in. wide. (Christie's) $682

A 19th century lacquer writing set comprising a writing table and a writing box, 61 x 33cm. and 25.1 x 22.5cm. respectively. (Christie's) $37,400

An apple green and mottled white jade carving of Guanyin, 18in. high, fixed pierced stand. (Christie's) $66,000

A needlework pocketbook worked in Queens stitch with silk yarns, Penn., circa 1818, 4 x 6in. (Robt. W. Skinner Inc.) $450

A builder's mirror back half model of the single screw cargo ship 'Persistence', 15 x 49¼ in. overall. (Christie's) $5,544

A fully planked un-rigged boxwood model of H.M.S. Circe, circa 1875, built by T. Wake, Stockwood, 5 x 17in. (Christie's) $1,201

A 19th century model of a Gloucester fishing schooner, 'Columbia', fully rigged with wooden sails, 20.3/8in. long. (Robt. W. Skinner Inc.) $900

A live steam spirit-fired wooden model of the paddle tug 'Alert' of Yarmouth, 21 x 39in. (Christie's) $2,679

A fully planked and rigged model of a 72-gun man-o'-war, built by P. Rumsey, Bosham, 26 x 37in. (Christie's) $2,772

An exhibition standard 1:384 scale model of H.M.S. Rattlesnake, circa 1781, built by J. Evans, Whyteleaf. (Christie's) $2,956

An exhibition standard 'One Metre' class steam boat 'Papua', BH 19, built by A. Broad, Bromley, 8 x 40in. (Christie's) $554

A well detailed wood and metal static display model of the Leander class frigate H.M.S. Aurora, Pennant No. F10, stand 14 x 16in. (Christie's) $1,016

A wood waterline model of the R.M.S. Edinburgh Castle built by Bassett-Lowke, the ship 30in. long, in glazed case. (Onslow's) $612

A contemporary model of Sir Henry Segrave's record breaking power boat Miss England, length of vessel 12in., in glazed case. (Onslow's) $520

A fully planked and rigged bone and wood model of a topsail schooner built by P. Rumsey, Bosham, 10 x 14in. (Christie's) $702

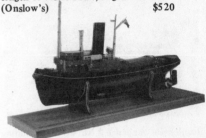

A model of the single screw tug 'Devonmoor', built by J. Gregory, Plymouth, 18 x 34in. (Christie's) $1,663

A 1:48 scale fibreglass, wood and metal, electric-powered model of the coastal cargo ship S.S. Talacre of Liverpool, built by R. H. Phillips, 13 x 33in. (Christie's) $739

A finely carved and detailed contemporary early 19th century boxwood model of the 28-gun man-o'-war H.M.S. Nelson, 13½ x 10½in. (Christie's) $15,708

A 1/24 scale fully planked electric powered model of the Herring Drifter 'Supernal', built by G. Wrigley, 1979/80 from drawings by R. Neville, 24 x 24in. (Christie's) $2,402

A contemporary mid 19th century model of the Paddle Steamer 'Atlanta', 18½ x 41in. (Christie's) $8,316

Marklin, gauge 1, clockwork 4-4-0 locomotive and tender No. 1031. (Phillips) $684

Marklin for Gamages, gauge 1, clockwork 0-4-0 G.N.R. locomotive and tender No. 294. (Phillips) $521

Hornby pre-war gauge 0 No. 0 vans, including two milk, ventilated refrigerator, perishable, meat; two No. 2 high capacity wagons and a Bing LNWR open wagon. (Christie's) $392

Marklin gauge 1 (e-rail) electric model of a Continental 4-4-0 'Compound' locomotive and six-wheeled tender No. 65/13041. (Christie's) $356

A Stevens's model dockyard, 3¼in. gauge live-steam spirit fired brass model of an early 2-2-0 locomotive, in original box, circa 1900. (Christie's) $338

A Hornby pre-war gauge 0 No. 2 tank Passenger train set, in original box. (Christie's) $748

Hornby No. 00 train, early 1920's clockwork tin printed MR locomotive and tender No. 483, with key. (Phillips) $138

Bing, gauge 1, clockwork 0-4-0 locomotive and tender No. 48, (unnamed). (Phillips) $456

A Bing for Bassett-Lowke gauge O clockwork model of the LMS 4-4-0 'Compound' locomotive and tender No. 1053 'George the Fifth', (James Norwich Auctions) $176

A Bassett-Lowke gauge 0, 3-rail, electric model of the GWR 2-6-0 'Mogul' locomotive and tender No. 4331, in original paintwork. (Christie's) $1,089

A gauge 0 clockwork model of the LNER 4-4-0 No. 2 special locomotive and tender No. 201, 'The Bramham Moor', by Hornby. (Christie's) $1,069

A 4in. gauge LMS model tank engine, heavy goods type, steam driven, on oak stand. (Woolley & Wallis) $1,944

A Hornby pre-war gauge 0 clockwork No. 2 tank goods set, in original box, and an M1 locomotive. (Christie's) $498

A 7¼in. gauge model of the Great Eastern Railway 0-4-0 locomotive No. 710, steel boiler with 7in. barrel and superheater, cylinders 2.1/8in. x 3¾in., driving wheels 8in. diam. (Onslow's) $3,519

A Bing gauge 0 clockwork model of the LNER 4-6-0 locomotive and tender No. 4472, 'Flying Fox', in original paintwork. (Christie's) $534

An early gauge 1 (3-rail) electric (4v) model of the LNWR 4-4-0 'Compound' locomotive and tender No. 2663, 'George The Fifth', by Marklin, circa 1912. (Christie's) $801

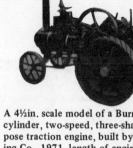

An early 20th century single cylinder horizontal mill engine, complete with mahogany lagged brass bound cylinder, 2½ x 3in. (Onslow's) $397

A 4½in. scale model of a Burrell single cylinder, two-speed, three-shaft general purpose traction engine, built by Lion Engineering Co., 1971, length of engine 68in. (Onslow's) $6,120

An exhibition standard 1½in. scale model of the Allchin single cylinder two-speed four-shaft General Purpose Traction Engine (Royal Chester'. (Onslow's) $2,295

A model of an early 20th century twin cylinder horizontal mill engine, complete with mahogany lagged copper bound cylinders, 2½ x 5in. (Onslow's) $734

A Stuart Major Beam engine, cylinder, 2¼ x 4in., on wood stand in glazed case. (Onslow's) $780

An early 20th century wood model of the 1860 horse-drawn goods wagon owned by Carter Paterson & Co, London and Suburban Express Carriers, 17in. long. (Onslow's) $489

Large monoplane model, made by Charles R. Witteman, Staten Island, New York, circa 1912, 62in. long, wingspan 78in. (Robt. W. Skinner Inc.) $2,000

An exhibition standard 2in. scale model of the Clayton Undertype Articulated wagon, built by E. W. D. Sheppard. (Onslow's) $2,295

A cast iron money bank of a golly, 15.5cm. high. (Phillips) $165

'Artillery', a cast-iron money-box, with a molded cannon, and a World War I tank, by Starkies, circa 1915, 10in. long. (Christie's) $254

'Tammany Bank', a cast iron mechanical bank, the seated gentleman with articulated right arm, 5¾in. high, by J. and E. Stevens Co., circa 1875. (Christie's)$175

'Bull Dog Bank', a cast-iron mechanical moneybox, by J. & E. Stevens, circa 1880, 7¾in. high. (Christie's) $326

'Trick Dog', a mechanical cast-iron moneybox, by J. & E. Stevens, circa 1888, 8¾ x 3in. (Christie's) $544

Late 19th century American cast iron mechanical bank, 'Stump Speaker', 9½in. high. (James Norwich Auctions) $168

'Stollwerck Bros. Post Savings-Bank', modelled as a chocolate dispenser, circa 1911, 6½in. high. (Christie's) $285

'United States and Spain', a mechanical cast-iron money-box, by J. & E. Stevens, circa 1898, 8½ x 2½in. (Christie's) $1,996

'Transvaal Moneybox', a mechanical cast-iron money-box of Paul Kruger. (Christie's) $235

Grenouille, a Lalique glass frog, script R. Lalique France marks (chips to leg and base), 2½in. high. (Onslow's) $1,094

An enamel, double sided, sign for Castrol Wakefield Motor Oil, 13 x 20in. (Onslow's) $136

'Coq Nain', a coloured car mascot, the topaz and satin finished glass molded as a cockerel, 20.2cm. high. (Christie's) $4,510

A nickel plated mascot of a girl bather standing in a seashell, 7in. high. (Onslow's) $209

A. Ward & Co. Ltd. sales leaflet for the N.A.G. 'My Darling', 13-15 H.P. Four Cylinder Car, together with other sales leaflets. (Onslow's) $38

Five publicity booklets by W. Heath Robinson, Connolly Land, Cattle Culture, Nothing Takes The Place of Leather and others; and two others similar by A. Leete and H. M. Bateman. (Onslow's) $193

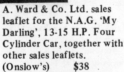

Brooklands Automobile Racing Club, an aluminium and enamel Junior Car Club badge, 3½in. high. (Onslow's) $177

Pratts, two gallon petrol can, repainted. (Onslow's) $57

A Smith's four position light switch and ammeter combined, with bezel action, suitable for Bentley, 3½in. diam. (Onslow's) $80

A Lalique clear and frosted glass car mascot of 'Victoire — Spirit of the Wind', 10in. long. (Prudential Fine Art) $9,454

Napier Motors British Made Throughout, enamel, double sided, 16 x 25in. (Onslow's) $322

'Tete de Belier', a Lalique car mascot, molded as a ram's head, 9.5cm. high. (Christie's)$27,060

A Doxa timepiece with second hand, nickel plated case, 6 o'clock side winder, 2½in. diam. (Onslow's) $193

A nickel plated Michelin type pressure gauge, contained in original printed tinplate box, with instructions. (Onslow's) $225

L'Allumage Moderne Magneto Lavalette Eisemann, hand-colored lithograph after E. Montaut, 17¾ x 35¼in. (Onslow's) $386

An early 20th century cold painted metal car mascot of a dragonfly golfer seated on a composition golf ball, 6in. high. (Woolley & Wallis) $693

Redline, two gallon petrol can, original black and gold paint. (Onslow's) $48

Tete de coq, a Lalique glass cockerel's head (chip to comb), 7in. high, on glass base. (Onslow's) $563

MOTORING ITEMS

Official programme to
the 7th Monte Carlo Rally,
1928. (Onslow's) $80

A chromium plated trophy,
modelled as a Bugatti radiator
grill and badge, mounted on
wood stand, 9in. high.
(Onslow's) $837

The late Hon. C. S. Rolls,
monochrome postcard.
(Onslow's) $32

A chromium plated and
enamelled Aero-Club Brooklands badge, stamped 418,
3½in. high. (Onslow's)
$853

Perche, a Lalique glass mascot,
script Lalique France marks,
4in. high. (Onslow's)
$402

A chromium plated speed
nymph, 5½in. high, mounted
on a radiator cap. (Onslow's)
$112

A Souvenir of Brooklands,
published by Temple Press,
1938; The Brooklands Year-
book, 1939; and Brooklands
Speed & Distance Tables,
revised edn. 1931. (Onslow's)
$161

'Archer', a Lalique car
mascot, in clear and grey
stained glass, with chrome
metal radiator mounts,
11.8cm. high. (Christie's)
$721

D. N. Ingles, Be Up-To-Date
— Shellubricate, printed tin,
with table of grades of oils
listing cars and aeroplane
engines, 25 x 17in. (Onslow's)
$161

Official programme to the 20th Annual 500 Mile Sweepstakes, Indianapolis, May 30th 1934. (Onslow's) $152

Join The R.A.C., printed tin-plate hanging leaflet box, 11in. high, with some membership leaflets. (Onslow's) $120

A circular enamel sign for Mercedes Benz, convex, 16in. diam. (Onslow's) $338

A chromium plated and enamelled B.A.R.C. Brooklands badge, stamped 803, 3½in. high. (Onslow's) $660

'Spirit of the Wind', a redashay car mascot on chromium plated metal mount, 11.5cm. high. (Christie's) $1,353

A brass electric Klaxon horn, suitable for Rolls-Royce, 9in. high. (Onslow's) $128

W. D. & H. O. Wills Ltd, Raymond Mays on the E.R.A. at Brooklands, cardboard advertising display for Will's Star Cigarettes, 27 x 19in. (Onslow's) $627

'Vitesse', a Lalique car mascot molded as a naked female, 18.5cm. high. (Christie's) $9,020

Le Sport & Le Tourisme Automobile, June 1925, French text, mounted plates. (Onslow's) $128

A Sublime Harmony musical box playing six operatic airs, trade label of C. Scotcher & Son, Birmingham, 21in. wide, the cylinder 13in. (Christie's) $3,207

A gramophone with 'The Gramophone Co., Maiden Lane, London, W.C.' label, a 7in. diam. turntable and four single sided E. Berliner's 7in. diam. records, circa 1900-10. (Hobbs & Chambers)$1,600

A key-wind part-overture musical box, No. 20420, playing 'Zampa' overture in two parts and ten other airs, 19in. wide, the cylinder 11½ x 3in. diam. (Christie's)$2,851

A Harmonia 16¼in. disc musical box with single comb movement and walnut veneered case, 23in. wide, with ten discs. (Christie's) $1,782

A 'Margot' forty-four-note piano orchestrion by H. Peters & Co., Leipsig, in oak case, 97in. high, with two barrels 24 x 10½in. diam. and weight. (Christie's) $6,771

A 9½in. Symphonium disc musical box with 'Sublime Harmony' combs, with one disc. (Christie's) $1,069

An Edison Amerola 1A phonograph, No. SM 950 in mahogany case with two-minute and four-minute traversing mandrel mechanism, 49in. high. (Christie's) $1,782

An Amourette organette in the form of a chalet, with seventeen discs, 14in. wide, the discs 9in. (Christie's) $801

A Symphonion musical mantel clock in walnut case, the hinged top concealing a 5¾in. periphery-drive double comb Symphonion movement, 18½in. high, with one disc. (Christie's) $855

MUSICAL BOXES & POLYPHONES

A forty-four key dumb organist pinned for six listed hymn tunes, in mahogany case with crank, 31in. wide. (Christie's) $1,158

An Edison Bell 'Commercial' electric phonograph, No. 21164, the motor in oak base with accessories drawer. (Christie's) $1,336

A mandolin musical box, No. 15838, playing six airs, 33in. wide overall, the cylinder 19½in. (Christie's) $4,633

 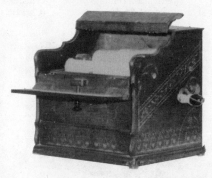 

An Edison Diamond Disc phonograph, Chippendale Laboratory Model (C19) No. SM 106640, 51½in. high, with nineteen discs. (Christie's) $748

A Melodia fourteen-note organ-ette by American Mercantile Co., on gilt stencilled walnut case with label of Bradford & Teale, London, with two rolls. (Christie's) $498

An oak Berliner 7in. record cabinet with folding lid, spaces for 32 records, containing seven American issue Berliners by Cal. Stewart and others. (Christie's) $712

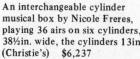

An interchangeable cylinder musical box by Nicole Freres, playing 36 airs on six cylinders, 38½in. wide, the cylinders 13in. (Christie's) $6,237

An EMG gramophone of compact Mark 10 design, with papier mache horn, 25in. diam. and approx. 300 classical records. (Christie's) $748

A bells and drum in view cylinder music box, by B. A. Bremond, circa 1875, box 21in. long. (Christie's) $2,530

An Edison Fireside phonograph, Model A No. 25426, the K reproducer, crane and 36 two-minute and four-minute wax cylinders in cartons. (Christie's) $748

A Polyphon 15.5/8in. periphery-drive disc musical box with winding handle and twelve discs. (Phillips) $1,440

A musical box by J. Thibouville Lamy & Co., No. 69701, playing twelve airs, 23in. wide, the cylinder 13in., 1890-1900. (Christie's) $1,514

A 24.5/8in. upright Polyphon with coin mechanism and drawer, in glazed walnut case, 46in. high, with twenty-seven discs. (Christie's) $8,019

An early Edison electric phonograph mechanism, in oak case with glass cover, with rear part of a Bettini carrier arm (lacks Edison carrier arm, Bettini reproducer and horn). (Christie's) $1,960

A 15.5/8in. Regina table disc musical box with double comb long bedplate movement in oak case and twelve zinc discs. (Christie's) $2,138

An Apollo horn gramophone with double-spring motor in oak case with part wood tonearm and laminated oak horn, circa 1912. (Christie's) $1,158

A Celestina twenty-note organette in gilt stencilled walnut case, with fourteen rolls and nineteen new rolls. (Christie's) $1,336

A musical box playing 12 airs, tune sheet and inlaid lid, 26in. wide, the cylinder 14in. (Christie's) $4,633

An HMV Intermediate Monarch gramophone with mahogany case and horn, 1911 (soundbox replaced). (Christie's) $1,158

A 19th century chased brass cased rectangular musical box with a hinged cover revealing a singing bird, 4.25in. long. (Woolley & Wallis) $495

A musical box by Ducommun Girod, playing eight operatic and other airs, in bevelled corner case, 23¾in. wide, the cylinder 13in. (Christie's) $1,692

An eighteen-key chamber barrel organ by Longhurst(?), London, with three barrels, drum, triangle and four musical stops, in mahogany case with simulated pipes to the Gothic front, 71in. high. (Christie's) $1,514

'Golden Marenghi', 46 key Fairground organ, circa 1905, 7ft. x 7ft. (Onslow's) $28,764

An HMV Model 203 cabinet gramophone, 5A soundbox and re-entrant tone chamber, the mahogany case with gilt internal fittings. (Christie's) $3,564

A 15.5/8in. table polyphone with twin combs and 17 discs. (Christie's) $2,316

A coin-operated table-top Buffet Tirelire musical box, the 17cm. cylinder with zither attachment, in walnut case, 47.5 x 42cm. (Osmond Tricks) $1,720

A 19.5/8in. upright Polyphon with coin mechanism and drawer, in glazed walnut case, 38in. high. (Christie's) $6,237

A Gramophone & Typewriter
Ltd. Style No. 6 gramophone
in panelled oak case and
Concert soundbox, travelling
arm and brass horn, circa 1901.
(Christie's) $1,603

Early HMV wind-up table
gramophone with original
gilt pleated circular diaphram.
(Lawrence Butler & Co.)
$820

A Gramophone & Typewriter
Ltd. New Style No. 3 gramophone with 7in. turntable,
now with Columbia soundbox
and brass horn. (Christie's)
$1,452

A 15¾in. Polyphon disc musical
box playing on single comb, in
walnut case, 19¼in. wide, complete with winding handle and
forty-one discs. (Hobbs &
Chambers) $1,408

An early Kammer & Rein-
hardt 5in. Berliner Gramophone, with three Berliner
records. (Phillips)
$2,080

A Britannia 'smoker's cabinet'
upright 9in. disc musical box in
walnut case, 26½in. high, with
fourteen discs. (Christie's)
$2,494

A Zither Marmonique Piccolo
musical box by Paillard, Vaucher
Fils, playing eight airs, 22in. wide,
the cylinder 13in. (Christie's)
$2,316

An Edison Home phonograph,
early Model A, with automatic
reproducer, and modern brass
witch's hat horn. (Christie's)
$427

A Sublime Harmony Tremelo
musical box with tune sheet
and bird's-eye maple case,
24½in. wide. (Christie's)
$1,782

A viola by Wm. H. Luff, London, dated 1971, 16½in. long. (Phillips) $6,048

A violoncello by Henry Jay, in London, circa 1760, 28.7/8in. long, with a lightweight case by Paxman. (Phillips) $8,064

A viola by G. Lucci, Roma, 1978, 16½in. long, with a bow in a modern shaped case. (Phillips) $2,856

A violin by N. Vuillaume, Paris, circa 1840, 14.1/8in. long, in case. (Phillips) $7,360

A violoncello by Ch. J. B. Collin-Mezin, length of back 30in. (Phillips) $7,160

A violin by Claude Pierray, in Paris, circa 1720, 14.5/16in. long, with a water-proof case by W. E. Hill & Sons. (Phillips) $4,200

A violin by G. A. Chanot, dated 1906, 14.3/16in. long, in case. (Phillips) $2,520

A violin by G. Pyne, London, 1921, 14in. long, with a silver mounted bow by J. Hel, in case. (Phillips) $1,680

A violin by Salomon of Reims, 1746, length of back 14. 13/16in., in an oblong, velvet-lined and fitted case. (Phillips) $2,970

A Florentine violin, circa 1770, bearing the label Lorenzo and Tommaso Carcassi, anno 1773, length of back 14in. (Phillips) $9,075

An English violin, bearing the label of G. Pyne, Maker London, 1888, 14.1/8in. long, with bow. (Phillips) $2,880

A viola, by B. Banks of Salisbury, circa 1770, length of back 15.3/8in., in a shaped and lined velvet case. (Phillips) $9,308

A violin by J. A. Chanot, 1899, length of back 14.1/8in., with a silver mounted bow, in case. (Phillips) $5,728

A violin by Wm. E. Hill & Sons, London, 1904, length of back 14in., in a mahogany case. (Phillips) $8,055

A violoncello by Wm. Forster, London, circa 1784, 29in. long, in wood case. (Phillips) $6,720

A violin by Carolus F. Landulphus, 1766, length of back 13. 15/16in., with a silver mounted bow, in an oak case. (Phillips) $57,280

A Neapolitan violoncello, circa 1750, attributed to G. Gagliano, 29.7/16in. long, with a silver mounted bow and cover. (Phillips) $58,800

A viola by F. Gagliano in Naples, 14½in. long, upper bouts 7.1/8in. long, lower bouts 9in. (Phillips) $17,600

A violoncello, circa 1750, of the Tyrolesse School, labelled Carlo Tunon, 1732, 29.3/16in. long, in wood case. (Phillips) $7,056

A violin by J. N. Leclerc, circa 1770, 14in. long, with two bows, in case. (Phillips) $2,520

A violin by Alfred Vincent, dated 1922, 13.14/16in. long, in a shaped case, by E. Withers. (Phillips) $3,024

A violin by Dom Nicolo Amati of Bologna, 1714, 14.1/16in. long, in case. (Phillips) $15,120

A viola, circa 1830, of the Kennedy School, 15.5/16in. long, with two bows, in an oblong case. (Phillips) $2,436

A violin attributed to R. Cuthbert, 1676, 13.7/8in. long, in case. (Phillips) $1,310

A viola, circa 1780, length of back 15¾in., in an oblong fitted case. (Phillips) $11,550

A violin by Richard Duke in London, circa 1770, length of back 14in. (Phillips) $6,930

A viola by Giuseppe Lucci, length of back 16½in., in a case lined in green velvet by Gewa. (Phillips) $3,795

A violin by Antonio Capela, 1972, length of back 14in., in shaped case. (Phillips) $198

A violin by William Glenister, 1904, length of back 14. 1/16in., with a bow. (Phillips) $1,567

A violin by Vincenzo Sannino, 1910, length of back 14.1/16in, with a shaped case and cover. (Phillips) $10,725

A violin by Joannes Gagliano of Naples, circa 1790, length of back 14in., in case. (Phillips) $9,308

A violin by Lorenzo Arcangioli of Florence, circa 1840, length of back 13.7/8in. (Phillips) $6,930

A violin by Ferd.
August Homolka,
length of back 13.
15/16in., with two
bows, in marquetry
case. (Phillips)
$5,012

A French viola, circa
1900, labelled
Joannes Baptista
Guadagnini, length
of back 15.7/8in.,
in fitted case.
(Phillips)
$3,300

A violin by J. Werro,
bearing the maker's
label Fecit a Berne
1922, length of back
14.1/8in. (Phillips)
$3,960

A violin by Joseph
Hill, 1756, length
of back 14in.
(Phillips)
$5,940

A violin by Charles
J. B. Collin-Mezin,
length of back 14.
1/8in., with two
bows in case.
(Phillips)
$2,805

A violin by F. W.
Chanot, London,
A.D. 1890, length
of back 14in., with
two bows, in water-
proof case. (Phillips)
$4,833

A violoncello by H.
Derazey in Mirecourt,
circa 1860, length of
back 29in., with a
silver mounted French
bow. (Phillips)
$6,444

A violin by H. L. Hill,
London, circa 1825,
length of back 14in.,
with a bow in leather
case. (Phillips)
$7,160

Early 19th century brass mounted mahogany sedan clock, 7in. diam. (Christie's) $306

A silver medallion by B. Andrieu, circa 1800, 2in. diam. (Christie's) $288

A bronze bust of Napoleon on spreading plinth, signed 'Noel R', 12¼in. high. (Christie's) $1,082

A 19th century ivory rotunda with stepped roof and fluted columns framing a statuette of Napoleon, 7in. high, 5½in. diam. (Christie's) $7,576

Napoleon I: Letter signed 'Napoleon', to the Archduke Charles, Compiegne, 24 March 1810, one page, sm. 4to, mounted beside a color printed engraving of Napoleon's head. (Christie's) $3,427

A 19th century brass carriage clock with enamel dial and statuette of Napoleon, 8in. high. (Christie's) $721

After Vauthier: Notables de a France revolutionaire, by E. Bovinet, engravings, 400 x 273mm. (Christie's) $1,082

A Continental biscuit porcelain equestrian group of Napoleon crossing the Alps after the painting by David, mid 19th century, 8in. wide, 10½in. high. (Christie's) $2,164

Napoleon I: Document signed 'Napol', one page, large folio, printed heading the crest, Moscow, 12 October 1812. (Christie's) $1,353

An Empire ormolu mounted mahogany fauteuil de bureau with revolving circular seat covered in ochre leather, 21½in. diam. (Christie's) $99,220

Early 19th century circular tortoiseshell box, the cover painted with Napoleon on horseback, 3in. diam. (Christie's) $541

A trooper's helmet of the French Cuirassiers (Second Empire) with chin-chain, mane and tuft, 18in. high. (Christie's) $1,804

A 19th century bronze bust of Napoleon as First Consul, 36cm. high. (Christie's) $635

Napoleon I: Document signed 'Nap', granting a pardon to Jean-Marie Merle, who had been sentened to 5 years hard labour in 1805 for desertion, one page, oblong folio, 395 x 505mm. (Christie's) $1,984

An ivory statuette of Frederick the Great on eight-sided base carved with relief portraits of ladies, 7¼in. high. (Christie's) $4,690

Napoleon I: Endorsement signed 'N', 26 May, 1813, one page, folio, printed heading of Ministere de la Guerre, Bureau de la Gendarmerie. (Christie's) $631

One of two early 19th century French shallow circular boxes, possibly Grenoble, 3½in. diam. (Christie's) $270

Early 19th century marquetry coach panel inlaid in shaded woods with Napoleon on horseback, 27¾ x 19½in. (Christie's) $1,262

A 19th century French bronze bust of Napoleon, inscribed on the reverse J. Berthoz, 24cm. high. (Christie's) $689

An Empire scarlet morocco leather despatch box with brass hasp backplate, clips and angles, 27in. wide. (Christie's) $7,216

A Continental biscuit porcelain bust inscribed 'Napoleon I', 16½in. high. (Christie's) $2,886

After Jean Baptiste Isabey: Napoleon a Malmaison, by C. L. Lingee and J. Godefroy, mixed method engraving, 637 x 433mm. (Christie's) $505

A bronze equestrian statue of Napoleon issuing instructions from a galloping horse, on a breccia marble base, 10in. wide, 11½in. high. (Christie's) $631

An Empire ormolu toilet mirror, with inscription '. . . taken by a Sergeant of the 11th Lt. Dragoons from Napoleon's Carriage dressing case . . .', 12 x 8in. (Christie's) $1,102

A 19th century bronze bust of Napoleon, signed 'Linedon' on verde antico marble plinth, 18½in. high. (Christie's) $1,713

A 19th century ormolu and porphyry encrier, the pentray centered by a bust of the Emperor with initial N below, 14½in. wide. (Christie's) $2,886

A 19th century French bronze figure of Napoleon, the base inscribed Vela. F. 1867, and on the reverse F. Barbedienne, 28cm. high. (Christie's) $1,361

A 19th century French bronze bust of Napoleon The First, after Ambrogio Colombo, 32cm. high. (Christie's) $998

A 19th century bronze, ormolu and verde antico paperweight mounted with a trophy of Napoleon's hat, sword and scroll, 6in. wide. (Christie's) $1,984

A bronze bust of Napoleon, signed 'Noel Ruffier', 11½in. high. (Christie's)
$1,443

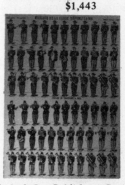

After Robert Lefevre: Joseph Napoleon, Roi de Naples et de Sicile, by L. C. Rouolle, colored mixed method engraving, 436 x 324mm. (Christie's) $396

A 19th century French bronze statue of Napoleon on Horseback, on rouge marble base, 61cm. high. (Christie's) $2,755

Pellerin & Co., Publishers: Genie; Musique de la Garde Republicane; Fanfare de Dragons; Hussards; Chasseurs; and Musique de Hussards, colored engravings, 373 x 265mm. (Christie's) $144

After Cornillet: Napoleon au Palais des Tuileries; and Napoleon assis, after F. Flameng, 304 x 210mm. (Christie's)
$505

A 19th century bronze group of Napoleon and a French soldier, 6½in. wide, 7in. high. (Christie's) $631

A 19th century bronze bust of Napoleon signed 'Noel R', on spreading verde antico marble plinth, 6½in. high. (Christie's) $216

A 20th century ivory netsuke, Boyasha Sonjiro, signed Nasatoshi, 5 cm. high. (Christie's) $6,692

An ivory netsuke of a grazing deer, unsigned, circa 1800, 6.2cm. high. (Christie's) $4,833

An 18th century ivory netsuke of Shoki and Oni, unsigned, 7.7cm. high. (Christie's) $2,974

A 19th century cloudy amber netsuke of Fukuro-kuju, 6.3cm. high. (Christie's) $1,301

Early 18th century wood netsuke of a bitch and puppies, signed Matsuda Sukenaga, 6.8cm. long. (Christie's) $1,673

A boxwood netsuke of Daruma, signed Sansho (1871-1936), 4.3cm. high. (Christie's) $7,807

A 19th century boxwood netsuke of a large snake holding a rat in its jaws, signed Masanori, 5cm. wide. (Christie's) $2,992

Late 18th century wood netsuke of Roshi seated on a mule (seal netsuke), 7cm. high. (Christie's) $1,766

An ivory seal netsuke carved as a well-known foreigner who came to Nagasaki, signed Mitsumasa, circa 1880, 4.8cm. high. (Christie's) $792

A 19th century Hirado ware netsuke of Gama Sennin, impressed signature Masakazu, 8.1cm. high. (Christie's) $1,022

An 18th century ivory netsuke of a grazing horse, unsigned, 7cm. high. (Christie's) $3,346

A 20th century ivory netsuke of Ryujin, signed Masatoshi, 9.2cm. high. (Christie's) $6,506

A 19th century metal netsuke of a Kendo mask, signed Nagayasu saku, 3.8cm. high. (Christie's) $3,718

Early 19th century wood netsuke of an ostler trying to shoe a horse, 4.8cm. long. (Christie's) $2,416

A 20th century stag-antler netsuke of an owl, signed Masatoshi, 4.5cm. high. (Christie's) $5,948

A wood netsuke of a dog with one foot on a clam shell, Kyoto School, circa 1780, 3.4cm. high. (Christie's) $1,936

Late 18th century ivory netsuke of Moso and bamboo shoot, signed Awataguchi, 8.4cm. high. (Christie's) $5,205

A 19th century wood netsuke of three human skulls, signed Yoshiharu, 5.3cm. wide. (Christie's) $2,602

Late 19th century Imari
ware netsuke of the monkey
showman, 5.5cm. high.
(Christie's) $1,115

A 19th century zelkova
wood Karashishi mask,
5.2cm. long. (Christie's)
$780

An ivory netsuke of Rakan,
signed Kuya, 4.5cm. high,
with tomobako. (Christie's)
$5,019

A 19th century ivory netsuke
of a cherry tree and morning
mist (ryusa manju), signed
with a kao, 4.3cm. diam.
(Christie's) $1,394

A wood netsuke of the
demon's arm, signed Kyusai,
7.2cm. long. (Christie's)
$3,346

A 19th century ivory netsuke
of a nine-tailed fox, signed
Baihosai, with seal Naomitsu,
7.4cm. diam. (Christie's)
$2,788

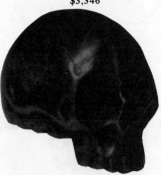

An ivory netsuke of a
seated kirin, signed Yoshi-
masa, circa 1800, 10.5cm.
high. (Christie's)
$44,616

A 19th century metal
netsuke of a human skull,
signed Yoshihide, 3.5cm.
long. (Christie's)
$2,044

A 19th century ivory
netsuke of Songoku the
magical monkey, signed
Mitsuhiro, 5.2cm. high.
(Christie's)
$13,013

A wood netsuke of Yamabushi, signed Soko (1879-1942), 5.3cm. high, with tomobako. (Christie's) $22,308

Early 19th century wood netsuke Ko-omote mask, 5.9cm. high. (Christie's) $1,022

A 19th/20th century colored and inlaid ivory netsuke of a courtier, signed Yasuaki, with seal Kodama, 4.6cm. high. (Christie's) $4,461

Mid 19th century ivory netsuke of a tsuba, signed Hojitsu, 4.4cm. high. (Christie's) $3,532

An 18th century ivory netsuke of an Amagatsu doll, signed Masanao (of Kyoto), 5.5cm. high. (Christie's) $48,334

A 19th century ivory, shishiaibori and kebori netsuke of Asahina Saburo and Sogo No Goro, signed Kosai Moritoshi and kao, 6.1cm. diam. (Christie's) $2,230

Early 19th century lacquered wood netsuke of Tososei, unsigned, 6.3cm. high. (Christie's) $1,580

An ivory netsuke carved as a tsuitate depicting Tekkai Sennin exhaling his spiritual essence, circa 1840, 5cm. high. (Christie's) $880

A 19th century ivory netsuke of a rat on a corn cob, 9.4cm. long. (Christie's) $2,230

An 18th century ivory netsuke of a dog and awabi shell, signed Tomotada, 3.5cm. high. (Christie's) $12,083

A wood netsuke of a recumbent camel, signed Sosui, 4.3cm. long. (Christie's) $13,942

A 19th century wood netsuke of Hideyoshi playing horse, 4cm. high. (Christie's) $2,602

A 19th century wood netsuke of Jurojin and stag, signed Masakatsu, 4.3cm. wide. (Christie's) $17,660

An ivory netsuke of Omori Hikoshichi and the witch, signed Shoko, 5.2cm. high, with tomobako. (Christie's) $13,013

A 19th century boxwood netsuke of a seated figure of a monster-man, 4.8cm. high. (Christie's) $3,718

A 19th century boxwood netsuke of a Bugaku mask, signed Shugetsu saku, 3.9cm. high. (Christie's) $1,487

A 19th century wood netsuke of a dragon in thunder clouds, signed Homi, 3.9cm. diam. (Christie's) $1,208

A 19th century ivory netsuke of an Otafuku mask, signed with a kao, 4cm. high. (Christie's) $2,044

A 19th century ivory netsuke of Yuramosuke, signed Anrakusai, 3.4cm. high. (Christie's) $2,974

An 18th century wood netsuke of two goats, signed Tametaka, 3.5cm. high. (Christie's) $13,013

A 19th century ivory netsuke of Karashishi and young with a tama, signed Eijusai Masayoshi, 4cm. wide. (Christie's) $13,942

Late 19th century ivory, stained and inlaid netsuke of a Temple servant, signed Yasumasa, 4.9cm. high. (Christie's) $3,532

Early 19th century wood netsuke of a demon mask, signed Gyokuzan, 6.3cm. high. (Christie's) $892

Early 19th century wood netsuke of a mushroom cluster, traces of signature, 4.7cm. high. (Christie's) $1,301

A 19th century wood netsuke of rats on an otafuku mask, signed Tadahisa, 4cm. long. (Christie's) $2,602

A 19th century ivory netsuke, Takaramono, 4.5cm. diam. (Christie's) $2,044

An ivory netsuke of a Daruma doll, signed Mitsu-hiro and kao (1810-75), 4cm. high. (Christie's) $4,089

1928 Bank of Australasia £1. (Phillips)
$356

Canada: 1897 Dominion $1. (Phillips)
$518

Zanzibar: 1916 20 rupees. (Phillips)
$1,620

Southern Rhodesia: 1951 10/-. (Phillips)
$251

1857 Mosenthal Brothers £5 issued at Cape
Town. (Phillips) $469

Gibraltar: 1914 (6 August) £1. (Phillips)
$550

£1 1915 overprinted for use in the Dardanelles.
(Phillips) $1,944

Barbados: 1938 Royal Bank of Canada $5.
(Phillips) $170

Mauritius: 1919 1 rupee. (Phillips) $275

Jersey: Jersey Mercantile Union Bank £1 uniface color trial in blue by Charles Skipper & East. (Phillips) $777

Hong Kong: 1929 Hong Kong & Shanghai Banking Corporation $10 specimen. (Phillips) $243

1916 Mercantile Bank of India $10. (Phillips) $324

Malaya: 1942 $100. (Phillips) $267

Zanzibar: 1928 (1st February) Government 10 rupees. (Phillips) $2,025

Ireland: Northern Bank £100, 1919. (Phillips) $194

Australia: c. 1900 Bank of New South Wales £100 unissued. (Phillips) $745

A rectangular pewter-rimmed kobako, unsigned, circa 1800, 9.3 x 8.3cm. (Christie's) $1,320

One of a pair of Art Nouveau pewter vases, attributed to WMF, with glass liners, stamped A K & Cie, 36cm. high. (Christie's) $1,713

German pewter three-handled soup tureen with boar mount, by Kayserzinn, 15in. high. (Worsfolds) $420

A Victorian pewter egg cruet with four spoons. (G. A. Key) $126

A Glasgow style pewter and enamel cigar box, with an enamel plaque of a maiden holding an apron of fruit, 8¾in. wide. (Christie's) $288

A Swedish art pewter inkwell by Svenskt Tenn, Stockholm, 12.5cm. high. (David Lay) $68

Liberty & Co. Tudric pewter two-handled motto cup, London, circa 1910, 7.7/8in. high. (Robt. W. Skinner Inc.) $225

A glass jar with pewter cover and mounting, after a design by Peter Behrens, 6¼in. high. (Robt. W. Skinner Inc.) $450

An 18th century large baluster pewter pitcher (hallmarked with two sets of cross keys). (J. M. Welch & Son)$486

A 19th century American Dixon & Son pewter teapot, with wooden handle. (Du Mouchelles) $150

A Liberty Tudric pewter biscuit box, the lid with twin handle over square section base, 11cm. high. (Phillips) $171

A 19th century pewter salt dip, on claw feet with hinged lids. (Du Mouchelles) $150

A WMF pewter centerpiece with rectangular clear glass tank, stamped marks, 55.5cm. wide, 31.4cm. high. (Christie's) $1,353

One of a pair of WMF pewter and glass vases, stamped marks, 48cm. high. (Christie's) $902

A WMF pewter centerpiece, cast as a young girl with flowing robe forming an irregular-shaped tray, 22.5cm. high. (Christie's) $721

A pewter bell-based candlestick, with flaring drip-pan above a cylindrical candlecup, 9in. high. (Christie's) $66

A pewter-rimmed kobako decorated with chrysanthemums by the East Fence, box 17th century, 7.9cm. long. (Christie's) $1,144

A Chinese octagonal pewter wine pot, glass panels depicting domestic scenes. (Du Mouchelles) $350

PHOTOGRAPHS

'Journal of my trip to Ceylon, Australia and Tasmania, W. G. Hardy, 1894', disbound album containing approx. 120 albumen prints, majority 6½ x 9½in., small 4to. (Christie's) $577

'The Expression of the Emotions in Man and Animals', by Charles Darwin with seven heliotype plates, 8vo., London: John Murray, 1872. (Christie's) $104

Three Midgets, whole plate tin-type, gilt highlights, gilt edged oval paper matt, 1850s/60s; and another. (Christie's) $90

F.E. Currey, Iris and chrysanthemum, two platinum prints, 7½ x 5½in. and 8 x 6in., unmounted (1880s or early 90s). (Christie's) $376

A pair of portrait photographs of George VI and Queen Elizabeth, by Dorothy Wilding, in original fitted cases, 26cm. x 35cm. (Phillips) $5,440

The Far East, Australasia, South America, South Africa and Europe, two albums, containing 360 albumen prints, 240 cartes-des-visites, oblong 4to. and half morocco, 1860s and 1870s. (Christie's) $1,804

Bill Brandt, Parlormaid and under-parlormaid ready to serve dinner, gelatin silver print, 35¼ x 30in., with photographer's ink stamp and initials 'B.B.' on reverse, 1930s. (Christie's) $1,985

Francis Frith (1822-1898), Egypt and Sinai, ten albumen prints, each 6 x 8in., six signed, 1857. (Christie's) $459

Bill Brandt (1906-1984), Antonio Tapies' left eye, gelatin silver print, 28 x 24in., with photographer's ink stamp and initials 'B.B.' on reverse, 1964. (Christie's)$731

Silvy, Caldesi, Notman, Robinson and others, a collection of cartes-des-visite and cabinet cards, 29 albums, majority full morocco,1850s/ 1890s. (Christie's) $1,443

6th Inniskilling Dragoons, an album of 24 photographs, majority salt prints and oval 5¼ x 4¼in., cont. half red morocco, 4to. (Christie's) $324

One of a collection of ambrotypes and daguerreotypes, quarter-plate portrait of a butcher hand-tinted in pink to emphasise the raw meat and his cheeks. (Christie's) $902

Angus McBean, 'Toumanova 'surrealized' as La Sylphide', gelatin silver print, 19¼ x 14¾in., signature and date 'London '38' in pencil on card. (Christie's) $271

Jane Brown, Edith Sitwell, gelatin silver print, 15 x 11in., mounted on card, 1959. (Christie's) $167

J. Dupont, Foot artist at work, albumen print, 9¾ x 7¾in., signature 'J. Dupont Phot. Anvers' (1870s). (Christie's) $585

Japanese costume portraits and topography, album of forty-six albumen prints and a three-print panorama, oblong 4to, dated 1896. (Christie's) $469

Yousuf Karsh, Ernest Hemingway, gelatin silver print, 12 x 10in., titled and credited, 1957. (Christie's)$271

James Linton, calotype, 7½ x 5½in., unmounted, letter 'A' stamped in ink on reverse, 1844-45. (Christie's) $940

An Operaphone cabinet gramophone in the form of a grand piano, in mahogany case with Thorens soundbox, internal horn enclosed by the 'keyboard fall', 34in. long. (Christie's) $891

A spinet by Longman Lukey & Co., London, circa 1771. Overall length 75in. (Phillips) $1,023

A Steinway upright oak piano, circa 1903, Serial 107781, decorated by Edwin Willard Deming. (Christie's) $28,600

An overstrung boudoir grand pianoforte, seven and a quarter octaves, by John Broadwood & Sons, in a satinwood case. (Christie's) $2,178

A classical rosewood and mahogany pianoforte, labelled by A. Babcock, Boston, circa 1820, 67in. wide. (Christie's) $2,860

An Aeolian Grand 58-note player organ with 19 musical stops and walnut case, 64in. wide. 1898. (Christie's) $1,782

Late 18th century wing-shaped spinet, the hardwood case stained dark walnut, overall length 73in. (Phillips) $5,370

A 48-note street barrel piano in veneered case, playing 10 airs, on painted hand-cart. (Christie's) $1,960

A fine single manual Harpsichord, by Jacob & Abraham Kirkman, in a cross banded mahogany case, 87 x 37¼in. on modern trestle stand. (Christie's) $23,628

An Eavestaff overstrung under-dampered 'mini-piano' with green drag point slab shaped deco case, also matching stool. (Peter Wilson) $1,134

An important Steinway parlour concert grand piano, circa 1904, 91in. long, together with a duet stool, 44in. long. (Christie's)
$66,000

A forty-seven note coin-slot barrel piano with ten-air barrel in varnished birch case and engraved glass panel, 40in. wide. (Christie's)
$855

Gernard Lens, a gentleman facing right in beige coat, signed with gold monogram, gilt metal mounts, rectangular wood frame, oval 2.7/8in. high. (Christie's) $1,069

James Peale, a lady in white shawl and bonnet, signed with initials and dated 1800, oval 3in. high. (Christie's) $1,960

Thomas Flatman, a self-portrait, on vellum, signed and dated 1678, gold frame, oval 2½in. high. (Christie's) $10,335

George Engleheart, a miniature of Capt. John Cummings in the uniform of The 8th Dragoons, signed and dated 1806, oval 3½in. high. (Christie's) $6,237

George Engleheart, a lady in decollete white dress with frilled border, gold frame, oval 2.7/8in. high. (Christie's) $5,346

John Cox Dillman Engleheart, a gentleman in dark blue coat with gold buttons, signed on the reverse and dated 1814, oval 2.5/8in. high. (Christie's) $980

Philip Jean, a gentleman in blue coat with gold buttons, gold frame with plaited hair reverse, oval 2¾in. high. (Christie's) $1,336

Attributed to Pierre Chasselat, a a lady seated on a bench in a landscape, set in the lid of a tortoiseshell box with gold rims, 2.5/8in. diam. (Christie's) $3,920

John Cox Dillman Engleheart, a gentleman in black coat and waistcoat, gold frame, oval 2.7/8in. high. (Christie's) $534

Andrew Plimer, an officer in scarlet uniform with blue facings and silver lace, gold frame, oval 3in. (Christie's) $3,207

John Smart, a miniature of Miss Elizabeth Cottingham of County Clare, signed and dated 1777, gold frame, oval 2in. high. (Christie's) $10,335

James Green, a gentleman possibly the Rt. Hon. Edward Ellice, gold frame, oval 3.1/8in. high. (Christie's) $981

Philip Jean, a gentleman in blue coat with gold buttons, gold frame, oval 2.5/8in. high. (Christie's) $715

David Des Granges, a miniature of a lady in black dress with lace border and white lace collar, on vellum, oval 2.3/8in. high. (Christie's) $8,019

Studio of Richard Gibson, a gentleman believed to be Sir John Germaine, on vellum, oval 3.1/8in. high. (Christie's) $1,782

George Place, a miniature of an officer of the Weymouth Vol. Artillery, gilt metal frame, oval 4¾in. high. (Christie's) $5,346

John Smart, Jane Palmer in ermine-bordered pale blue surcoat, signed with initials and dated 1777, gold frame, oval 1¾in. high. (Christie's) $7,128

John Comerford, Capt. James Hughes in the blue uniform of The 18th Dragoons (Hussars), signed and dated 1807, oval 3in. high. (Christie's) $2,138

After Pierre Adolph Hall, a
gentleman in white-lined
blue coat with gold borders,
gilt metal frame with split
pearl border, 2¾in. diam.
(Christie's) $1,158

English School, circa 1800,
a gentleman in black coat
with large lace ruff, set in
the lid of a tortoiseshell box,
1¾in. diam. (Christie's)
$712

In the manner of Charles
Henard, a lady seated in a
green chair mixing poison,
2½in. diam. (Christie's)
$2,316

Richard Gibson, a gentleman
facing right in armor and
white linen collar, on vellum,
gilt metal frame with reeded
border, oval 2¼in. high.
(Christie's) $2,494

Captain and Mrs. Wm. Croome, by
G. Engleheart, both signed and
dated 1811 and 1812, later gold
frames, ovals, 3¼in. high.
(Christie's) $8,316

Thomas Flatman, a nobleman
called John Maitland, 2nd Earl
and Duke of Lauderdale, on
vellum, signed with initial, oval
2.1/8in. high. (Christie's)
$7,128

Mme. Aimee Zoe Lizinka de
Mirbel (nee Rue), a miniature,
possibly of Queen Adelaide,
signed and dated 1830,
rectangular 4.1/8in. high.
(Christie's) $5,346

Continental School, a nobleman in gold bordered crimson
coat, oil on copper, oval 3in.
high. (Christie's) $356

Ozias Humphrey, after Sir
Godfrey Kneller, Lionel, 1st
Duke of Dorset, gold frame,
6½in. high. (Christie's)
$1,247

Jacques Charlier, after
Francois Boucher, two
nymphs and two putti,
ormolu frame with beaded
border, 2¾in. diam.
(Christie's) $4,633

Jean Baptiste Isabey, a
miniature of a gentleman in
brown coat, signed, gilt metal
frame, 2¾in. diam. (Christie's)
$8,553

Andrew Plimer, a miniature of
an officer in scarlet uniform,
gold frame, oval 2¼in. high.
(Christie's) $4,455

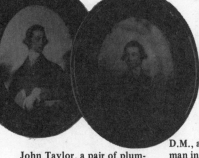

Christian Frederick Zincke, a
portrait of a lady, enamel,
gilt metal frame, oval 1¾in.
high. (Christie's) $1,564

John Taylor, a pair of plum-
bagos of William and Cyril
Jackson, oval 5in. high.
(Christie's) $1,960

D.M., a miniature of a gentleman in blue coat with large
buttons, on vellum, signed in
gold with monogram and
dated 1665, oval 2.3/8in. high.
(Christie's) $2,494

John Smart, a miniature of
Peter Johnston, signed
with initials and dated 1803,
gold frame, oval 3½in. high.
(Christie's) $10,692

Aldani, a miniature of a
gentleman seated on a stone
wall, signed, gilt metal frame,
rectangular 3.1/8in. high.
(Christie's) $1,782

William Grimaldi, a portrait
of a child seated beside a
tree with a blue finch on his
hand, signed, gold frame, oval
2¾in. high. (Christie's)
$6,237

PRINTS

Yoshijuro Urishibawa: Paeonies and Fresias, one of four woodcuts printed in colors, circa 1910, 303 x 201mm. and smaller. (Christie's) $2,032

Albrecht Durer: St. Jerome in his Study, engraving, watermark Three Balls (?), 245 x 189mm. (Christie's) $5,913

Henry Moore: Reclining Figures and Reclining Mother and Child, lithograph printed in colors, 1971 and 1974, 299 x 239mm. (Christie's) $1,386

Pierre-Auguste Renoir: La Danse a la Campagne, Deuxieme Planche, soft-ground etching, circa 1890, on wove paper, 220 x 135mm. (Christie's) $8,553

Henry Moore: Girl Seated At Desk VII, lithograph printed in colors, 1974, on J. Green wove paper, 242 x 175mm. (Christie's) $1,570

Dame Elisabeth Frink: Geoffrey Chaucer, etching illustrating Chaucer's Canterbury Tales, Leslie Waddington Prints Ltd., London, 1972, 588 x 694mm. (Christie's) $702

David Hockney: Black Tulips, lithograph, 1980, signed, dated and numbered 80/100, published by Waddington, 112 x 76cm. (Phillips) $5,670

Laura Knight: At The Fair, aquatint, signed in pencil, mount-stained, taped to front mount, 26 x 21cm. (Phillips) $486

Andy Warhol: Hand-colored Flower, lithograph, signed with initials, 102 x 68cm. (Phillips) $1,944

Henry Moore: Three reclining Figures on Pedestals, lithograph printed in colors, 1966, on Arches, signed and dated in pencil, 312 x 263mm. (Christie's) $2,656

Jacques Villon: L'Italienne, after A. Modigliani, aquatint printed in colors, circa 1927, on wove paper, signed, 497 x 309mm. (Christie's) $6,771

David Hockney: Rue de Seine, etching, 1971, on J. Green mold-made wove paper, numbered 92/150, 537 x 435mm. (Christie's) $8,019

Three, Les Maitres de l'Affiche, Volumes I-V, Imprimerie Chaix, Paris 1896-1900, sheet 403 x 315mm. (Christie's) $21,384

David Hockney: Potted Daffodils, lithograph, 1980, signed, dated and numbered 81/95 in pencil, 112 x 76cm. (Phillips) $5,670

Shuho Yamakawa, oban tate-e, okubi-e of a young woman, signed, entitled Yukimoyoi, dated 1927, 38.5 x 26.5cm. (Christie's) $1,108

Marc Chagall: Cirque avec Clowne-jaune, lithograph printed in colors, 1967, on Arches, numbered 83/150, 675 x 496mm. (Christie's) $7,484

Jacques Villon: Le Paysan, after V. van Gogh, aquatint printed in colors, 1927, on wove paper, signed, 400 x 317mm. (Christie's) $1,692

Kathe Kollwitz: Zwei Schwatzende Frauen mit zwei Kindern, lithograph, 1930, on wove paper, 296 x 262mm. (Christie's) $5,346

Alexei Gan: Twenty Years of Works by Vladimir Mayakovsky. lithograph printed in colors, 1930, on wove paper, 614 x 438mm. (Christie's) $891

Marc Chagall: Ile Saint-Louis (M. 225), lithograph printed in colors, 1959, on Arches, 517 x 668mm. (Christie's) $17,820

Norman Wilkinson: A Land Locked Salmon, etching, signed in pencil, 21.5 x 30cm. (Phillips) $178

Alphonse Maria Mucha: Reverie, lithograph printed in colors, 1896, on wove paper, 639 x 477mm. (Christie's) $3,920

El Lissitsky: Pro Dva Kvadrata (Of Two Squares), Skythen Verlag, Berlin, 1922, album of lithographs printed in colors, 1920, 280 x 225mm. (Christie's) $8,910

Otto Dix: Kupplerin, lithograph printed in red, yellow and blue, 1923, numbered 5/65, 482 x 367mm. (Christie's) $35,640

Erich Heckel: Hockende,
woodcut, 1913, on soft wove
paper, watermark Saskia, first
state of two, 417 x 306mm.
(Christie's) $11,583

George Braque, Composition
(Nature morte I) (V. 8),
etching, 1911, on Arches,
350 x 215mm. (Christie's)
$21,222

Jacques Villon: Nu, after P. A.
Renoir, aquatint printed in
colors, 1923, on Arches,
signed in pencil, numbered
193/200, 602 x 450mm.
(Christie's) $3,920

Marc Chagall: L'Odyssee, two volumes, printed
on Arches, containing 43 color lithographs
and 39 lithographs printed in gray in the text,
the next text being a translation of Homer.
(Phillips) $38,880

Marc Chagall: Hymen, from Daphne et Chloe
(M. 349), lithograph printed in colors, 1961,
on Arches, numbered 52/60, 422 x 643mm.
(Christie's) $40,986

Paul Delvaux: La Reine de
Saba, screenprint in colors,
1982, on Arches, 596 x
431mm. (Christie's)
$1,336

Erich Heckel: Mannerbildnis,
woodcut printed in black,
olive-green, brown and blue,
1919, second state of three,
463 x 327mm. (Christie's)
$92,664

Marc Chagall: Femme de
l'Artiste, lithograph printed
in colors, 1971, on Arches,
649 x 503mm. (Christie's)
$33,858

Utamaro, a triptych, signed, published
by Yamaguchiya Tobei, each sheet
approx. 36 x 24cm. (Christie's)
$7,392

One of seven etchings with aquatint
by George Barbier, 'La Paresse',
'L'Envie', 'La Luxure', 'L'Orgeuil',
'La Colere', 'L'Avarice' and 'La
Gourmandise', dated 1924, 28.3 x
19.4cm. and smaller. (Christie's)·
$432

David Hockney: Rue de Seine,
etching, 1971, on J. Green
mould-made wove paper, signed
and dated '72 in pencil, 536 x
434mm. (Christie's)
$8,870

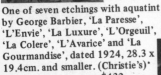

Jean Morin: Tete de Mort,
after P. Champaigne,
engraving, watermark pro-
prietary, 315 x 324mm.
(Christie's) $2,217

Jacques Villon: Portrait de
jeune Femme, drypoint,
1913, on BFK Rives, watermark Eug Delatre, numbered
7, from the edition of approx.
30, 651 x 498mm.
(Christie's) $53,460

Mikhail Larionov, N. Goncharova,
V. Tatlin and I. Rogovin: Alexei
Kruchenykh and Velimir Khleb-
nikov, Mirskontsa (Worldbackwards),
paper collage and lithographs, 1912,
189 x 154mm. (Christie's)
$14,256

Christopher Richard Wynne Nevinson: After
a German Retreat, Labour Battalion making
a Road through a captured Village, lithograph
printed in dark brown, 1918, 235 x 308mm.
(Christie's) $2,032

Rolf Nesch: Negerrevue, etching with
drypoint and aquatint printed in black,
orange-red and deep mustard yellow, 1930,
on thick fibrous Japan, 353 x 555mm.
(Christie's) $32,076

Edward Wadsworth: Mine-sweepers in Ports, woodcut, on thin Japan, signed and dated 'Liverpool 1918', 50 x 135mm. (Christie's) $6,468

Louis Icart: Mimi, drypoint with aquatint printed in colors, 1927, on wove paper published by Les Graveurs Modernes, Paris, 534 x 356mm. (Christie's) $1,016

Conrad Felixmuller: Ich zeichnend (Selbstbildnis mit Akt), woodcut, 1924, on wove paper, 545 x 335mm. (Christie's) $2,494

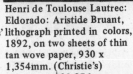

A Walt Disney celluloid depicting 'Turtle and Chipmunk', from 'Snow White and the Seven Dwarfs' 1934, 5 x 5¼in. (Robt. W. Skinner Inc.) $950

Henri de Toulouse Lautrec: Eldorado: Aristide Bruant, lithograph printed in colors, 1892, on two sheets of thin tan wove paper, 930 x 1,354mm. (Christie's) $32,076

Henri de Toulouse-Lautrec: Le Jockey, lithograph, 1899, on Chine, second (final) state, from the edition of 100, 504 x 359mm. (Christie's) $18,711

Utamaro, hashira-e, the famous lovers Koharu and Jihei, signed, published by Murataya, 64.1 x 13.6cm. (Christie's) $2,112

James Abbott McNeill Whistler: Thames Police, etching with drypoint, on laid paper, third (final) state, 149 x 224mm. (Christie's) $1,293

Paul Cesar Helleu: Madame Wolffe, drypoint, printed in colors, signed in pencil, 54 x 33.6cm. (Phillips) $3,888

Tsuguji Foujita: Le Songe, lithograph, circa 1964, on wove paper, signed in pencil, 510 x 660mm. (Christie's) $1,386

Roy Lichtenstein: Crak!, offset lithograph printed in colors, 1964, on wove paper, signed and dated in pencil, 474 x 687mm. (Christie's) $5,544

Georges Roualt: Christ en Croix, aquatint printed in colors, 1936, on Montval, 657 x 495mm. (Christie's) $53,460

Ernst Ludwig Kirchner: Halbakt, lithograph, 1909, on smooth wove paper, 256 x 149mm. (Christie's) $39,204

Henri Matisse: Marie-Jose en Robe jaune, aquatint printed in five colors, 1950, on Arches, numbered 50/100, 538 x 418mm. (Christie's) $71,280

Louis Icart: Parfum des Fleurs (Le Divan), etching with drypoint and aquatint printed in colors, 1937, 447 x 643mm. (Christie's) $1,848

Pablo Picasso: Personnages masques et Femme Oiseau, etching with aquatint, 1934, on Montval, watermark Vollard, from the edition of 250, 249 x 348mm. (Christie's) $5,346

Richard Hamilton: I'm dreaming of a Black Christmas, silkscreen and collotype printed in colors, 1971, on wove paper, signed in pencil, numbered 40/150, published by Petersburg Press, London, with margins, 517 x 760mm. (Christie's) $1,755

Henry Moore: Reclining Figure Point, etching with aquatint, 1976, on wove paper, watermark Bisonte, second (final) state, signed in pencil, numbered 41/100, 170 x 245mm. (Christie's) $2,032

Jacob Kramer: Vorticist Figure, lithograph, circa 1920, on laid paper, 417 x 252mm. (Christie's) $2,402

Marc Chagall: Now the King loved Science and Geometry, Plate X from Four Tales from the Arabian Nights, lithograph printed in colors, 1948, 380 x 286mm. (Christie's) $27,621

Theodore Alexandre Steinlen: Motocycles Comiot, lithograph printed in colors, 1899, on two joined sheets of thin tan wove paper, 1,885 x 1,280mm. (Christie's) $13,365

Pablo Picasso: Minotaure caressant une Femme, etching, 1933, on Montval, watermark Vollard, from the edition of 250, 299 x 370mm. (Christie's) $13,810

Jacques Villon: Les Joueurs de Cartes, after P. Cezanne, aquatint printed in colors, 1929, on Arches, signed, 487 x 601mm. (Christie's) $2,851

Appliqued quilt, America, late 19th century, red cotton patches arranged in a 'Princess Feather' pattern, 96 x 98in. (Robt. W. Skinner Inc.) $1,100

Mid 19th century pieced and appliqued quilt, the calico patches arranged in 'conventional rose' pattern, 80 x 84in. (Robt. W. Skinner Inc.) $425

Mid 19th century crib quilt, the red, yellow and green calico patches arranged in the 'Star of Bethlehem' pattern, 28in. square. (Robt. W. Skinner Inc.) $400

Mid 19th century patchwork crib quilt, worked in mosaic pattern with various calicos, American, 42 x 44in. (Robt. W. Skinner Inc.) $1,800

An appliqued album quilt, cross stitch name in corner 'Miss Lydia Emeline Keller, 1867', American, 84 x 86in. (Robt. W. Skinner Inc.) $2,100

An Amish pieced cotton quilt, Lancaster County, Penn., circa 1900, with later embroidery JEB, 1920, 83½ x 85in. (Christie's) $352

Bryan Ferry, 'Don't Stop the Dance' promotional poster, Limited Edition 52/100, signed, 97 x 66cm. (Phillips) $701

A black peaked 'Boy' cap, decorated by Boy George, together with a publicity photograph of Boy George. (Phillips) $3,674

Elvis Presley, signed color photo of Elvis, 10 x 8in. (Onslow's) $182

A black, turquoise, green and purple fluorescent body suit worn by Kim Wilde on her video for 'The Second Time'. (Phillips) $300

The Who, John Entwhistle's Guild 'Brown' solid brass guitar, Serial No. 102232, with case. (Phillips) $2,171

Ivor Novello Award Certificate of Honour, 1974/75, presented to Mike Batt, The Wombles. (Phillips) $250

A presentation silver disc for 'Blondes Have More Fun', 1978, presented to Rod Stewart by B.P.I. for U.K. sales of £150,000. (Phillips) $1,169

Paul McCartney Live Aid, 1985, a 20 x 16in. silver print, Limited Edition 2/3, signed, signed on the front by David Bailey. (Phillips) $2,505

Status Quo, a presentation silver disc 'Blue for You', 1976, presented to Phonogram Ltd. for U.K. sales of more than £100,000. (Phillips) $567

Phil Collins Live Aid, 1985, a 20 x 16in. silver print, Limited Edition 8/8, signed by David Bailey on the reverse. (Phillips)$1,252

Elvis Presley: 'I'm left, You're right, She's Gone/Baby lets Play House', 45 rpm record on the Sun label, (Sun 217), circa May 1955. (Phillips) $411

A good signed publicity photograph of The Beatles, 21.5 x 15cm. (Phillips) $673

A superb pair of Michael Jackson's purple lace-up dancing shoes, heavily studded with purple glass stones. (Phillips) $7,480

The Who, Pete Townshend's Fender Telecaster three-colour sunburst guitar AO25167 Japanese. (Phillips)$2,338

Hot Chocolate, Errol Brown's Yamaha six-string guitar FG 140, with etched titles of the band's hit songs on the front. (Phillips) $2,004

An extremely rare drawing by Michael Jackson in blue ball point pen entitled 'Your Girlfriend' and signed, 18 x 11.5cm. (Phillips) $1,870

A poster, John's Children, produced by Track Records, to promote a new single 'Desdemona', released in 1967, 51cm. sq. (Phillips) $66

An excellent handwritten letter from Jimi Hendrix to a member of the Universal Autograph Collector's Club, written in red biro, circa 1967. (Phillips) $2,992

A black and white photograph of Elvis Presley, signed on the front, 10 x 18in. (Phillips) $374

Led Zeppelin: John Bonham's Ludwig drum set, together with a charity ball invitation, signed on the back by John Bonham, circa July 1978. (Phillips) $5,610

The Rolling Stones: Keith Richard. An original black and white photograph, mounted, framed and glazed, 43 x 37cm. (Phillips) $121

 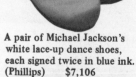

M.T.V. 'Man on the Moon' video music award, awarded to Jack Sonni, rhythm guitarist for Dire Straits, for Best Video of the Year, 'Money for Nothing', 31cm. high. (Phillips) $634

A six-string electric Aria guitar, PE R80 Model, with a personal note from Robin Le Mesurier. (Phillips) $835

A pair of Michael Jackson's white lace-up dance shoes, each signed twice in blue ink. (Phillips) $7,106

Elvis Presley's full length Eastern style green and gold bedrobe. (Phillips) $2,992

John Lennon and Yoko Ono, a promotional poster 'Hair Peace' for 'Wedding Album', released in 1969, 79cm. sq. (Phillips) $267

Bee Gees, a presentation gold disc for the single 'Night Fever', presented to Polydor Ltd. to recognize the sale in the U.K. of more than 500,000 copies. (Phillips) $634

Late 19th century Anatolian Yastik, possibly Mudjur, 2ft. 10in. x 1ft.10in. (Robt. W. Skinner Inc.) $375

Late 19th/early 20th century Kazak rug, the brick-red field with four deep and pale blue abrashed medallions, 8ft. x 4ft.7in. (Robt. W. Skinner Inc.) $1,800

Late 19th century Serapi carpet, 8ft.7in. x 11ft.8in. (Robt. W. Skinner Inc.) $6,000

Late 19th/early 20th century cloudband Kazak rug, 8ft.8in. x 4ft.1in. (Robt. W. Skinner Inc.) $1,900

A Heriz carpet, the ivory field set with stepped medallion, 135 x 175in. (Giles Haywood) $1,910

A Shirvan rug with short kilim strip at each end, (slight overall wear), 10ft.2in. x 4ft.6in. (Christie's) $1,752

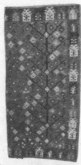

An Agra rug, the magenta field woven with a palmette trellis in pink, blue, green and cream, 7ft.7in. x 5ft.1in. (Lawrence Fine Art) $1,566

A Kelim, the tomato red field woven with a stylized blue tree bearing lozenge flowers, 12ft. x 5ft.10in. (Lawrence Fine Art) $391

A 19th century needlework carpet with colored geometric foliage on a black ground, 14ft.7in. x 9ft. (Christie's) $25,454

Late 19th/early 20th century Heriz carpet, 7ft.10in. x 11ft. (Robt. W. Skinner Inc.) $2,400

A Soumac small carpet, the tomato red field with four elongated lozenge medallions and half medallions in green, cream and magenta, 9ft.3in. x 6ft.3in. (Lawrence Fine Art) $1,135

Marion Dorn, an abstract small carpet woven in khaki and pale blue green, 8ft. x 4ft. 2in. (Lawrence Fine Art) $783

Late 19th century Kazak rug, Southwest Caucasus, 7ft.11in. x 4ft.5in. (Robt. W. Skinner Inc.) $750

A hooked rug, the beige field centering a brown spotted dog, dated 1892, America, 27in. wide, 53in. long. (Robt. W. Skinner Inc.) $275

A Kazak runner, the indigo field with five sunburst medallions, 44 x 118in. (Hy. Duke & Son) $1,980

A Hamadan small carpet, the camel field with rows of beige boteh and centered by a blue lozenge pole medallion, 10ft. 1in. x 5ft.7in. (Lawrence Fine Art) $626

A Kazak Karatchoph rug, the tomato red field woven with a cream octagon within diced spandrels, dated 1862, 4ft.5in. x 4ft.9in. (Lawrence Fine Art) $12,139

A Tabriz rug, the honey field woven with a flower filled vase within mille fleur spandrels, 6ft.6in. x 4ft.7in. (Lawrence Fine Art) $1,958

A Fereghan rug, 6ft.4in. x 4ft.7in. (Christie's) $2,510

Early 20th century Yomud Asmalyk, the pale ivory field with a repeating rust, coral, red and turquoise trellis, 2ft.2in. x 3ft.10in. (Robt. W. Skinner Inc.) $325

Late 19th century kuba rug, East Caucasus, 3ft. 9in. x 3ft.2in. (Robt. W. Skinner Inc.) $550

A Qashqai Kilim, the brick-red field with diagonal rows of multi-colored radiating hooked lozenges, 9ft.10in. x 5ft.2in. (Christie's) $1,179

A hand-knotted rug attributed to Henry van de Velde, 146.5cm. long, 95.9cm. wide. (Christie's) $1,533

A Shirvan rug with a broad kilim strip at each end, dated AH1321 (1905AD), 10ft.7in. x 5ft.5in. (Christie's) $1,972

A Bergama rug, the rust field with a stepped ivory and cruciform central panel and stellar cochineal medallions, 1.85 x 1.44m. (Phillips) $984

A Perepedil rug, the indigo field with traditional 'wurma' motifs, stylized peacocks and all over angular designs, 1.56 x 1.06m. (Phillips) $2,624

A Herez carpet, the terra-cotta field with green pal-mette pendant indigo medallion with all over angular designs, 3.76 x 2.78m. (Phillips) $8,200

Late 19th century Soumak bagface in shades of blue, turquoise and camel, 1ft.7in. x 1ft.8in. (Robt. W. Skinner Inc.) $300

A Karabagh Kilim, the black field with three large bouquets surrounded by sprays with perching birds and stylized human figures, 12ft.1in. x 5ft.2in. (Christie's) $1,542

A Mahal carpet, the ivory field with an all over design with palmettes, lanceolate leaves and panels, 4.38 x 3.42m. (Phillips) $4,920

A Melas rug, the indigo field with three large brick lobed and hooked medallions, 6ft.5in. x 3ft.9in. (Woolley & Wallis) $544

A 19th century rectangular hooked rug, American, 2ft. 7in. x 5ft.2in. (Robt. W. Skinner Inc.) $1,100

Late 19th century Bordjalou kazak, 6ft.2in. x 3ft.7in. (Robt. W. Skinner Inc.) $400

Early 20th century Heriz carpet, N.W. Persia, 11ft. 7in. x 7ft.9in. (Robt. W. Skinner Inc.) $3,700

A hand-woven Art Deco carpet, the powder-pink field with circle and triangle motif, in beige, emerald green and eau de nile, 273 x 296cm. (Christie's) $1,804

Early 20th century Heriz carpet, N.W. Persia, 11ft. 7in. x 8ft.1in. (Robt. W. Skinner Inc.) $2,700

A Kashan pictorial Natanz rug, silk pile, circa 1920, 4ft.6in. x 6ft.6in. (Peter Wilson) $1,539

A Kashan rug with central medallion on a deep pink field within a deep blue floral border, 6ft. x 4ft. (Lots Road Chelsea Auction Galleries) $1,377

One of a pair of Kirman rugs, the ivory field with center medallion and three line border, 6ft.2in. x 3ft.11in. (Worsfolds) $672

An Agra rug, the cream field woven with palmettes and floral sprays, 7ft.8in. x 4ft. 11in. (Lawrence Fine Art) $8,811

A Louis Philippe Aubusson rug woven with floral sprays on a chocolate ground, 6ft.1in. x 6ft.6in. (Christie's) $4,699

Late 19th century Bidjar rug, Northwest Persia, 5ft.2in. x 8ft.6in. (Robt. W. Skinner Inc.) $1,900

A Kazak runner, the madder field with four pale green medallions, 49in. wide, 142in. long. (Hy. Duke & Son) $468

Late 19th/early 20th century Bidjar carpet, Northwest Persia,with red Herati filled field, 9ft. x 12ft. (Robt. W. Skinner Inc.) $7,500

Early 20th century Heriz carpet, Northwest Persia, 10ft.4in. x 8ft. (Robt. W. Skinner Inc.) $3,100

Late 19th/early 20th
century East Caucasian
rug, 5ft.5in. x 4ft.3in.
(Robt. W. Skinner Inc.)
$1,700

Mid 19th century Aubusson
carpet woven with a central
floral spray on a celadon
ground, 6ft.8½in. x 6ft.4½in.
(Christie's) $5,874

A Karabagh Kilim, the black
ground with two bouquets in
a floral spray frame, 13ft.8in.
x 6ft.2in. (Christie's)
$3,894

Late 19th century Sewan
Kazak, Southwest Caucasus,
5ft.5in. x 6ft.11in. (Robt. W.
Skinner Inc.) $1,600

A 19th century needlework
carpet, in mainly autumnal
shades of a beige ground,
6ft.4½in. x 6ft.7in.
(Christie's) $17,622

A wool pile carpet, signed on
reverse 'Orendi', circa 1900-
20, 7ft.7in. by 10ft.6in.
(Robt. W. Skinner Inc.)
$4,500

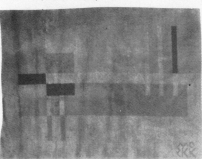

A Persian rug, possibly Shiraz,
the camel flat weave field with
brown finger indents, 5ft.6in.
x 3ft.1in. (Lawrence Fine Art)
$744

Edward McKnight Kauffer, an
abstract rug woven in shades of
brown, yellow and blue, 5ft.3in.
x 3ft.10in. (Lawrence Fine Art)
$783

A Caucasian Kilim, the
shaded blue field with
diagonal rows of stepped
lozenges, 9ft.8in. x 5ft.1in.
(Christie's) $428

A needlework sampler, 'Sina Halls Sampler Wrought at Wallingford, August 10, 1811', worked in a variety of stitches on moss-green linsey-woolsey ground, 15¾ x 17½in. (Robt. W. Skinner Inc.) $14,000

A sampler 'Wrought by Harriot Wethrell May Aged 10 years, Plymouth Massachusetts, June 10th 1830', 16¼ x 16½in. (Robt. W. Skinner Inc.) $1,900

A mid 19th century Armenian needlework sampler by Souepile Kedeasian, the linen ground embroidered in red and pink threads, 45 x 58cm. (Phillips) $160

A needlework sampler by Eliz. Matilda Whitcombe aged 11, 1846, embroidered in colored silks on a wool ground, 43 x 32cm. (Phillips) $569

Needlework sampler, 'Rhoda Roger's Sampler wrought in the 11 years of her age 1804', Mass. (Robt. W. Skinner Inc.) $6,000

A mid 19th century needlework sampler by Sarah Redfern, 1.04 x 0.77m., framed and glazed. (Phillips) $890

Needlework picture, entitled 'The Beggar's Petition', by Sarah Hadley, 1841, 24 x 24in. (Robt. W. Skinner Inc.) $2,800

An 18th century sampler, by Kezi Ladell, July 11, 1799, 37 x 21cm. (David Lay) $358

A needlework family register, 'Wrought by Hannah Winchell, 1822', 22½ x 23½in. (Robt. W. Skinner Inc.) $2,600

A needlework picture, signed Anne Oram and dated 1824, worked in polychrome threads on natural ground, 10 x 12in. (Christie's) $440

An early 18th century needlework sampler, the linen ground embroidered in colored silks, 46 x 21cm. (Phillips) $1,513

A needlework sampler made by 'Anna Braddock . . . A work wrought in the 14th year of her age, 1826', 22½ x 26in. (Robt. W. Skinner Inc.) $38,000

Late 18th century framed needlework sampler, by Charlotte Richardson 13 years, Dec. 1786, American, 17 x 20in. (Robt. W. Skinner Inc.) $1,500

A needlework sampler 'Susannah Styles finished this work in the 10 years of her age 1800', worked in silk yarns on wool ground, 13in. square. (Robt. W. Skinner Inc.) $1,000

Sampler with alphabet verse and figures of plants and birds, dated 1824, 17 x 13in. (Lots Road Chelsea Auction Galleries) $501

A needlework sampler by Mary Ann Cash, 1801, the linen ground worked in colored silks, 37 x 30cm. (Phillips) $356

A 17th century needlwork sampler by Anna Stone, the linen ground worked in pink, green and blue silk threads, 41 x 19cm. (Phillips) $1,176

Needlework sampler, 'Betsey Stevens, her sampler wrought in 10th year of her age AD 1796', silk yarns on linen, 15 x 16in. (Robt. W. Skinner Inc.) $3,000

Folkestone Pier and Lift Co. 1888 £10 shares, vignette of Queen Victoria, Red seal. (Phillips) $51

The Mediterranean Electric Telegraph, 1854, Bearer certificate for 1 x £10 share. (Phillips) $58

Waveney Steam Drift Fishing Co. Ltd. 1909-18. Ord. £1 shares. (Phillips) $72

The London & Brighton Railway Co. 1847, fixed interest bearer certificate No. 4 for £50 at 5%. (Phillips) $939

Pullman's Palace Car Company 1898, $100 shares. Vignette of St. Pancras Station and The Pullman Car Works, Detroit. (Phillips) $98

The North American Land Company, 1795, two shares. Handsigned by Robt. Morris, a signatory of the Declaration of Independence. (Phillips) $518

A pair of glace black kid slippers, embroidered with bouquets of flowers, trimmed with pale blue silk, circa 1840. (Christie's) $924

A pair of shoes of mustard colored ribbed silk with 3in. heels, English, circa 1770, inscribed Miss Alsorne. (Christie's) $2,117

A pair of glace black kid slippers embroidered with flowers in colored silks on the front and heel, lined and trimmed with pink silk, circa 1840. (Christie's) $962

A pair of ladies' high heeled shoes of crimson damask, trimmed with gold lace with 2in. heels, 9in. long, early 18th century. (Christie's) $1,455

A pair of ladies' high heeled shoes of ivory silk, circa 1730. (Christie's) $3,118

A pair of early 18th century lady's shoes of duck-egg-blue silk worked with gold thread embroidery and sequin decoration. (Phillips) $2,670

A pair of early 19th century plum kid shoes with silk ruffle trim and ties. (Phillips) $1,352

A pair of mid 19th century boots of brown and white leather, lined with pink kid, and a pair of white kid boots. (Christie's) $1,540

A pair of lady's shoes of dark blue morocco, with low wedge heels, circa 1790. (Christie's) $1,663

BASKETS

A George III oval bread-basket on spreading foot, by Henry Nutting or Hannah Northcote, 1801, 14in. long, 26ozs. (Christie's) $2,024

One of a pair of George III silver gilt oval dessert baskets and covers, by Wm. Pitts, 1803, with frosted glass liners, 12½in. long, 95oz. (Christie's) $15,147

A George III shaped oval bread basket, on molded oval foot, by John Vere and William Lutwyche, 1766, 14in. long, 32ozs. (Christie's) $5,348

A George II shaped oval bread basket on four lion's mask and claw feet, the handle engraved with a crest, by Peter Archambo, 1741, 14½in. long, 63ozs. (Christie's) $11,313

A Wiener Werkstätte electro-plated basket, designed by Josef Höffmann, 26cm. high. (Christie's) $1,623

A George II shaped oval bread basket, by Benjamin Godfrey, 1741, 11¾in. long, 51oz. (Christie's) $12,474

A George III beaded and pierced oval swing-handle cake basket, London 1777, 13in. 21.75oz. (Christie's) $1,275

A pierced and engraved fruit basket, by Robert Hennell, London, 1788, 14in. long. (Brown & Merry) $3,005

A George III oval cake basket, by Michael Plummer, 1793, 36.9cm., 24.6oz. (Lawrence Fine Art) $1,851

BASKETS

A George III oval bread basket, by William Plummer, 1782, 15in. long, 42oz. (Christie's) $9,266

A George III oval cake basket, the spreading foot and rim pierced with slats, by Robert Hennell, 1787, 14¼in. long, 25ozs. (Christie's) $2,944

George III oblong cake basket with reeded swing handle, Dublin, 1806. (Reeds Rains) $734

A George III oval cake basket on molded foot, by Paul Storr, 1799, 14¾in. long, 34oz. (Christie's) $6,930

A cake basket with pierced foliate handle, by Udall & Ballou, circa 1900-10, 11in. high overall, 14¾in. long, 49oz. (Christie's) $2,860

A Victorian oval cake basket, pierced fret sides in George III style, by Henry Hyde, London, 1859. (Woolley & Wallis) $1,353

A George III shaped oval bread basket, by William Kidney, 1745, 15in. long, 83oz. (Christie's) $13,860

A George III sugar basket with concave corners, reeded borders and swing handle, by John Robins, London, 1796, 6¾in., 8.1/3oz. (Dreweatt Neate) $935

A George III shaped oval bread basket, on rim foot, with openwork sides, by John Vere and William Lutwyche, 1765, 13¼in. long, 29ozs. (Christie's) $3,291

BOWLS

A George II circular fluted bowl, by Benjamin Godfrey, 1739, 6¾in. diam., 12oz. 7dwt. (Christie's) $4,719

A shaped rectangular center-piece bowl, by Tiffany & Co., 1878-91, 4½in. high, 18.3/8in. wide, 8½in. deep, 67oz.10dwt. (Christie's) $15,400

A nut bowl, in the form of a barrel-stave bucket, by Gorham Manuf. Co., 1869, 2¼in. high, 4¾in. wide, 3oz. (Christie's) $418

A George I Irish plain circular Monteith bowl, by David King, Dublin, 1715, 10¾in. high, 63oz. (Christie's) $39,930

A George I plain circular sugar bowl and pear-shaped cream jug, by George G. Jones, 1726, 15oz.15dwt. (Christie's) $12,830

Large plated punch bowl by Viners with embossed decoration. (G. A. Key) $78

A yachting trophy punch bowl, by Gorham Manuf. Co., 1884, the interior gilt, 9¼in. high, 18¼in. wide, 117oz. (Christie's) $41,800

A Monteith bowl, by Samuel Kirk & Son, Baltimore, 1880-90, 5½in. high, 9½in. diam., 25oz. (Christie's) $1,430

A George II Irish small circular punch bowl, by Robert Calderwood, Dublin, 1732, 7.5/8in. diam., 23oz. (Christie's) $12,705

BOWLS

An Edwardian hammered sugar bowl, in Art Nouveau style, by A. E. Jones, Birmingham, 1908, 4¼in. diam., 4.5oz. (Hobbs & Chambers) $165

An Italian white metal punch bowl, by Gannazzi, stamped 800 (circa 1940), 46.9cm. diam., 1.464kg. (Christie's) $2,886

A sterling silver bowl, by Arthur Stone, 1910-37, 5.3/8in. diam., 7 troy oz. (Robt. W. Skinner Inc.) $1,300

A Georg Jensen footed bowl, stamped marks GJ 925.S 4, 7.6cm. high, 129.2gr. (Christie's) $613

A George I sugar bowl and cover, possibly by James Goodwin, London, 1719, 4in. diam. (Woolley & Wallis) $3,712

A Georg Jensen bowl and cover, stamped with C. F. Heise assay mark 100B and with London import marks for 1925, 11.9cm. high, 242gr. (Christie's) $1,172

A large two-handled circular bowl, by Elkington & Co., Birmingham, 1908, 13½in. diam., 100oz. (Christie's) $2,673

A silver gilt bowl, by Gorham Manuf. Co., Providence, 1884, 3¾in. high, 6oz. (Christie's) $1,210

A bowl, circular with flaring rim, by Josiah Austin, Boston, circa 1750-70, 3in. high, 5¾in. diam., 6oz. (Christie's) $14,300

SILVER

A Victorian casket of square bombe form, by S. S. Drew and E. Drew of J. Drew & Sons, 1890, 20.5cm. (Lawrence Fine Art) $1,028

Early 20th century German silver singing bird box, 4in. long. (Christie's) $2,640

A silver cigar box, cedar lined, double container, central cutter and tools with spirit light, London, 1899. (Brown & Merry) $1,055

A George III silver gilt circular box and cover, by Joseph Ash, 1810, 4½in. diam., 10oz.16dwt. (Christie's) $3,385

A small silver spice box in the form of a skull, the hinged back revealing six compartments, ¾in. wide. (Christie's) $544

One of a pair of George III silver gilt oval toilet boxes, by D. Smith and R. Sharp, 1783, 7.5/8in. long, 55oz. (Christie's) $20,872

A Victorian fisherman's creel vesta case, the interior with Essex crystal depicting two trout, by Thos. Johnson, 1882, 5.5cm. long. (Phillips) $3,062

An Arts & Crafts hammered silver box, by Chas. Horner, Birmingham hallmarks for 1902, 15.3cm. long, 5oz. 12dwt. (Christie's) $721

A French silver gilt casket of bombe triangular form on four scroll feet, by Lhote, the miniatures by Paillet, 7½in. wide. (Christie's) $3,993

BOXES

A silver gilt box, the lid inset with an enamel plaque, Birmingham hallmarks for 1922 and maker's monogram SB, 9cm. long, 2oz.17dwt. gross wt. (Christie's) $252

A box, the lid pierced and embossed with figures, a carriage and horses, bells, scrolls and flowers, by Wm. Comyns, London, 1903, 5¾in. long. (Dreweatt Neate) $336

A 19th century Swiss shaped oblong silver gilt and enamel singing bird box, the movement by Chas. Bruguier, 3½in. long. (Christie's) $5,082

A Dutch silver gilt shaped square tobacco box and cover, by Pieter Meeter, Leewarden, 1770, 5in. sq., 20oz. (Christie's) $7,128

A French circular blonde tortoiseshell box, the cover with a grisaille miniature of Napoleon, Marie-Louise and the King of Rome, circa 1815, 2¾in. diam. (Christie's) $907

An Arts & Crafts rectangular silver box, by W. Hutton & Sons Ltd., London hallmarks for 1901, 11.1cm. long, 11oz. 4dwt. gross weight. (Christie's) $396

A sterling silver box with pierced enamel hinged cover, Worcester, Mass., 1925, 3¾in. wide. (Robt. W. Skinner Inc.) $475

A German silver and enamel singing bird box, struck with English import hallmarks for 1926, 4in. long. (Christie's) $3,300

A green stained box, by George Anton Scheidt, with pierced and chased white metal mount of scrolling tendrils, 6.3cm. long. (Christie's) $396

CANDELABRA

One of two plated candelabra
with two lights on swept
reeded arms, not matching.
(G. A. Key) $141

One of a pair of five-light
candelabra, by Tiffany & Co.,
New York, 1885-91, 18¾in.
high, 133oz.10dwt.
(Christie's) $18,700

Hallmarked silver three-light
candelabrum, Birmingham
Assay. (G. A. Key)
                     $175

One of a pair of George II
two-light candelabra, by
Wm. Cripps, 1750, the
branches unmarked, the
branch sockets and drip-pans
probably later replacements.
(Christie's) $18,150

A pair of George I style three
light candelabra, each on
hexagonal base with scroll
branches, by Richard
Comyns, 1964, 71ozs, 11¼in.
high. (Christie's)
                  $2,879

One of a pair of George III
cast candelabra, by Wm.
Eaton, London, 1816,
380oz., 51cm. high.
(Wellington Salerooms)
                  $4,032

One of a pair of ormolu twin-
light candelabra of Louis XVI
style, 13in. high. (Christie's)
                  $2,204

A pair of George III three-light
candelabra and two matching
candlesticks, by John Scofield,
1792 and 1795, 19½in. high,
weight of branches 96oz.
(Christie's) $71,280

One of a pair of large five-
light candelabra with four
detachable scroll branches,
30¼in. high. (Christie's)
                  $3,63⁷

CANDELABRA

One of a pair of Georg Jensen five-branch candelabra, designed by Harald Nielsen, 40cm. high. (Christie's) $25,256

A pair of Old Sheffield plate three-light candelabra, each on circular base and with fluted tapering column, by Matthew Boulton and Co., circa 1815, 21in. high. (Christie's)
$1,840

A massive Victorian ten-light candelabrum, by John Mortimer and John S. Hunt, circa 1843, 38in. high. (Christie's)
$82,280

A Victorian five-light candel-abrum, by Robert Garrard, 1841, 30½in. high, 254oz. (Christie's) $7,260

A pair of three light candelabra, each on oval fluted base, with two reeded branches and central light, Birmingham, 1950, 18½in. high. (Christie's)
$3,291

One of a pair of George III three-light candelabra, by Richard Cooke, 1800 and 1804, 16¾in. high, 128oz. (Christie's) $16,929

One of a pair of late 19th century German cast rococo style seven-light candelabra, by J. D. Schleissner & Sons, Hanau, 54cm. high, 234.5oz. (Phillips) $6,125

Pair of Sheffield plated three-light candelabra, 55cm. high. (Lawrence Fine Art)
$2,159

One of two Victorian ten-light candelabra, by Barnard Bros, 1846 and C. F. Hancock, 1895, 32¼in. high, 458oz. (Christie's) $21,384

CANDLESTICKS

Two of four George IV table candlesticks, by J. & T. Settle, Sheffield, 1824, 11¾in. high. (Christie's) $4,455

Pair of silver candlesticks, decorated in the Adam style, by John Round & Sons Ltd., Sheffield, 1902, 6½in. tall. (G. A. Key) $676

Two of four George II table candlesticks, by John Cafe, 1747, 9¾in. high, 84oz. (Christie's) $8,910

A pair of George III Irish table candlesticks, by A. Boxwell, Dublin, 1781, 10½in. high, 45oz. (Christie's) $3,742

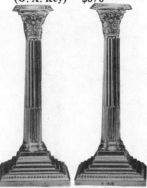

Pair of late Victorian candlesticks, formed as Corinthian columns, by Charles Stuart Harris, London, 1898, 29cm. high, weighted. (Osmond Tricks) $1,496

A pair of Queen Anne tapering baluster candlesticks, by Wm. Turell, 1713, 19.5cm. high, 30oz. (with later nozzles). (Phillips) $25,375

A pair of George III table candlesticks on square bases with detachable nozzles, by Jonathan Alleine, 1777, 10½in. high, 56oz. (Christie's) $6,897

A pair of Louis XV Provincial candlesticks, 8.5in. high, Lille, circa 1765. (Woolley & Wallis) $4,125

A pair of Victorian, Adam style Corinthian column table candlesticks, by H. Wilkinson of Sheffield, London, 1871, 13in. high. (Hy. Duke & Son) $1,692

CANDLESTICKS

Two of a set of four George II cast candlesticks, by James Gould, 1738, two nozzles by J. Baddeley, 1821, 7¾in. high, 72oz. (Christie's) $15,427

Two of four George II table candlesticks, by Samuel Courtauld, 1757, 10¾in. high, 86oz. (Christie's) $11,583

A pair of James Dixon & Sons silver candlesticks, Sheffield hallmarks for 1904, 22cm. high. (Christie's) $1,262

A pair of George III silver reeded and fluted column candlesticks, maker's mark I.P. & Co., John Parsons & Co., Sheffield, 1783, 11¼in. high. (Geering & Colyer) $1,557

Two of a set of four George III table candlesticks, by John Romer, 1763, 11½in. high, 139oz. (Christie's) $22,687

A pair of George IV table candlesticks, by S. C. Younge & Co., Sheffield, 1821, 11¾in. high. (Christie's) $2,851

Two of a set of four George III Corinthian column candlesticks, by Emick Romer, 1762, 11½in. high. (Christie's) $9,801

A pair of Old Sheffield plate candlesticks, designed to commemorate famous and contemporary British Admirals and their naval victories over the French during the late 18th century, 21cm. high. (Phillips) $1,715

Two of a set of four George II table candlesticks, by Wm. Cafe, 1757, 9¾in. high, 57oz. (Christie's) $25,839

CASTERS

One of a pair of Dutch silver gilt octagonal pear-shaped casters, by Albert de Thomese, The Hague, 1733, 7¾in. high, 22oz. (Christie's) $4,989

A pair of William IV vase-shaped casters, by Robert Hennell, London, 1834, 5¾in. high, 10.75oz. (Christie's) $712

A Queen Anne sugar caster, by Simon Pantin I, 1709, 19cm. high, 10oz. (Phillips) $2,362

One of a pair of George IV casters, by William, Charles and Henry Eley, 1824, 11.8cm. high. (Lawrence Fine Art) $925

A set of three Charles II casters, the smaller casters, 1682, 6in. high, the larger 1683, 7in. high, 22oz. (Christie's) $71,280

An amber, coral and malachite sugar caster, designed by Anton Rosen, stamped marks GJ 826 GJ, 19.9cm. high. (Christie's) $3,608

An Edwardian plain baluster sugar caster, by Elkington & Co., Birmingham, 1909, 8in. high, 12oz. (Christie's) $249

A set of three George I plain octagonal casters, by Edward Vincent, 1716, 5.7/8in. and 7½in. high, 27oz. (Christie's) $11,253

An early 18th century style lighthouse sugar caster on a skirted foot, London, 1932, 7in. high, 9oz. (Christie's) $213

CENTERPIECES

A WMF electroplated centerpiece with cut glass liner of oval section modelled in full relief with young lovers, 21in. across. (Christie's) $1,017

A sterling silver Martele oval centerpiece, by Gorham Mfg. Co., dated 1881 to 1906, 38 troy oz., 12¾in. long. (Robt. W. Skinner Inc.) $2,750

A WMF plated centerpiece of twin-handled boat-shape with clear glass liner, 46cm. long. (Phillips) $672

A George III epergene with four scroll branches each with detachable dish, by Thomas Pitts, 1766, 98oz. (Christie's) $13,612

A French centerpiece, by Christofle, Paris, 24¾in. high, 8,947gr. (Christie's) $13,860

A Victorian plated centerpiece, the simulated coral mount supported by three dolphins, 11in. high, together with a matching pair of single dolphin centerpiece bases, 8in. high. (Christie's) $541

A baroque style centerpiece, Sheffield, 1903, approx. 20in. high, approx. 158oz. (Peter Wilson) $5,104

A centerpiece bowl, by Gorham Manuf. Co., 1880, 3.1/8in. high, 7½in. diam., 11oz.10dwt. (Christie's) $605

An Austro-Hungarian brightly colored silver gilt centerpiece finely modelled as a crowned ostrich, by Hermann Bohm, Vienna, circa 1880, 15in. high. (Christie's) $35,640

CHAMBERSTICKS

SILVER

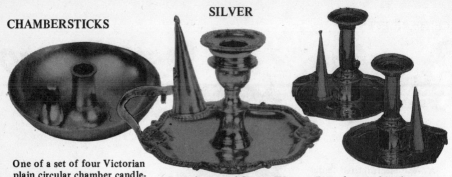

One of a set of four Victorian plain circular chamber candlesticks, by Robt. Garrard, 1878, 7in. diam., 63oz. (Christie's) $6,930

One of a pair of George III shaped circular chamber candlesticks, by B. & J. Smith, 1808, the nozzles 1809, 6in. diam., 28oz. (Christie's) $3,762

Part of a set of twelve George III circular chamber candlesticks, by M. Boulton, Birmingham 1803, 125oz. (Christie's) $30,294

CHOCOLATE POTS

A George II plain cylindrical chocolate pot, on molded spreading foot, by Isaac Cookson, Newcastle, 1731, 9¾in. high, 29ozs. (Christie's) $6,592

A sterling silver Martele chocolate pot, by Gorham Mfg. Co., circa 1900, 11½in. high, 23 troy oz. (Robt. W. Skinner Inc.) $3,500

A George II plain tapering cylindrical chocolate pot, on molded circular foot, 1738, 9¼in. high, 24ozs. (Christie's) $3,496

A George I Irish plain tapering cylindrical chocolate pot, by Thos. Williamson, Dublin, 1715, 11¼in. high, gross 32oz. (Christie's) $8,167

A Louis XV plain pear-shaped chocolate pot, by Jean Gouel, Paris, 1734, 9.5/8in. high, weight without handle 840gr. (Christie's) $5,808

A Queen Anne plain tapering cylindrical chocolate pot, by Robt. Timbrell and J. Bell I, 1709, 10¼in. high, gross 27oz. (Christie's) $6,336

CIGARETTE CASES

A late Victorian cigarette case enamelled on cover with a coaching scene, by J. Wilmot, Birmingham, 1896. (Phillips) $509

A good 19th century Russian niello cigarette case, cover depicting a despatch carrier being driven by a peasant in a horse-drawn carriage, Gustav Klingert, Moscow, 1888, 8.5cm. long. (Phillips) $618

A Russian cigarette case with separate hinged vesta compartment, probably by Dmitri Nikolaiev, Moscow, circa 1890. (Phillips) $402

CLARET JUGS

A William IV pear-shaped claret jug, by James Franklin, 1835, 11½in. high, 31oz. (Christie's) $1,692

A pair of Victorian silver gilt mounted glass claret jugs, by W. & G. Sissons, Sheffield, 1872, 11in. high. (Christie's) $3,385

A William IV large vase-shaped claret jug, 1837, maker's mark IW overstriking another, perhaps that of Chas. Fox, 17in. high, 65oz. (Christie's) $5,808

One of a pair of French silver mounted glass claret jugs, circa 1880, 10¼in. high. (Christie's) $4,174

One of a pair of Victorian silver mounted glass claret jugs, by Henry Wilkinson & Co., Sheffield, 1862, 9in. high. (Christie's) $3,920

An early Victorian vase-shaped claret jug, by Henry Wilkinson & Co., Sheffield, 1838, 12¾in. high, 23oz. (Christie's) $1,692

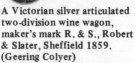

A pair of George III silver wine coasters, by Rebecca Emes and Edward Barnard, London, 1815, 6.1/8in. diam. (Christie's)
$2,420

One of a pair of George III coasters, by Thos. Nash I, London, 1767, 12cm. diam. (Osmond Tricks)
$3,300

A Victorian silver articulated two-division wine wagon, maker's mark R. & S., Robert & Slater, Sheffield 1859. (Geering Colyer)
$3,115

One of a pair of George III decanter stands, by Rebecca Emes and E. Barnard, London, 1802. (Woolley & Wallis)
$2,310

Two George III silver wine coasters, the first by S. Herbert & Co., London, 1765, the second Dublin, circa 1765, 5½in. diam. (Christie's)
$2,750

A pair of George IV circular wine coasters, by S. C. Younge & Co., Sheffield, 1821, 14.8cm. diam. (Lawrence Fine Art)
$3,268

One of a pair of George IV wine coasters, by Rebecca Emes and Edward Barnard, London, 1825, 7in. diam. (Christie's) $2,860

One of four George IV wine coasters, by Smith, Tate, Hoult & Tate, Sheffield, 1823. (Christie's) $5,940

One of a pair of George III wine coasters, by Wm. Burwash, London, 1814, 6½in. diam. (Christie's)
$2,420

Pair of George III circular wine coasters, by William Plummer, 1782. (Christie's)
$4,356

One of a pair of decanter stands on turned wood bases, by Elkington & Co. (Woolley & Wallis)
$577

Pair of George III coasters with wrigglework band decoration, by Robt. Hennell, London, 1792. (Reeds Rains) $1,503

COFFEE POTS

A George III oval coffee pot, stand and lamp, on three reeded scroll feet, by Benjamin and James Smith, 1811, 10¼in. high, 37ozs. (Christie's) $1,851

A Georgian style coffee pot, the domed hinged cover with ivory oval mushroom knop, Sheffield, 1891, 24½oz. (Lalonde Fine Art) $627

A George II Provincial coffee pot with scroll embellished spout and acorn finial, by Wm. Partis, Newcastle, 1743, 24cm. high, 32.5oz. (Phillips) $2,887

A George I plain tapering cylindrical coffee pot, by Wm. Spackman, 1718, 9¼in. high, gross 21oz. (Christie's) $4,989

A George II plain tapering cylindrical coffee pot, by Peze Pilleau, 1732, 8¾in. high, gross 28oz. (Christie's) $4,989

A George I Irish plain tapering cylindrical coffee pot, by J. Hamilton, Dublin, 1715, 9½in. high, gross 29oz. (Christie's) $7,920

A George III plain pear-shaped coffee pot, by Francis Crump, 1765, 10½in. high, gross 29oz. (Christie's) $3,207

A William IV pear-shaped coffee pot, by Paul Storr, 1836, finial by J. S. Hunt, 8¾in. high, 32oz. (Christie's) $3,630

A George I plain tapering cylindrical coffee pot, by Robt. Timbrell and Joseph Bell, 1714, 9½in. high, gross 30oz. (Christie's) $14,520

COFFEE POTS

A French coffee pot of ovoid form, the spout terminating in a ram's head, Paris, circa 1825, 24cm. high, 15.5oz. (Phillips) $1,137

A George III cylindrical coffee biggin, stand and lamp, by J. Wakelin and R. Garrard, 1798, 11in. high, 28oz. (Christie's) $1,452

A George III beaded pear-shaped coffee pot on spreading circular foot, with fluting and rococo flowers and foliage, 12¼ in. high, 25.5oz. (Christie's) $1,748

A George II tapering cylindrical coffee pot, by Daniel Piers, 1754, 9in. high, gross 22oz. (Christie's) $2,450

A 1960's silver coffee pot and hot water jug, by H. Brown, Birmingham·hall-marks for 1963, 29cm. high, 40oz.12dwt. gross weight. (Christie's) $902

A Queen Anne plain tapering cylindrical coffee pot, by T. Holland, 1710, 10½in. high, gross 29oz. (Christie's) $8,910

A George I plain tapering cylindrical coffee pot, by Thomas Partis, Newcastle, 1725, 9in. high, gross 22oz. (Christie's) $5,702

A George I small tapering cylindrical coffee pot, by Wm. Darker, 1724, 7¼in. high, gross 14oz.2dwt. (Christie's) $3,920

A George II Irish tapering cyl-indrical coffee pot, on molded circular foot, Dublin, circa 1740. 9in. high, 31ozs. (Christie's) $4,114

CREAM JUGS

A Georgian silver baluster
cream jug on three shaped
legs, London, 1748, 3½in.
tall, 2oz. (J. M. Welch & Son)
$410

A cream pitcher, urn-shaped,
by Isaac Woodcock, Mary-
land, circa 1790-1810, 6¾in.
high, 5oz. (Christie's)
$3,300

A George II silver creamer,
London, 1756, 3½in. tall.
(J. M. Welch & Son)
$247

CRUETS

A shaped oblong bright cut
cruet on shell feet, fitted
with seven cut glass condiment
bottles, 9½in. (Christie's)
$198

A five-part division Warwick
cruet (2 oil bottles missing),
by Samuel Wood, London,
1757, 46oz., 27.5cm. high.
(Wellington Salerooms)
$2,856

A George III Sheffield Plate
oval cruet, the base on shell
panel feet, circa 1785.
(Woolley & Wallis)
$561

A Victorian cruet frame, by
Robert Garrard, 1839, 5¾in.
wide, the frame 22oz.10dwt.
(Christie's) $4,719

A French 19th century oblong
oil and vinegar stand on ball
feet, 8¼in. high. (Christie's)
$316

A Victorian condiment cruet,
by James Dixon of Sheffield.
(Woolley & Wallis)
$396

CUPS

A Charles II plain tumbler cup, by Robert Williamson, York, 1669, 3½in. diam., 3oz.13dwt. (Christie's) $4,900

A George III silver gilt fox mask stirrup cup, by Thomas Pitts, 1771, 5½in. long, 5oz. 13dwt. (Christie's) $4,174

A Kalo sterling silver tumbler, Chicago, Illinois, 1914-18, 3.5/8in. high, approx. 3½ troy oz. (Robt. W. Skinner Inc.) $75

A George III silver gilt two handled cup and cover, on spreading circular foot, by Rebecca Emes and Edward Barnard, 1817, London, 11½in. high, 66ozs. (Christie's) $8,228

A silver gilt replica of the Norton Cup In The Fishmonger's Company, dated 1925, by Gerrard and Co Ltd., 1918, 14in. high, 49ozs. (Christie's) $1,645

A George II two-handled cup and cover on circular molded foot, by John White, 1728, 12½in. high, 82oz. (Christie's) $9,075

The Richmond Race Cup, 1764: a George III silver gilt two-handled cup and cover, designed by Robert Adam; by D. Smith and Robert Sharp, 1764, 19in. high, 142oz. (Christie's) $106,920

A 19th century Continental silver betrothal cup in the form of Queen Elizabeth I, 20cm. high. (Henry Spencer & Sons) $525

A George III silver gilt two handled cup and cover on spreading circular foot, by John Emes, 1798, 13in. high, 36ozs. (Christie's) $3,702

CUPS

A cup and cover in the early 17th century style, the gold plaque engraved 'The Manchester Cup 1924', 1923, 15ct., in fitted case, 17¼in. high, 54oz. (Christie's) $35,640

Part of a set of six beakers and two footed cups, by John Targee, N.Y., 1809-14, beakers 3¾in. high, footed cups 5½in. high, 48oz. (Christie's) $7,700

A George III two-handled partly-fluted cup and cover, by Andrew Fogelberg and Stephen Gilbert, 1789, 18¼in. high, 104oz. (Christie's) $6,237

A presentation loving cup, by Dominick & Haff, Newark, for J. E. Caldwell & Co., 1895, in original mahogany box, 11½in. high, 82oz. (Christie's) $9,900

A William IV silver stirrup cup, cast and chased as a fox mask, by C. G. Gordon, London, 1833, 6½in. long, 12oz. (Christie's) $8,250

A German white metal large three-handled cup and cover, by J. H. Werner, circa 1905, 26½in. high, 10kg. (Christie's) $8,910

The Richmond Race Cup, 1768: a George III silver gilt two-handled cup and cover, by D. Smith and R. Sharp, 1768, 17¼in. high, 112oz.17dwt. (Christie's) $16,929

A George I Irish plain inverted pear-shaped two-handled cup, by Anthony Stanley, Dublin, 1715, 9½in. high, 62oz. (Christie's) $4,537

A Victorian silver gilt cup, by Alfred Clark, in the manner of J. H. Hunt, 19in. high, London, 1879. (Woolley & Wallis) $1,567

SILVER

A mid Victorian Sheffield plated oval venison dish, two-handled and with gravy channels and well, 26in. long. (Lalonde Fine Art) $1,188

A pair of Edwardian bon-bon dishes, Chester, 1901, 172gr. total. (Henry Spencer & Sons) $245

One of a set of three George III oval meat dishes, by Wm. Bennett, London, 1807, 67oz. (Woolley & Wallis) $2,062

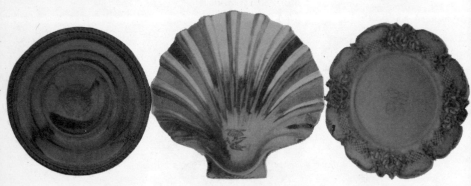

One of a pair of George I large plain circular basins, by David Willaume, 1726, 15in. diam., 112oz. (Christie's) $24,410

One of a pair of George I shell-shaped butter dishes, 1726, maker's mark perhaps IE a coronet above, a crescent below, 9oz.17dwt. (Christie's) $5,445

One of a set of twelve plates, by Redlich & Co., New York, circa 1900, 9¾in. diam., 160oz. (Christie's) $5,280

A tureen with domed cover, by Black, Starr & Frost, New York, circa 1900, 9½in. high, 14in. wide overall, 73oz.10dwt. (Christie's) $3,520

Two of a set of four George III octagonal entree dishes, covers and handles, by Robert Sharp, 1788, 10½in. long, 155oz. (Christie's) $12,474

Early 20th century plated bacon dish of oval form complete with revolving lid. (G. A. Key) $231

DISHES

A Joel F. Hewes sterling silver hand-raised, footed candy dish, circa 1908, 6in. diam., approx. 10 troy oz. (Robt. W. Skinner Inc.) $400

A late Victorian oval dish, by Gilbert Marks, 1899-1900, 15in. long, 30oz. (Christie's) $3,085

An enamelled sterling silver and glass jam dish and spoon, by Mary P. Winlock, 4.5/8in. diam., approx. 5 troy oz. (Robt. W. Skinner Inc.) $500

One of a set of six Charles II shell-shaped dishes, by S. Hood, 1675, 4¾in. wide, 10oz.7dwt. (Christie's) $57,024

A George IV shaped oval meat dish with gadrooned, shell and foliage border, by Philip Rundell, 1821, 19¾in. long, 74oz. (Christie's) $6,897

A shell-shaped bonbonniere on triple ball feet, Sheffield, 1910, 6½in. long, 6oz. (Hy. Duke & Son) $270

A late Victorian dish, by Walker & Hall, Sheffield, 1898, 24cm. diam., 330gr. (Henry Spencer & Sons) $297

One of a pair of Victorian dessert stands, by J. S. Hunt, 1857, 7½in. high, 72oz. (Christie's) $3,168

One of a pair of Georgian silver gilt oval dishes, by William Pitts, London, 1817, 45oz., 10in. diam. (Wellington Salerooms) $3,192

FLATWARE

A Charles II Puritan spoon, by Jeremy Johnson, 1662. (Christie's) $2,087

An Elizabeth I apostle spoon, with fig-shaped bowl and tapering hexagonal stem, by Wm. Cawdell, 1599, 7in. long. (Christie's) $1,425

A William III dog-nose spoon, by Richard Wilcocks, Exeter, 1701, 7½in. long. (Christie's) $801

An Elizabeth I seal top spoon with partly fluted baluster top, by Wm. Rawnson, York, 1589. (Christie's) $1,542

A set of four parcel gilt serving pieces, by Tiffany & Co., circa 1880-85, ladle 13½in. long, 18oz.10dwt. (Christie's) $9,350

Part of an International Co. partial sterling silver flatware service, Meriden, Conn., circa 1934, consisting of 53 pieces, weight approx. 110 troy oz. (Robt. W. Skinner Inc.) $1,200

Part of a Georg Jensen 36-piece 'Acorn' pattern table service, designed by Johan Rohde. (Christie's) $3,066

Part of a 146-piece flatware service, by Tiffany & Co., New York, 1878-1900, in the original fitted oak box, 230oz. excluding knives. (Christie's) $7,700

FLATWARE

A pair of grape shears, by Tiffany & Co., circa 1880-85, of shaped scissor-form, 8in. long, 5oz. (Christie's) $4,400

A caddy spoon with hammered fig-shaped bowl and stylized flower handle set at center with a cornelian boss, 1921. (Phillips) $665

A Charles II trefid spoon, the stem surmounted with the cast figure of a prancing greyhound and ring attachment, by Thomas Cory, 1684. (Phillips) $1,137

A Charles II slip top spoon, engraved with initials HS, by Jeremy Johnson, 1664. (Christie's) $1,415

Three of seven parcel gilt condiment servers, by Tiffany & Co., circa 1880-85, serving spoon 9½in. long, sauce ladles each approx. 7in. long, 13oz. (Christie's) $6,050

Part of a 113-piece Victorian Queen's pattern table service by George Adams, 1869, 1870, 1872, soup ladle, 1902, 284oz. (Christie's) $12,705

Part of a 140-piece mixed metal flatware service, by Tiffany & Co., 1880-85, dinner fork, 8.1/8in. long, ladel 13in. long, 201oz. 10dwt. excluding knives. (Christie's) $99,000

Part of a 24-piece set of parcel gilt dessert knives and forks, by Tiffany & Co., circa 1880-85, knives 8¼in. long, 48oz.10dwt. (Christie's) $4,950

GOBLETS

An American silver wine goblet, a footed beaker and a cann, the first by Robert & Wm. Wilson, Phila., the second by W. W. Hannah, Hudson, New York, the third circa 1850. (Christie's) $770

Two late 19th century Chinese Colonial silver wine goblets, struck with maker's mark WF and an ideogram, 7½in. and 7.5/8in. high, 20oz.10dwt. (Christie's) $935

An American silver wine goblet, by Samuel Kirk, Baltimore, circa 1840, 6.1/8in. high, and a beaker 4½in. high, 118oz.10dwt. (Christie's) $1,045

A Victorian silver gilt goblet, by George Angell, 1863, 16.3cm. high. (Lawrence Fine Art) $781

Two American silver wine goblets, by W. Adams, New York, circa 1825, 5.7/8in. and 6.7/8in. high, 15oz.10dwt. (Christie's) $715

A George III silver wine goblet, by Robert Hennell, 1778, 6.3/8in. high. (Christie's) $605

One of two American silver wine goblets, by C. Bard & Son, one 5¾in. high, the other 6¼in. high, 9oz.10dwt. (Christie's) $660

A pair of George III Irish silver wine goblets, by Joseph Jackson, Dublin, 1801, 6½in. high, 12oz. (Christie's) $2,750

Mid 19th century Chinese Colonial silver wine goblet, by Khecheong, 6¼in. high, 9oz. (Christie's) $1,210

INKSTANDS

A Victorian shaped oval inkstand, by Thomas Smily, fully marked 1859, 28.2cm. long, 15oz. (Lawrence Fine Art)
$1,398

A George III silver-gilt circular inkstand, with scroll handle and three quill holders, by Robert Garrard, 1817, 5in. wide, 14ozs. (Christie's)
$8,832

A shaped rectangular inkstand, the cut glass bottles with shaped circular silver caps, Sheffield, 1905, maker's mark WM&S, 27.6cm. long, 20.8oz. (Lawrence Fine Art)
$905

A Victorian silver-mounted gadrooned heart-shaped tortoiseshell ink stand with loop handle, William Comyns, London 1889, 4¾in. long. (Christie's) $539

An Elkington electrotype circular inkstand commemorating the Great Exhibtion of 1851 pattern, 9in. diam. (Woolley & Wallis)
$330

A late Victorian shaped oblong inkstand on hoof feet, fitted with two silver topped cut-glass square inkwells, W. G. & J. L., London 1898, 10¾in. wide., 33oz. (Christie's)
$1,828

A silver desk stand fitted with two glass and silver topped bottles, Chester, 1913, 15oz. (J. M. Welch & Son)
$516

A large Victorian shaped oblong inkstand on leaf-capped claw feet with two cylindrical ink pots, Messrs Barnard, London 1868, 11in. 33oz. free. (Christie's)
$2,262

An 18th century Victorian gadrooned rounded oblong inkstand, on curved legs, Goldsmiths & Silversmiths Co. Ltd., London 1899, 8¾in., 22oz. free. (Christie's) $929

A pitcher of baluster form, by Samuel Kirk, Baltimore, assay marks for 1824, 8¼in. high, 25oz.10dwt. (Christie's) $2,090

A 19th century embossed and worked silver wine jug with four silver pictorial panels, Sheffield, 1857. (J. M. Welch & Son) $1,968

One of a pair of William IV plain pear-shaped wine jugs, by Paul Storr, 1835, 7¾in. high, 30oz. (Christie's) $6,237

A George IV silver gilt wine ewer, in the style of Francois Briot, by Wm. Eaton, 1827, 11½in. high, 37oz. (Christie's) $2,541

A Queen Anne silver baluster hot water jug with scrolled thumb-piece, London, 1707, 23oz. (Dacre, Son & Hartley) $1,722

A George III vase-shaped hot-water jug, by Andrew Fogelberg and Stephen Gilbert, 1782, 12¼in. high, 24oz. (Christie's) $2,178

Early 20th century Arthur Stone sterling silver water pitcher, Gardner, Mass., 9in. high, 31 troy oz. (Robt. W. Skinner Inc.) $2,000

A George III helmet-shaped milk jug, probably by Benjamin Mordecai or Benjamin Mountigue, London, 1790, 6¼in. high, 3¾oz. (Dreweatt Neate) $355

A George II plain oval pear-shaped shaving jug, by Paul Crespin, 1749, 7¾in. high, 18oz.15dwt. (Christie's) $8,553

MISCELLANEOUS

A George III silver gilt oval basin, 1764, and Victorian ewer, with the makers mark, the basin 13¼in. long, the ewer 8¾in. high, 50oz. (Christie's) $6,897

An Old Sheffield plate cruciform mirror plateau, in five sections, circa 1830, 49¾in. long. (Christie's) $7,623

Edwardian novelty desk clip and pen brush in the form of a muzzled bear, Birmingham, 1908. (Prudential Fine Art) $462

A Georg Jensen tazza, stamped marks 264B GJ 925 S and London import marks for 1928, 30.5cm. high, 1.701kg. (Christie's) $5,772

A Victorian cast model of a whippet, after Jiji by Jules-Pierre Mene, Sheffield, circa 1860, maker's mark WB, 6¼in. high overall. (Christie's) $1,815

A late 19th century English electrotype shield with scenes from John Bunyan's 'Pilgrim's Progress', electroformed from the original by L. Morel-Ladeuil by Elkington & Co. (Christie's) $2,388

Late 19th century Continental silver plated decanting cradle, in the form of a field gun, overall length 15in. (Christie's) $990

Pair of Spanish Colonial silver spurs, 8½in. long, rhondell diam. 2¾in. (Robt. W. Skinner Inc.) $800

A George III ivory biscuit barrel with Old Sheffield plate Greek key pattern base and hinged cover, 4½in. high. (Hy. Duke & Son) $576

SILVER

An American silver bottle cradle by the Gorham Co., 1890, oval with gadrooned borders, 13½in. long. (Christie's) $1,760

A William IV silver barrel spigot, by Wm. Wheatcroft, London, 1830, 6¼in. long, 16oz.10dwt. (Christie's) $880

A Victorian cast whistle formed as the head of a dog, by Samson Mordan, London, 1886, 2½in. long. (Christie's) $739

A late 19th century English electrotype shield with scenes from Milton's 'Paradise Lost', electroformed by Elkington & Co., Birmingham, 1887. (Christie's) $2,388

A Continental silver metal figure of a curly haired youth, on black marble plinth, 29.5cm. high, and another group of a younger child, 30cm. high. (Phillips) $1,385

A large easel mirror with bevelled rectangular plate in ornamental trellis and scroll, Chester, 1898, makers J.D. and W.D., 19 x 12½in. (Graves Son & Pilcher) $716

A circular, gilt lined love token box, probably French, 2½in. diam. (Christie's) $492

A George III plain vase-shaped argyle, by John Wakelin and Wm. Taylor, circa 1780, 8¼in. high, gross 16oz.13dwt. (Christie's) $1,247

A Victorian shaped dressing table mirror with easel support, by William Comyns, London, 1893, 10¾in. high. (Christie's) $616

MISCELLANEOUS

A strainer with ring handle, by John Brevoort, N.Y., 1742-75, 3½in. diam., 1oz.10dwt. (Christie's) $1,540

Mid 19th century Dutch table bell with fluted handle, 5¾in. high. (Christie's) $616

A German parcel gilt ewer and basin, by Johann Mittnacht, Augsburg, circa 1690, 24in. long, and 13in. high, 84oz. (Christie's) $32,076

A Hukin & Heath electro-plated toast rack, designed by C. Dresser, 5¼in. high. (Christie's) $2,316

A George III Scottish silver two-handled punch strainer, by Robt. Gray & Sons, Edinburgh, 1811, 11¾in. long, 8oz. (Christie's) $3,520

A Tiffany sterling silver sealing wax set, N.Y., circa 1891-1902, 8½in. sq., wt. approx. 20 troy oz. (Robt. W. Skinner Inc.) $800

Late 19th century Victorian silver plated three-bottle decanter stand, by Martin Hall & Co., 13½in. high. (Christie's) $495

A George III two-bottle stand, by William Eaton, 1815, 22.4cm. high, 19oz. (Lawrence Fine Art) $863

A 19th century American loud-hailer of trumpet shape, 52cm. high, circa 1850, 23oz. (Phillips) $3,675

MUGS

A George III gilt-lined tapering mug with molded rim and bracket handle, London 1806, 2½in., (Christie's) $426

A George II plain baluster mug on a spreading circular foot, Fuller White, London 1748, 4¼in., 9.5oz. (Christie's) $623

A good 19th century Chinese Export mug of tapering shape, by Cutshing of Canton, circa 1870, 11cm. high, 8.5ozs. (Phillips) $748

A Victorian gilt-lined tapering christening mug with molded rim and loop handle, Robert Hennell, London 1878, 3¾in. high. (Christie's) $325

A Victorian gilt-lined baluster christening mug on spreading circular foot, engraved with a monogram and date, circa 1891, 4in. high. (Christie's) $400

A George III mug, probably by Thomas Ollivant, 1804, 15.2cm. high, 23.4oz. (Lawrence Fine Art) $1.069

MUSTARDS

A French mustard pot with clear glass liner, Paris, circa 1825, 3.5oz. (Phillips) $367

A George III mustard pot, by Samuel Wheatley, 1816, 9.2cm. high. (Lawrence Fine Art) $534

An early Victorian pierced drum mustard pot, fitted with a blue glass liner, by Charles Fox, London, 1838, 4in. high. (Christie's) $422

POMANDERS

Early 18th century German silver pear-shaped pomander in three threaded sections, 2.5/8in. high. (Christie's) $798

A silver pomander with eight compartments, circa 1700, 2in. high. (Christie's) $4,452

Early 18th century German silver pomander with entwined foliage stem, 2in. high. (Christie's) $272

Early 18th century silver gilt pomander of threaded acorn shape, 2½in. high. (Christie's) $1,052

A silver gilt pomander, the six-hinged segments engraved with flowers and foliate sprays, circa 1600, probably German, 1¾in. high. (Christie's) $4,950

Early 18th century German silver pear-shaped pomander with perforated interior, 2½in. high. (Christie's) $816

PORRINGERS

A James II plain circular two-handled porringer and cover, 1685, maker's mark PM, star above and below, 5in. high, 11oz.19dwt. (Christie's) $5,808

An important Commonwealth two handled porringer, cover and stand, by Arthur Mainwaring, 1657, salver 13in. diam. porringer 5¼in, 44ozs 4dwts. (Christie's) $47,311

An early Charles II two-handled porringer and cover, on three cast gilt spread scallop feet, circa 1670, 23ozs. (Phillips) $74,800

SALTS

A pair of Adam style boat-shaped salts, by Robert and Samuel Hennell, London, 1803, 6oz. (Hy. Duke & Son) $648

One of a set four George III salts, by Thos. Robins, London, 1819, 2¾in. diam., 18oz. (Hobbs & Chambers) $742

A Victorian drum mustard pot and a pair of oval salt cellars, by Henry Wilkinson & Co., Sheffield, 1851 and 1853, mustard pot 2¾in. high. (Christie's) $457

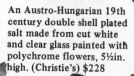

Pair of late Victorian salt cellars by Hunt & Roskell Ltd., 1901, 6½in. high, 34oz. (Christie's) $9,504

An Austro-Hungarian 19th century double shell plated salt made from cut white and clear glass painted with polychrome flowers, 5½in. high. (Christie's) $228

Pair of Victorian peppers, with detachable heads, by Frederick Edmonds of Johnson, Sons & Edmonds, 6cm. high. (Lawrence Fine Art) $1,131

A set of four George III style Edwardian silver salts, London, 1909, with matching spoons, 43oz. (Hetheringtons Nationwide) $1,023

A pair of knife rests and open salts, by Tiffany & Co., 1878-91, also a set of four butter plates, each approx. 3in. wide, 13oz. (Christie's) $3,080

Two of a set of four Victorian gilt lined shell salt cellars with four matching spoons, in a fitted case, Sheffield 1872 and 1873. (Christie's) $427

SAUCEBOATS

A fine pair of George II style shaped oval sauceboats and ladles, by D. & J. Welby, 1959 and 1960, 7¾in. long, 41oz. (Christie's) $2,904

Pair of Edwardian silver sauceboats of Georgian style, London 1905, 6¼in. wide, 17oz. (Hobbs & Chambers) $608

Pair of Victorian fluted shaped sauceboats, by John S. Hunt, 1846, 7¾in. long, 36oz. (Christie's) $7,128

SNUFF BOXES

A William IV silver-gilt castle-top snuff box, chased in high relief with a view of 'Abbotsford House', 8 x 4.5cm, by Joseph Willmore, Birmingham, 1832, 4.25ozs. (Phillips) $1,159

Late 19th century French silver and gold snuff box, maker's initials JL, Paris, 3½in. long. (Christie's) $1,452

A George IV rectangular silver gilt snuff box, London, 1823, maker's mark TP possibly for Thos. Peacock or Thos. P. Prothero, in red leather case, 3¼in. long. (Christie's) $1,179

A George III silver gilt musical snuff box, playing two tunes, by S. Pemberton, Birmingham, 1816, with key, 3¼in. long. (Christie's) $1,452

A George III oblong silver gilt snuff box, by Thomas Phipps, James Phipps II and E. Robinson II, London, 1815, 2¾in. long. (Christie's) $1,452

A George III silver gilt snuff box, by Daniel Hockly, London, 1816, 3¼in. long. (Christie's) $998

A George I plain tapering cylindrical tankard on molded rim foot, with scroll handle, by William Fawdrey, 1716, 7½in. high, 32ozs. (Christie's) $5,348

A William III tapering cylindrical tankard, on reeded rim foot, by John Edwards, 1699, 8in. high, 39ozs. (Christie's) $13,987

A Victorian cylindrical tankard and cover, by John Figg, 1839, 12¼in. high, 45oz. (Christie's) $6,237

A George II baluster tankard, by Thomas Cooke II and Richard Gurney, 1752, 19.8cm. high, 31oz. (Lawrence Fine Art) $3,394

A George I flagon, maker's mark of Richard Bayley overstriking another, 1717, 29.5cm. high, 40.5oz. (Lawrence Fine Art) $1,748

A silver mounted leather 'blackjack', by Gorham Manuf. Co., Providence, circa 1905, 7½in. high. (Christie's) $330

A George III tapering cylindrical tankard, by Solomon Hougham, 1792, 7½in. high, 27oz. (Christie's) $1,996

A Charles II plain tapering cylindrical tankard, date letter indistinct, maker's mark OS, pellets above, trefoil slipped below, 6in. high, 25oz. (Christie's) $7,484

A Queen Anne plain tapering cylindrical tankard, by Timothy Ley, 1710, 6in. high, 21oz. (Christie's) $5,082

TANKARDS

A Danish cylindrical peg tankard on three crowned lion and ball feet, by Peder Brock, Randers, circa 1753, 8½in. high, 40oz. (Christie's) $4,633

A silver mounted serpentine tankard and cover, circa 1670, maker's mark only struck three times, IC a star below, 5½in. high. (Christie's) $1,815

An early 18th century Norwegian peg tankard, with ball and claw feet, by Anders Nielsen Borg, Trondheim, probably 1723, 16cm. high, 15.5ozs. (Phillips) $9,350

A plain tapering cylindrical tankard, the body probably by K. Mangy, Hull, circa 1700, the cover by H. Brind, London, 1750, 6½in. high, 19oz. (Christie's) $1,782

A Queen Anne plain cylindrical tankard and cover, on molded foot, by Adam Billon, Cork, circa 1710, 7¾in. high, 21ozs. (Christie's) $6,171

A large George II baluster tankard, by William Soame, 1758, 26cm. high overall, 44.5oz. (Phillips) $6,650

A German large tapering flagon, by Korner & Proll, Berlin, late 19th century, 15¼in. high, 3330gr. (Christie's) $5,142

A repousse tankard, by Tiffany & Co., N.Y. finished March 10, 1893, for the World's Columbian Exposition, Chicago, 1893, 10in. high, 52oz. 10dwt. (Christie's) $28,600

A George III partly-fluted pear-shaped tankard, by James Barber, York, 1812, 9in. high, 38oz. (Christie's) $3,564

TEA & COFFEE SETS

A Victorian three-piece tea service, all with leaf capped harp handles and on conforming pedestal bases, by Robert Harper, 1873, 21.5cm. height of teapot, 50.5oz. (Lawrence Fine Art) $1,769

A five-piece tea service and tray, by Tiffany & Co., New York, circa 1881, comprising a coffee pot, a covered sugar bowl, a cream pitcher, a waste bowl and a large two-handled tray, coffee pot 8½in. high, tray 27¼in. long, gross weight 306oz. (Christie's)
$41,800

A George IV pear-shaped tea and coffee service, each on four mask, shell and scroll feet and chased overall with scrolls, foliage and shells, 1825, maker's mark IW, height of coffee pot 7½in., 98oz. (Christie's) $4,537

TEA & COFFEE SETS

A Victorian three-piece silver tea service comprising pumpkin-shaped teapot with embossed scroll decoration, 11½in. wide, and matching sugar basin and cream jug, Edinburgh, 1842, 65oz.10dwt. (Dacre, Son & Hartley) $1,485

A Victorian tea and coffee service, comprising pear-shaped teapot, coffee pot, hot water jug, sugar basin and cream jug, on a two-handled shaped oval tray, by Elkington & Co., Birmingham 1897 and 1898, the tray 24¾in. long, gross 234oz. (Christie's) $10,890

A five-piece tea and coffee service, by George B. Sharp for Bailey & Co., Phila., circa 1848-50, comprising a kettle on stand, a coffee pot, a teapot, a covered cream pitcher and a covered sugar bowl, coffee pot 15¼in. high, 231oz.10dwt. (Christie's) $19,800

TEA CADDIES

A George III cube shaped tea caddy, with hinged flat cover, by John Vere and William Lutwyche, 1767, 3¾in. high, 15ozs. 13dwts. (Christie's) $5,759

A George III oval tea caddy with central hinge, two covers and plain divider, by Henry Chawner, 1788, 7in. high, 15oz.10dwt. (Christie's) $3,811

One of a pair of George I plain octagonal tea caddies, by S. Pantin, 1715, 4½in. high, 25oz. (Christie's) $9,801

A George II plain octagonal tea caddy, Exeter, 1730, 4in. high, and another similar. (Christie's) $3,366

A set of George II plain vase-shaped tea caddies and circular sugar bowl and cover, by Samuel Taylor, 1752, in oval satinwood box, circa 1790, 28oz. (Christie's) $8,167

A Queen Anne octagonal tea caddy, by Thos. Ash, 1711, the base struck twice with the maker's mark of J. Farnell, 5in. high, 8oz.17dwt. (Christie's) $2,376

A George III oval serpentine side tea caddy, 5.5in. high, by Thos. Satchell, London, 1791. (Woolley & Wallis) $3,135

A George III Sheffield Plate oval tea caddy, the hinged cover with a Dutch drop handle, 4in. high. (Woolley & Wallis) $676

A George III shaped tea caddy, with hinged domed cover and urn-shaped finial, by Henry Chawner, circa 1792. 5½in. high, 10ozs. 18dwts. (Christie's) $3,085

TEA KETTLES

A Victorian compressed large tea kettle chased with flowers and foliage, complete with stand, 18¼in. overall. (Christie's) $610

A William IV melon-shaped tea kettle, stand and lamp, engraved with a coat-of-arms and crest by Paul Storr, 1835, gross 68oz. (Christie's) $5,445

A Victorian style part-fluted compressed tea kettle with a burner, probably George Fox, London 1912, 11½in., 45oz. (Christie's) $1,017

Late 19th century silver plated kettle on stand with spirit burner. (Brown & Merry) $582

A George III plain oval tea-kettle, stand and burner, by Edward Fernell, 1789, 13¼in. high, gross 68oz. (Christie's) $3,960

A George III plain tapering cylindrical tea kettle, stand and lamp, by Chas. Wright, 1780, the stand and lamp, 1782, 15in. high overall, gross 56oz. (Christie's) $2,722

A Victorian swing-handle compressed tea kettle engraved with scrolling foliage, with a burner, 13¾in. high. (Christie's) $591

A Victorian inverted pear-shaped tea kettle, stand and lamp, by Harris Bros., 1896, gross 63oz. (Christie's) $1,425

A Victorian circular kettle on stand, the underframe with a spirit heater, maker's mark two bells, 16.5in. high. (Woolley & Wallis) $693

TEAPOTS

A George III teapot and cover, by John and Henry Lias, London, 1819, 6½in. high, 22oz. (Hy. Duke & Son) $414

A George III rectangular section teapot on four ball feet with hinged lid, London, 1789, approx. 18oz. (Peter Wilson) $598

A George II Scottish bullet shaped teapot, on circular moulded foot, by William Aytoun, Edinburgh, 1743, 20ozs. (Christie's) $2,879

A William IV plain circular teapot, by Paul Storr, 1831, 7in. high, 31oz. (Christie's) $2,138

A silver repousse teapot, probably Boston, circa 1835, 9½in. high, approx. 39 troy oz. (Robt. W. Skinner Inc.) $425

A George IV inverted pear-shaped teapot and coffee pot, by John Bridge, 1823, height of coffee pot 8in., gross 48oz. (Christie's) $1,692

A Georgian silver teapot with gadrooned rim, Exeter, 1814 or 1834, 22.3oz. (Dee & Atkinson) $421

A William IV circular compressed melon panel teapot, by Wm. Burwash, London, 1837. (Woolley & Wallis) $462

TEAPOTS

A George III Irish oval pointed end teapot
with domed cover and ebonized handle, by
Peter Wills, Cork, circa 1790, 20½oz. gross.
(Dreweatt Neate) $1,402

A George III shaped oval teapot and stand,
by Robert and David Hennell, 1795, 7¼in.
high, gross 20oz. (Christie's)$3,207

A teapot, pyriform, with a high domed cover,
marked 'HM', N.Y., 1715-25, 5¾in. high,
gross weight 16oz.10dwt. (Christie's)
$41,800

An early Victorian circular teapot, by Reilly
& Storer, London, 1839, 23.5oz. all in.
(Woolley & Wallis) $495

A W. M. Hutton & Sons electroplated teapot
and hot-water jug, designed by H. Stabler,
15.7cm. high. (Christie's) $336

A teapot, urn-shaped, the conical cover with
a pineapple finial, by Charles Westphal,
Phila., circa 1790-1800, 11in. high, gross
weight 25oz. (Christie's) $8,250

George III bullet-shaped teapot with baluster
finial , by Francis Crump, London, 1769.
(Reeds Rains) $417

A George I Scottish plain circular teapot, by
Charles Blair, Edinburgh, 1722, 5¼in. high,
gross 20oz.10dwt. (Christie's)$4,989

TRAYS & SALVERS

A silver footed salver having fancy border, London, 1912, 15in. diam., 46 troy oz. (Giles Haywood)$861

A large shaped silver salver on four cabriole legs and ball-and-claw feet, Sheffield, 1934, 14in. diam., 45oz. (J. M. Welch & Son) $759

A George II Scottish shaped circular salver on three hoof feet, by Robert Lowe, Edin., 1751, 8¾in. diam., 16oz.7dwt. (Christie's) $726

George III Irish shaped circular salver on four hoof feet, by John Nicolson, Cork, circa 1785, 16¼in. diam. (Christie's) $2,406

A George III shaped circular salver and a pair of matching smaller salvers, by John Carter, 1772, 14¼in. and 7in. diam., 65oz. (Christie's) $5,263

George III salver, circular with raised beaded border, maker possibly John Crouch, London, 1772, 14½in. diam., 44oz. (Hobbs & Chambers) $957

A plain George II large shaped circular salver, by Robert Abercrombie, 1734, 18in. diam., 73oz. (Christie's) $8,553

A silver footed two-handled tray with rope edge, Birmingham, 1930, 21 x 13in., 56 troy oz. (Giles Haywood) $754

An inlaid waiter with an everted brim, on four cast feet, by Tiffany & Co., 1878-91, 9½in. diam., gross weight 10oz. (Christie's) $19,800

TRAYS & SALVERS

A George III plain circular
salver on slightly curved
feet, by John Crouch and
Thos. Hannam, 1785, 15¾in.
diam., 48oz. (Christie's)
$2,851

A Victorian octafoil-shaped
tray with beaded handles and
border, London, 1874. (Reeds
Rains) $4,175

A George III shaped circular
salver, by John Carter, 1773,
15in. diam., 52oz. (Christie's)
$5,702

A George II shaped square
salver, by Lewis Pantin I,
1735, 12½in. wide, 52oz.
(Christie's) $9,801

Silver salver on three feet,
London, 1876, 25oz. (Brown
& Merry) $800

A sterling silver strapwork tray,
signed Shreve & Co. San
Francisco Sterling, circa 1918,
12½in. diam., 26 troy oz.
(Robt. W. Skinner Inc.)
$700

A Victorian shaped circular
presentation salver, by
William Hunter, 1872, 41cm.
diam., 56.4oz. (Lawrence
Fine Art) $1,563

A silver footed salver having
fancy border, Sheffield,
1934, 12in. diam., 27 troy
oz. (Giles Haywood)
$492

Late 19th century silver
mounted shibayama inlaid
lacquer tray, signed Yasuaki,
24cm. diam. (Christie's)
$2,805

SILVER

A George III two handled soup tureen and cover on four scroll feet, by John Parker and Edward Wakelin, 1769, 16½in. long, 91ozs. (Christie's) $14,399

A pair of George IV two handled circular soup tureens and covers, engraved by John Bridge, circa 1825, 12in. diam. 322ozs. (Christie's) $57,596

One of a pair of George III two-handled sauce tureens and covers, engraved with a coat of arms and crests, by Joseph William Story and William Elliott, circa 1810, 10in. long. (Christie's) $6,376

George IV two-handled oval soup-tureen and cover on four acanthus foliage and paw feet, by John Craddock and William Reid, 1823, width 16½in. 155 ozs. . (Christie's) $17,480

A George III two handled circular soup tureen and cover, on spreading circular foot, by Paul Storr, 1803, 12in. high, 113ozs. (Christie's) $22,627

An Old Sheffield plate molded oval two-handled soup tureen and cover with scrolling foliate handle, on shell feet, Blagden, Hodgson & Co., circa 1820, 14¼in. high. (Christie's) $1,006

One of a set of four George III two-handled oval sauce tureens and covers, by Robt. Sharp, 1788, 6in. high, 125oz. (Christie's) $3,564

A pair of George IV two handled oval sauce tureens and covers, each on four cast lion's paw and foliage feet, Paul Storr, 1821, 8½in. long, 68ozs. (Christie's) $19,541

One of a pair of George IV two-handled oblong sauce tureens and covers, by J. Angell, 1825, 72oz. (Christie's) $3,029

URNS

A George III vase-shaped two-handled tea urn, by John Denziloe, 1784, 21¼in. high, gross 106oz. (Christie's) $3,294

A tea urn, by Eoff & Shepherd for Ball, Black & Co., N.Y., 1839-51, 18in. high, 15in. wide, 112oz.10dwt. (Christie's) $3,520

A fine George III two handled vase shaped tea urn, on four foliate scroll bracket feet, with a coat-of-arms and a crest, by Andrew Fogelberg, 1773, 20½in. high, 107ozs. (Christie's) $10,285

Silver sugar urn, by Joseph Lownes, Phila., 1758-1820, 10in. high. (Robt. W. Skinner Inc.) $1,700

An Art Deco chromium plated tea urn of tapering form, 42cm. high, stamped 'REG 849217'. (Phillips) $832

An English Georgian Sheffield cannonball samovar, circa 1803. (Du Mouchelles) $300

A 19th century plated samovar of globular form with lion ring handles, on four ball feet, 14in. high. (G.A. Key) $141

An 1820 Sheffield samovar, by D. G. Holy & Co, with claw feet. (Du Mouchelles) $2,775

An English Sheffield Russian style samovar, on square plinth, with bracket feet. (Du Mouchelles) $200

VASES

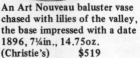

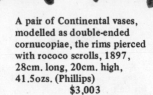

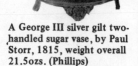

An Art Nouveau baluster vase
chased with lilies of the valley,
the base impressed with a date
1896, 7¼in., 14.75oz.
(Christie's) $519

A pair of Continental vases,
modelled as double-ended
cornucopiae, the rims pierced
with rococo scrolls, 1897,
28cm. long, 20cm. high,
41.5ozs. (Phillips)
$3,003

A George III silver gilt two-
handled sugar vase, by Paul
Storr, 1815, weight overall
21.5ozs. (Phillips)
$9,100

An urn-shaped vase, by Ball,
Black & Co., N.Y., 1851-76,
9½in. high, 6oz.10dwt.
(Christie's) $528

A pair of Georg Jensen vases,
stamped marks Dessin G J
925.S Georg Jensen 107A,
13.2cm. high, 332.5gr.
(Christie's) $631

A bud vase, the body inlaid
in copper and niello with
butterflies and cherry blos-
soms, by Tiffany & Co.,
1872-91, 5in. high, 3oz.10dwt.
(Christie's) $3,080

Late 19th century shaped
octagonal silver vase and
cover with eight oval lacquer
panels, signed Haruaki,
46cm. high. (Christie's)
$20,570

Hallmarked silver posy holder,
with blue glass liner, Sheffield,
1904. (G. A. Key) $140

An ovoid vase, by Tiffany &
Co., N.Y., 1878-90, 6.5/8in.
high, 14oz. (Christie's)
$7,150

VINAIGRETTES

A silver gilt engine turned vinaigrette, by Nathaniel Mills, Birmingham, 1825, 1¾in. long. (Christie's)　　　$580

An attractive 19th century gold and champleve enamel vinaigrette, circa 1840. (Phillips)　　　$328

A Victorian oblong silver-gilt castle-top vinaigrette, with a view of a large church, Yapp & Woodward, Birmingham 1844. (Christie's) $544

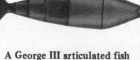

An attractive late Victorian vinaigrette, the cover set with turquoise and incised with a name in Persian script, by William Summers, 1888. (Phillips)　　　$147

A George III articulated fish vinaigrette, 7.25cm. long, by Samuel Pemberton, Birmingham 1817. (Phillips)　　　$598

A large silver gilt castletop vinaigrette, the hinged cover chased with a view of Warwick Castle, by Nathaniel Mills, Birmingham, 1839, 1¾in. long. (Christie's)　　　$1,452

An early 19th century gold engine-turned rectangular vinaigrette, 3 x 2.2cm unmarked, circa 1830. (Phillips)　　　$935

A Victorian shaped oval gilt-lined vinaigrette, the lid depicting a river scene with tree-lined banks and buildings, Nathaniel Mills, Birmingham 1846, 1½in. (Christie's)　　　$471

A silver gilt vinaigrette, the cover repousse and chased with four pheasants in a wooded landscape, by Ledsam, Vale & Wheeler, Birmingham, 1829, 1¾in. long. (Christie's)　　　$1,089

A parcel gilt vinaigrette, the cover repousse and chased with a man in 17th century dress, by Nathaniel Mills, Birmingham, 1835(?), 1¾in. long. (Christie's)　　　$907

A small oblong gold vinaigrette, the cover with a winged putto holding a butterfly. (Christie's)　　　$1,416

A silver gilt vinaigrette with engine turned sides and base, London, 1829, maker's initials A.D. possibly for Allen Dominy, 1.5/8in. long. (Christie's)　　　$635

WINE COOLERS

An Old Sheffield plate tapering two-handled wine cooler on rococo shell and scroll feet with detachable liner, unmarked circa 1810, 10in. high. (Christie's) $503

An oval two-handled wine cistern, in the Queen Anne style, Britannia Standard, maker's mark RR, 24in. long, 239oz. (Christie's) $21,384

A Victorian silver plated ice bucket, by Elkington & Co., circa 1880, 8½in. high, together with three other ice buckets. (Christie's) $1,100

One of a pair of plated wine coolers or jardinieres modelled as sacks with molded rims and rope-twist ties, each with two ring handles, 9in. high. (Christie's) $460

A pair of Sheffield plated wine coolers, engraved with a shield of arms, 24cm. high. (Lawrence Fine Art) $2,005

An Elkington plate wine cooler and stand, stamped Cunard White Star, 18¼in. high. (Christie's) $702

One of a pair of Old Sheffield two-handled partly fluted campana-shaped wine coolers, circa 1820, 8¼in. high. (Christie's) $3,385

An Old Sheffield plate gadrooned two-handled compressed vase-shaped wine cooler on a rising circular foot, 9¼in. high. (Christie's) $619

One of a pair of wine coolers with lion mask drop ring side handles, detachable rims and tinned liners, 22.5cm. diam., circa 1775. (Phillips) $3,675

WINE FUNNELS

A George III part-fluted wine funnel with curved spigot and reeded rim, maker's initials I.C., London, 1811, 4¾in. long, 5.75oz. (Christie's) $712

A George III silver wine funnel, by N. Middleton, London, 1805, 4½in. long, 3oz. (Christie's) $2,970

A George III Provincial silver wine funnel, by Richard Richardson, Chester, 4½in. long, 2oz. (Christie's) $1,650

A George III Scottish silver wine funnel, circa 1800, 6.1/8in. long, the stand part-marked for Edinburgh, 1809, maker's mark GMH, 4¼in. diam., 5oz. (Christie's) $880

A George IV silver wine funnel, by John James Keith, London, 1828, 6¼in. long, 4oz. (Christie's) $1,540

A Victorian silver wine funnel, by A. & J. Savory, London, 1854, 5½in. long, 3oz. (Christie's) $1,375

A George III Scottish silver wine funnel, maker's mark WA, probably for Wm. Auld, Edinburgh, 1813, 5in. long, 4oz.10dwt. (Christie's) $1,100

Early 19th century Chinese Export silver wine funnel, by Sunshing, Canton, 5¾in. long, 4oz. (Christie's) $3,520

A George III Irish silver wine funnel, maker's mark AG, probably for Andrew Goodwin, circa 1768, 4¼in. long, the stand by Wm. Bond, 1798, 3½in. diam., 3oz. (Christie's) $935

WINE LABELS

A George III cast openwork wine label with a reclining satyr beside a barrel, by Phipps & Robinson, probably 1817. (Phillips) $210

One of a pair of George IV Irish oval wine labels, by James Scott, Dublin, circa 1825. (Phillips) $560

A Victorian Provincial escutcheon wine label, possibly by Thomas Wheatley of Newcastle, circa 1850. (Phillips) $113

A Victorian silver bottle ticket for Sherry, in the form of a bat, English or Indian Colonial, circa 1880, 4¼in. wide. (Christie's) $880

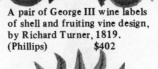

A pair of George III wine labels of shell and fruiting vine design, by Richard Turner, 1819. (Phillips) $402

A George IV armorial wine label of openwork ribbed disk form, by Riley & Storer, 1829. (Phillips) $630

A set of four Victorian wine labels, each engraved with a crest, by Rawlings & Sumner, London, 1859 and 1860. (Christie's) $281

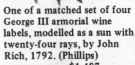

One of a matched set of four George III armorial wine labels, modelled as a sun with twenty-four rays, by John Rich, 1792. (Phillips) $1,487

A George III wine label modelled as a putto, by Peter, Anne and William Bateman, 1799. (Phillips) $1,435

A George II Provincial wine label, formed as two putti, by Isaac Cookson, Newcastle, circa 1750. (Phillips) $367

A George III Provincial rectangular thread-edge wine label, by Hampston & Prince, York, 1784/5. (Phillips) $122

A Victorian wine label of fruiting vine and leafy scroll design, circa 1840. (Phillips) $210

WINE TASTERS

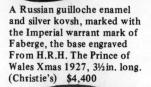

A Russian silver gilt and champleve enamel wine taster, probably Moscow, circa 1900, maker's mark KA, 3.7/8in. diam. (Christie's) $1,760

A Russian guilloche enamel and silver kovsh, marked with the Imperial warrant mark of Faberge, the base engraved From H.R.H. The Prince of Wales Xmas 1927, 3½in. long. (Christie's) $4,400

A Charles II two handled circular wine taster, punched with bunches of grapes, 1675, 3¾in. diam. (Christie's) $2,057

A Louis XVI silver wine taster, Provincial, circa 1780, maker's mark PF over P crowned, 4in. long, 1oz.10dwt. (Christie's) $880

A George III silver wine taster, maker's mark apparently that of Joseph Steward II, London, 1764, 4.1/8in. diam., 2oz. (Christie's) $9,350

A Louis XVI silver wine taster, Provincial, circa 1780, possibly Angers, 3.5/8in. long, 1oz. (Christie's) $880

A Louis XVI silver wine taster, maker's mark TN, cockerel between, Reims, 1781-89, 4in. long, 1oz.15dwt. (Christie's) $1,870

An Austrian silver parcel gilt wine taster, Vienna, 1676, maker's mark FV, also struck with later control marks, 5½in. long, 3oz. (Christie's) $1,980

A Louis XV silver wine taster, possibly by Chas. Despots, with the charge and discharge of A. Leschaudel, 4½in. long. (Christie's) $1,045

A George IV silver wine taster, London, 1828, maker's mark IH, probably for Joseph Hodgson, 4½in. diam., 1oz. 10dwt. (Christie's) $1,045

A Louis XVI silver wine taster, Provincial, circa 1780, with stylized snake handle, 4in. long, 1oz.5dwt. (Christie's) $880

A Russian shaded enamel and silver gilt kovsh, marked the 11th Artel, St. Petersburg, 1908-17, 4½in. long. (Christie's) $2,200

A 19th century nine-color
glass overlay snuff bottle.
(Christie's) $544

Late 18th/early 19th century
embellished celadon jade
snuff bottle, with fitted wood
stand. (Christie's) $907

An 18th century black and
white jade snuff bottle,
Suzhou School. (Christie's)
$50,820

Late 18th/early 19th century
glass overlay snuff bottle of
flattened spherical form.
(Christie's) $871

A carved white jade snuff
bottle, both faces carved in
low relief depicting a seated
Pharaoh surrounded by
simulated hieroglyphics, late
Qing Dynasty. (Christie's)
$1,179

A two-color glass overlay
snuff bottle, the opaque
white ground with black
and caramel overlay.
(Christie's) $1,815

A rock crystal snuff bottle
of rounded rectangular form,
mid Qing Dynasty.
(Christie's) $2,722

A glass overlay seal-type
snuff bottle of ovoid
shape, Yangzhou School.
(Christie's) $3,630

A mottled glass snuff bottle
of ovoid form, mid Qing
Dynasty. (Christie's)
$635

An 18th century white jade snuff bottle, Suzhou School, the even stone with minor inclusions. (Christie's) $3,630

Mid 19th century famille rose snuff bottle of pilgrim flask form, Qianlong six-character mark. (Christie's) $3,448

A 19th century Baltic amber snuff bottle of rounded rect-angular form. (Christie's) $1,815

A 19th century embellished copper snuff bottle of flattened baluster form, Qianlong four-character seal mark. (Christie's) $1,542

An inside-painted and carved rock crystal snuff bottle, signed Ye Zhongsan and dated 1933. (Christie's) $1,179

An inside-painted rock crystal snuff bottle with flaring sides by Ye Zhongsan, signed and dated 1916. (Christie's) $2,722

Late 18th/early 19th century pink glass snuff bottle, the rim with jewel festoons. (Christie's) $11,797

A 19th century aquamarine snuff bottle, the translucent pale bluish stone of gem-like color with minor cloudy inclusions. (Christie's) $3,448

An enamelled copper European subject snuff bottle of bulbous pear shape, blue enamel Qian-long four-character mark and of the period. (Christie's) $23,595

A conglomerate agate snuff bottle, the stone of varied brown and ochre tones with striations of wood-grain patterns, mid Qing Dynasty. (Christie's) $2,722

An inside-painted smoky crystal snuff bottle, probably by Ye Zhongsan, signed and dated 1925. (Christie's) $834

An 18th century chalcedony agate snuff bottle, the surface carved in relief with three carp interlocked with a goldfish. (Christie's) $3,267

An important and rare Famille Rose gilt-copper enamel snuff bottle, an oval panel inset with a European lady, 18th/19th century. (Christie's) $36,300

A chalcedony agate snuff bottle, Suzhou School, the stone highly translucent. (Christie's) $27,225

A 19th century molded and reticulated porcelain snuff bottle, seal mark. (Christie's) $816

Late 18th/early 19th century chloromelanite snuff bottle, the stone of dark spinach tone with emerald-green mottling. (Christie's) $3,630

A 19th century banded agate snuff bottle, the translucent stone with attractive bold opaque ochre, white and brown striations. (Christie's) $635

Late 18th/early 19th century glass overlay snuff bottle, the oviform body with a bubble-glass ground with blue overlay. (Christie's) $1,815

A pale apple and emerald-green jade snuff bottle, late Qing Dynasty, wood stand. (Christie's) $544

Early/mid 19th century embellished pale celadon jade snuff bottle, fitted wood stand. (Christie's) $1,452

An 18th century glass snuff bottle of spherical shape, probably Beijing workshops. (Christie's) $2,722

A coral snuff bottle of ovoid form, carved in relief with a profusion of jars, vases and pots, mid Qing Dynasty. (Christie's) $3,630

Late 18th/early 19th century glass overlay snuff bottle, the dense snowstorm ground with blue overlay. (Christie's) $453

Late 18th/early 19th century shadow agate snuff bottle of ovoid form, the body well hollowed. (Christie's) $2,178

Late 18th/early 19th century shadow agate snuff bottle, well hollowed. (Christie's) $4,356

Early 19th century large white jade snuff bottle, signed Zigang. (Christie's) $1,270

An inside-painted glass portrait snuff bottle, by Ma Shaoxuan, signed and dated Winter 1909. (Christie's) $18,150

High Wheel Robot, clockwork mechanism, moveable legs, with visible rotating wheels, sparks in chest, with box, by Yoshiya (mk. 4), Japanese, 1960's, 25cm. high. (Christie's) $770

Planet Robot, battery operated with remote control, rotating antenna on top, with box, by Yoshiya, Japanese, 1950's, 23cm. high. (Christie's) $949

Television Spaceman, battery operated, moveable arms and legs, rotating eyes, screen in chest revealing a space scene, by Alps, Japanese, 1950's, 38.5cm. high. (Christie's) $949

Attacking Martian, battery operated, moveable legs, chest opens to reveal flashing guns, with box, by Horikawa (mk. 6), Japanese, 1960's, 23cm. high. (Christie's)$1,009

Sparky Robot, clockwork mechanism, moveable legs and sparking eyes, with box, by Yoshiya, Japanese, 1950's, 19.5cm. high. (Christie's) $562

Answer-Game, battery operated immobile, executes simple mathematics, flashing eyes, by Ichida (mk. 3), Japanese, 1960's, 35.5cm. high. (Christie's) $2,494

Gear Robot, battery operated, moveable legs with colored wheel rotating chest and flashing head, possibly by Horikawa, Japanese, 1960's, 22.5cm. high. (Christie's) $622

Busy Cart Robot, battery operated, pushing and lifting a wheelbarrow, with box, by Horikawa (mk. 6), Japanese, 1960's/1970's, 30cm. high. (Christie's) $1,187

Ultraman, clockwork mechanism, moveable arms and legs, with box, by Bullmark (mk. 5), Japanese, 1960's, 23cm. high. (Christie's) $355

Sparky Jim, battery operated with remote control, moveable legs and flashing eyes, Japanese, 1950's, 19.5cm. high. (Christie's)$1,247

Nando, the mechanism activated by air pressure through remote control, moveable legs and head, with box, by Opset, Italian, circa 1948, 13cm. high. (Christie's)$2,197

Astoman, clockwork mechanism, moveable arms and legs, by Nomura (mk. 1), Japanese, 1960's, 23.5cm. high. (Christie's)$1,067

Space Explorer, battery operated box transforms into Robot, revealing '3-D' television screen, with box, by Yonezawa (mk. 2), Japanese, 1960's, 29.5cm. high. (Christie's) $2,434

Mr. Robot, clockwork mechanism and battery activated, with box, by Alps, Japanese, 1950's, 20cm. high. (Christie's) $1,602

Dyno Robot, battery operated, moveable legs, opening mask to reveal a flashing red dinosaur's head, with box, by Horikawa, Japanese, 1960's, 28.5cm. high. (Christie's) $770

Confectionary Dispenser, battery operated, with coinslot, transparent chest showing sweets, Italian, late 1960's, 139cm. high. (Christie's) $2,257

Giant Robot, battery operated, moveable legs, chest opening to reveal flashing gun, possibly by Horikawa, Japanese, 1960's, 41cm. high. (Christie's) $1,187

Talking Robot, battery powered, mobile, speaks four different messages, with box, by Yonezawa (mk. 2), Japanese, 1950's, 28cm. high. (Christie's) $1,542

TAPESTRIES

A Royal Aubusson silk and wool tapestry, depicting The Pageant of Man's Redemption, circa 1784. (Christie's) $44,000

Late 16th century Brussels silk and wool garden tapestry based on the courtship of Vertumnus and Pomona, 11ft.1in. x 12ft. 8in. (Christie's) $74,800

Early 18th century Flemish tapestry with a traveller and two companions beneath trees, 8ft.8in. x 5ft.8in. (Christie's)$5,874

Late 16th century Brussels tapestry woven in wools and silks with King Numitor, 10ft. x 12ft.8in. (Christie's) $31,328

Mid 17th century Brussels tapestry woven with polychrome silk, wool and metallic threads depicting Moses at the rock, 13ft. 6in. x 15ft.2in. (Christie's)$29,370

Late 16th century Brussels silk and wool garden tapestry. (Christie's) $57,200

A Mortlake tapestry depicting Diogenes seated, teaching the Academy of Plato, 3.15 x 2.87m. (Phillips) $7,380

Mid 19th century Aubusson tapestry woven in silks and wools with Louis XIV and his army in a landscape defeating the Spanish, 6ft. x 7ft.8in. (Christie's) $4,895

A 17th century Brussels mythological tapestry depicting a banquet with Dionysus and Ceres, 3.85 x 2.62m. (Phillips) $5,904

Mid 16th century Flemish feuille de choux tapestry woven with a parrot and other birds, a snail and dragonfly amid flowerheads, Enghien, 11ft.10in. x 12ft.8in. (Christie's) $43,076

A Mortlake tapestry depicting Diogenes lying beside his bath tub with two followers, 3.23 x 2.65m. (Phillips) $7,380

A wall tapestry depicting Georgian woodland hunting scene, 70 x 100in. (J. M. Welch & Son) $456

A 19th century patchwork coverlet worked in plain and printed cottons, 2.80 x 2.60m. (Phillips) $291

A late 18th century oval silk-work picture depicting a country lass gathering wheat-sheafs in her apron, 34 x 28cm. (Phillips) $806

A late 18th century Benares cover of red silk gauze woven in gold thread with a central shaped medallion, 1.08 x 1.14m. (Phillips) $297

A 19th century Chinese coverlet of crimson silk, lined and fringed, 2.32 x 2.14m. (Phillips) $288

A shaped panel of 19th century Chinese silk, the blue ground embroidered with colored silks in pekin knot and satin stitch, 2.08m. high, joined. (Phillips) $648

A late 18th century embroidered picture, the ivory silk ground worked mainly in satin stitches, 65 x 70.50cm. (Phillips) $604

A silk embroidered picture, Mass., 1807, worked in silk yarns on ivory silk satin ground fabric, 8 x 8½in. (Robt. W. Skinner Inc.) $2,200

A late 19th century Japanese wall hanging of K'o-ssu woven in pastel colored silks and gold thread, 3.04 x 1.80m. (Phillips) $3,240

An Oriental panel, the fuchsia ground worked in colored silk threads with butterflies, flowers and Oriental figures, 2.60 x 2.40m. (Phillips) $972

A 17th century Turkish bocha, the linen ground embroidered in shades of red, blue, yellow and green silks, 1.10 x 1.04m. (Phillips) $1,260

A pair of 19th century oval silkwork pictures, the ivory silk ground embroidered in black and cream silks with lakeside scenes, 11cm. high. (Phillips) $436

An 18th century Anatolian embroidered panel, work in silk on beige silk fabric, 45 x 38in. (Robt. W. Skinner Inc.) $1,300

One of a pair of crewelwork curtains, one signed Mary Fincher 1703, 65 x 86in., another pair 41 x 52in. and two pelmets. (Christie's) $2,887

An early 18th century Kashmir shawl of crimson pashmina, 2.40 x 1.26m. (Phillips) $1,848

A length of mid 17th century Italian brocade woven in crimson and yellow silk, 2.12m. x 53cm., and a fragment similar. (Phillips) $324

A mid 18th century gros et petit point arched firescreen panel worked in colored wools with a garden scene of musicians, 87.50 x 67cm. (Phillips) $806

An early 18th century needlework picture embroidered with colored wools and silks in mainly tent stitch, 24 x 21cm. (Phillips) $1,512

A 19th century Rescht cover of red worsted decorated with multi-colored insertions and applique, 2.24 x 1.45m., fringed, lined. (Phillips) $672

TEXTILES

A needlework picture worked in polychrome silk threads on a natural ground, by Lois Burnham, Mass., 1775, 15¾ x 22in. (Christie's) $2,420

A 19th century Japanese wall hanging, worked in applied floss silk and cord mainly in pastel shades, 2.5m. x 90cm. (Phillips) $324

A mid 19th century Kashmir shawl, having a central medallion of fawn pashmina, 1.98m. square, reversible. (Phillips) $4,704

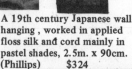

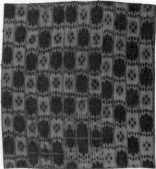

A rectangular needlework cushion with summer flowers on a brown ground, 18in. wide. (Christie's) $311

A needlework picture worked in petit-point, circa 1660, 13½ x 17in. (Christie's) $9,625

Two of four panels from an embroidered screen, worked in colored silks with various scenes, mid 18th century, two panels 51 x 16in., the other two 56 x 16in. (Christie's) $731

An early 19th century needlework picture of A Map of England & Wales, 49 x 44cm. (Phillips) $436

A mid 17th century stumpwork picture, the ivory silk ground embroidered in colored silks with mainly French knot, needlepoint and satin stitches, 55 x 58cm. (Phillips) $5,208

A 19th century Uzbek silk ikat cover designed with bold red and yellow guhl motifs and green stripes, 1.55m. square, lined. (Phillips) $672

Needlework picture, 'Mary Anne Rowe's Work, Reading, 1834', Penn., silk yarns on canvas, 18 x 22½in. (Robt. W. Skinner Inc.) $15,000

A rectangular cushion worked with silver thread and crimson velvet, 18in. wide. (Christie's) $292

'Borboleta de Noite', by Genaro de Carvalho, a gros point needlework picture embroidered in brilliant wools and signed Genaro, 1.05 x 1.22m. (Phillips) $100

A Chinese coverlet of black silk embroidered in couched gold thread and colored silks, 1.74m. square, lined. (Phillips) $1,134

A mid 19th century needlework picture by Ann Wright, designed with a tablet showing 'The Given Chap. of Exodus', The Ten Commandments, Moses and Aaron, 46.50 x 31.50cm. (Phillips) $1,596

A rectangular cushion worked with metal thread strapwork and foliage on a green silk velvet ground, 26in. (Christie's) $233

An early 18th century English linen coverlet worked in colored silks and applied silver thread with embroidered and applique motifs, 2.33m. square. (Phillips) $5,208

A late 17th century stumpwork picture, the ivory silk ground embroidered mainly in green and brown silks and metal thread in needlepoint, 24 x 39cm. (Phillips) $1,440

A mid 19th century Japanese fukusa, of blue silk with embroidered, applied and couched silks in pastel shades, 78 x 66cm. (Phillips) $745

White Star Line Triple-Screw R.M.S. Olympic and Titanic 45,000 tons each, The Largest Steamers in the World, a color postcard from R. Phillips to Mr. Wm. Squires, 4 Northfield Cottages, Ilfracombe, Devonshire, postmarked Queenstown 5.45pm 11 April. (Onslow's) $3,260

White Star Royal Mail Steamer Titanic, artist drawn, pre-sinking color postcard, postmarked 1st August 1912, State Series, Liverpool. (Onslow's) $228

A contemporary watercolor drawing of R.M.S. Titanic Leaving Southampton April 12th 1912 Sunk April 15th 1912, signed J. Nicholson, in oval satin mount, 13 x 24cm. (Onslow's) $195

White Star Line Olympic and Titanic Smoke Room, a monochrome postcard to Master Tom Richmond, 14 Lennox Road, Crookston, Paisley, Lothian, postmarked Queenstown 3.45pm 11 April. (Onslow's) $2,445

'The Iceberg', a contemporary bromide photograph with ink inscription, 'Iceberg taken by Capt. Wood S.S. Etonian 12 April 1912 in 41° 56N 49° 51W S.S. Titanic Struck 14 April and sank in three hours', 200 x 255mm. (Onslow's) $374

Launch of White Star Royal Mail Triple-Screw Steamer Titanic at Belfast, Wednesday, 31 May 1911, at 12.15pm, a printed card admission ticket in two portions, each numbered 1246, overall size 84 x 136mm. (Onslow's)
$1,793

A typed letter to Mr R Penny from W. T. Stead, dated 9 April 1912, on The Review of Reviews writing paper. (Onslow's)
$1,467

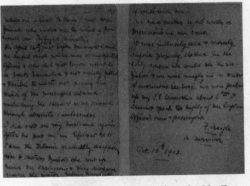

A contemporary account written by Mrs F. Angle of the disaster dated 15 October 1913, on two sheets. (Onslow's)
$978

S.S. Titanic, the cast brass nameplate from Lifeboat No. 12, 322mm. long x 39mm. wide. (Onslow's) $9,128

Titanic Leaving Southampton, glossy mono-chrome postcard, published by Nautical Photo Agency, N.W.7. (Onslow's)
$228

'Unterseeboot', a painted metal submarine, by Bing, circa 1902, 17¾in. long. (Christie's) $998

A tin toy car, modelled as two-seater Model A with leather wheels and painted details, 6in. high, 6in. wide, 20in. long. (Christie's) $154

Tipp Co., clockwork lithographed bomber bi-plane TC-1029, wing span 36.5cm., 25.5cm. long, key, lacking pilot, three bombs. (Phillips) $537

A Gunda-Werke lithograph tinplate motor-cycle and sidecar with clockwork mechanism, 6½in. long, circa 1920, and a tinplate monkey moneybox. (Christie's) $1,361

Lesney Massey Harris 745D tractor. (Hobbs & Chambers) $210

'Echo', EPL 725, an early printed and painted tinplate motorcyclist with clockwork mechanism operating a metal painted spoked wheel, by Lehmann, circa 1910, 8¾in. long. (Christie's) $2,904

Biplane No. 24, with clockwork mechansim, Deutsche Lufthansa markings, wingspan 20¼in. long, by Tipp, circa 1939. (Christie's) $653

A boxed set of six green and cream Tipper lorries with drivers. (Phillips) $358

'Mac 700', a printed and painted tinplate motorbike and rider with clockwork mechanism, causing the rider to hop on and off, 7¼in. long, by Arnold, W. Germany, circa 1955. (Christie's) $471

An Ingap four-door limousine with clockwork mechanism, driving rear axle and operating front head lamps, 11¼in. long, circa 1930. (Christie's) $635

Pre-war tinplate model of a two-seater tourer car, 9½in. long, and a cardboard model of a 'Daily Mail' pre-war aircraft. (Reeds Rains) $50

'Strato Clipper', a printed and painted tinplate four-engine airliner with battery mechanism, by Gama, circa 1956, wingspan 20in. (Christie's) $172

Six turned polychrome Ring Toss Game figures, New England, late 19th century, 14½in. high. (Robt. W. Skinner Inc.) $3,250

Set 2052, Anti-Aircraft Unit with AA gun, searchlight and instruments and operating crew of eight men, in original box, 1959 Britain's. (Phillips) $1,072

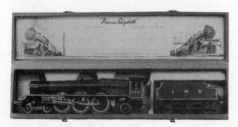

Hornby, 3.R.E. Princess Elizabeth and tender, boxed. (Phillips) $1,969

A Schuco 6080 Elektro-Construction tinplate fire engine, in original box, circa 1955. (Osmond Tricks) $412

A German clockwork flying car, 19.5cm., and a Hungarian open tourer in blue, 26cm. (Phillips) $125

Britain's set of Indian Army Cavalry, one bugler and four troopers at the gallop, bearing swords (one sword missing), on original card but no box. (James Norwich Auctions)
$159

Vertunni original paint, Louis XV of France, with his wife, mistress, mother, two Royal Guards and a gentleman. (Phillips) $264

Pelham Puppets, Mickey Mouse and Minnie Mouse. (Phillips) $107

Corgi 803 The Beatles Yellow Submarine, with the four famous members of the band, open hatches and revolving periscopes, in original box. (Christie's) $108

A constructor Racing Car, probably French, with battery operated remote control, 29cm. long. (Phillips) $250

Britain's Set No. 2, The Royal Horse Guards, one officer and four troopers, at the trot, bearing swords (one sword missing), box torn but with label intact. (James Norwich Auctions) $132

'Cadillac', a printed and painted tinplate car, with friction-drive mechanism, rubber tyred wheels and tinted windows, by Ichiko, circa 1967, 28in. long. (Christie's) $651

Britain's Farm, horse-drawn milk float with milkman and two churns, No. 131F, in original box. (Milkman has broken neck.) (James Norwich Auctions) $84

A Harlequin set of nine Steiff skittles, circa 1908, on circular wooden bases. (Lawrence Fine Art) $9,615

Dinky Guy 'Spratts' van, no. 514, boxed. (Hobbs & Chambers) $350

A painted wood Noah's Ark on wheels, with opening roof, door and windows, German, circa 1890, 31in. long. (Christie's) $338

Britain's Farm, single-horse plough with plough-man, No. 4/8, in original box. (James Norwich Auctions) $115

A 2in. scale model of a Garrett 'undertype three-way tipper, live-steam wagon, 30in. long. (Anderson & Garland) $1,805

Late 19th century Folk Art painted and carved mechanized wooden model of five bearded men at work, America, base 18½in. long. (Robt. W. Skinner Inc.) $1,200

A plush covered lion cub, 9in. long, circa 1925 with Steiff button. (Christie's) $146

Roger Berdou original 54mm. mounted figure entitled 'Garde Imperiale Tartares Lithuaniens Trompette 1812', signed R.B. (Phillips) $297

A German clockwork Drummer Boy dressed as a soldier in busby, 28cm. high. (Phillips) $116

Jigsaw Puzzle, John Wallis's chronological Tables of English History for the Instruction of Youth, 1788, one piece missing. (James Norwich Auctions) $212

A musical teddy bear with swivelling head operated via his tail, 43cm. high. (David Lay) $360

A live steam, spirit fired tinplate vertical steam engine, by Bing, circa 1928, 12½in. high, in original box. (Christie's) $160

German made, a tinplate sentry box with 120mm. Sentry of the Foot Guards, in original box, 1890. (Phillips) $429

Y 11 series 2, 1912 Packard Landaulet, in original box. (James Norwich Auctions) $23

A carved and painted wooden paddle boat, 26in. long. (Christie's) $462

Lehmann, early flywheel driven 'Africa', EP2 No. 170. (Phillips) $447

A Falk tinplate painted clockwork battleship, HMS Invincible, 37cm. long. (Phillips) $751

Tut-Tut or A Run In A Motor Card, A New and Exciting Game, with forty-eight cards depicting an Edwardian open tourer, contained in original box. (Onslow's) $112

A Lehmann 'Lo and Li' tinplate toy. (Hobbs Parker) $1,674

Y5 series 1, 1929 4½ litre Le Mans Bentley, in original box. (James Norwich Auctions) $49

Marx, Walt Disney's Donald Duck Duet, boxed. (Phillips) $396

A 70mm. scale figure of the Colonel-in-Chief, the Welsh Guards, with painted legend 'South Africa 1947' on the base, in original box, Britain's. (Phillips) $1,980

A clockwork fur covered giraffe with clown rider, 31cm. high, and an HK, Fipps, clockwork nodding puppy. (Phillips) $90

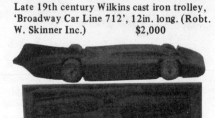

Early 20th century miniature Eskimo model of dogsled and team, wooden sled, and four rabbit skin covered papier mache dogs, sled 12.3/8in. long. (Robt. W. Skinner Inc.) $475

Late 19th century Wilkins cast iron trolley, 'Broadway Car Line 712', 12in. long. (Robt. W. Skinner Inc.) $2,000

Hess, clockwork flywheel driven open tourer, 1920's, 23.5cm. long, pressed wheel version. (Phillips) $358

Britains Bluebird, in original box. (James Norwich Auctions) $248

Dinky pre-war set No. 50, 'Ships of the British Navy', together with five other warships and 'Famous Liners'. (Christie's) $267

Dinky Supertoys, 919 Guy van, advertising 'Golden Shred', in original paintwork, with golly, in original box. (Christie's) $712

Corgi, Gift Set No. 23, Chipperfields Circus Models, in original presentation box. (Christie's) $427

JEP: No. 3, clockwork streamline speedboat painted in pale blue and cream with driver, 36cm. long. (Phillips) $81

Dinky Supertoy, No. 514C Guy van, advertising 'Weetabix', in original paintwork and box. (Christie's) $463

A painted tinplate river paddle steamer with clockwork mechanism, 11in. long, by Uebelacker, Nuremberg, circa 1902. (Christie's) $801

A Fleischmann No. 855 oil tanker, a painted tinplate model, 26in. long, circa 1936. (Christie's) $855

A Schuco Ingenico electric remote control car 5311/56, and a Carreto 5330 trailer, in original boxes. (Christie's) $338

A clockwork German cow finished in brown and cream, the mechanism causing the animal to walk and nod, 18.5cm. long. (Phillips) $163

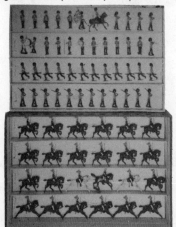

Spot-On, set No. 260, The Royal Presentation Set, in original box. (Christie's) $388

Large display box Set 93, containing Coldstream Guards with mounted officer, four pioneers, thirteen-piece band, two officers, twelve marching, twelve running, two trumpeters, six troopers and fifteen normal troopers, 1938, Britain's. (Phillips) $11,550

Dinky Supertoys, 514B Guy Van, advertising 'Lyons Swiss Rolls', in original paintwork and box. (Christie's) $570

Tyrannosaurus Rex and Triceratops. (Phillips) $214

Late 19th century boxed Marklin wind-up train set, sold by F.A.O. Schwartz, New York. (Robt. W. Skinner Inc.) $2,100

Fleischmann tinplate clockwork model of a two-funelled ocean liner, 10½in. long. (Prudential Fine Art) $247

Mettoy, a large four-door Saloon finished in bright lime-green with cream lining, the interior with chaffeur at the wheel, in box, 35cm. long.   (Phillips) $132

SH-Japanese battery operated Space Station, boxed. (Phillips) $440

Marx, Armored Floating Tank Transporter, boxed. (Phillips) $74

An early 20th century doll's house, paper covered to simulate brickwork, 88cm. high. (Osmond Tricks) $542

A German post-war clockwork Boxing Match, boxed (no lid). (Phillips) $115

Tekno, Mercedes Tuborg Pilsner Delivery lorry, boxed. (Phillips) $99

A battery-operated four-door Cadillac State Service Car, boxed, 49cm. long. (Phillips) $363

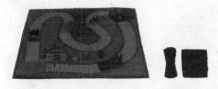

'The Game of Motoring', by Chad Valley, circa 1908, with original box. (Christie's) $169

A model of a horse-drawn cart by Benefink & Co. (Lots Road Chelsea Auction Galleries) $643

A painted wood Noah's Ark, by Erzegebirge, Germany, circa 1870, 23¾in. long, approx. 205 animals. (Christie's) $1,514

Karl-Bub, clockwork Atom Rocket Ship, boxed. (Phillips) $181

A mixed collection of 15 lead models, including soldiers, cowboys and red indians, Spanish warship blowing up, two men-of-war, etc., circa early 1920's. (James Norwich Auctions) $34

A collection of 38 French soldiers and Zouaves, including ski troops and one mule, made in France, circa 1940. (James Norwich Auctions) $108

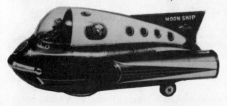

TM, battery operated Supersonic Moon Ship, boxed. (Phillips) $181

Set 68, 2nd Bombay Native Infantry, First Version, in original unmarked early printer's type box, 1896. (Phillips) $1,072

An English leaping clock-work hare. (Phillips) $75

Spot-On, 265 Tonibell Ice Cream van, with server, in original box. (Christie's) $71

'Bulky Mule, The Stubborn Donkey', EPL 425, by Lehmann, circa 1920, 7½in. long. (Christie's) $178

'Our New Clergyman', a stained and carved wood, metal and tinplate preacher, probably by F. Martin, circa 1890, 10½in. high. (Christie's) $2,494

Marx, clockwork Moon Mullins and Kayo hand car, 1935, boxed. (Phillips) $244

'The Juba Dancers', carved and stained wood mechanical toy, by Ives, U.S.A., circa 1874, 10in. high. (Christie's) $463

A golden plush covered teddy bear with pronounced hump, pointed snout and with Steiff button in ear, 29in. high. (Christie's) $4,719

A printed paper on wood doll's house, by Lines Bros., 43in. wide. (Christie's) $1,542

A golden plush covered teddy bear with boot button eyes, cut muzzle, hump and elongated limbs, with Steiff button in left ear, 19in. high. (Christie's) $871

A honey plush covered pull-along bear on metal wheels, 6in. high, circa 1908, probably Steiff. (Christie's) $471

Spot-On, 271 Express Dairy van, with driver and milk crates, in original box. (Christie's) $35

A small German clockwork leaping Kangaroo. (Phillips) $75

Linemar, battery operated Bubble Blowing Popeye. (Phillips) $391

Two wooden rod puppets with painted faces. (Worsfolds) $164

Marx, clockwork Hi-Yo-The Lone Ranger, boxed. (Phillips) $146

A clockwork somersaulting teddy bear dressing in gold felt jacket, blue trouser and white vest, by Bing of Nuremberg, 9in. high. (Christie's) $943

A painted wooden doll's box-type town house of three bays and three storeys, 25in. high. (Christie's) $544

A golden plush covered teddy bear in the form of a child's muff, 15in. high. (Christie's) $290

TOYS

A Daimler Sedanca motor car, in the original box. (Geering & Colyer) $576

Nurnberger Blechspielwarenfabric, clockwork novelty toy in the form of a circus elephant with roller ball shute, 1950, 24cm. high. (Phillips) $125

A searchlight lorry with adjustable electric searchlight, in the original box. (Geering & Colyer) $342

Early 19th century rooster squeak toy, molded papier mache body on coiled wire legs, 5in. high. (Robt. W. Skinner Inc.) $225

An early 20th century two-storeyed doll's house, facade 20 x 18in., depth 12in. (James Norwich Auctions) $448

A gold plush teddy bear, with metal Steiff disk in left ear, German, circa 1907, 25in. high. (Hobbs & Chambers) $3,200

A Le Praxinoscope optical toy with shade and ten picture strips, by Emile Reynaud, drum with sellers label. (Christie's) $221

A 20th century wooden rocking horse, painted black, leather bridle and saddle and mounted on a boat-shaped rocker base, 6ft.7in. long. (Lawrence Fine Art) $469

An early Lehmann automobile 'Tut Tut', EPL marque, circa 1910, 6¾in. long. (James Norwich Auctions) $566

Dinky 28/3a Hornby Trains Delivery Van, finished in red, advertising 'Hornby Trains British and Guaranteed', in gold decals. (Christie's) $363

A carved wooden paddle toy, modelled as a peacock, 9½in. high. (Christie's) $175

Gunthermann, post-war tramcar finished in orange, cream and pale yellow. (Phillips) $143

A German printed tinplate musical cathedral, printed marks DRGM, Made in Germany, 17.5cm. high. (David Lay) $126

An early gold plush tumbling teddy bear, the body of wood and cardboard, containing a key-wind mechanism, 9in. high. (Lawrence Fine Art) $97

A German made tinplate sentry box with 60mm. mounted sentry of The Royal Horse Guards, in original box, 1890. (Phillips) $544

German straw-filled teddy bear with hump back, pad feet, long nose and button eyes, 11in. high. (Giles Haywood) $311

An early Lehmann, EPL marque, 'Paddy riding his pig to market', with clockwork mechanism, circa 1910, 5½in. long. (James Norwich Auctions) $566

A Doll & Co. printed and painted carousel with a handcranked clockwork mechanism, 11½in. long, circa 1914. (Christie's) $508

1955 Citroen Light 15 four-door saloon, Reg. No. WFX 436, Chassis No. 657720, 1,911 c.c., 56 b.h.p. (Christie's) $8,217

1967 Morgan plus four open Sportscar, Reg. No. PUV 316F, Chassis/Engine Nos. not known, engine, Triumph TR4, 2,138 c.c., 104 b.h.p. (Christie's) $5,478

1974 Alfa-Romeo 2000 Spider Veloce 2 + 2 open Sportscar, coachwork by Pininfarina, Reg. No. GLT 87N, Chassis No. 247/0730, Engine No. AROS 12/519285, 1,962 c.c., 131 b.h.p. (Christie's) $6,938

1957 Ford Thunderbird Sports two-seater with hard and soft tops, Reg. No. KRV 1P, Chassis No. D7FH 302275, 352 cu. ins. (5,769 c.c.), 130 b.h.p. (Christie's) $19,602

1935 Bentley 3½-litre four-door Sports saloon, coachwork by Hooper, Reg. No. BLE 714, Chassis No. B40CR, Engine No. U2 BH, 3,669 c.c., 105 b.h.p. (Christie's) $23,166

1938 Rolls-Royce Phantom III two-door fixed head Coupe, coachwork by Hooper, Reg. No. 11 DPW, Chassis No. 3CM173, Engine No. P98N, 7,340 c.c., 50.7 h.p. (Christie's) $98,010

1930 Austin Seven open two-seater, Reg. No. PG 5934, Chassis No. 105171, Engine No. 105002, 747 cc., 7.8 h.p., right-hand drive. (Christie's) $4,455

1957 Mercedes-Benz 300SL two-seat Roadster, Reg. No. CSU 418, Chassis No. 7500143, Engine No. 198042, 2,996 c.c., 215 b.h.p. (Christie's) $76,692

1949 Aston Martin DB1 open Sports two-seater, coachwork by Swallow, Reg. No. MKE 836, Chassis No. AMC 49/8, Engine No. LB6B/50/630, 2,580 c.c.. (Christie's) $31,042

1932 Mercedes-Benz 170 four-door saloon, Reg. No. GP 6387, Chassis No. U88418, Engine No. 88418, 1,692 c.c., 32 b.h.p. (Christie's) $7,669

1937 MG VA four-seat drophead Coupe, coachwork by Tickford, Reg. No. COR 331, Chassis No. VA 0850, Engine No. TPBG 1099, 1,549 c.c., 55 b.h.p. (Christie's) $16,929

1930 Rolls-Royce Phantom II Sedanca De Ville, coachwork by Barker, Reg. No. USV 694, Chassis No. 202 GN, Engine No. J65, 7.7-litre, 40/50 h.p. (Christie's) $94,952

1937 Mercedes-Benz 540K Supercharged Cabriolet B, coachwork by Daimler-Benz, Sindelfingen, Reg. No. Not registered in U.K., Chassis No. 154119, 5,401 c.c., 115 b.h.p. (Christie's) $182,600

1954 Jaguar XK 120 Roadster To Rally Specification, Reg. No. RJH 400, Chassis No. S661165, Engine No. F2111/85, 3,442 c.c., 160 b.h.p. (Christie's) $63,910

1956 Bentley S1 four-door Sports saloon, Reg. No. JTL 717, Chassis No. B80 CK, Engine No. BC40, 3,887 c.c. (Christie's) $12,830

1952 Aston Martin DB2 two-seat Sports saloon, Reg. No. NGO 655, Chassis No. LML/50/218, 2,580 c.c., 107 b.h.p. in standard tune. (Christie's) $12,474

Leyland 36 H.P. platform lorry, circa 1920, Reg. No. UV 6025, Engine No. 26860, (Christie's) $8,217

1959 Jaguar XK150 fixed head Coupe, Reg. No. 499 KBH, Chassis No. 8247620-W, Engine No. V6429-8, 3,442 c.c., 210 b.h.p. (Christie's) $15,147

1899 De Dion-Bouton D1 3½ H.P. Vis-A-Vis, Reg. No. PM 643, Chassis No. 73, Engine No. 228, 400 c.c.. (Christie's) $24,057

1926 Austin Seven Chummy two-door open tourer, Reg. No. PN 2231, Chassis No. 17973, Engine No. 7H2 TIA 38AF2, 747 c.c., 11 b.h.p. (Christie's) $7,669

1921 Hillman 11 'Peace Model' two-seat drop-head Coupe with dickey, Reg. No. BY 3898, Chassis No. 1686, Engine No. 1686, 1,580 c.c., 10.4 b.h.p. (Christie's) $17,529

1946 Rover Twelve four-door saloon, Reg. No. LSV 897, Chassis No. BA1372, Engine No. N/A, 1,496 c.c., 12 h.p. (Christie's) $2,739

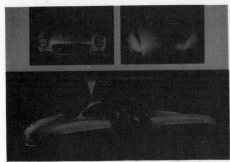

1954 Mercedes-Benz 300 SL two-seat Gull-wing Coupe, Reg. No. KVE 886F, Chassis No. 1980404500122, Engine No. 198980, Bosch fuel injection, 2,996 c.c., 215 b.h.p. (Christie's) $151,470

Leyland ¾ ton chassis/cab, circa 1923, Reg. No. DY 4227, Chassis/Engine No. 13662, 30/36 h.p. (Christie's) $7,304

1947 MG 1¼-litre Y-type four-door Sports saloon, Reg. No. MG 7180, Chassis No. YO297, Engine No. XPAG SC10051, 1,250 c.c., 46 b.h.p. (Christie's) $5,478

1930 Lea-Francis P type 12/40 drophead Coupe with dickey, coachwork by Cross & Ellis, Reg. No. KX 4497, Chassis No. 13953, Engine No. 9982, 1,496 c.c., 40 b.h.p. (Christie's) $13,365

1962 Mercedes-Benz 300 SL Roadster, Reg. No. Not Registered in the U.K., Chassis No. 1980421000298, Engine No. 19898010003022, Bosch fuel injection, 2,996 c.c., 215 b.h.p. (Christie's) $101,574

1929 Austin Seven 'Top Hat' two-door saloon, Reg. No. KR 1019, Chassis Nos. 102226, Engine No. 84995, 747.5 c.c., 11 b.h.p. (Christie's) $10,225

1968 ISO Grifo A3L 2 + 2 Sports Coupe, Not Registered in U.K., Chassis No. 820 202, Engine No. 1067Y0323HT, 5,359 c.c., 350 b.h.p. (Christie's) $17,820

1955 Triumph TR2 two-seat Sportscar, Reg. No. RXV 318, Chassis No. TS 7707, Engine No. TS 8003, 1,991 c.c., 90 b.h.p. (Christie's) $7,304

1953 Alvis-Healey G-type 3-litre convertible Sports 2/3 seater, Reg. No. NXR 829, Chassis No. G518, Engine No. 25318, 2,993 c.c. (Christie's) $10,956

1931 Rolls-Royce 20/25 Doctor's Coupe, coachwork by Windover, Reg. No. GP 5803, Chassis No. GO510, Engine No. D9E, 3.7-litres, 20/25 h.p. (Christie's) $60,588

1968 Aston Martin DB6 Superleggera Grand touring four-seater, Reg. No. SKK 714G, Chassis No. DB6L/L001R, Engine No. 400/406, 3,996 c.c., 282 b.h.p. (Christie's) $17,820

1953 Jaguar XK120 Special Equipment two-seat Roadster, Reg. No. IRXB 240 (USA), Chassis No. S673307, Engine No. W6896-85, 3,442 c.c., 160 b.h.p. (Christie's) $24,057

1963 Chevrolet Corvette Stingray 'Split-Window' Sports Coupe, Reg. No. ABK 747A, Chassis No. 30837S102721, 327 cu. ins. (5,350 c.c.). (Christie's) $28,512

1927 Austin Seven four-seat Chummy tourer, Reg. No. WW 753, Chassis No. A4-2041, Engine No. 33977, 747 c.c., 7.8 h.p. (Christie's) $5,346

1938 Daimler Light Straight Eight four-door Sports saloon, coachwork by Charlesworth, Reg. No. RN6265, Chassis No. 4770, Engine No. 88611, 3,421 c.c., 26 h.p. (Christie's) $24,651

1956 Jaguar XK 140 two-door fixed head Sports Coupe, Reg. No. SDA 898, Chassis No. 804705, Engine No. 67855-8, 3,442 c.c., 190 b.h.p. (Christie's) $16,251

1948 Rolls-Royce Silver Wraith Sedanca De Ville, coachwork by H. J. Mulliner, Reg. No. Not registered in U.K., Chassis No. WYA 32, Engine No. W197A, 4,256 c.c., approx. 125 b.h.p. (Christie's) $19,173

1960 MGA 1600 two-seat Sports Coupe, Reg. No. YLT 629, Chassis No. CHD 82813, Engine No. 16JEUL 11195, 1,588 c.c. (Christie's) $4,747

1950 MG TD Midget 2 + 2 seat Sportscar, Reg. No. KSM 567, Chassis No. TO TD 0509, Engine No. XPAG/TD/867, 1,250 c.c., 54 b.h.p. (Christie's) $10,225

1949 HRG Sports two-seater, Reg. No. KYD 103, Chassis No. S96, Engine No. 7160986, 2,088 c.c., 90 b.h.p. (Christie's) $15,147

1953 MG TF Midget two-seat Sportscar, Reg. No. OGN 866, Chassis No. HDA 261736, Engine No. XPAG/TF/30443, 1,250 c.c., 57 b.h.p. (Christie's) $18,260

1923 Daimler CK 2/3 ton dropside lorry, Reg. No. BK 8749, Chassis No. CK 4269, Engine No. 46315, 22 h.p. (Christie's) $12,782

Sheet copper weathervane, America, late 19th century, silhouette of a cannon, 24in. wide. (Robt. W. Skinner Inc.) $750

Mid 19th century cut out sheet iron banner weathervane, Lafayette, Rhode Island, 50in. long. (Robt. W. Skinner Inc.) $2,500

Late 19th century molded copper and zinc running horse weathervane, 'Smuggler', America, 46in. high, 31in. long. (Robt. W. Skinner Inc.) $1,200

Copper bull weathervane, America, late 19th century, full-bodied figure standing bull, 18½in. high. (Robt. W. Skinner Inc.) $750

Cast iron horse weathervane, Rochester, New Hampshire, late 19th century, full bodied figure of a prancing horse, 36in. wide. (Robt. W. Skinner Inc.) $11,000

Mid 19th century molded copper and zinc leaping stag weathervane, New England, 27in. high, 30in. long. (Robt. W. Skinner Inc.) $5,500

A large sheet iron horse weathervane, long. (Christie's) $550

A 19th century molded copper and zinc trotting horse weathervane, America, 23¼in. high, 34in. long. (Robt. W. Skinner Inc.) $3,400

WEATHERVANES

Rare fire hose wagon weathervane, Mass., last quarter 19th century, full-bodied figure of copper horse pulling copper and iron hose wagon. (Robt. W. Skinner, Inc.) $55,000

Early 20th century copper train weathervane, America, 60in. long, 12½in. high. (Robt. W. Skinner Inc.) $11,000

Sheet iron train weathervane, America, late 19th/early 20th century, silhouette of Locomotive and tender on railroad track, 22in. long. (Robt. W. Skinner Inc.) $650

Late 19th century copper and zinc quill weathervane, New England, with traces of gold leaf, 25½in. high, 24½in. long. (Robt. W. Skinner Inc.) $1,800

Late 19th century gilded copper leaping stag weathervane with zinc head, 30in. long, mounted on display stand. (Robt. W. Skinner Inc.) $4,100

A trumpeting angel silhouette weathervane, constructed of sheet iron, supported by wrought-iron strapping, New England, circa 1800, 59in. long. (Robt. W. Skinner Inc.) $40,000

Mid 19th century copper telescope weathervane, New England, 62in. high, 49in. long. (Robt. W. Skinner Inc.) $4,500

Late 19th century copper horse and trainer weathervane, America, traces of gold leaf under yellow ochre paint, 29in. long. (Robt. W. Skinner Inc.) $4,000

1 bottle Chateau Haut-Brion—
Vintage 1899, Pessac, Graves,
1er cru classe, Recorked by
Whitwham & Co., 1979,
excellent neck level and deep
colour, label soiled. (Christie's)
$902

Two bottles of Chateau
Haut-Brion—Vintage 1906,
Pessac, Graves, 1er cru classe,
one recorked by Whitwham &
Co., 1980, top-shoulder level,
excellent deep color and
good labels. (Christie's)
$572

1 bottle Chateau Lafite—
Vintage 1858, Pauillac, 1er
cru classe, Recorked by
Whitwham & Co., 1980,
with a neck level and deep
color . (Christie's)
$2,420

1 magnum Chateau Mouton-
Rothschild—Vintage 1878,
Pauillac, 1er cru classe, Recorked by Whitwham & Co.,
1980, neck level and deep
color , label soiled. (Christie's)
$2,860

1 double magnum Chateau
Lafite—Vintage 1865, Pauillac,
1er cru classe, with deep color
and level in the neck, with
Christie's slip label. (Christie's)
$17,050

1 bottle Chateau d'Yquem—
Vintage 1921, Sauternes, 1er
grand cru classe, top-shoulder
level and deep amber gold
color . (Christie's) $902

1 bottle Chateau Mouton-
Rothschild—Vintage 1899,
Pauillac, 1er cru classe,
Chateau-embossed capsule,
neck level and deep color .
(Christie's) $902

Six bottles of Barolo
Riserva—Vintage 1947, Pied-
mont, Giacomo Borgogno
& Figli. (Christie's) $858

1 bottle Chateau Lafite-
Vintage 1888, Pauillac, 1er
cru classe, Recorked by
Whitwham & Co., 1980,
and with neck level.
(Christie's) $792

1 bottle Chateau Lafite—
Vintage 1945, Pauillac, 1er
cru classe, neck level.
(Christie's) $682

Two bottles of Chateau
d'Yquem—Vintage 1940,
Sauternes, 1er grand cru classe,
excellent honey gold color,
neck level, labels slightly
stained. (Christie's)
$1,012

1 bottle Chateau Latour—
Vintage 1874, Pauillac, 1er
cru classe, Recorked by
Whitwham & Co., 1982,
excellent color .(Christie's)
$1,485

1 jeroboam Chateau Lafite—
Vintage 1949, Pauillac, 1 er cru
classe, with a neck level, deep
color, and pristine label.
(Christie's) $2,420

1 double magnum Chateau
Petrus—Vintage 1953,
Pomerol, neck level and
pristine label. (Christie's)
$3,630

1 bottle, with original cork
attached, Chateau Mouton-
Rothschild—Vintage 1888,
Pauillac, 1er cru classe,
Recorked by Whitwham &
Co., 1980, level in neck.
(Christie's) $682

1 bottle Chateau Petrus—
Vintage 1945, Pomerol,
excellent top-shoulder level,
label slightly tattered and
soiled. (Christie's)
$1,650

Three bottles of Chateau
Cheval-Blanc—Vintage 1929,
Saint-Emilion, 1er grand cru
classe (A), two recorked by
Whitwham & Co., 1982.
(Christie's) $1,045

1 jeroboam, in original case,
Chateau Mouton-Rothschild—
Vintage 1929, Pauillac, 1er
cru classe, high-shoulder level,
garnet color and pristine
label. (Christie's)
$8,800

WINE

1 bottle Chateau Mouton—Vintage 1870, Pauillac, 1er cru classe, Bordeaux-bottled, neck level, deep garnet color , clean label . (Christie's) $2,530

Two bottles of Romanee-Conti—Vintage 1919, Recorked by Whitwham & Co., level only 1in.-1½in. below corks, deep color . (Christie's) $1,265

1 bottle Chateau Lafite Blanc—Vintage 1934, Pauillac, top-shoulder level and honey gold color , excellent label, slightly soiled. (Christie's) $682

1 bottle Romanee-Conti—Vintage 1924, Domaine de la Romanee-Conti, excellent level only 1½in. below cork, deep color maturing at rim. (Christie's) $605

Three magnums of Clos des Lambrays—Vintage 1947, Cote de Nuits, Heritiers Cosson, levels very high, only 1in.-2in. below corks. (Christie's) $682

1 bottle Chateau Mouton-Rothschild—Vintage 1874, Pauillac, 1er cru classe, Chateau-embossed capsule, neck level, deep color and pristine labels. (Christie's) $1,320

1 bottle Chateau Margaux—Vintage 1888, Margaux, 1er cru classe, Recorked by Whitwham & Co., 1981, with neck level, original cork attached to neck of bottle. (Christie's) $418

Two bottles of Romanee-Conti—Vintage 1934, Domaine de la Romanee-Conti, excellent level on 1in.-2in. below corks, deep color to rim, labels slightly soiled. (Christie's) $902

1 bottle Les Gaudichots—Vintage 1929, Domaine de la Romanee-Conti, excellent level only 1in. below cork, deep color , label soiled. (Christie's) $572

1 bottle Chateau Latour-Vintage 1896, Pauillac, 1er cru classe , Recorked by Whitwham & Co., 1981, neck level and deep color , label soiled and worn. (Christie's) $462

Two bottles of La Tache—Vintage 1945, Domaine de la Romanee-Conti, levels only 1½in.-2in. below corks, deep color , labels slightly soiled. (Christie's) $1,045

1 bottle Beaulieu Vineyard Napa Valley Cabernet Sauvignon—Vintage 1961, Private Reserve, Georges de Latour. (Christie's) $137

1 bottle Chateau Petrus—Vintage 1943, Pomerol, top-shoulder level, label slightly soiled, resealed capsules. (Christie's) $550

Three bottles, neck level, Chateau Cheval-Blanc—Vintage 1947, Saint-Emilion, 1er grand cru classe (A), top-shoulder levels and deep color . (Christie's) $1,540

1 bottle Chateau d'Yquem—Vintage 1928, Sauterns, 1er grand cru classe, top-shoulder levels and honey gold color . (Christie's) $682

1 magnum, neck level, Chateau Haut-Brion—Vintage 1947, Pessac, Graves, 1er cru classe, label with minor stains and soil. (Christie's) $792

Two bottles of Chateau d'Yquem—Vintage 1937, Sauternes, 1er grand cru classe, top-shoulder levels and medium honey gold color . (Christie's) $1,155

1 magnum Chateau Lafite-Vintage 1869, Pauillac, 1er cru classe, excellent mid-shoulder level. (Christie's) $3,740

A 19th century boxwood wrist-rest, unsigned, 5.5cm. long. (Christie's) $880

A walnut carving of a horse-drover and horse pulling a section of tree, carved by A. L. B. Huggler, circa 1900, plinth 34in. x 8½in. (Prudential Fine Art) $1,541

Early 19th century carved dark wood mask of Hannya, 5.8cm. high. (Christie's) $281

Carved oak fire surround and overmantel, 5ft. long, 4ft 4ft. high. (Giles Haywood) $451

A Maori wood fish hook, 12cm. high, and another two 9cm. and 10cm. high. (Phillips) $196

One of a pair of giltwood jardinieres with overhanging reeded lips, 11in. wide. (Christie's) $1,837

A 19th century lacquered. wood mask of Ayagiri, 4.6cm. high. (Christie's) $1,487

A Netherlandish oak panel carved in relief with the Adoration of the Magi, 17th/18th century, 71 x 81cm. (Phillips) $2,934

One of a pair of Italian carved pine girandoles, 27½in. high. (Christie's) $2,204

WOOD

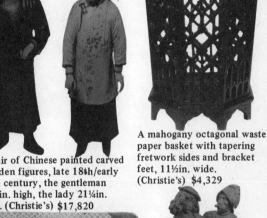

Late 19th/early 20th century, Continental wood window display, probably French, in the form of a cask-rack, 22½in. high. (Christie's) $1,760

Two African wood carvings, Benin, an incised double bell, 4in. high, and a standing figure holding serpent, 6in. high. (Robt. W. Skinner Inc.) $1,200

Early 20th century primitive carved eagle, American, the body carved from a single block of pine, 21in. long. (Robt. W. Skinner Inc.) $375

A Gustav Stickley round slat-sided waste basket, no. 94, circa 1907, 14in. diam. (Robt. W. Skinner Inc.) $1,200

A pair of Chinese painted carved wooden figures, late 18th/early 19th century, the gentleman 46¼in. high, the lady 21¼in. high. (Christie's) $17,820

A mahogany octagonal waste paper basket with tapering fretwork sides and bracket feet, 11½in. wide. (Christie's) $4,329

A Chinese carved hardwood figure of a sage with inset ivory eyes and teeth, 17in. high. (Dacre, Son & Hartley) $147

A large shaped rectangular framed wooden panel, unsigned, Meiji period, 82 x 60cm. (Christie's) $2,805

A 16th century Flemish oak relief carved group of a moustachioed soldier and his female companion, 42cm. high. (Phillips) $5,542

Early 19th century George
III mahogany wine tray, with
twenty-two square divisions
in two sizes, 18in. long.
(Christie's) $1,210

A Maori wood feather box
of oval form, the lid carved
with a tiki figure at each end,
45cm. long. (Phillips)
$738

Early 19th century George
III mahogany bottle carrier,
15½in. by 14¼in.
(Christie's) $1,210

One of a pair of giltwood
wall brackets of rococo
design, 13½in. high.
(Christie's) $4,989

A late 16th century poly-
chromed and carved lime-
wood relief panel of a
bearded saint, possibly St.
Christopher, 37cm. high.
(Phillips) $652

One of a pair of George III
giltwood and composition
wall brackets, 16½in. high.
(Christie's) $8,910

An 18th century German
carved boxwood group of
the Madonna and Child,
19cm. high. (Phillips)
$2,037

A pair of Chinese carved hardwood
figures of laughing boy musicians,
15½in. high. (Dacre, Son & Hartley)
$164

A Shaker miniature lidded
pail with strap handle and
two fingers, 2.3/8in. high.
(Christie's) $550

A treen barrel-form tobacco canister, the lift-off cover set with a wine bottle and two glasses, 7in. high. (Christie's) $330

A wooden group of miniature human and animal figures, platform 5 x 9in. (Robt. W. Skinner Inc.) $360

An ancient Egyptian wood carving of a rower, 6½in. high. (Robt. W. Skinner Inc.) $275

A carved hardwood Indian figure of a man with feathered head-dress, 18½in. high. (Dacre, Son & Hartley) $65

Two late 19th century Noh masks of Ko-Omote and Obeshimi, 22cm. long. (Christie's) $1,408

An Easter Island wood carving of male ribbed figure, 'Moai Kavakava', 14in. long. (Robt. W. Skinner Inc.) $2,600

A 19th century mahogany wine tray, with six square divisions, 10¾in. long. (Christie's) $605

A 16th/17th century carved and polychromed limewood group of the Madonna and Child, 52cm. high. (Phillips) $1,630

A Mission oak magazine/wood carrier, circa 1910, 18in. high, 15¼in. wide. (Robt. W. Skinner Inc.) $450

A scene from Tam O'Shanter, 'The Beginning of the Evening', wood carving by Gerrard Robinson, 13 x 14in. (Anderson & Garland) $1,026

A well carved figure of the head of a man, 30in. long. (Christie's) $1,478

One of two 19th century painted burlwood bowls, oval, 12in. wide, the second circular, 13in. diam. (Christie's) $352

A painted cherrywood and gesso group of a couple dancing, 'Tango', 36in. high, by Elie Nadelman. (Christie's) $2,860,000

A 19th century Japanese carved hardwood okimono of humorous deity, 5½in. high. (Hobbs & Chambers) $264

An ebony and oval panelled shaped jelly mold , 6in high. (Woolley & Wallis) $66

A carved and painted ship's head figure, modelled as a partially clad mermaid, 38in. high. (Christie's) $1,320

A wooden framed wire bird cage. (Worsfolds) $268

A 19th century carved and polychrome allegorical figure, America, 52in. high. (Robt. W. Skinner Inc.) $5,500

Early 19th century carved and polychrome figurehead, New England, 23in. high. (Robt. W. Skinner Inc.) $3,500

One of three 19th century burlwood bowls, each circular with molded rim, two 13in. diam., the third 8in. diam. (Christie's) $935

A Dutch mahogany birdcage, the stepped front with four compartments, late 18th century, 41in. wide. (Christie's) $30,525

Late 19th century painted wooden sled, America, 48½in. long, 12in. wide. (Robt. W. Skinner Inc.) $1,600

A Portuguese or Spanish carved walnut panel, 'The Adoration of the Magi', circa 1600. (Woolley & Wallis) $759

Late 19th/early 20th century carved and painted wooden hanging clock shelf, possibly Virginia, 21½in. high, 14¾in. wide. (Christie's) $495

A carved and painted wooden spoonrack, 22½in. high, 9in. wide. (Christie's) $352

A stylized figure of a carved wooden horse, America, 23in. high, 23in. long. (Robt. W. Skinner Inc.) $1,200

A 20th century carved wooden tobacconist figure, America, overall height 77½in. (Robt. W. Skinner Inc.) $2,500

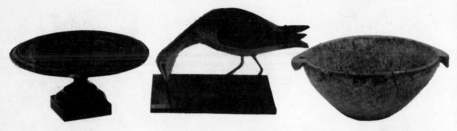

A Regency rosewood tazza with molded ring-turned bowl, 10¼in. wide. (Christie's) $484

Early 20th century Summer Yellow Legs carving, G. Shaw, Chatham, Mass., 5in. high, 9in. long. (Robt. W. Skinner Inc.) $1,100

Late 18th century carved burl bowl, with carrying handles, America, 22½in. diam. (Robt. W. Skinner Inc.) $1,600

Early 20th century standing male figure, 28in. high. (Robt. W. Skinner Inc.) $300

Small carousel stander, mounted as a rocking horse, circa 1900, 27in. high, 29in. long. (Robt. W. Skinner. Inc.) $1,500

Late 19th century 'Factory Girl' large painted sled, America, 3ft.8½in. long, 19in. wide. (Robt. W. Skinner Inc.) $3,200

An Egyptian Anthropoid wood mask, 18cm. high, Ptolemaic Period. (Phillips) $254

A 19th century American carved wood butter stamp, depicting a standing pig on grass, and a cylindrical cover, top 5¾in. diam. (Christie's) $264

A 19th century American carved wood butter stamp, 4¼in. diam. (Christie's) $242

A 19th century Swiss carved
wood life-size model of a
brown bear, 3ft.9in. long,
2ft.6in. high. (Capes Dunn)
$7,697

A 19th century painted and
carved pine eagle, possibly
taken from the stern of a
ship, America, 28in. long.
(Robt. W. Skinner Inc.)
$1,900

A Continental carved oak
relief wall plaque, 32in. high,
44in. wide. (J. M. Welch &
Son) $638

A painted wooden caricature
figure of Charlie Chaplin, by
Betterway, Vienna, 52cm.
high, circa 1930. (Phillips)
$272

A 19th century American
large polychrome woven
splint market basket, 19in.
wide. (Christie's) $286

Late 19th century carved
and painted black figure of
a male acrobat, possibly
Italy, 31in. high. (Robt. W.
Skinner Inc.) $2,900

Late 19th century painted
wooden architectural model,
America, 32in. long, 33in.
high. (Robt. W. Skinner Inc.)
$575

Early 19th century carved
wooden dove, American,
10¾in. high. (Robt. W.
Skinner Inc.) $350

One of five carved wood butter
stamps with turned handles,
4½in. diam. (Christie's)
$198

WOOD

One of two carved wooden friction toys, the first modelled as a bird, the second as a grasshopper, 8in. and 8½in. long respectively. (Christie's) $275

A polychrome woven splint lunch basket, probably Maine, 12in. high, 15in. long, 7½in. wide. (Christie's) $132

A miniature Canada goose, by A. Elmer Crowell, Mass., original paint. (Robt. W. Skinner Inc.) $1,000

A painted wood caricature figure of Douglas Fairbanks, Snr., by Betterway, Vienna, 51cm. high, circa 1930. (Phillips) $320

A Charles X period carved walnut cradle on foliate scroll dolphin supports. (Phillips) $7,000

Late 18th century carved hard pine spoon rack with chip carved decoration, New Jersey, 21in. high. (Robt. W. Skinner Inc.) $1,800

A nickel and wood decanting cradle, on oval ebonized base, overall length 14in. (Christie's) $880

A pair of late 19th century Italian limewood figures, Apollo and Peace, after Jacopo Sansovino, 94in. high, including wood pedestals. (Christie's) $33,000

A 19th century crimping machine of Thomas Clark type. (David Lay) $187

INDEX